THE FAMILY TRADE

Charles Stross lives with his wife in Edinburgh. His short fiction has been nominated for both the Hugo and Nebula awards. *The Family Trade* is his third novel.

'*The Family Trade* is one of those rare delights – a book that is fun, intelligently written, and which leaves a reader breathlessly wondering what will happen next. Readers Beware: Stross weaves a tale that continually builds to an engrossing climax . . . you'll find yourself hooked'

David Farland

The FAMILY TRADE

BOOK ONE OF THE MERCHANT PRINCES

CHARLES STROSS

First published 2004 by Tor, Tom Doherty Associates, NY

First published in Great Britain in paperback 2007 by Tor
an imprint of Pan Macmillan Ltd
Pan Macmillan, 20 New Wharf Road, London N1 9RR
Basingstoke and Oxford
Associated companies throughout the world
www.panmacmillan.com

ISBN 978-0-330-45193-2

1 3 5 7 9 8 6 4 2

A CIP catalogue record for this book is available from
the British Library.

Printed and bound in Great Britain by
Mackays of Chatham plc, Chatham, Kent

For Steve and Jenny Glover

ACKNOWLEDGMENTS

No novelist works in a creative vacuum. Whatever we do, we owe a debt to the giants upon whose shoulders we stand. This book might not have happened if I hadn't read the works of H. Beam Piper and Roger Zelazny.

Nor would this book have been written without the intervention of several other people. My agent, Caitlin Blaisdell, nudged me to make a radical change of direction from my previous novels. David Hartwell of Tor encouraged me further, and my wife, Feorag, lent me her own inimitable support while I worked on it. Other friends and critics helped me in one way or another; I'd like to single out for their contributions my father, Jan Goulding, Paul Cooper, Steve Glover, Andrew Wilson, Robert "Nojay" Sneddon, Cory Doctorow, Sydney Webb, and James Nicoll. Thank you all.

PART 1

PINK SLIP

WEATHERMAN

Ten and a half hours before a mounted knight with a machine gun tried to kill her, tech journalist Miriam Beckstein lost her job. Before the day was out, her pink slip would set in train a chain of events that would topple governments, trigger civil wars, and kill thousands. It would be the biggest scoop in her career, in any journalist's career— bigger than Watergate, bigger than 9/11—and it would be Miriam's story. But as of seven o'clock in the morning, the story lay in her future: All she knew was that it was a rainy Monday morning in October, she had a job to do and copy to write, and there was an editorial meeting scheduled for ten.

The sky was the color of a dead laptop display, silver-gray and full of rain. Miriam yawned and came awake to the Monday morning babble of the anchorman on her alarm radio.

"—Bombing continues in Afghanistan. Meanwhile, in business news, the markets are down forty-seven points on the word that Cisco is laying off another three thousand employees," announced the anchor. "Ever since 9/11, coming on top of the collapse of the dot-com sector, their biggest customers are hunkering down. Tom, how does it look from where you're sitting—"

"Shut *up*," she mumbled and killed the volume. "I don't want to hear this." Most of the tech sector was taking a beating. Which in turn meant that *The Industry Weatherman*'s readers—venture capitalists and high-tech entrepreneurs, along with the wannabe day traders—would be taking a beating. Her own beat, the biotech firms, were solid, but the collapsing internet sector was making waves. If something didn't happen to relieve the plummeting circulation figures soon, there would be trouble.

Trouble. Monday. "I'll give you trouble," she muttered, face forming a grin that might have frightened some of those readers, had they been able to see it. "Trouble is my middle name." And trouble was good news, for a senior reporter on *The Industry Weatherman*.

She slid into her bathrobe, shivering at the cold fabric, then shuffled along stripped pine boards to the bathroom for morning ablutions and two minutes with the electric toothbrush. Standing before the bathroom mirror under the merciless glare of the spotlights, she shivered at what she saw in it: every minute of her thirty-two years, in unforgiving detail. "Abolish Monday mornings and Friday afternoons," she muttered grimly as she tried to brush some life into her shoulder-length hair, which was stubbornly black and locked in a vicious rear-guard action against the ochre highlights she bombarded it with on a weekly basis. Giving up after a couple of minutes, she fled downstairs to the kitchen.

The kitchen was a bright shade of yellow, cozy and immune to the gloom of autumn mornings. Relieved, Miriam switched on the coffee percolator and made herself a bowl of granola—what Ben had always called her rabbit-food breakfast.

Back upstairs, fortified by an unfeasibly large mug of coffee, she had to work out what to wear. She dived into her closet and found herself using her teeth to tear the plastic bag off one of the three suits she'd had dry-cleaned on Friday—only to discover it was her black formal interview affair, not at all the right thing for a rainy Monday pounding the streets—or at least doing telephone interviews from a cubicle in the office. She started again and finally managed to put together an outfit. Black boots, trousers, jacket, turtleneck, and trench coat: as black as her Monday morning mood. *I look like a gangster,* she thought and chuckled to herself. "Gangsters!" *That* was what she had to do today. One glance at her watch told her that she didn't have time for makeup. It wasn't as if she had to impress anyone at the office anyway: They knew damned well who she was.

She slid behind the wheel of her four-year-old Saturn, and thankfully it started first time. But traffic was backed up, one of her wiper blades needed replacing, the radio had taken to crackling erratically, and she couldn't stop yawning. *Mondays,* she thought. *My favorite day! Not.* At least she had a parking space waiting for her—one of the handful reserved for senior journalists who had to go places and interview thrusting new economy executives. Or money-laundering gangsters, the *nouveau riche* of the pharmaceutical world.

Twenty minutes later she pulled into a crowded lot behind an anonymous office building in Cambridge, just off Somerville Avenue, with satellite dishes on the roof and fat cables snaking down into the basement. Headquarters of *The Industry Weatherman,* journal of the tech VC community and Miriam's employer for the past three years. She swiped her pass-card, hit the elevator up to the third floor, and stepped out into cubicle farm chaos. Desks with PCs and drifts of paper that overflowed onto the floor: A couple of harried Puerto Rican cleaners emptied garbage cans into a trolley laden with bags, to a background of phones ringing and anchors gabbling on CNN, Bloomberg, Fox. Black space-age Aeron chairs everywhere, all wire and plastic, electric chairs for a fully wired future.

" 'Lo, Emily," she nodded, passing the departmental secretary.

"Hi! With you in a sec." Emily lifted her finger from the "mute" button, went back to glassy-eyed attention. "Yes, I'll send them up as soon as—"

Miriam's desk was clean: The stack of press releases was orderly, the computer monitor was polished, and there were no dead coffee cups lying around. By tech journalist standards, this made her a neat freak. She'd always been that way about her work, even when she was a toddler. Liked all her crayons lined up in a row. Occasionally she wished she could manage the housework the same way, but for some reason the skill set didn't seem to be transferable. But this was work, and work was always under control. *I wonder where Paulie's gotten to?*

"Hi, babe!" As if on cue, Paulette poked her head around the side of the partition. Short, blonde, and bubbly, not even a rainy Monday morning could dent her enthusiasm. "How's it going? You ready to teach these goodfellas a lesson?"

" 'Goodfellas?' " Miriam raised an eyebrow. Paulette took the cue, slid sideways into her cubicle, and dropped into the spare chair, forcing Miriam to shuffle sideways to make room. Paulie was obviously enjoying herself: It was one of the few benefits of being a research gofer. Miriam waited.

"Goodfellas," Paulette said with relish. "You want a coffee? This is gonna take a while."

"Coffee." Miriam considered. "That would be good."

"Yeah, well." Paulette stood up. "Read this, it'll save us both some time." She pointed out a two-inch-thick sheaf of printouts and photocopies to Miriam, then made a beeline for the departmental coffeepot.

Miriam sighed and rubbed her eyes as she read the first page. Paulie had done her job with terrifying efficiency yet again: Miriam had only worked with her on a couple of investigations before—mostly Miriam's workload didn't require the data mining Paulette specialized in—but every single time she'd come away feeling a little dizzy.

Automobile emissions tests in California? Miriam squinted and turned the page. Failed autos, a chain of repair shops buying them for cash and shipping them south to Mexico and Brazil for stripping or resale. "What's this got to do with—" she stopped. "Aha!"

"Nondairy creamer, one sweetener," said Paulie, planting a coffee mug at her left hand.

"This is great stuff," Miriam muttered, flipping more pages. *Company accounts.* A chain of repair shops that— "I was hoping you'd find something in the small shareholders. *How* much are these guys in for?"

"They're buying about ten, eleven million in shares each year." Paulette shrugged, then blew across her coffee and pulled a face. "Which is crazy, because their business only turns over about fifteen mill. What kind of business puts eighty percent of its gross into a pension fund? One that bought two hundred and seventy-four autos last year for fifty bucks a shot, shipped them south of the border, and made an average of forty *thousand* bucks for each one they sold. And the couple of listed owners I phoned didn't want to talk."

Miriam looked up suddenly. "You phoned them?" she demanded.

"Yes, I—oh. Relax, I told them I was a dealership in Vegas and I was just doing a background check."

" 'Background check.' " Miriam snorted. "What if they've got caller-ID?"

"You think they're going to follow it up?" Paulette asked, looking worried.

"Paulie, you've got *eleven million* in cash being laundered through this car dealership and you think they're not going to sit up and listen if someone starts asking questions about where those beaters are coming from and how come they're fetching more than a new Lexus south of the border?"

"Oh. Oh shit."

"Yes. 'Oh shit' indeed. How'd you get into the used car trail anyway?"

Paulette shrugged and looked slightly embarrassed. "You asked me to follow up the shareholders for Proteome Dynamics and Biphase Technologies. Pacific Auto Services looked kind of odd to me—why would a car dealership have a pension fund sticking eight digits into cutting-edge proteome research? And there's another ten like them, too. Small mom-and-pop businesses doing a lot of export down south with seven- or eight-digit stakeholdings. I traced another—flip to the next?"

"Okay. Dallas Used Semiconductors. Buying used IBM mainframe kit? That's not our—and selling it to—oh shit."

"Yeah." Paulie frowned. "I looked up the book value. Whoever's buying those five-year-old computers down in Argentina is paying ninety percent of the price for new kit in cash greenbacks—they're the next thing to legal currency down there. But up here, a five-year-old mainframe goes for about two cents on the dollar."

"And you're *sure* all this is going into Proteome and Biphase?" Miriam shook the thick sheaf of paper into shape. "I can't believe this!"

"Believe it." Paulette drained her coffee cup and shoved a stray lock of hair back into position.

Miriam whistled tunelessly. "What's the bottom line?"

" 'The bottom line?' " Paulette looked uncomfortable. "I haven't counted it, but—"

"Make a guess."

"I'd say someone is laundering between fifty and a hundred million dollars a year here. Turning dirty cash into clean shares in Proteome Dynamics and Biphase Technologies. Enough to show up in their SEC filings. So your hunch was right."

"And nobody in Executive Country has asked any questions," Miriam concluded. "If I was paranoid, I'd say it's like a conspiracy of silence. Hmm." She put her mug down. "Paulie. You worked for a law firm. Would you call this . . . circumstantial?"

" 'Circumstantial?' " Paulette's expression was almost pitying. "Who's paying you, the defense? This is enough to get the FBI and the DA muttering about RICO."

"Yeah, but . . ." Miriam nodded to herself. "Look, this is heavy. Heavier than usual anyway. I can guarantee you that if we spring this story we'll get three responses. One will be flowers in our hair, and the other will be a bunch of cease-

and-desist letters from attorneys. Freedom of the press is all very well, but a good reputation and improved circulation figures won't buy us defense lawyers, which is why I want to double-check everything in here *before* I go upstairs and tell Sandy we want the cover. Because the third response is going to be oh-shit-I-don't-want-to-believe-this, because our great leader and teacher thinks the sun shines out of Biphase and I think he's into Proteome too."

"Who do you take me for?" Paulette pointed at the pile. "That's *primary,* Miriam, the wellspring. SEC filings, public accounts, the whole lot. Smoking gun. The summary sheet—" she tugged at a Post-it note gummed to a page a third of the way down the stack—"says it all. I was in here all day yesterday and half the evening—"

"I'm sorry!" Miriam raised her hand. "Hey, really. I had no idea."

"I kind of lost track of time," Paulette admitted. She smiled. "It's not often I get something *interesting* to dig into. Anyway, if the boss is into these two, I'd think he'd be glad of the warning. Gives him time to pull out his stake before we run the story."

"Yeah, well." Miriam stood up. "I think we want to bypass Sandy. This goes to the top."

"But Sandy needs to know. It'll mess with his page plan—"

"Yeah, but someone has to call Legal before we run with this. It's the biggest scoop we've had all year. Want to come with me? I think you earned at least half the credit . . ."

They shared the elevator up to executive row in silence. It was walled in mirrors, reflecting their contrasts: Paulette, a short blonde with disorderly curls and a bright red blouse, and Miriam, a slim five-foot-eight, dressed entirely in black. The business research wonk and the journalist, on their way to see the editorial director. *Some Mondays are better than others,* thought Miriam. She smiled tightly at Paulette in the mirror and Paulie grinned back: a worried expression, slightly apprehensive.

The Industry Weatherman was mostly owned by a tech venture capital firm who operated out of the top floors of the building, their offices intermingled with those of the magazine's directors. Two floors up, the corridors featured a better grade of carpet and the walls were genuine partitions covered in oak veneer, rather than fabric-padded cubicles. That was the only difference she could see—that and the fact that some of the occupants were assholes like the people she wrote glowing profiles of for a living. *I've never met a tech VC who a shark would bite,* Miriam thought grumpily. *Professional courtesy among killers.* The current incumbent of the revolving door office labeled EDITORIAL DIRECTOR—officially a vice president—was an often-absent executive by the name of Joe Dixon. Miriam led Paulette to the office and paused for a moment, then knocked on the door, half-hoping to find he wasn't there.

"Come in." The door opened in her face, and it was Joe himself, not his secretary. He was over six feet, with expensively waved black hair, wearing his suit jacket over an open-necked dress shirt. He oozed corporate polish: If he'd been ten years older, he could have made a credible movie career as a captain of industry. As it was, Miriam always found herself wondering how he'd climbed into the boardroom so young. He was in his mid-thirties, not much older than she was. "Hi." He took in Miriam and Paulette standing just behind her and smiled. "What can I do for you?"

Miriam smiled back. "May we have a moment?" she asked.

"Sure, come in." Joe retreated behind his desk. "Have a chair, both of you." He nodded at Paulette. "Miriam, we haven't been introduced."

"Oh, yes. Joe Dixon, Paulette Milan. Paulie is one of our heavy hitters in industrial research. She's been working with me on a story and I figured we'd better bring it to you first before taking it to the weekly production meeting. It's a bit, uh, sensitive."

" 'Sensitive.' " Joe leaned back in his chair and looked straight at her. "Is it big?"

"Could be," Miriam said noncommittally. *Big? It's the*

biggest I've ever worked on! A big story in her line of work might make or break a career; this one might send people to jail. "It has complexities to it that made me think you'd want advance warning before it breaks."

"Tell me about it," said Joe.

"Okay. Paulie, you want to start with your end?" She passed Paulette the file.

"Yeah." Paulie grimaced as she opened the file and launched into her explanation. "In a nutshell, they're laundries for dirty money. There's enough of a pattern to it that if I was a DA in California I'd be picking up the phone to the local FBI office."

"That's why I figured you'd want to know," Miriam explained. "This is a big deal, Joe. I think we've got enough to pin a money-laundering rap on a couple of really big corporations and make it stick. But last November you were talking to some folks at Proteome, and I figured you might want to refer this to Legal and make sure you're fire-walled before this hits the fan."

"Well. That's very interesting." Joe smiled back at her. "Is that your file on this story?"

"Yeah," said Paulette.

"Would you mind leaving it with me?" he asked. He cleared his throat. "I'm kind of embarrassed," he said, shrugging a small-boy shrug. The defensive set of his shoulders backed his words. "Look, I'm going to have to read this myself. Obviously, the scope for mistakes is—" he shrugged.

Suddenly Miriam had a sinking feeling: *It's going to be bad.* She racked her brains for clues. *Is he going to try to bury us?*

Joe shook his head. "Look, I'd like to start by saying that this isn't about anything you've done," he added hurriedly. "It's just that we've got an investment to protect and I need to work out how to do so."

"Before we break the story." Miriam forced another, broader, smile. "It was all in the public record," she added. "If we don't break it, one of our competitors will."

"Oh, I don't know," Joe said smoothly. "Listen, I'll get

back to you in an hour or so. If you leave this with me for
now, I just need to go and talk to someone in Legal so we can
sort out how to respond. Then I'll let you know how we're
going to handle it."

"Oh, okay then," said Paulette acceptingly.

Miriam let her expression freeze in a fixed grin. *Oh shit,*
she thought as she stood up. "Thanks for giving us your
time," she said.

"Let yourselves out," Joe said tersely, already turning the
first page.

Out in the corridor, Paulette turned to Miriam. "Didn't
that go *well*?" she insisted.

Miriam took a deep breath. "Paulie."

"Yeah?"

Her knees felt weak. "Something's wrong."

"What?" Paulette looked concerned.

"Elevator." She hit the "call" button and waited in silence,
trying to still the butterflies in her stomach. It arrived, and
she waited for the doors to close behind them before she
continued. "I may just have made a bad mistake."

"'Mistake?'" Paulette looked puzzled. "You don't think—"

"He didn't say anything about publishing," Miriam said
slowly. "Not one word. What were the other names on that
list of small investors? The ones you didn't check?"

"The list? He's got—" Paulette frowned.

"Was Somerville Investments one of them?"

"Somerville? Could be. Why? Who are they?"

"Because that's—" Miriam pointed a finger at the roof
and circled. She watched Paulette's eyes grow round.

"I'm thinking about magazine returns from the newsstand
side of the business, Paulie. Don't you know we've got low
returns by industry standards? And people buy magazines
for cash."

"Oh."

"I'm sorry, Paulie."

When they got back to Miriam's cubicle, a uniformed security guard and a suit from Human Resources were already
waiting for them.

"Paulette Milan? Miriam Beckstein?" said the man from HR. He checked a notepad carefully.

"Yes?" Miriam asked cautiously. "What's up?"

"Would you please follow me? Both of you?"

He turned and headed for the stairwell down to the main entrance. Miriam glanced around and saw the security guard pull a brief expression of discomfort. "Go on, ma'am."

"Go on," echoed Paulette from her left shoulder, her face white.

This can't be happening, Miriam thought woodenly. She felt her feet carrying her toward the staircase and down, toward the glass doors at the front.

"Cards, please," said the man from Human Resources. He held out his hand impatiently. Miriam passed him her card reluctantly: Paulette followed suit.

He cleared his throat and looked them over superciliously. "I've been told to tell you that *The Industry Weatherman* won't be pressing charges," he said. "We'll clear your cubicles and forward your personal items and your final paycheck to your addresses of record. But you're no longer allowed on the premises." The security guard took up a position behind him, blocking the staircase. "Please leave."

"What's going *on*?" Paulette demanded, her voice rising toward a squeak.

"You're both being terminated," the HR man said impassively. "Misappropriation of company resources; specifically, sending personal e-mail on company time and looking at pornographic Web sites."

" 'Pornographic—' " Miriam felt herself going faint with fury. She took half a step toward the HR man and barely noticed Paulette grabbing her sleeve.

"It's not worth it, Miriam," Paulie warned her. "We both know it isn't true." She glared at the HR man. "You work for Somerville Investments, don't you?"

He nodded incuriously. "Please leave. *Now*."

Miriam forced herself to smile. "Better brush up your résumé," she said shakily and turned toward the exit.

Two-thirds of her life ago, when she was eleven, Miriam had been stung by a hornet. It had been a bad one: Her arm had swollen up like a balloon, red and sore and painful to touch, and the sting itself had hurt like crazy. But the worst thing of all was the sense of moral indignation and outrage. Miriam-aged-eleven had been minding her own business, playing in the park with her skateboard—she'd been a tomboy back then, and some would say she still was—and she hadn't done anything to provoke the angry yellow-and-black insect. It just flew at her, wings whining angrily, landed, and before she could shake it off it stung her.

She'd howled.

This time she was older and much more self-sufficient—college, pre-med, and her failed marriage to Ben had given her a grounding in self-sufficiency—so she managed to say good-bye to an equally shocked Paulie and make it into her car before she broke down. And the tears came silently—this time. It was raining in the car park, but she couldn't tell whether there was more water inside or outside. They weren't tears of pain: They were tears of anger. *That bastard—*

For a moment, Miriam fantasized about storming back in through the fire door at the side of the building, going up to Joe Dixon's office, and pushing him out of the big picture window. It made her feel better to think about that, but after a few minutes she reluctantly concluded that it wouldn't solve anything. Joe had the file. He had her computer—and Paulie's—and a moment's thought told her that those machines would be being wiped right now. Doubtless, server logs showing her peeking at porn on the job would be being fabricated. She'd spoken to some geeks at a dot-com startup once who explained just how easy it was if you wanted to get someone dismissed. "Shit," she mumbled to herself and sniffed. "I'll have to get another job. Shouldn't be too hard, even without a reference."

Still, she was badly shaken. Journalists didn't get fired for exposing money-laundering scams; that was in the rules somewhere. Wasn't it? In fact, it was completely crazy. She blinked away the remaining angry tears. *I need to go see Iris,* she decided. Tomorrow would be soon enough to start looking for a new job. Or to figure out a way to break the story herself, if she was going to try and do it freelance. Today she needed a shoulder to cry on—and a sanity check. And if there was one person who could provide both, it was her adoptive mother.

Iris Beckstein lived alone in her old house near Lowell Park. Miriam felt obscurely guilty about visiting her during day-time working hours. Iris never tried to mother her, being content to wander around and see to her own quiet hobbies most of the time since Morris had died. But Miriam also felt guilty about *not* visiting Iris more often. Iris was convalescent, and the possibility of losing her mother so soon after her father had died filled her with dread. Another anchor was threatening to break free, leaving her adrift in the world.

She parked the car in the road, then made a dash for the front door—the rain was descending in a cold spray, threatening to turn to penetrating sheets—and rang the doorbell, then unlocked the door and went in as the two-tone chime echoed inside.

"Ma?"

"Through here," Iris called. Miriam entered, closing the front door. The hallway smelled faintly floral, she noticed as she shed her raincoat and hung it up: *The visiting home help must be responsible.* "I'm in the back room."

Doors and memories lay ajar before Miriam as she hurried toward the living room. She'd grown up in this house, the one Morris and Iris had bought back when she was a baby. The way the third step on the staircase creaked when you put your weight on it, the eccentricities of the downstairs toilet, the way the living room felt cramped from all the bookshelves—the way it felt too big, without Dad. "Ma?" She pushed open the living room door hesitantly.

Iris smiled at her from her wheelchair. "So nice of you to visit! Come in! To what do I owe the pleasure?"

The room was furnished with big armchairs and a thread-bare sofa deep enough to drown in. There was no televi-sion—neither Iris nor Morris had time for it—but there were bookcases on each wall and a tottering tower of paper next to Iris's chair. Miriam crossed the room, leaned over, and kissed Iris on top of her head, then stood back. "You're look-ing well," she said anxiously, hoping it was true. She wanted to hug her mother, but she looked increasingly frail—only in her fifties, but her hair was increasingly gray, and the skin on the backs of her hands seemed to be more wrinkled every time Miriam visited.

"I won't break—at least, I don't think so. Not if you only hug me." Iris grimaced. "It's been bad for the past week, but I think I'm on the mend again." The chair she sat in was newer than the rest of the furniture, surrounded by the im-pedimenta of invalidity: a little side trolley with her crochet and an insulated flask full of herbal tea, her medicines, and a floor-standing lamp with a switch high up its stem. "Marge just left. She'll be back later, before supper."

"That's good. I hope she's been taking care of you well."

"She does her best." Iris nodded, slightly dismissively. "I've got physiotherapy tomorrow. Then another session with my new neurologist, Dr. Burke—he's working with a clinical trial on a new drug that's looking promising and we're going to discuss that. It's supposed to stop the pro-gressive demyelination process, but I don't understand half the jargon in the report. Could you translate it for me?"

"Mother! You know I don't do that stuff any more—I'm not current; I might miss something. Anyway, if you go telling your osteopath about me, he'll panic. I'm not a bone doctor."

"Well, if you say so." Iris looked irritated. "All that time in medical school wasn't wasted, was it?"

"No, Mom, I use it every day. I couldn't do my job with-out it. I just don't know enough about modern multiple scle-rosis drug treatments to risk second-guessing your specialist, all right? I might get it wrong, and then who'd you sue?"

"If you say so." Iris snorted. "You didn't come here just to talk about that, did you?"

Damn, thought Miriam. It had always been very difficult to pull one over on her mother. "I lost my job," she confessed.

"I wondered." Iris nodded thoughtfully. "All those dot-coms of yours, it was bound to be infectious. Is that what happened?"

"No." Miriam shook her head. "I stumbled across something and mishandled it badly. They fired me. And Paulie . . . Remember I told you about her?"

Iris closed her eyes. "Bastards. The bosses are bastards."

"Mother!" Miriam wasn't shocked at the language—Iris's odd background jumped out to bite her at the strangest moments—but it was the risk of misunderstanding. "It's not that simple; I screwed up."

"So you screwed up. Are you going to tell me you deserved to be fired?" asked Iris.

"No. But I should have dug deeper before I tried to run the story," Miriam said carefully. "I was too eager, got sloppy. There were connections. It's deep and it's big and it's messy; the people who own *The Weatherman* didn't want to be involved in exposing it."

"So that excuses them, does it?" asked Iris, her eyes narrowing.

"No, it—" Miriam stopped.

"Stop making excuses for them and I'll stop chasing you." Iris sounded almost amused. "They took your job to protect their own involvement in some dirty double-dealing. Is that what you're telling me?"

"Yeah. I guess."

"Well." Iris's eyes flashed. "When are you going to hang them? And how high? I want a ringside seat!"

"Ma." Miriam looked at her mother with mingled affection and exasperation. "It's not that easy. I think *The Weatherman*'s owners are deeply involved in something illegal. Money laundering. Dirty money. Insider trading too, probably. I'd like to nail them, but they're going to play dirty if I try. It took them about five minutes to come up with cause for dismissal, and they said they wouldn't press charges if I kept my mouth shut."

"What kind of charges?" Iris demanded.

"They say they've got logfiles to prove I was net-surfing pornography at work. They . . . they—" Miriam found she was unable to go on speaking.

"So were you?" Iris asked quietly.

"No!" Miriam startled herself with her vehemence. She caught Iris's sly glance and felt sheepish. "Sorry. No, I wasn't. It's a setup. But it's so easy to claim—and virtually impossible to disprove."

"Are you going to be able to get another job?" Iris prodded.

"Yes." Miriam fell silent.

"Then it's all right. I really couldn't do with my daughter expecting me to wash her underwear after all these years."

"Mother!" Then Miriam spotted the sardonic grin.

"Tell me about it. I mean, everything. Warm a mother's heart, spill the beans on the assholes who took her daughter's job away."

Miriam flopped down on the big overstuffed sofa. "It's either a very long story or a very short one," she confessed. "I got interested in a couple of biotech companies that looked just a little bit odd. Did some digging, got Paulette involved— she digs like a drilling platform—and we came up with some dirt. A couple of big companies are being used as targets for money laundering.

"Turns out that *The Weatherman's* parent company is into them, deep. They decided it would be easier to fire us and threaten us than to run the story and take their losses. I'm probably going to get home and find a SLAPP lawsuit sitting in my mailbox."

"So. What are you going to do about it?"

Miriam met her mother's penetrating stare. "Ma, I spent *three years* there. And they fired me cold, without even trying to get me to shut up, at the first inconvenience. Do you really think I'm going to let them get away with that if I can help it?"

"What about loyalty?" Iris asked, raising an eyebrow.

"I gave them mine." Miriam shrugged. "That's part of why this hurts. You earn loyalty by giving it."

"You'd have made a good feudal noble. They were big on loyalty, too. And blind obedience, in return."

"Wrong century, wrong side of the Atlantic, in case you hadn't noticed."

Now Iris grinned. "Oh, I noticed that much," she conceded. "No foreign titles of nobility. That's one of the reasons why I stayed here—that, and your father." Her smile slipped. "Never could understand what the people here see in kings and queens, either the old hereditary kind or the modern presidential type. All those paparazzi, drooling after monarchs. I like your line of work. It's more honest."

"Harder to keep your job when you're writing about the real world," Miriam brooded gloomily. She struggled to sit a little straighter. "Anyway, I didn't come around here to mope at you. I figure I can leave job-hunting until tomorrow morning."

"Are you sure you're going to be all right?" Iris asked pointedly. "You mentioned lawsuits—or worse."

"In the short term—" Miriam shrugged, then took a deep breath. "Yes," she admitted. "I guess I'll be okay as long as I leave them alone."

"Hmm." Iris looked at Miriam sidelong. "How much money are we talking about here? If they're pulling fake lawsuits to shut you up, that's not business as usual."

"There's—" Miriam did some mental arithmetic— "about fifty to a hundred million a year flowing through this channel."

Iris swore.

"Ma!"

"Don't you 'Ma' me!" Iris snorted.

"But—"

"Listen to your old ma. You came here for advice, I'm going to give it, all right? You're telling me you just happened to stumble across a money-laundering operation that's handling more money in a week than most people earn in their life. And you think they're going to settle for firing you and hoping you stay quiet?"

Miriam snorted. "It can't possibly be that bad, Ma, this isn't goodfellas territory, and anyway, they've got that faked evidence."

Iris shook her head stubbornly. "When you've got criminal activities and millions of dollars in cash together, there are no limits to what people can do." For the first time, Miriam realized with a sinking feeling, Iris looked worried. "But maybe I'm being too pessimistic—you've just lost your job and whatever else, that's going to be a problem. How are your savings?"

Miriam glanced at the rain-streaked window. *What's turned Ma so paranoid?* she wondered, unsettled. "They're not doing badly. I've been saving for the past ten years."

"There's my girl," Iris said approvingly.

"I put my money into tech-sector shares."

"No, you didn't!" Iris looked shocked.

Miriam nodded. "But no dot-coms."

"Really?"

"Most people think that all tech stocks are down. But biotech stocks actually crashed out in ninety-seven and have been recovering ever since. The bubble last year didn't even touch them. People need new medicines more than they need flashy Web sites that sell toys, don't they? I was planning on paying off my mortgage year after next. Now I guess it'll have to wait a bit longer—but I'm not in trouble unless I stay unemployed over a year."

"Well, at least you found a use for all that time in med school." Iris looked relieved. "So you're not hard up."

"Not in the short term," Miriam corrected instinctively. "Ask me again in six months. Anyway, is there anything I can get you while I'm here?"

"A good stiff drink." Iris clucked to herself. "Listen, I'm going to be all right. The disease, it comes and it goes—another few weeks and I'll be walking again." She gestured at the aluminum walking frame next to her chair. "I've been getting plenty of rest and with Marge around twice a day I can just about cope, apart from the boredom. I've even been doing a bit of filing and cleaning, you know, turning out the dusty old corners?"

"Oh, right. Turned anything up?"

"Lots of dustballs. Anyway," she continued after a moment. "There's some stuff I've been meaning to hand over to you."

"'Stuff.'" For a moment, Miriam couldn't focus on the problem at hand. It was too much to deal with. She'd lost her job and then, the very same day, her mother wanted to talk about selling her home. "I'm sorry, I'm not very focused today."

"Not very—" Iris snorted. "You're like a microscope, girl! Most other people would be walking around in a daze. It's not very considerate of me, I know, it's just that I've been thinking about things and there's some stuff you really should have right now. Partly because you're grown up and partly because it belongs to you—you might have some use for it. Stuff that might get overlooked."

Miriam must have looked baffled because Iris smiled at her encouragingly. "Yes. You know, 'stuff.' Photograph albums, useless things like Morris's folks' birth certificates, my old passport, my parents' death certificates, your adoption papers. Some stuff relating to your birth-mother, too."

Miriam shook her head. "My adoption papers—why would I want them? That's old stuff, and you're the only mother I've ever had." She looked at Iris fiercely. "You're not allowed to push me away!"

"Well! And who said I was? I just figured you wouldn't want to lose the opportunity. If you ever felt like trying to trace your roots. It belongs to you, and I think now is definitely past time for you to have it. I kept the newspaper pages too, you know. It caused quite a stir." Miriam made a face. "I *know* you're not interested," Iris said placatingly. "Humor me. There's a box."

"A box."

"A pink and green shoebox. Sitting on the second shelf of your father's bureau in the guest bedroom upstairs. Do me a favor and fetch it down, will you?"

"Just for you."

Miriam found the box easily enough. It rattled when she picked it up and carried it, smelling of mothballs, down to the living room. Iris had picked up her crochet again and was pulling knots with an expression of fierce concentration. "Dr. Hare told me to work on it," she said without looking up. "It helps preserve hand-eye coordination."

"I see." Miriam put the box down on the sofa. "What's this one?"

"A Klein-bottle cozy." Iris looked up defensively at Miriam's snort. "You should laugh! In this crazy inside-out world, we must take our comforts from crazy inside-out places."

"You and Dad." Miriam waved it off. "Both crazy inside-out sorts of people."

"*Bleeding hearts*, you mean," Iris echoed ominously. "People who refuse to bottle it all up, who live life on the outside, who—" she glanced around— "end up growing old disgracefully." She sniffed. "Stop me before I reminisce again. Open the box!"

Miriam obeyed. It was half-full of yellowing, carefully folded newsprint and elderly photocopies of newspaper stories. Then there was a paper bag and some certificates and pieces of formal paperwork made up the rest of its contents. "The bag contained stuff that was found with your birthmother by the police," Iris explained. "Personal effects. They had to keep the clothing as evidence, but nobody ever came forward and after a while they passed the effects on to Morris for safekeeping. There's a locket of your mother's in there—I think you ought to keep it in a safe place for now; I think it's probably quite valuable. The papers—it was a terrible thing. Terrible."

Miriam unfolded the uppermost sheet; it crackled slightly with age as she read it. UNKNOWN WOMAN FOUND STABBED, BABY TAKEN INTO CUSTODY. It gave her a most peculiar feeling. She'd known about it for many years, of course, but this was like seeing it for the first time in a history book, written down in black and white. "They *still* don't know who she was?" Miriam asked.

"Why should they?" Iris looked at her oddly. "Sometimes they can reopen the case when new evidence comes to light, or do DNA testing, but after thirty-two years most of the witnesses will have moved away or died. The police officers who first looked into it will have retired. Probably nothing happens unless a new lead comes up. Say, they find another body or someone confesses years later. It's just one of those terrible things that sometimes happen to people. The only unusual thing about it was you." She looked at Miriam fondly.

"Why they let two radicals, one of them a resident alien and both of them into antiwar protests and stuff like that, adopt a baby—" Miriam shook her head. Then she grinned. "Did they think I would slow you down or something?"

"Possibly, possibly. But I don't remember being asked any questions about our politics when we went to the adoption agency—it was much easier to adopt in those days. They didn't ask much about our background except whether we were married. We didn't save the newspapers at the time, by the way. Morris bought them as morgue copies later."

"Well." Miriam replaced the news clipping, put the lid back on the box, and contemplated it. "Ancient history."

"You know, if you wanted to investigate it—" Iris was using *that* look on her, the penetrating diamond-tipped stare of inquisition, the one Miriam tried to think herself into when interviewing difficult customers—"I bet a journalist of your experience would do better than some doughnut stuffed policeman on a routine job. Don't you think?"

"I think I really ought to help my real mother figure out what she's going to do about not going stir-crazy while she gets better," Miriam replied lightly. "There are more immediate things to investigate, like whether your tea is cold and if there are any cookies in the kitchen. Why don't we leave digging up the dead past for some other time?"

PINK SLIPPERS

Miriam drove away slowly, distractedly, nodding in time to the beat of the windshield wipers. Traffic was as bad as usual, but nothing untoward penetrated her thoughts.

She parked, then hunched her shoulders against the weather and scurried to her front door. As usual, her keys got muddled up. *Why does this always happen when I'm in a hurry?* She wondered. Inside, she shook her way out of her raincoat and jacket like a newborn moth emerging from its sodden cocoon, hung them on the coat rail, then dumped her shoulder bag and the now-damp cardboard box on the old telephone table and bent to unzip her boots. Free of the constraints of leather, her feet flexed luxuriously as she slid them into a pair of battered pink slippers. Then she spotted the answering machine's blinking light. "You have *new* messages," she sang to herself, slightly manic with relief at being home. "Fuck 'em." She headed for the kitchen to switch on the coffeepot, then poured a mug and carried it into her den.

The den had once been the dining room of this suburban home, a rectangular space linked to the living room by an archway and to the kitchen by a serving hatch. Now it was a cramped office, two walls jammed with bookcases and a third occupied by a huge battered desk. The remaining wall was occupied by a set of french windows opening onto the rear deck. Rain left twisting slug trails down the windows, kicking up splashes from the half-submerged ceramic pots outside. Miriam planted the coffee mug in the middle of the pile of stuff that accumulated on her desk and frowned at the effect. "It's a mess," she said aloud, bemused. "How the hell did it get this untidy?"

"This is *bad*," she said, standing in front of her desk. "You hear me?" The stubborn paperwork and scattering of gadgets stubbornly refused to obey, so she attacked them, sorting the letters into piles, opening unopened mail and discarding the junk, hunting receipts and filing bills. The desk turned out to be almost nine months' deep in trivia, and cleaning it up was a welcome distraction from having to think about her experience at work. When the desk actually showed a clear surface— and she'd applied the kitchen cleaner to the coffee rings—she started on the e-mail. That took longer, and by the time she'd checked off everything in her in-box, the rain battering on the windows was falling out of a darkening sky as night fell.

When everything was looking shipshape, another thought struck her. "Paperwork. Hmm." She went through into the hall and fetched the pink and green shoebox. Making a face, she upended it onto the desk. Papers mushroomed out, and something clattered and skittered onto the floor. "Huh?"

It was a paper bag. Something in it, a hard, cold nucleus, had spilled over the edge of the desk. She hunted around for a few seconds, then stooped and triumphantly deposited bag and contents next to the pile of yellowing clippings, rancid photocopies, and creamy documents. One of which, now that she examined it, looked like a birth certificate—no, one of those forms that gets filled in in place of a birth certificate when the full details are unknown. Baby Jane Doe, age approximately six weeks, weight blah, eye color green, sex female, parents unknown . . . for a moment Miriam felt as if she was staring at it down a dark tunnel from a long way away.

Ignoring the thing-that-rattled, Miriam went through the papers and sorted these, too, into two stacks. Press clippings and bureaucracy. The clippings were mostly photocopies: They told a simple—if mysterious—tale that had been familiar to her since the age of four. A stabbing in the park. A young woman—apparently a hippie or maybe a Gypsy, judging by her strange clothes—found dead on the edge of a wooded area. The cause of death was recorded as massive blood loss caused by a deep wound across her back and left shoulder, inflicted by some kind of edged weapon, maybe a machete. That was unusual enough. What made it even more unusual was the presence of the six-week-old baby shrieking her little heart out nearby. An elderly man walking his dog had called the police. It was a seven-day wonder.

Miriam knew the end to that story lay somewhere in Morris and Iris Beckstein's comforting arms. She'd done her best to edit this other dangling bloody end to the story out of her life. She didn't want to be someone else's child: She had two perfectly good parents of her own, and the common assumption that blood ties must be thicker than upbringing rankled. Iris's history taught better—the only child of Holocaust refugees settled in an unfriendly English town after the war, she'd emigrated at twenty and never looked back after meeting and marrying Morris.

Miriam shook out the contents of the paper bag over the not-quite birth certificate. It was a lens-shaped silver locket on a fine chain. Tarnished and dull with age, its surface was engraved with some sort of crest of arms: a shield and animals. It looked distinctly cheap. "Hmm." She picked it up and peered at it closely. *This must be what Ma told me about,* she thought. *Valuable?* There was some sort of catch under the chain's loop. "I wonder . . ."

She opened it.

Instead of the lover's photographs she'd half-expected, the interior of the shell contained a knotwork design, enamel painted in rich colors. Curves of rich ochre looped and interpenetrated, weaving above and beneath a branch of turquoise. The design was picked out in silver—it was far brighter than the exposed outer case had suggested.

Miriam sighed and leaned back in her sprung office chair. "Well, there goes *that* possibility," she told the press clippings gloomily. No photographs of her mother or long-lost father. Just some kind of tacky cloissoné knotwork design.

She looked at it closer. Knotwork. Vaguely Celtic knotwork. The left-hand cell appeared to be a duplicate of the right-hand one. If she traced that arc from the top left and followed it under the blue arc—

Why had her birth-mother carried this thing? What did it mean to her? (The blue arc connected through two interlinked green whorls.) What had *she* seen when she stared into it? Was it some kind of meditation aid? Or just a pretty picture? It certainly wasn't any kind of coat of arms.

Miriam leaned back further. Lifting the locket, she dangled it in front of her eyes, letting the light from the bookcase behind her catch the silver highlights. Beads of dazzling blue-white heat seemed to trace their way around the knot's heart. She squinted, feeling her scalp crawl. The sound of her heart beating in her ears became unbearably loud: There was a smell of burning toast, the sight of an impossible knot twisting in front of her eyes like some kind of stereoisogram forming in midair, trying to turn her head inside out—

Three things happened simultaneously. An abrupt sense of nausea washed over her, the lightbulb went out, and her chair fell over backward.

"*Ouch!* Dammit!" Something thumped into Miriam's side, doubling her over as she hit the ground and rolled over, pulling her arms in to protect her face. A racking spasm caught her by the gut, leaving her feeling desperately sick, and the arm of the chair came around and whacked her in the small of her back. Her knees were wet, and the lights were out. "Shit!" Her head was splitting, the heartbeat throb pounding like a jackhammer inside her skull, and her stomach was twisting. A sudden flash of fear: *This can't be a migraine. The onset is* way *too fast. Malignant hypertension?*

The urge to vomit was strong, but after a moment it began to ebb. Miriam lay still for a minute, waiting for her stomach to come under control and the lights to come back on. *Shit, am I having an aneurism?* She gripped the locket so tightly that it threatened to dig a hole in her right fist. Carefully she tried to move her arms and legs: Everything seemed to be working and she managed a shallow sigh of relief. Finally, when she was sure her guts were going to be alright, she pushed herself up onto her knees and saw—

Trees.

Trees everywhere.

Trees inside her den.

Where did the walls go?

Afterward, she could never remember that next terrible minute. It was dark, of course, but not totally dark: She was in twilight on a forested slope, with beech and elm and other familiar trees looming ominously out of the twilight. The ground was dry, and her chair lay incongruously in a thicket of shrubbery not far from the base of a big maple tree. When she looked around, she could see no sign of her house, or the neighboring apartments, or of the lights along the highway. *Is there a total blackout?* she wondered, confused. *Did I sleepwalk or something?*

She stumbled to her feet, her slippers treacherous on leaf mulch and dry grass stems. She shivered. It was cold—not quite winter-cold but too damned chilly to be wandering around in pants, a turtleneck, and bedroom slippers. And—

"Where the hell *am* I?" she asked the empty sky. "What the *hell*?"

Then the irony of her situation kicked in and she began to giggle, frightened and edgy and afraid she wouldn't be able to stop. She did a twirl, in place, trying to see whatever there was to see. *Sylvan idyll at nightfall, still-life with deranged dot-com refugee and brown office furniture.* A gust of wind rattled the branches overhead, dislodging a chilly shower of fat drops: A couple landed on Miriam's arms and face, making her shudder.

The air was fresh—too fresh. And there was none of the

subliminal background hum of a big city, the noise that never completely died. It didn't get this quiet even out in the country—and indeed, when she paused to listen, it wasn't quiet; she could hear distant birdsong in the deepening twilight.

She took a deep breath, then another. Forced herself to thrust the hand with the locket into her hip pocket and let go of the thing. She patted it obsessively for a minute, whimpering slightly at the pain in her head. *No holes,* she thought vaguely. She'd once worn pants like this where her spare change had worn a hole in the pocket lining and eventually spilled on the ground, causing no end of a mess.

For some reason, the idea of losing possession of the locket filled her with a black terror.

She looked up. The first stars of evening were coming out, and the sky was almost clear of cloud. It was going to be a cold night.

"Item," she muttered. "You are not at home. *Ouch.* You have a splitting headache and you don't think you fell asleep in the chair, even though you were in it when you arrived here." She looked around in wild surmise. She'd never been one for the novels Ben occasionally read, but she'd seen enough trashy TV serials to pick up the idea. *Twilight Zone, Time Squad,* programs like that. "Item: I don't know where or when I am, but this ain't home. Do I stay put and hope I automagically snap back into my own kitchen or . . . what? It was the locket, no two ways about it. Do I look at it again to go back?"

She fumbled into her pocket nervously. Her fingers wrapped around warm metal. She breathed more easily. "Right. Right."

Just nerves, she thought. Alone in a forest at night—what lived here? Bears? Cougars? There could be anything here, anything at all. Be a fine joke if she went exploring and stepped on a rattler, wouldn't it? Although in this weather . . . "I'd better go home," she murmured to herself and was about to pull the locket out when she saw a flicker of light in the distance.

She was disoriented, tired, had just had a really bad day, and some cosmic trickster-god had dumped a magic amulet on her to see what she'd do with it. That was the only explanation, she reasoned afterward. A *sane* Miriam would have sat down and analyzed her options, then assembled a plan of action. But it wasn't a sane Miriam who saw those flickers of orange light and went crashing through the trees downhill toward them.

Lights. A jingle, as of chains. Thudding and hollow clonking noises—and low voices. She stumbled out into the sudden expanse of a trail—not a wide one, more of a hiking trail, the surface torn up and muddy. *Lights!* She stared at them, at the men on horseback coming down the trail toward her, the lantern held on a pole by the one in the lead. Dim light glinted off reflecting metal, helmet, and breastplate like something out of a museum. Someone called out something that sounded like: "Curl!" *Look. He's riding toward me,* she thought dazedly. *What's that he's—*

Her guts liquid with absolute fright, she turned and ran. The flat crack of rifle fire sounded behind her, repeated short bursts firing into the night. Invisible fingers ripped at the branches overhead as Miriam heard voices raised in hue and cry behind her. Low branches scratched at her face as she ran, gasping and crying, uphill away from the path. More bangs, more gunshots—astonishingly few of them, but any at all was too many. She ran straight into a tree, fell back winded, brains rattling around inside her head like dried peas in a pod, then she pushed herself to her feet again faster than she'd have believed possible and stumbled on into the night, gasping for breath, praying for rescue.

Eventually she stopped. Somewhere along the way she'd lost her slippers. Her face and ribs felt bruised, her head was pounding, and she could barely breathe. But she couldn't hear any sounds of pursuit. Her skin felt oddly tight, and everything was far too cold. As soon as she was no longer running, she doubled over and succumbed to a fit of racking coughs, prolonged by her desperate attempts to muffle them.

Her chest was on fire. *Oh god, any god. Whoever put me here. I just want you to know that I hate you!*

She stood up. Somewhere high overhead the wind sighed. Her skin itched with the fear of pursuit. *I've got to get home,* she realized. Now her skin crawled with *another* fear—fear that she might be wrong, that it wasn't the locket at all, that it was something else she didn't understand that had brought her here, that there was no way back and she'd be stranded—

When she flicked it open, the right-hand half of the locket crawled with light. Tiny specks of brilliance, not the phosphorescence of a watch dial or the bioluminescence of those plastic disposable flashlights that had become popular for a year or two, but an intense, bleached blue-white glare like a miniature star. Miriam panted, trying to let her mind drift into it, but after a minute she realized all she was achieving was giving herself a headache. "What did I *do* to make it work?" she mumbled, puzzled and frustrated and increasingly afraid. "If *she* could make it—"

Ah. That was what she'd been doing. Just relaxing, meditating. Wondering what the hell her birth-mother had seen in it. Miriam gritted her teeth. How was she going to re-create that sense of detached curiosity? Here in a wild forest at night, with strangers shooting at her in the dark? *How*—she narrowed her eyes. The headache. *If I can see my way past it, I could*—

The dots of light blazed up for a moment in glorious conflagration. Miriam jackknifed forward, saw the orange washout of streetlights shining down on a well-mowed lawn. Then her stomach rebelled and this time she couldn't keep it down. It was all she could do to catch her breath between heaves. Somehow her guts had been replaced by a writhing snake, and the racking spasms kept pulsing through her until she began to worry about tearing her esophagus.

Noise of a car slowing—then speeding up again as the driver saw her vomiting. A yell from the window, inarticulate, something like "Drunk fucking bums!" Something clattered into the road. Miriam didn't care. Dampness and cold clenched their icy fingers around her, but she didn't care: She was back in civilization, away from the threatening trees

and her pursuer. She stumbled off the front lawn of somebody's house and sensed harsh asphalt beneath her bare feet,
stones digging into her soles. A road sign said it was somewhere she knew. One of the other side roads off Grafton
Street, which her road also opened off. She was less than
half a mile from home.

Drip. She looked up. *Drip*. The rain began to fall again,
sluicing down her aching face. Her clothes were stained and
filthy with mud and vomit. Her legs were scratched and felt
bruised. *Home*. It was a primal imperative. *Put one foot in
front of another*, she told herself through the deafening hammering in her skull. Her head hurt, and the world was spinning around her.

An indefinite time—perhaps ten minutes, perhaps half an
hour—later, she saw a familiar sight through the downpour.
Soaked to the skin and shivering, she nevertheless felt like a
furnace. Her house seemed to shimmer like a mirage in the
desert when she looked at it. And now she discovered another problem—she'd come out without her keys! *Silly me,
what was I thinking?* she wondered vaguely. *Nothing but this
locket*, she thought, weaving its chain around her right index
finger.

The shed, whispered a vestige of cool control in the back
of her head.

Oh, yes, the shed, she answered herself.

She stumbled around the side of her house, past the
cramped green rug that passed for a yard, to the shed in
back. It was padlocked, but the small side window wasn't actually fastened and if you pulled just *so* it would open outward. It took her three tries and half a fingernail—the rain
had warped the wood somewhat—but once open she could
thrust an arm inside and fumble around for the hook with the
key dangling from it on a loop. She fetched the key, opened
the padlock—dropping it casually on the lawn—and found,
taped to the underside of the workbench, the spare key to the
french doors.

She was home.

WALK ON
THE WILD SIDE

Somehow Miriam found her way upstairs. She worked this out when she awakened sprawled on her bed, feet freezing and hot shivers chasing across her skin while a platoon of miners with pickaxes worked her head over. It was her bladder that woke her up and led her still half-asleep to the bathroom, where she turned on all the lights, shot the deadbolt on the door, used the toilet, and rummaged around for an Advil to help with the hangover symptoms. "What you need is a good shower," she told herself grimly, trying to ignore the pile of foul and stinking clothes on the floor that mingled with the towels she'd spilled everywhere the night before. Naked in a brightly lit pink and chromed bathroom, she spun the taps, sat on the edge of the bathtub, and tried to think her way past the haze of depression and pain.

"You're a big girl," she told the scalding hot waterfall as it gushed into the tub. "Big girls don't get bent out of shape by little things," she told herself. Like losing her job. "Big girls deal with divorces. Big girls deal with getting pregnant while they're at school, putting the baby up for adoption, finishing med school, and retraining for another career when they don't like the shitty options they get dealt. Big girls cope with marrying their boyfriends, then finding he's been sleeping with their best friends. Big girls make CEOs shit themselves when they come calling with a list of questions. They don't go crazy and think they're wandering around a rainy forest being shot at by armored knights with assault rifles." She sniffed, on the edge of tears.

A first rational thought intruded: *I'm getting depressed and that's no good.* Followed rapidly by a second one: *Where's the bubble bath?* Bubble bath was fun. Bubble bath was a *good* thought. Miriam didn't like wallowing in self-pity, although right now it was almost as tempting as a nice warm shower. She went and searched for the bubble bath, finally found the bottle in the trashcan—almost, but not entirely, empty. She held it under the tap and let the water rinse the last of the gel out, foaming and swirling around her feet.

Depression would be a perfectly reasonable response to losing my job, she told herself, *if it was actually my fault. Which it wasn't.* Lying back in the scented water and inhaling steam. *But going nuts? I don't think so.* She'd been through bad times. First the unplanned pregnancy by Ben, in her third year at college, too young and too early. She still couldn't fully articulate her reasons for not having an abortion; maybe if that bitch from the student counseling service hadn't simply assumed . . . but she'd never been one for doing what everyone expected her to do, and she'd been confident—maybe too confident—in her relationship with Ben. Hence the adoption. And then, a couple of years later when they got married, that hadn't been the smartest thing she'd ever done either. With twenty-twenty hindsight it had been a response to a relationship already on the rocks, the kind that could only end in tears. But she'd weathered it all without going crazy or even having a small breakdown. *Iron control, that's me.* But this new thing, the stumbling around the woods being shot at, seeing a *knight*, a guy in armor, with an M-16 or something—that was scary. *Time to face the music.* "Am I sane?" she asked the toilet duck.

Well, whatever this is, it ain't in DSM-IV. Miriam racked her memory for decade-old clinical lectures. No way was this schizophrenia. The symptoms were all wrong, and she wasn't hearing voices or feeling weird about people. It was just a single sharp incident, very vivid, realistic as—

She stared at her stained pants and turtleneck. "The chair," she muttered. "If the chair's missing, it was real. Or at least *something* happened."

Paradoxically, the thought of the missing chair gave her something concrete to hang on to. Dripping wet, she stumbled downstairs. Her den was as she'd left it, except that the chair was missing and there were muddy footprints by the french doors. She knelt to examine the floor behind her desk. She found a couple of books, dislodged from the shelf behind her chair when she fell, but otherwise no sign of anything unexpected. "So it was real!"

A sudden thought struck her and she whirled then ran upstairs to the bathroom, wincing. *The locket!*—

It was in the pocket of her pants. Pulling a face, she carefully placed it on the shelf above the sink where she could see it, then got into the bathtub. *I'm not going nuts,* she thought, relaxing in the hot water. *It's real.*

An hour later she emerged, feeling much improved. Hair washed and conditioned, nails carefully trimmed and stripped of the residue of yesterday's polish, legs itching with mild razor-burn, and skin rosy from an exfoliating scrub, she felt clean, as if she'd succeeded in stripping away all the layers of dirt and paranoia that had stuck to her the day before. It was still only lunchtime, so she dressed again: an old T-shirt, jeans that had seen better days, and an old pair of sneakers.

The headache and chills subsided slowly, as did the lethargy. She headed downstairs slowly and dumped her dirty clothing in the washing machine. Then she poured herself a glass of orange juice and managed to force down one of the granola bars she kept for emergencies. This brought more thoughts to mind, and as soon as she'd finished eating she headed downstairs to poke around in the gloom of the basement.

The basement was a great big rectangular space under the floor of the house. The furnace, bolted to one wall, roared eerily at her; Ben had left lots of stuff with her, her parents had passed on a lot of their stuff too, and now one wall was faced in industrial shelving units.

Here was a box stuffed with old clothing that she kept meaning to schlep to a charity shop: not her wedding dress—which had gone during the angry month she filed for divorce—but ordinary stuff, too unimportant to repudiate. *There* was an old bag full of golf clubs, their chromed heads dull and speckled with rust. Ben had toyed with the idea of doing golf, thinking of it as a way up the corporate ladder. There was a dead lawn mower, an ancient computer of Ben's—probably a museum piece by now—and a workbench with vice, saws, drill, and other woodworking equipment, and maybe the odd bloodstain from his failed attempts to be the man about the house. *There* on that high shelf was a shotgun and a box of shells. It had belonged to Morris, her father. She eyed it dubiously. Probably nobody had used it since Dad bought it decades ago, when he'd lived out west for a few years, and what she knew about shotguns could be written on one side of a postage stamp in very large letters, even though Morris had insisted on teaching her to use a handgun. Some wise words from the heavyweight course on industrial espionage techniques the Weatherman HR folks had paid for her to take two years ago came back: *You're a journalist, and these other folks are investigators. You're none of you cops, none of you are doing anything worth risking your lives over, so you should avoid escalating confrontations. Guns turn any confrontation into a potentially lethal one. So keep them the hell out of your professional life!* "Shotgun, no," she mused. "But. Hmm. Handgun." *Must stop talking to myself,* she resolved.

"Do I really expect them to follow me here?" she asked

the broken chest freezer, which gaped incomprehendingly at her. "Did I just dream it all?"

Back upstairs, she swiped her leather-bound planner from the desk and poured another glass of orange juice. *Time to worry about the real world,* she told herself. She went back to the hall and hit the "play" button on the answering machine. It was backed up with messages from the day before.

"Miriam? Andy here. Listen, a little bird told me about what happened yesterday and I think it sucks. They didn't have any details, but I want you to know if you need some freelance commissions you should give me a call. Talk later? Bye."

Andy was a junior editor on a rival tech-trade sheet. He sounded stiff and stilted when he talked to the telephone robot, not like a real person at all. But it still gave her a shiver of happiness, almost a feeling of pure joy, to hear from him. Someone cared, someone who didn't buy the vicious lie Joe Dixon had put out. *That bastard really got to me,* Miriam wondered, relief replaced by a flash of anger at the way she'd been treated.

Another message, from Paulette. Miriam tensed. "Miriam, honey, let's talk. I don't want to rake over dead shit, but there's some stuff I need to get straight in my head. Can I come around?"

She hit the "pause" button. Paulette sounded severely messed up. It was like a bucket of ice water down her spine. *I did this. I got us both fired,* she began thinking, and her knees tried to turn to jelly. Then she thought, *Hold on. I didn't fire anybody!* That switched on the anger again, but left her feeling distinctly shaky. Sooner or later she'd have to talk to Paulie. Sooner or—

She hit the "next message" button again.

Heavy breathing, then: "Bitch. We know where you live. Heard about you from our mutual friend Joe. Keep your nose out of our business or you'll be fucking sorry"—*click.*

Wide-eyed, she turned and looked over her shoulder. But the yard was empty and the front door was locked. *"Bastards,"* she spat. But there was no caller-ID on the message and probably not enough to get the police interested in it. Especially not if Joe's minions at *The Weatherman* started mud slinging with forged fire-wall logs: They could make her look like the next Unabomber if they wanted to. For a moment, outrage blurred her vision. She forced herself to stop panting and sit down again, next to the treacherous, venomous answering machine. "Threaten me in my own home, will you? *Fuck*."

The gravity of her situation was only just sinking in. "Better keep a gun under my pillow," she muttered under her breath. "Bastards." The opposite wall seemed to be pulsing slightly, a reaction to her fury. She felt her fingers clenching involuntarily. *"Bastards."* Kicking her out of her job and smearing her reputation wasn't enough for them, was it? She'd show them—

—Something.

After a minute she calmed down enough to face the remaining message on the answering machine. She had difficulty forcing herself to press the button. But the next message wasn't another threat—quite the opposite. "Miriam, this is Steve from *The Herald*. I heard the news. Get in touch."

For that, she hit the "pause" button yet again, and this time frowned and scribbled a note to herself. Steve wasn't a chatty editor, like Andy; Steve treated words like dollar bills. And he wouldn't be getting in touch if it didn't involve work, even freelance work. A year ago he'd tried to head-hunt her, offering a big pay raise and a higher position. Taking stock of her options—and when they were due to mature—she'd turned him down. Now she had reason to regret it.

That was the end of her mailbox, and she hit the "erase" button hard enough to hurt her finger. Two editors talking about work, a former office mate wanting to chew over the corpse—and what sounded like a death threat. *This isn't going to go away,* she realized. *I'm in it up to my neck now.* A stab of guilt: *So is Paulie. I'll have to talk to her.* A ray of hope: *For someone who's unemployed, I sure get a lot of business calls.* A conclusion: *Just as long as I stay sane I should be all right.*

The living room was more hospitable right now than the chairless den, its huge french doors streaked with rain falling from a leaden sky. Miriam went through, considered building a fire in the hearth, and collapsed into the sofa instead. The combination of fear, anger, and tension had drained most of her energy. Opening her planner, she turned to a blank page and began writing:

I NEED WORK
Call Andy and Steve. Pass "Go." Collect freelance commissions. Collect two hundred dollars. Keep up the mortgage payments.

I AM GOING CRAZY
Well, no. This isn't schizophrenia. I'm not hearing voices, the walls aren't going soft, and nobody is beaming orbital mind control lasers at me. Everything's fine except I had a weird fugue moment, and the office chair is missing.

DID SOMEONE SLIP ME SOMETHING?
Don't be silly: Who? Iris? Maybe she and Morris tripped when they were younger, but she just wouldn't *do* that to me. Joe Dixon is a sleazebag with criminal connections, but he didn't offer me a drink. And who else have I seen in the past day? Anyway, that's not how hallucinogens work.

MAGIC
That's silly, too, but at least it's testable.

Miriam's eyes narrowed and she chewed the cap of her pen. This was going to take planning, but at least it was beginning to sound like she had her ducks lined up in a row. She began jotting down tasks:

1. Call Andy at *The Globe*. Try to sell him a feature or three.

2. Make appointment to see Steve at *The Herald*. See what he wants.

3. See Paulie. Check how she's doing. See if we can reconstruct the investigation without drawing attention. See if we can pitch it at Andy or Steve. Cover the angles. If we do this, they *will* turn nasty. Call FBI?

4. See if whatever I did last night is repeatable. Get evidence, then a witness. If it's me, seek help. If it's not me . . .

5. Get the story.

That afternoon Miriam went shopping. It was, she figured, retail therapy. Never mind the job-hunting, there'd be time for that when she knew for sure whether or not she was going insane in some obscurely nonstandard manner. It was October, a pretty time of year to go hiking, but fall had set in and things could turn nasty at the drop of a North Atlantic depression. Extensive preparations were therefore in order. She eventually staggered home under the weight of a load of camping equipment: tent, jacket, new boots, portable stove. Getting it all home on the T was a pain, but at least it told her that she could walk under the weight.

A couple of hours later she was ready. She checked her watch for the fourth time. She'd taken two ibuprofen tablets an hour ago and the propionic acid inhibitor should be doing its job by now.

She tightened the waist strap of her pack and stretched nervously. The garden shed was cramped and dark and there didn't seem to be room to turn around with her hiking gear and backpack on. *Did I put the spare key back?* she asked herself. A quick check proved that she had. Irrelevant thoughts were better than *Am I nuts?*—as long as they weren't an excuse for prevarication.

Okay, here goes nothing.

The locket. She held it in her left hand. With her right she patted her right hip pocket. The pistol was technically illegal—but as Ben had pointed out, he'd rather deal with an unlicensed firearms charge than his own funeral. The rattling memory of a voice snarling at her answering machine, the echo of rifle fire in the darkness, made her pause for a moment. "Do I really want to do this?" she asked herself. Life was complicated enough as it was.

Hell yes! Because either I'm mad, and it doesn't matter, or my birth-mother was involved in something huge. Something much bigger than a billion-dollar money-laundering scam through Proteome and Biphase. And if they killed her because of it— A sense of lingering injustice prodded her conscience. "Okay," she told herself. "Let's do it. I'm right behind myself." She chuckled grimly and flicked the locket open, half-expecting to see a photograph of a woman, or a painting, or something else to tell her she needed help—

The knot tried to turn her eyes inside out, and then the hut wasn't there any more.

Miriam gasped. The air was cold, and her head throbbed—but not as badly as last time.

"Wow." She carefully pushed the locket into her left pocket, then pulled out her pocket dictaphone. "Memo begins: Wednesday, October 16, 8 P.M. It's dark and the temperature's about ten degrees colder . . . here. Wherever the hell 'here' is." She turned around slowly. Trees, skeletal, stretched off in all directions. She was standing on a slope, not steep but steep enough to explain why she'd skidded. "No sign of people. I can either go look for the chair or not. Hmm. I think not."

She looked up. Wind-blown clouds scudded overhead, beneath a crescent moon. She didn't turn her flashlight on. *No call for attracting attention,* she reminded herself. *Just look around, then go home . . .*

"I'm an astronaut," she murmured into the dictaphone. She took a step forward, feeling her pack sway on her back, toward a big elm tree. Turning around, she paused, then knelt and carefully placed an old potsherd from the shed on the leafy humus where she'd been standing. "Neil and Buzz only spent eight hours on the moon on that first trip. Only about four hours on the surface, in two excursions. This is going to be *my* moonwalk." *As long as I don't get my damn fool self shot,* she reminded herself. *Or stuck.* She'd brought her sleeping bag and tent, and a first-aid kit, and Ben's pistol (just in case, and she felt wicked because of it). But this didn't feel like home. This felt like the wild woods—and Miriam wasn't at home in the woods. Especially when there were guys with guns who shot at her like it was hunting season and Jewish divorcées weren't on the protected list.

Miriam took ten paces up the hill, then stopped and held her breath, listening. The air was chilly and damp, as if a fog was coming in off the river. There was nothing to hear—no traffic noise, no distant rumble of trains or jets. A distant avian hooting might signify an owl hunting, but that was it. "It's really quiet," Miriam whispered into her mike. "I've never heard it so silent before."

She shivered and looked around. Then she took her small flashlight out and slashed a puddle of light across the trees, casting long sharp shadows. "There!" she exclaimed. Another five paces and she found her brown swivel chair lying on a pile of leaf mold. It was wet and thoroughly the worse for wear, and she hugged it like a long-lost lover as she lifted it upright and carefully put it down. "Yes!"

Her temples throbbed, but she was overjoyed. "I found it," she confided in her dictaphone. "I found the chair. So this is the *same* place." But the chair was pretty messed up. Almost ruined, in fact—it had been a secondhand retread to begin with, and a night out in the rainy woods hadn't helped any.

"It's real," she said quietly, with profound satisfaction. "I'm not going mad. Or if I'm confabulating, I'm doing it so damn *consistently*—" She shook her head. "My birth-mother came here. Or from here. Or something. And she was stabbed, and nobody knows why, or who did it." That brought her back to reality. It raised echoes of her own situation, hints of anonymous threatening phone calls, and other unfinished business. She sighed, then retraced her steps to the potsherd. Massaging her scalp, she sat down on the spot, with her back to the nearby elm tree.

She stopped talking abruptly, thrust the dictaphone into her hip pocket, pulled out the locket, and held her breath.

The crunch of a breaking branch carried a long way in the night. Spooked, she flicked the locket open, focused on its depths, and steeled herself to face the coming hangover: She really didn't want to be out in the woods at night—at least, not without a lot more preparation.

The next morning—after phoning Andy at *The Globe* and securing a commission for a business supplement feature on VC houses, good for half a month's income, with the promise of a regular weekly slot if her features were good enough—Miriam bit the bullet and phoned Paulette. She was nerving herself for an answering machine on the fifth ring when Paulette answered.

"Hello?" She sounded hesitant—unusual for Paulie.

"Hi, Paulie! It's me. Sorry I didn't get back to you yesterday, I had a migraine and a lot of, uh, issues to deal with. I'm just about getting my head back together. How are you doing? Are you okay?"

A brief silence. "About as well as you'd expect," Paulette said guardedly.

"Have you had any, uh, odd phone calls?"

"Sort of," Paulette replied.

Miriam tensed. *What's she concealing?*

"They sent me a reemployment offer," Paulie continued, guardedly.

"They did, did they?" asked Miriam. She waited a beat. "Are you going to take it?"

"Am I, like hell!" Miriam relaxed slightly. Paulette sounded furious. She hadn't expected Paulie to roll over, but it was good to get this confirmation.

"That bad, huh? Want to talk about it? You free?"

"My days are pretty open right now—listen, are you busy? How about I come over to your place?"

"Great," Miriam said briskly. "I was worried about you, Paulie. After I got past being worried about me, I guess."

"Well. Should I bring a pizza?"

"Phew . . ." Miriam took stock. *Just a bitch session together? Or something more going on?* "Yeah, let's do that. I'll lay on the coffee right away."

"That'd be wonderful," Paulette said gratefully.

After she'd put the phone down, Miriam pondered her motives. She and Paulette had worked together for three years and had hung out together in their off-hours. Some people you met at work, socialized with, then lost contact after moving on; but a few turned into friends for life. Miriam wasn't sure which Paulie was going to turn out to be. *Why did she turn the reemployment offer down?* Miriam wondered. Despite being shell-shocked from the crazy business with the locket, she kept circling back to the Monday morning disaster with a rankling sense of injustice. The sooner they blew the lid off it in public, the sooner she could go back to living a normal life. But then the locket kept coming back up. *I need a sanity check,* Miriam decided. *Why not Paulie?* Better to have her think she'd gone nuts than someone whose friendship went back a long way and who knew Iris. Or was it?

An hour later the doorbell rang. Miriam stood up and went to answer it, trying to suppress her worries about how Paulette might be coming. She was waiting on the doorstep, impatiently tapping one heel, with a large shopping bag in hand. "Miriam!" Paulette beamed at her.

"Come in, come in." Miriam retreated. "Hey, what's that? Have you been all right?"

"I've been worse." Paulie bounced inside and shut the door behind her, then glanced around curiously. "Hey, neat. I was worried about you, after I got home. You didn't look real happy, you know?"

"Yeah. Well, I wasn't." Miriam relieved her of her coat

and led her into the living room. "I'm really glad you're taking it so calmly. For me, I put in three years and nothing to show for it but hard work and junk bonds—then some asshole phoned me and warned me off. How about you? Have you had any trouble?"

Paulette peered at her curiously. "What kind of warning?"

"Oh, he kind of intimated that he was a friend of Joe's, and I'd regret it if I stuck my nose in any deeper. Playing at goodfellas, okay? I'd been worrying about you . . . What's this about a job offer?"

"I, uh—" Paulette paused. "They offered me my job back with strings attached," she said guardedly. "Assholes. I was going to accept till they faxed through the contract."

"So why didn't you sign?" Miriam asked, pouring a mug of coffee while Paulette opened the pizza boxes.

"I've seen nondisclosure agreements, Miriam. I used to be a paralegal till I got sick of lawyers, remember? This wasn't a nondisclosure agreement; it was a fucking straitjacket. If I'd signed it, I wouldn't even own the contents of my own head—before and *after* working for them. Guess they figured you were the ringleader, right?"

"Hah." There was a bitter taste in Miriam's mouth, and it wasn't from the coffee. "So. Found any work?"

"Got no offers yet." Paulette took a bite of pizza to cover her disquiet. "Emphasis on the *yet*. You?"

"I landed a freelance feature already. It's not going to cover the salary, but it goes a hell of a way. I was wondering—"

"You want to carry on working the investigation."

It wasn't a question. Miriam nodded. "Yeah. I want to get the sons of bitches, now more than ever. But something tells me moving too fast is going to be a seriously bad idea. I mean, there's a lot of money involved. If we can redo the investigative steps we've got so far, I figure this time we ought to go to the FBI first—and then pick a paper. I think I could probably auction the story, but I'd rather wait until the feds are ready to start arresting people. And I'd like to disappear for a bit while they're doing that." A sudden bolt of realization struck Miriam, so that she almost missed Paulette's reply: *The locket! That's one place they won't be able to follow me! If—*

"Sounds possible." Paulie looked dubious. "It's not going to be easy duplicating the research—especially now that they know we stumbled across them. Do you really think it's that dangerous?"

"If it's drugs money, you can get somebody shot for a couple of thousand bucks. This is way bigger than that, and thanks to our friend Joe, they now know where we live. I don't want to screw up again. You with me?"

After a moment, Paulette nodded. "I want them too." A flash of anger. "The bastards don't think I matter enough to worry about."

"But first there's something I need to find out. I need to vanish for a weekend," Miriam said slowly, a fully formed plan moving into focus in her mind—one that would hopefully answer several questions. Like whether someone else could see her vanish and reappear, and whether she'd have somewhere to hole up if the anonymous threats turned real—and maybe even a chance to learn more about her enigmatic birth-mother than Iris could tell her.

"Oh?" Paulette perked up. "Going to think things over? Or is there a male person in play?" Male persons in play were guaranteed to get Paulie's notice: Like Miriam, she was a member of the early thirties divorcée club.

"Neither." Miriam considered her next words carefully. "I ran across something odd on Monday night. Probably nothing to do with our story, but I'm planning on investigating it and I'll be away for a couple of days. Out of town."

"Tell me more!"

"I, um, can't. Yet." Miriam had worked it through. The whole story was just too weird to lay on Paulie without some kind of proof to get her attention. "However, you can do me a big favor, okay? I need to get to a rest area just off a road near Amesbury with some hiking gear. Yeah, I know that sounds weird, but it's the best way to make sure nobody's following me. If you could ride out with me and drive my car home, then put it back there two days later, that would be really good."

"That's . . . odd." Paulette looked puzzled. "What's with the magical mystery tour?"

Miriam improvised fast. "I could tell you, but then I'd have to get you to sign a nondisclosure agreement that would make anything *The Weatherman* offered you look liberal. And the whole thing is supersecret; my source might spike the whole deal if I let someone in on it without prior permission. I'll be able to tell you when you pick me up afterward, though." If things went right, she'd be able to tell a more-than-somewhat-freaked Paulie why she'd vanished right in front of her eyes and then reappeared in front of them. "And I want you to promise to tell nobody about it until you pick me up again, okay?"

"Well, okay. It's not as if I don't have time on my hands." Paulette frowned. "When are you planning on doing your disappearing act? And when do you want picking up?"

"I was—they're picking me up tomorrow at 2 P.M. precisely," said Miriam. "And I'll be showing up *exactly* forty-eight hours later." She grinned. "If you lie in wait—pretend to be eating your lunch or something—you can watch them pick me up."

Friday morning dawned cold but clear, and Miriam showered then packed her camping equipment again. The doorbell rang just after noon. It was Paulette, wearing a formal black suit. "My God, is it a funeral?"

"Had a job interview this morning." Paulette pulled a face. "I got sick of sitting at home thinking about those bastards shafting us and decided to do something for number one in the meantime."

"Well, good for you." Miriam picked up her backpack and led Paulie out the front door, then locked up behind her. She opened her car, put the pack in, then opened the front doors. "Did it go well?" she asked, pulling her seat belt on.

"It went like—" Paulette pulled another face. "Listen, I'm a business researcher, right? Just because I used to be a paralegal doesn't mean that I want to go back there."

"Lawyers," Miriam said as she started the engine. "Lots of work in that field, I guarantee you."

"Oh yeah," Paulette agreed. She pulled the sun visor down and looked at herself in the mirror. "Fuck, do I really look like that? I'm turning into my first ex-boss."

"Yes indeed, you look just like—naah." Miriam thought better of it and rephrased: "Congresswoman Paulette Milan, from Cambridge. You have the floor, ma'am."

"The first ex-boss is in politics now," Paulie observed gloomily. "A real dragon."

"Bitch."

"You didn't know her."

They drove on in amiable silence for the best part of an hour, out into the wilds of Massachusetts. Up the coast, past Salem, out toward Amesbury, off Interstate 95 and on to a four-lane highway, then finally a side road. Miriam had been here before, years ago, with Ben, when things had been going okay. There was a rest area up on a low hill overlooking Browns Point, capped by a powder of trees, gaunt skeletons hazed in red and auburn foliage at this time of year. Miriam pulled up at the side of the road just next to the rest area and parked. "Okay, this is it," she said. There were butterflies in her stomach again: *I'm going to go through with it,* she realized to her surprise.

"This?" Paulette looked around, surprised. "But this is *nowhere!*"

"Yeah, that's right. Best place to do this." Miriam opened the glove locker. "Look, I brought my old camcorder. No time for explanations. I'm going to get out of the car, grab my pack, and walk over there. I want you to film me. In ten minutes either I'll tell you why I asked you to do this and you can call me rude names—or you'll know to take the car home and come back the day after tomorrow to pick me up. Okay?"

"Miriam, this is nuts—"

She got out in a hurry and collected her pack from the trunk. Then, without waiting to see what Paulette did, she walked over to the middle of the parking lot. Breathing deeply, she hiked the pack up onto her back and fastened the chest strap—then pulled the locket out of the outer pocket where she'd stashed it.

Feeling acutely self-conscious, she flicked it open and turned her back on the parked car. Raised it to her face and stared into the enameled knot painted inside it. *This is stupid,* a little voice told her. *And you're going to have your work cut out convincing Paulie you don't need to see a shrink.*

Someone was calling her name sharply. She screened it out. Something seemed to move inside the knot—

hIDE-AND-SEEK

This time it was raining gently.

Miriam winced at the sudden stabbing in her head and pocketed the locket. Then she did what she'd planned all along: a three-sixty-degree scan that took in nothing but autumn trees and deadfall. Next, she planted her pack, transferred the pistol to her right hip pocket, retrieved her camera and the recorder, and started taking snapshots as she dictated a running commentary.

"The time by my watch is fourteen twelve hours. Precipitation is light and intermittent, cloud cover is about six-sevenths, wind out of the northwest and chilly, breeze of around five miles per hour. I think."

Snap, snap, snap: The camera had room for a thousand or so shots before she'd have to change hard disks. She slung it around her neck and shouldered the pack again. With the Swiss army knife Ben had given her on their second wedding anniversary—an odd present from a clueless, cheating husband with no sense of the difference between jewelry and real life—she shaved a patch of bark above eye level on the four nearest trees, then fished around for some stones to pile precisely where she'd come through. (It wouldn't do to go back only to come out in the middle of her own car. If that was possible, of course.)

As she worked, she had the most peculiar sensation: *I'm on my second moon mission,* she thought. *Did any of the Apollo astronauts go to the moon more than once?* Here she was, *not* going crazy, recording notes and taking photographs to document her exploration of this extraordinary place that simply wasn't like home. Whatever "home" meant, now that gangsters had her number.

"I still don't know why I'm here," she recorded, "but I've got the same alarming prefrontal headache, mild hot and cold chills, probable elevated blood pressure as last time. Memo: Next time bring a sphygmomanometer; I want to monitor for malignant hypertension. And urine sample bottles." The headache, she realized, was curiously similar to a hangover, itself caused by dehydration that triggered inflammation of the meninges. Miriam continued: "Query physiological responses to . . . whatever it is that I do. When I focus on the knot. Memo: Scan the locket, use Photoshop to rescale it and print it on paper, then see if the pattern works as a focus when I look at it on a clipboard. More work for next time."

They won't be able to catch me here, she thought fiercely as she scanned around, this time looking for somewhere suitable to pitch her tent and go to ground. *I'll be able to nail them and they won't even be able to find me to lay a finger on me!* But there was more to it than that, she finally admitted to herself as she hunted for a flat spot. The locket had belonged to her birth-mother, and receiving it had raised an unquiet ghost. Somebody had stabbed her, somebody who had never been found. Miriam wouldn't be able to lay that realization to rest again until she learned what this place had meant to her mother—and why it had killed her.

With four hours to go before sunset, Miriam was acutely aware that she didn't have any time to waste. The temperature would dip toward frost at night and she planned to be well dug-in first. Planting her backpack at the foot of the big horse chestnut tree, she gathered armfuls of dry leaves and twigs and scattered them across it—nothing that would fool a real woodsman, but enough to render it inconspicuous at a distance. Then she walked back and forth through a hundred-yard radius, pacing out the forest, looking for its edge. That there was an edge came as no surprise: The steep escarpment was in the same place here as on the hiking map of her own world that she'd brought along. Where the ground fell away, there was a breathtaking view of autumnal forest marching down toward a valley floor. The ocean was probably eight to ten miles due east, out of sight beyond hills and dunes, but she had a sense of its presence all the same.

Looking southwest, she saw a thin coil of smoke rising—a settlement of some kind, but small. No roads or telegraph poles marred the valley, which seemed to contain nothing but trees and bushes and the odd clearing. She was alone in the woods, as alone as she'd ever been. She looked up. Thin cirrus stained the blue sky, but there were no jet contrails.

"The area appears to be thinly populated," she muttered into her dictaphone. "They're burning something—coal or wood—at the nearest settlement. There are no telegraph poles, roads, or aircraft. The air doesn't smell of civilization. No noise to speak of, just birds and wind and trees."

She headed back to her clearing to orient herself, then headed on in the opposite direction, down the gentle slope away from her pack. "Note: Keep an eye open for big wildlife. Bears and stuff." She patted her right hip pocket nervously. Would the pistol do much more than annoy a bear? She hadn't expected the place to be quite this desolate. There were no bears, but she ran across a small stream—nearly fell into it, in fact.

There was no sign of an edge to the woods, in whichever direction she went. Nor were there signs of habitation other than the curl of smoke she'd seen. It was four o'clock now. She returned to her clearing, confident that nobody was around, and unstrapped her tent from the backpack. It took half an hour to get the dome tent erected, and another half-hour with the netting and leaves to turn it into something that could be mistaken for a shapeless deadfall. She spent another fifteen minutes returning to the stream to fill her ten-liter water carrier. Another half-hour went on digging a hole nearby, then she took ten minutes to run a rope over a bough and hoist her bag of food out of reach of the ground. Darkness found her lighting her portable gas stove to boil water for her tea. *I did it,* she thought triumphantly. *I didn't forget anything important!* Now all she had to do was make it through tomorrow and the morning of the next day without detection.

The night grew very cold without a fire, but her sleeping bag was almost oppressively hot with the tent zipped shut. Miriam slept lightly, starting awake at the slightest noise—worried at the possibility of bears or other big animals wandering through her makeshift camp, spooked by the sigh of wind and the patter of a light predawn rainfall. Once she dreamed of wolves howling in the distance. But dawn arrived without misadventure and dragged her bleary-eyed from the tent to squat over the trench she'd remembered to dig the day before. "The Girl Scout training pays off at last," she dictated with a sardonic drawl.

A tin of sausages and beans washed down with strong black coffee made a passable breakfast. "Now what?" she asked herself. "Do I wait it out with the camp or go exploring?"

For a moment, Miriam quailed. The enormity of the wilderness around her was beginning to grind on her nerves, as was the significance of the situation she'd thrown herself into. "I could break a leg here and nobody would ever find me. Or—" *Gunfire in the night.* "Someone stabbed my mother, and she *didn't* come here to escape. There must be a reason why. Mustn't there?"

Something about the isolation made her want to chatter, to fill up the oppressive silence. But the words that tumbled out didn't tell her much, except that she was— *Let's face it. I'm scared. This wasn't the sensible thing to do, was it? But I haven't been doing sensible properly since I got myself fired on Monday.*

Unzipping the day pack from her backpack, she filled it
with necessities, then set out for the escarpment.

It was a clear, cold morning, and the wisp of smoke she'd
seen yesterday had disappeared. But she knew roughly
where she'd seen it, and a careful scan of the horizon with
binoculars brought it into focus once more—a pause in the
treeline, punctuated by nearly invisible roofs. At a guess, it
was about three miles away. She glanced at the sky and
chewed on her lower lip: *Doable,* she decided, still half-
unsure that it was the right thing to do. *But I'll go out of my
skull if I wait here two days, and Paulie won't be back until
tomorrow.* Bearing and range went into her notepad and onto
the map, and she blazed a row of slashes on every fifth tree
along the ridgeline to help her on the way back. The scarp
was too steep to risk on her own, but if she went along the
crest of the ridge, she could take the easy route down into the
valley.

Taking the easy route was not, as it happened, entirely
safe. About half a mile farther on—half a mile of plodding
through leaf mounds, carefully bypassing deadfalls, and
keeping a cautious eye open—an unexpected sound made
Miriam freeze, her heart in her mouth and ice in her veins.
Metal, she thought. *That was a metallic noise! Who's there?*
She dropped to a squat with her back against a tree as a
horse or mule snorted nearby.

The sound of hooves was now audible, along with a
creaking of leather and the occasional clatter or jingle of
metalwork. Miriam crouched against the tree, very still,
sweat freezing in the small of her back, trying not to breathe.
She couldn't be sure, but it sounded like a single set of
hooves. With her camouflage-patterned jacket, knitted black
face mask, and a snub-nosed pistol clutched in her right
hand, she was a sight to terrify innocent eyes—but she was
frightened half out of her own wits.

She held perfectly still as a peculiarly dressed man led a
mule past, not ten yards away from her. The animal was
heavily overloaded, bulging wicker baskets towering over its
swaying back. Its owner wore leggings of some kind, but

was swathed from head to knees in what looked like an ancient and moth-eaten blanket. He didn't look furtive; he just looked dirt-poor, his face lined and tanned from exposure to the weather.

The mule paused. Almost absently, its owner reached out and whacked it across the hindquarters with his rod. He grunted something in what sounded like German, only softer, less sibilant.

Miriam watched, fear melting into fascination. That was a knife at his belt, under the blanket—a great big pigsticker of a knife, almost a short sword. The mule made an odd sort of complaining noise and began moving again. *What's in the baskets?* she wondered. *And where's he taking it?*

There were clearly people living in these woods. *Better be careful,* she told herself, taking deep breaths to calm down as she waited for him to pass out of sight. She pondered again whether or not she shouldn't go straight back to her campsite. In the end curiosity won out—but it was curiosity tempered by edgy caution.

An hour later, Miriam found a path wandering among the trees. It wasn't a paved road by any stretch of the imagination, but the shrubbery to either side had been trampled down and the path itself was muddy and flat: Fresh road-apples told her which way the man with the mule had gone. She slashed a marker on the tree where her path intersected the road, crudely scratching in a bearing and distance as digits. If her growing suspicion was true, these people wouldn't be able to make anything of it. She picked her way through the trees along one side of the path, keeping it just in sight. Within another half-mile the trees ended in a profusion of deadfalls and stumps, some of which sprouted amazing growths of honey fungus. Miriam picked her way farther away from the path, then hunkered down, brought out binoculars and dictaphone, and gave voice to her fascination.

"This is incredible! It's like a museum diorama of a medieval village in England, only— Eww, I sure wouldn't drink from that stream. The stockade is about two hundred yards away and they've cleared the woods all around it.

There are low stone walls, with no cement, around the field.
It's weird, all these rows running across it like a patchwork
quilt made from pin-stripe fabric."

She paused, focusing her binoculars in on a couple of figures walking in the near distance. They were close enough to
see her if they looked at the treeline, so she instinctively
hunched lower, but they weren't paying attention to the forest. One of them was leading a cow—a swaybacked beast
like something from a documentary about India. The buildings were grayish, the walls made of stacked bundles of
something or other, and the roofs were thatched—not the
picturesque golden color of the rural English tourist trap
she'd once stayed in outside Oxford, but the real thing, gray
and sagging. "There are about twelve buildings; none of
them have windows. The road is unpaved, a mud track.
There are chickens or some kind of fowl there, pecking in
the dirt. It looks sleazy and tumbledown."

She tracked after the human figures, focused on the stockade. "There's a gate in the stockade and a platform or tower
behind it. Something big's in there, behind the wall, but I
can't see it from here. A long house? No, this doesn't
look . . . wrong period. These aren't Vikings, there's, uh—"

Around the curve of the stockade an ox came into view,
dragging some kind of appliance—a wooden plow, perhaps.
The man walking behind it looked as tired as the animal.
"They're all wearing those blankets. Women too. That was a
woman feeding the chickens. With a headscarf wrapped
around her face like a Muslim veil. But the men wear pretty
much the same, too. This place looks so *poor*. Neglected.
That guy with the mule—it must be the equivalent of a
BMW in this place!"

Miriam felt distinctly uneasy. History book scenes were
outside her experience—she was a creature of the city,
raised with the bustle and noise of urban life, and the sordid
poverty of the village made her feel unaccountably guilty.
But it left questions unanswered. "This could be the past; we
know the Vikings reached New England around the eleventh
century. Or it could be somewhere else. How can I tell if I

can't get in and see what's inside the stockade? I think I need an archaeologist."

Miriam crouched down and began to snap off photographs. *Here* three hens pecked aimlessly at the dirt by an open doorway, the door itself a slab of wood leaning drunkenly against the wall of the hut. *There* a woman (or a man, the shapeless robe made it impossible to be sure) bent over a wooden trough, emptying a bucket of water into it and then lifting and pounding something from within. Miriam focused closer—

"Wer find thee?" Someone piped at her.

Miriam jolted around and stared: The someone stared right back, frozen, eyes wide. He looked to be about fourteen or fifteen years old, dressed in rags and barefoot: He was shorter than she was. Pipecleaner arms, legs like wire, big brown eyes, and a mess of badly trimmed hair in a pudding-bowl cut. Time slowed to a crawl. *That's a skin infection,* she realized, her guts turning to ice as she focused on a red weal on the side of his neck. He was skinny, not as thin as a famine victim but by no means well-fed. He had a stick, clenched nervously in his hands, which he was bringing up—

Miriam glared at him and straightened up. Her right hand went to her hip pocket, and she fumbled for the treacherous opening. "You'll be sorry," she snapped, surprised at herself. It was the first thing that entered her head. Her hand closed on the butt of the pistol, but she couldn't quite draw it—it was snagged on something.

Oh shit. She yanked at her pocket desperately, keeping her eyes on his face, despite knees that felt like jelly and a churning cold in her gut. She had a strong flashback to the one time she was mugged, a desperate sense of helplessness as she tried to disentangle the gun from her pocket lining and bring it out before the villager hit her with his stick.

But he didn't. Instead, his eyes widened. He opened his mouth and shouted, "An solda'des Koen!" He turned, dropping the stick, and darted away before Miriam could react. A moment later she heard him wailing, "An solda!"

"Shit." The gun was in her hand, all but forgotten. Terror

lent her feet wings. She clutched her camera and ran like hell, back toward the forest, heedless of any noise she might make. *He nearly had me! He'll be back with help! I've got to get out of here!* Breathless fear drove her until branches scratched at her face and she was panting. Then the low apple trees gave way to taller, older trees and a different quality of light. She staggered along, drunkenly, as behind her a weird hooting noise unlike any horn she'd heard before split the quiet.

Ten minutes later she stopped and listened, wheezing for breath as she tried to get her heart under control. She had run parallel to the path, off to one side. Every instinct was screaming at her to *run* but she was nearly winded, so she listened instead. Apart from the horn blasts, there were no sounds of pursuit. *Why aren't they following me?* She wondered, feeling ill with uncertainty. *What's wrong?* After a moment she remembered her camera: She'd lost the lens cap in her mad rush. "Damn, I could have broken my ankle," she muttered. "They'd have caught me for—" she stopped.

"That look in his eye." Very carefully, she unslung the camera and slid it into a big outer hip pocket. She glanced around the clearing sharply, then spent a moment untangling the revolver from her other pocket. Now that she had all the time in the world, it was easy. "He was *scared*," she told herself, wondering. "He was *terrified* of me! What was that he was shouting? Was he warning the others off?"

She began to walk again, wrapped in a thoughtful silence. There were no sounds of pursuit. Behind her the village hid in the gloom, like a terrified rabbit whose path had just crossed a fox on the prowl. "Who are you hiding from?" she asked her memory of the boy with the stick. "And who did you mistake me for?"

It was raining again, and the first thing she noticed once she crossed over—through the blinding headache—was that Paulette was bouncing up and down like an angry squirrel, chattering with indignation behind the camcorder's view-finder. "Idiot! What the *hell* do you think you were doing?" she demanded as Miriam opened the passenger door and dumped her pack on the backseat. "I almost had a heart attack! That's the second time you've nearly given me one this week!"

"I said it would be a surprise, right?" Miriam collapsed into the passenger seat. "God, I reek. Get me home and once I've had a shower I'll explain everything. I promise."

Paulette drove in tight-lipped silence. Finally, during a moment when they were stationary at a traffic light, she said: "Why me?"

Miriam considered for a moment. "You don't know my mother."

"That's—oh. I see, I think. Anything else?"

"Yeah. I trusted you to keep your mouth shut and not to panic."

"Uh-huh. So what have you gotten yourself into this time?"

"I'm not sure. Could be the story of the century—the second one this week. Or it could be a very good reason indeed for burying something and walking away fast. I've got some ideas—more, since I spent a whole day and a half over there—but I'm still not sure."

"Where's *over there?* I mean, where did you go?" The car moved forward.

"Good question. The straight answer is: I'm not sure—the geography is the same, the constellations are the same, but the landscape's different in places and there's an honest-to-god medieval village in a forest. And they don't speak English. Listen, after I've had my shower, how about I buy supper? I figure I owe you for dropping this on your lap."

"You sure do," Paulette said vehemently. "After you vanished, I went home and watched the tape six times before I believed what I'd seen with my own two eyes." Her hands were white on the steering wheel. "Only *you* could fall into something this weird!"

"Remember Hunter S. Thompson's First Law of Gonzo Journalism: 'When the going gets tough, the tough get weird'?" Miriam chuckled, but there was an edge to it. Everywhere she looked there were buildings and neon lights and traffic. "God, I feel like I spent the weekend in the Third World. Kabul." The car smelled of plastic and deodorant, and it was heavenly—the stink of civilization. "Listen, I haven't had anything decent to eat for days. When we get home I'm ordering take out. How does Chinese sound?"

"I can cope with that." Paulette made a lazy right turn and slid into the slow-moving stream of traffic. "Don't feel like cooking?"

"I've got to have a shower," said Miriam. "Then I've got a weekend of stuff to put in the washing machine, several hundred pictures to download and index, memos to load into the computer, and an explanation. If you figure I can do all that and a pot roast too, then you don't know me as well as I think you do."

"That," Paulette remarked as she pulled over into the parking space next to Miriam's house, "was a very mixed metaphor."

"Don't listen to what I say; listen to what I mean, okay?"

"I get the picture. Dinner's on you."

After half an hour in the bathroom, Miriam felt human, if not entirely dry. She stopped in her bedroom for long enough to find some clean clothes, then headed downstairs in her bare feet.

Paulette had parked herself in the living room with a couple of mugs of coffee and an elegant-looking handbag. She raised an eyebrow at Miriam: "You look like you've been dry-cleaned. Was it that bad?"

"Yeah." Miriam settled down on the sofa, then curled her legs up beneath her. She picked up one of the mugs and inhaled deeply. "Ah, that's better."

"Ready to tell me what the hell is going on?"

"In a moment." Miriam closed her eyes, then gathered up the strands of still-damp hair sticking to her neck and wound them up, outside her collar. "That's better. It happened right after they screwed us over, Paulie. I figured you'd think I'd gone off the deep end if I just told you about it, which is why I didn't call you back the same day. Why I asked you to drive. Sorry about the surprise."

"You should be: I spent an hour in the woods looking for you. I nearly called the police twice, but you'd said precisely when you'd be back and I thought they'd think *I* was the one who was nuts. 'Sides, you've got a habit of dredging up weird shit and leaving me to pick up the pieces. Promise me there are no gangsters in this one?"

"I promise." Miriam nodded. "Well, what do *you* think?"

"I think I'd like some lemon chicken. Sorry." Paulette grinned impishly at Miriam's frown. "Okay, I believe you've discovered something very weird indeed. I actually videoed you vanishing into thin air in front of the camera! And when you appeared again—no, I didn't get it on tape, but I saw you out of the corner of my eye. Either we're both crazy or this is for real."

"Madness doesn't come in this shape and size," Miriam said soberly. She winced. "I need a painkiller." She rubbed her feet, which were cold. "You know I'm adopted, right? My mother didn't quite tell me everything until Monday. I went to see her after we were fired . . ."

For the next hour Miriam filled Paulette in on the events of the past week, leaving out nothing except her phone call to Andy. Paulette listened closely and asked the right questions. Miriam was satisfied that her friend didn't think she was mad, wasn't humoring her. "Anyway, I've now got tape of my vanishing, a shitload of photographs of this village, and dictated notes. See? It's beginning to mount up."

"Evidence," said Paulette. "That would be useful if you want to go public." Suddenly she looked thoughtful. "Big *if* there."

"Hmm?" Miriam drank down what was left of her coffee.

"Well, this place you go to—it's either in the past or the future, or somewhere else, right? I think we can probably rule out the past or future options. If it was the past, you wouldn't have run across a village the way you described it; and as for the future, there'd still be some sign of Boston, wouldn't there?"

"Depends how far in the future you go." Miriam frowned. "Yeah, I guess you're right. It's funny; when I was a little girl I always figured the land of make-believe would be *bright* and *colorful*. Princesses in castles and princes to go around kissing them so they turned into frogs—and dragons to keep the royalty population under control. But in the middle ages there were about a thousand peasants living in sordid poverty for every lord of the manor, who actually had a sword, a horse, and a house with a separate bedroom to sleep in. A hundred peasants for every member of the nobility—the lords and their families—and the same for every member of the merchant or professional classes."

"Sounds grimly real to me, babe. Forget Hollywood. Your map *was* accurate, wasn't it?"

"What are you getting at? You're thinking about . . . What was that show called: *Sliders*? Right?"

"Alternate earths. Like on TV." Paulette nodded. "I only watched a couple of episodes, but . . . well. Suppose you *are* going sideways, to some other earth where there's nobody but some medieval peasants. What if you, like, crossed over next door to a bank, walked into *exactly* where the vault would be in our world, waited for the headache to go away, then crossed back again?"

"I'd be inside the bank vault, wouldn't I? *Oh*."

"That, as they say, is the sixty-four-thousand-dollar question," Paulette commented dryly. "Listen, this is going to be a long session. I figure you haven't thought all the angles through. What were you planning on doing with it?"

"I—I'm." Miriam stopped. "I told you about the phone call."

Paulette looked at her bleakly. "Yeah. Did I tell you—"

"You too?"

She nodded. "The evening after I told them to go fuck themselves. Don't know who it was: I hung up on him and called the phone company, told them it was a nuisance call, but they couldn't tell me anything."

"Bastards."

"Yes. Listen. When I was growing up in Providence, there were these guys . . . it wasn't a rich neighborhood, but they always had sharp suits. Momma told me never to cross them—or, even talk to them. Trouble is, when *they* talk to *you*— I think I need a drink. What do you say?"

"I say there're a couple of bottles in the cabinet," said Miriam, massaging her forehead. "Don't mind if I join you."

Coffee gave way to a couple of modest glasses of Southern Comfort. "It's a mess," said Paulette. "You, uh—we didn't talk about Monday. Did we?"

"No," Miriam admitted. "If you want to just drop it and forget the whole business, I'm not going to twist your arm." She swallowed. She felt acutely uneasy, as if the whole comfortable middle-class professional existence she'd carved out for herself was under threat. Like the months when she'd subliminally sensed her marriage decaying, never quite able to figure out exactly what was wrong until . . .

" 'Drop it?' " Paulette's eyes flashed, a momentary spark of anger. "Are you crazy? These hard men, they're really easy to understand. If you back down, they own you. It's simple as that. *That's* something I learned when I was a kid."

"What happened—" Miriam stopped.

Paulie tensed, then breathed out, a long sigh. "My parents weren't rich," she said quietly. "Correction: They were poor as pigshit. Gramps was a Sicilian immmigrant, and he hit the bottle. Dad stayed on the wagon but never figured out how to get out of debt. He held it together for Mom and us kids, but it wasn't easy. Took me seven years to get through college, and I wanted a law degree so bad I could taste it. Because lawyers make lots of money, that's numero uno. And for seconds, I'd be able to tell the guys Dad owed where to get off."

Miriam leaned forward to top off her glass.

"My brother Joe didn't listen to what Momma told us," Paulette said slowly. "He got into gambling, maybe a bit of smack. It wasn't the drugs, but one time he tried to argue with the bankers. They held him down and used a cordless drill on both his kneecaps."

"Uh." Miriam felt a little sick. "What happened?"

"I got as far as being a paralegal before I figured out there's no point getting into a job where you hate the guts of everybody you have to work with, so I switched track and got a research gig. No journalism degree, see, so I figured I'd work my way up. Oh, you meant to Joe? He OD'd on heroin. It wasn't an accident—it was the day after they told him he'd never walk again." She said it with the callous disregard of long-dead news, but Miriam noticed her knuckles tighten on her glass. "That's why I figure you don't want to ever let those guys notice you. But if they do, you don't *ever* back off."

"That's—I'm really sorry. I had no idea."

"Don't blame yourself." Paulette managed an ironic smile. "I, uh, took a liberty with the files before I printed them." She reached inside her handbag and flipped a CD-ROM at Miriam.

"Hey, what's this?" Miriam peered at the greenish silver surface.

"It's the investigation." Paulie grinned at her. "I got *everything* before you decided to jump Sandy's desk and get Joe to take an unhealthy interest in us."

"But that's stealing!" Miriam ended on a squeak.

"And what do you call what they did to your job?" Paulette asked dryly. "I call this insurance."

"Oh."

"Yes, *oh*. I don't think they know about it—otherwise we'd be in way deeper shit already. Still, you should find somewhere to hide it until we need it."

Miriam looked at the disk as if it had turned into a snake. "Yeah, I can do that." She drained her glass, then picked up the disk and carried it over to the stereo. "Gotcha." She pulled a multidisk CD case from the shelf, opened it, and slid the extra disk inside. "*The Beggar's Opera*. Think you can remember that?"

"Oh! Why didn't I think of doing that?"

"Because." Miriam grinned at her. "Why didn't I think of burning that disk in the first place?"

"We each need a spare brain." Paulette stared at her. "Listen, that's problem number one. What about problem number two? This crazy shit from another world. What were you messing around with it for?"

Miriam shrugged. "I had some idea that I could hide from the money laundry over there," she said slowly. "Also, to tell the truth, I wanted someone else to tell me I wasn't going crazy. But going totally medieval isn't going to answer my problem, is it?"

"I wouldn't say so." Paulette put her glass down, half-empty. "Where were we? Oh yeah. You cross over to the other side, wherever that is, and you wander over to where your bank's basement is, then you cross back again. What do you *think* happens?"

"I come out in a bank vault." Miriam pondered. "They're wired inside, aren't they? After my first trip I was a total casualty, babe. I mean, projectile vomiting—" she paused, embarrassed. "A fine bank robber I'd make!"

"There is that," said Paulette. "But you're not thinking it through. What happens when the alarm goes off?"

"Well. Either I go back out again too fast and risk an aneurism or . . ." Miriam trailed off. "The cops show and arrest me."

"And what happens after they arrest you?"

"Well, assuming they don't shoot first and ask questions later, they cuff me, read me my rights, and haul me off to the station. Then book me in and stick me in a cell."

"And *then?*" Paulette rolled her eyes at Miriam's slow uptake.

"Why, I call my lawyer—" Miriam stopped, eyes unfocused. "No, they'd take my locket," she said slowly.

"Sure. Now, tell me. Is it your locket or is it the pattern in your locket? Have you tested it? If it's the design, what if you've had it tattooed on the back of your arm in the meantime?" Paulette asked.

"That's—" Miriam shook her head. "Tell me there's a flaw in the logic."

"I'm not going to do that." Paulette picked up the bottle and waved it over Miriam's glass in alcoholic benediction. "I think you're going to have to test it tomorrow to find out. And *I'm* going to have to test it, to see if it works for me—if that's okay by you," she added hastily. "If it's the design, you just got your very own 'Get Out of Jail Free' card. Doesn't matter if you can't use it to rob bank vaults, there's any number of other scams you can run if you can get out of the fix instantaneously. Say, uh, you walk into a bank and pull a holdup. No need for a gun, just pass over a note saying you've got a bomb and they should give you all the money. Then, instead of running away, you head for the staff rest room and just *vanish* into thin air."

"You have got a larcenous mind, Paulie." Miriam shook her head in awe. "You're wasted in publishing."

"No, I'm not." Paulette frowned seriously. "Y'see, you haven't thought this through. S'pose you've got this super power. Suppose nobody else can use it—we can try me out tomorrow, huh? Do the experiment with the photocopy of the locket on you, then try me. See if I can do it. I figure it's going to be you, and not me, because if just anybody could do it it would be common knowledge, huh? Or your mother would have done it. For some reason somebody stabbed your mother and she *didn't* do it. So there must be some kind of gotcha. But anyway. What do you think the cops would make of it if instead of robbing banks or photographing peasant villagers you, uh, donated your powers to the forces of law and order?"

"Law and order consists of bureaucracies," Miriam said with a brisk shake of her head. "You've seen all those tedious FBI press conferences I sat in on when they were lobbying for carnivore and crypto export controls, huh?" A vision unfolded behind her eyes, the poisonous fire blossom of an airliner striking an undefended skyscraper. "Jesus, Paulie, imagine if Al Qaida could do this!"

"They don't need it: They've got suicide volunteers. But

yeah, there are other bad guys who . . . if you can see it, so can the feds. Remember that feature about nuclear terrorism that Zeb ran last year? How the NIRT units and FEMA were able to track bombs as they come in across the frontier if there's an alert on?"

"I don't want to go there." The thought made Miriam feel physically ill. "There is *no way in hell* I'd smuggle a nuclear weapon across a frontier."

"No." Paulette leaned forward, her eyes serious: "But if *you* have this ability, who else might have it? And what could they do with it? There are some very scary, dangerous national security implications here, and if you go public the feds will bury you so deep—"

"I said I *don't* want to go there," Miriam repeated. "Listen, this is getting deeply unfunny. You're frightening me, Paulie, more than those assholes with their phone calls and their handle on the pharmaceutical industry. I'm wondering if maybe I should sleep with a gun under my pillow."

"Get frightened fast, babe; it's your ass we're talking about. I've had two days to think about your vanishing trick and our goodfella problem, and I tell you, you're still thinking like an honest journalist, not a paranoid. Listen, if you want to clean up, how about the crack trade? Or heroin? Go down to Florida, get the right connections, you could bring a small dinghy over and stash it on the other side, no problems—it'd just take you a while, a few trips maybe. Then you could carry fifty, a hundred kilos of coke. Sail it up the coast, then up the Charles. Bring it back over right in the middle of Cambridge, out of fucking nowhere without the DEA or the cops noticing. They say one in four big shipments gets intercepted—that's bullshit—but maybe one in five, one in eight . . . you could smuggle the stuff right under their noses in the middle of a terrorist scare. And I don't know whether you'd do that or not—my guess is not, you've got capital-P principles—but that is the *first* thing the cops will think of."

"Hell." Miriam stared into the bottom of her glass, privately aghast. "What do you suggest?"

Paulette put her own glass down. "Speaking as your legal adviser, I advise you to buy guns and move fast. Mail the disk to another newspaper and the local FBI office, then go on a long cruise while the storm breaks. That—and take a hammer to the locket and smash it up past recognition."

Miriam shook her head, then winced. "Oh, my aching head. I demand a second opinion. Where is my recount, dammit?"

"Well." Paulette paused. "You've made a good start on the documentation. We can see if it's just you, run the experiments, right? I figure the clincher is if you can carry a second person through. If you can do *that*, then not only do you have documents, you've got witnesses. If you go public, you want to do so with a splash—so widespread that they can't put the arm on you. They've got secret courts and tame judges to try national security cases, but if the evidence is out in the open they can't shut you up, especially if it's international. I'd say Canada would be best." She paused again, a bleak look in her eye. "Yeah, that might work."

"You missed something." Miriam stabbed a finger in Paulette's direction. "You. What do you get?"

"Me?" Paulette covered her heart with one hand, pulled a disbelieving face. "Since when did I get a vote?"

"Since, hell, since I got you into this mess. I figure I owe you. Noblesse oblige. You're a friend, and I don't drop friends in it, even by omission."

"Friendship and fifty cents will buy you a coffee." Paulie paused for a moment, then grinned. "But I'm glad, all the same." Her smile faded. "I didn't get the law job."

"I'm sorry."

"Will you stop *doing* that? Every chance you get to beat yourself up for getting me fired, you're down on your knees asking for forgiveness!"

"Oh, sorry. I didn't realize it was getting on your nerves," Miriam said contritely.

"Fuck off!" Paulette giggled. "Pardon my French. Anyway. Think about what I said. Tomorrow you can mail that disk to the FBI if you want, then go on a long vacation. Or stick around and we'll work on writing a story that'll get you the Pulitzer. You can catch all the bullets from the goodfella hit men while I'll be your loyal little gofer, get myself a star-spangled reference and a few points of the gross. Like, fifty percent. Deal?"

"Deal. I think my head hurts." Miriam shuffled around and stood up. She felt a little shaky: Maybe it was the alcohol hitting her head on an empty stomach. "Where's that takeout?"

Paulette looked blank. "You ordered it?"

"No." Miriam snapped her fingers in frustration. "I'll go do that right now. I think we have some forward planning to do." She paused unevenly in the doorway, looking at Paulette.

"What?"

"Are you in?" she asked.

"Am I in? Are you nuts? I wouldn't miss this for anything!"

PART 2

MEET THE FAMILY

ҺOTEL ᗰAFIOSI

They came for her in the early hours, long after Paulette had called a taxi and Miriam had slunk into bed with a stomach full of lemon chicken and a head full of schemes. They came with stealth, black vans, and Mac-10s: They didn't know or care about her plans. They were soldiers. They had their orders; this was the house the damp brown chair was colocated with, and so this was the target. That was all they needed.

Miriam slept through the breaking of the french window in her den because the two men on entry detail crowbarred the screens open, then rolled transparent sticky polyurethane film across the glass before they struck it with rubber mallets, then peeled the starred sheets right out of the frame. The phone line had been cut minutes before; there was a cell-phone jammer in the back garden.

The two break-and-enter men took point, rolling into the den and taking up positions at either side of the room. The light shed by the LEDs on her stereo and computer glinted dimly off their night-vision goggles and the optics of their guns as they waited tensely, listening for any sign of activity.

Hand signals relayed the news from outside, that Control hadn't seen any signs of motion through the bedroom curtains. His short-wavelength radar imager let him see what the snatch crew's night-vision gear missed: It could pinpoint the telltale pulse of warm blood right through a drywall siding. Two more soldiers in goggles, helmets, and flak jackets darted through the opening and into the hall, cautiously extending small mirrors on telescoping arms past open doorways to see if anyone was inside. Within thirty seconds they had the entire ground floor swept clean. Now they moved the thermal imager inside: Control swept each ceiling carefully before pausing in the living room and circling his index finger under the light fitting for the others to see. *One body, sleeping, right overhead.*

Four figures in black body armor ghosted up the staircase, two with guns, and two behind them with specialist equipment. The master bedroom opened off the small landing at the top of the stairs—the plan was to charge straight through and neutralize the occupant directly.

However, they hadn't counted on Miriam's domestic untidiness. Living alone and working a sixty-hour week, she had precious little time for homemaking: All her neat-freakery got left behind at work each evening. The landing was crowded, an overflowing basket of dirty clothing waiting for a trip down to the basement beside a couple of bookcases that narrowed the upstairs hall so that they had to go in single-file. But there were worse obstacles to come. Miriam's house was full of books. Right now, a dog-eared copy of *The Cluetrain Manifesto* lay facedown at one side of the step immediately below the landing. It was precisely as cold as the carpet it lay on, so to the night-vision goggles it was almost invisible. The first three intruders stepped over it without noticing, but the fourth placed his right boot on it, and the effect was as dramatic as if it had been a banana skin.

Miriam jolted awake in terror, hearing a horrible clatter-
ing noise on the landing. Her mind was a blank, the word *intruder* running through it in neon letters the size of
headlines—she sat bolt upright and fumbled on the dressing
table for the pistol, which she'd placed there when she found
she could feel it through the pillow. The noise of the bedroom door shoving open was infinitely frightening and as
she brought the gun around, trying to get it untangled from
the pillowcase—Brilliant light lanced through her eyelids, a
flashlight: *"Drop it, lady!"*

Miriam fumbled her finger into the trigger guard—

"Drop it!" The light came closer, right in her face. "Now!"

Something like a freight locomotive came out of the darkness and slammed into the side of her right arm.

Someone said, "Shee-it" with heartfelt feeling, and a huge
weight landed on her belly. Miriam gathered breath to
scream, but she couldn't feel her right arm and something was
pressing on her face. She was choking: The air was acrid and
sweet-smelling and thick, a cloying flowery laboratory stink.
She kicked out hard, legs tangled in the comforter, gasping
and screaming deep in her throat, but they were muffling her
with the stench and everything was fuzzy at the edges.

She couldn't move. "Not funny," someone a long way
away at the end of a black tunnel tried to say. The lights were
on now, but everything was dark. Figures moved around her
and her arm hurt—distantly. She couldn't move. Tired.
There was something in her mouth. *Is this an ambulance?*
she wondered. Lights out.

The dogpile on the bed slowly shifted, standing up. Specialist A worked on the subject with tongue depressor and
tubes, readying her for assisted ventilation. The chloroform
pad sitting on the pillow was an acrid nuisance: For the journey ahead, something safer and more reliable was necessary.
Specialist B worked on her at the same time, sliding the col-
lapsible gurney under her and strapping her to it at legs,
hips, wrists, and shoulders.

"That was a *fucking* mess," snarled Control, picking up the little snub-nosed revolver in one black-gloved hand. "Safety catch was on, luckily. Who screwed up on the landing?"

"Sir." It was Point B. "There was a book. On the stairs."

"Bitchin'. Okay, get little Miss Lethal here loaded and ready to move. Bravo, start the cleanup. I want her personal files, wherever she keeps them. *And* her computer, and all the disks. Whoever the hell was with her this evening, I want to know who they are too. And everything else. Charlie, pack her bags like she's going on vacation—a long vacation. Clothing, bathroom stuff. Don't make a mess of it. I want to be ready to evacuate in twenty minutes."

"Sir. Yes, sir." Control nodded. Point B was going to pull a shitwork detail when they got home, but you didn't discipline people in the field unless they'd fucked up bad enough to pull a nine-millimeter discharge. And Point B hadn't. A month cleaning the latrines would give him time to think on how close he'd come to getting plugged by a sleepy woman with a thirty-eight revolver.

Spec A was nearly done; he and Spec B grunted as they lifted the coffin-shaped framework off the bed. Miriam was unconscious and trussed like a turkey inside it. "Is she going to be okay?" Control asked idly.

"I think so," said Spec A. "Bad bruising on her right arm, and probably concussed, but I don't expect anything major. Worst risk is she pukes in her sleep and chokes on her own vomit, and we can deal with that." He spoke confidently. He'd done paramedic training and Van Two was equipped like an ambulance.

"Then take her away. We'll be along in half an hour when we're through sanitizing."

"Yeah, boss. We'll get her home."

Control looked at the dressing table, strewn with underwear, month-old magazines, and half-used toiletries. His expression turned to disgust at the thought of searching through piles of dirty clothing. "Sky father, what a mess."

There was an office not far from Miriam's cell. The office was quiet, and its dark oak paneling and rich Persian carpets gave it something of the ambiance of a very exclusive Victorian gentleman's club. A wide walnut desk occupied the floor next to the window bay. The top of the desk was inlaid with a Moroccan leather blotter, upon which lay a banker's box full of papers and other evidence.

The occupant of the office sat at the desk, reading the mess of photocopies and memos from the file box. He was in his early fifties, thickset with the stomach of middle age, but tall enough to carry it well. His suit was conservative: He might have been a retired general or a corporate chairman. Neither guess would be wrong, but neither would be the full truth, either. Right now he looked as if he had a headache; his expression was sour as he read a yellowing newspaper clipping. "What a mess," he murmured. "What a blessed mess . . ."

A buzzer sounded above the left-hand door.

The officeholder glanced at the door with wintry gray eyes. "Enter," he called sharply. Then he looked back at the papers.

Footsteps, the sound of male dress shoes—leather-soled—on parquet, were abruptly silenced as the visitor reached the carpeted inner sanctum.

"You summoned me, uncle? Is there any movement on my proposal? If anyone wants me to—"

Angbard Lofstrom looked up again and fixed his nephew with a long icy stare. His nephew shuffled, discomfited: a tall, blond fellow whose suit would not have been out of place in an advertising agency's offices. "Patience," he said in English.

"But I—"

"I said *patience*." Angbard laid the newspaper clipping flat on his blotter and stared at his nephew. "This is not the time to discuss your proposal. About which there is no news, by the way. Don't expect anything to happen soon; you need to learn timing if you want to make progress, and the changes you are suggesting we make are politically difficult."

"How much longer?" The young man sounded tense.

"As long as I deem necessary." Angbard's stare hardened. "Remember why you are here."

"I—yes, my lord. If it pleases you to accept my apologies . . ."

"How is the prisoner?" Angbard asked abruptly.

"Oh. Last time I checked—fifteen minutes ago—she was unconscious but sleeping normally. She is in one of the doppelgänger cells. I removed the mnemonic she was wearing on her person and had one of the maids search her for tattoos. Her cell has no mirror, no shaving apparatus. I left instructions that I am to be called when she awakens."

"Hmm." Angbard chewed on his upper lip with an expression of deep disapproval. "What does the doctor say?"

"The doctor says that he might have to splint her arm, later—there is bruising—but she sustained no serious harm in the course of the pickup."

"Well." Angbard waved one hand in the direction of the chairs positioned before his desk. "Sit down." His nephew sat with alacrity, his back stiff. "Do we have any known loose ends, Earl Roland?"

"Yes, sir, but nothing critical. We have retrieved the documents, camera, recorder, personal computer, and all the other effects that we could find. Her house was untidy, but we are fairly sure we were able to locate everything—her office was well-organized. The windows have been repaired, and the neighbors informed indirectly that she is on assignment away from home. She is unmarried and has few attachments." Roland looked faintly disapproving. "There is reference to an elderly mother who lives alone. The only possible problem is referred to in the contractor's report. Evidently on her last excursion a woman, identity unknown, arrived, collected her car, then her person, and drove her home. Presumably a friend. The problem is that she left the stakeout by taxi without any notice—I assume she summoned it by means of a mobile telephone—and our contractor team was too short-staffed to dispatch a tail. I have therefore instructed them to continue surveillance and rein-

state the line tap, in the hope that the friend reappears. Once
she does so—"

Roland shrugged.

"See that you do—I want them in custody as soon as possible." Angbard harrumphed. "As to the prisoner's disposition . . ." He paused, head cocked slightly to one side.

"Sir?" Roland was a picture of polite attentiveness.

"The prisoner is to be treated with all the courtesy due to
one of your own station, indeed, as a senior Clan member, I
say. As a respected guest, detained for her own protection."

"Sir!" Roland couldn't contain his shock.

Angbard stared at him. "You have something to say, my
earl?" he asked coldly.

Roland swallowed. "I hear and . . . and will of course obey,"
he said. "Just, please permit me to say, this is a surprise—"

"Your surprise is *noted*," Angbard stated coldly. "Nevertheless, I will keep my reasons to myself for the time being.
All you need to know at present is that the prisoner must be
treated with, as they say, kidskin gloves." He stared at the
young officer intently, but he showed no sign of defiance:
and after a moment Angbard relented slightly. "This—" he
gestured at the box before him—"raises some most disturbing possibilities." He tapped one finger on the topmost sheet.
"Or had you noticed any strangers outwith the Clan who are
gifted with the family talent?"

"Mm, no, sir, I had not." Roland looked suddenly thoughtful. "What are you thinking?"

"Later," Angbard said tersely. "Just see she's transferred
to a comfortable—but securely doppelgängered—suite. Be
polite and hospitable, win her trust, and treat her person with
the utmost respect. And notify me when she is ready to answer my questions."

"I hear and obey," Roland acknowledged, less puzzled,
but clearly thoughtful.

"See that you do," Angbard rumbled. "You are dismissed."

His nephew rose, straightened his suit jacket, and strode
toward the door, a rapier banging at his side. Angbard stared

at the door in silence for a minute after he had gone, then turned his eye back to the items in the file box. Which included a locket that he had seen before—almost a third of a century ago.

"Patricia," he whispered under his breath, "what has become of you?"

Daylight. That was the first thing that Miriam noticed. That—and she had the mother of all hangovers. Her head felt as if it was wrapped in cotton wool, her right arm hurt like hell, and everything around her was somehow wrong. She blinked experimentally. Her head *was* wrapped in cotton wool—or bandages. And she was wearing something unfamiliar. She'd gone to bed in her usual T-shirt, but now she was wearing a nightgown—but she didn't own one! *What's going on?*

Daylight. She felt muzzy and stupid and her head was pounding. She was thirsty, too. She rolled over and blinked at where the nightstand should have been. There was a whitewashed wall six inches from her nose. The bed she was lying in was jammed up against a rough cinder-block wall that had been painted white. It was as weird as that confused nightmare about the light and the chemical stink—

Nightmare?

She rolled the other way, her legs tangling up in the nightgown. She nearly fell out of the bed, which was far too narrow. It wasn't her own bed, and for a moment of panic she wondered what could possibly have happened. Then it all clicked into place. "Gangsters or feds? Must be the feds," she mumbled to herself. *They must have followed me. Or Paulie. Or something.*

A vast, hollow terror seemed to have replaced her stomach. *They'll 'bury you so deep,'* she remembered. *'So deep' that—*

Her throat felt sore, as if she'd spent the entire night screaming. Odd, that. Maybe it was anticipation.

Somehow she swung her legs over the side of the strange

bed. They touched the floor much too soon, and she sat up, pushing the thin comforter aside. The far wall was too close, and the window was set high up; in fact, the whole room was about the size of a closet. There was no other furniture except for a small stainless-steel sink bolted to the wall opposite the door. The door itself was a featureless slab of wood with a peephole implanted in it at eye level. She noted with a dull sense of recognition that the door was perfectly smooth, with no handle or lock mechanism to mar its surface: It was probably wood veneer over metal.

Her hand went to her throat. The locket was gone.

Miriam stood, then abruptly found that she had to lean against the wall to keep upright. Her head throbbed and her right arm was extremely sore. She turned and looked up at the window, but it was above the top of her head, even if she had the energy to stand on the bed. High and small and without curtains, it looked horribly like the skylight of a prison cell. *Am I in prison?* she wondered.

With that thought, Miriam lost what calm she had. She leaned against the door and pounded it with her left hand, setting up a hollow racket, but stopped when her hand began to throb and the fear swept back in a suffocating wave, driving a storm surge of rage before it. She sat down and buried her face in her hands and began to sob quietly. She was still in this position a few minutes later when the door frame gave a quiet click and opened outward.

Miriam looked up suddenly as the door opened. "Who the fuck are you?" she demanded.

The man standing in the doorway was perfectly turned out, from his black loafers to the ends of his artfully styled blond hair: He was young (late twenties or early thirties), formally dressed in a fashionable suit, clean-shaven, and his face was set in neutral lines. He could have been a Mormon missionary or an FBI agent. "Miss Beckstein, if you'd be so good as to come with me, please?"

"Who *are* you?" She repeated. "Aren't you guys supposed to read me my rights or something?" There was something odd about him, but she couldn't quite get her head around it.

Past his shoulder she could see a corridor, blurry right now—then she realized what it was that she was having trouble with. *He's wearing a sword,* she told herself, hardly believing her eyes.

"You seem to be laboring under a misapprehension." He smiled, not unpleasantly. "We don't have to read you your rights. However, if you'll come with me, we can go somewhere more comfortable to discuss the situation. Unless you're entirely happy with the sanitary facilities here?"

Miriam glanced behind her, suddenly acutely aware that her bladder was full and her stomach was queasy. "Who are you?" she asked uncertainly.

"If you come with me, you'll get your answers," he said soothingly. He took a step back and something made Miriam suspect there was an implicit *or else* left dangling at the end of his last sentence. She lurched to her feet unsteadily and he reached out for her elbow. She shuffled backward instinctively to avoid contact, but lost her balance against the edge of the bed: She sat down hard and went over backward, cracking her head against the wall.

"Oh dear," he said. She stared up at him through a haze of pain. "I'll bring a wheelchair for you. Please don't try to move."

The ceiling pancaked lazily above her head. Miriam felt sick and a little bit drowsy. Her head was splitting. *Migraine or anesthesia hangover?* she wondered. The well-dressed man with the sword sticking incongruously out from under his suit coat was back, with a wheelchair and another man wearing a green medical smock. Together they picked her up and planted her in the chair, loose as a sack of potatoes. "Oww," she moaned softly.

"That was a nasty bash," said her visitor. He walked beside the chair. Lighting strips rolled by overhead, closed doorways to either side. "How do you feel?"

"Lousy," she managed. Her right arm had come out in sympathy with her skull. "Who're you?"

"You don't give up, do you?" he observed. The chair turned a corner: More corridor stretched ahead. "I'm

Roland, Earl Lofstrom. Your welfare is my responsibility for now." The chair stopped in front of burnished stainless-steel panels—an elevator. Mechanisms grumbled behind the door. "You shouldn't have awakened in that isolation cell. You were only there due to an administrative error. The individual responsible has been disciplined."

A cold chill washed down Miriam's spine, cutting through the haze of pain. "Don't want your name," she muttered. "Want to know who you people *are*. My rights, dammit."

The elevator doors opened and the attendant pushed her inside. Roland stepped in beside her, then waved the attendant away. Then he pushed a button out of sight behind her head. The doors closed and the elevator began to rise, but stopped only a few seconds later. "You appear to be under a misapprehension," he repeated. "You're asking for your rights. The, uh, Miranda declaration, yes?"

She tried to look up at him. "Huh?"

"That doesn't apply here. Different jurisdiction, you know." His accompanying smile left Miriam deeply unnerved.

The elevator doors opened and he wheeled her into a silent, carpeted corridor with no windows—just widely spaced doors to either side, like an expensive hotel. He stopped at the third door along on the left and pushed it open, then turned her chair and rolled it forward into the room within. "There. Isn't this an improvement over the other room?"

Miriam pushed down on the wheelchair arms with both hands, wincing at a stab of pain in her right forearm. "Shit." She looked around. "This isn't federal."

"If you don't mind." He took her elbow, and this time she couldn't dodge. His grip was firm but not painful. "This is the main reception room of your suite. You'll note the windows don't actually open, and they're made of toughened glass for your safety. The bathroom is through that door, and the bedroom is over there." He pointed. "If you want anything, lift the white courtesy phone. If you need a doctor, there is one on call. I suggest you take an hour to recover, then freshen up and get dressed. There will be an interview in due course."

"What *is* this place? Who *are* you people?"

Finally Roland frowned at her. "You can stop pretending you don't know," he said. "You aren't going to convince anyone." Pausing in the doorway, he added, "The war's over, you know. We won twenty years ago." The door closed behind him with a solid-sounding *click,* and Miriam was unsurprised to discover that the door handle flopped limply in her hand when she tried it. She was locked in.

Miriam shuffled into the white-tiled bathroom, blinked in the lights, then sat down heavily on the toilet. "Holy shit," she mumbled in disbelief. It was like an expensive hotel—a fiendishly expensive one, aimed at sheikhs and diplomats and billionaires. The floor was smooth, a very high grade of Italian marble if she was any judge of stonework. The sink was a molded slab of thick green glass and the taps glowed with a deep luster that went deeper than mere gilding could reach. The bath was a huge scalloped shell sunk into the floor, white and polished, with blue and green lights set into it amid the chromed water jets. An acre of fluffy white towels and a matching bathrobe awaited her, hanging above a basket of toiletries. She knew some of those brand names; she'd even tried their samplers when she was feeling extravagant. The shampoo alone was a hundred dollars a bottle.

This definitely isn't anything to do with the government, she realized. *I know people who'd pay good money to be locked up in here!*

She sat down on the edge of the bathtub, slid into one of the seats around its rim, and spent a couple of minutes puzzling out the control panel. Eventually she managed to coax half a dozen jets of aerated water into life. *This is a prison,* she kept reminding herself. Roland's words haunted her: *'Different jurisdiction, you know.'* Where was she? They'd taken the locket. That implied that they knew about it—and about her. But there was absolutely no way to square this experience with what she'd seen in the forest: the pristine wilderness, the peasant village.

The bedroom was as utterly over the top as the bathroom, dominated by a huge oak sleigh-bed in a traditional Scandinavian style, with masses of down comforters and pillows. Rather than fitted furniture there were a pair of huge oak wardrobes and a chest of drawers and other, smaller, furniture—a dressing table with mirror, an armchair, something that looked like an old linen press. Every piece of furniture in the bedroom looked to be an antique. The combined effect was overwhelming, like being expected to sleep in an auction house's display room.

"Oh wow." She looked around and spotted the windows, then walked over to them. A balcony outside blocked the view of whatever was immediately below. Beyond it she had a breathtaking view of a sweep of forested land dropping away toward a shallow valley with a rocky crag, standing proud and bald on the other side. It was as untainted by civilization as the site of her camping expedition. She turned away, disquieted. Something about this whole picture screamed: *Wrong!* at her, but she couldn't quite put her finger on it.

The chest of drawers held an unpleasant surprise. She pulled the top drawer open, half-expecting it to be empty. Instead, it contained underwear. *Her* underwear. She recognized the holes in one or two socks that she hadn't gotten around to throwing away.

"Bastards." She focused on the clothing, mind spinning furiously. *They're thorough, whoever they are.* She looked closer at the furniture. The writing desk appeared to be an original Georgian piece, or even older, a monstrously valuable antique. And the chairs, Queen Anne or a good replica—disturbingly expensive. *A hotel would be content with reproductions*, she reasoned. The emphasis would be on utility and comfort, not authenticity. If there were originals anywhere, they'd be on display in the foyer. It reminded her of something that she'd seen somewhere, something that nagged at the back of her mind but stubbornly refused to come to the foreground.

She stood up and confirmed her suspicion that the

wardrobes held her entire range of clothing. More words came back to haunt her: *'There will be an interview in due course.'* "I'm not in a cell," she told herself, "but I could be. They showed me that much. So they're playing head games. They want to play the stick-and-carrot game. That means I've got some kind of leverage. Doesn't it?" *Find out what they want, then get out of here fast,* she decided.

Half an hour later she was ready. She'd chosen a blouse the color of fresh blood, her black interview suit, lip gloss to match, and heels. Miriam didn't normally hold with makeup, but this time she went the whole hog. She didn't normally hold with power dressing either, but something about Roland and this setup suggested that his people were much more obsessed with appearances than the dot-com entrepreneurs and Masspike corridor startup monkeys she usually dealt with. Any edge she could get . . .

A bell chimed discreetly. She straightened up and turned to look at the door as it opened. *Here it comes,* she thought nervously.

It was Roland, who'd brought her up here from the cell. Now that she saw him in the daylight from the windows with a clear head, her confusion deepened. *He looks like a secret service agent,* she thought. Something about that indefinably military posture and the short hair suggested he'd been ordered into that suit in place of combat fatigues.

"Ah. You've found the facilities." He nodded. "How are you feeling?"

"Better," she said. "I see you ransacked my house."

"You will find that everything has been accounted for," he said, slightly defensively. "Would you rather we'd given you a prison uniform? No?" He sized her up with a glance. "Well, there's someone I have to take you to see now."

"Oh, *good.*" It slipped out before she could clamp down on the sarcasm. "The chief of secret police, I assume?"

His eyes widened slightly. "Don't joke about it," he muttered.

"Oh." Miriam dry-swallowed. "Right, well, we wouldn't want to keep him waiting, would we?"

"Absolutely not," Roland said seriously. He held the door open, then paused for a moment. "By the way, I really wouldn't want you to embarrass yourself trying to escape. This is a secure facility."

"I see," said Miriam, who didn't—but had made her mind up already that it would be a mistake to simply cut and run. These people had snatched her from her own bed. That suggested a frightening level of—competence.

She approached the door warily, keeping as far away from Roland as she could. "Which way?"

"Along the passage."

He headed off at a brisk march and she followed him, heels sinking into the sound-deadening carpet. She had to hurry to keep up. *When I get out of this mess, I'm buying a new interview outfit—one I can run in*, she promised herself.

"Wait one moment, please."

She found herself fetched up behind Roland's broad back, before a pair of double doors that were exquisitely paneled and polished. *Odd*, she wondered. *Where* is *everybody?* She glanced over her shoulder, and spotted a discreet video camera watching her back. They'd come around two corners, as if the corridor followed a rectangle: They'd passed a broad staircase leading down, and the elevator—there ought to be more people about, surely?

"Who am I—"

Roland turned around. "Look, just wait," he said. "Security calls." She noticed for the first time that he had the inside of his wrist pressed against an unobtrusive box in the wall.

"Security?"

"Biometrics, I think it's called," he said. There was a *click* from the door and he opened it slowly. "Matthias? Ish hafe gefauft des'usher des Angbard."

Miriam blinked—she didn't recognize the language. It sounded a bit like German, but not enough to make anything out; and her high school German was rusty, anyway.

"Innen gekomm', denn."

The door opened and Roland caught her right arm, tugged her into the room after him, and let the door close. She pulled her arm back and rubbed the sore spot as she glanced around.

"Nice place you've got here," she said. Thick draped curtains surrounded the window. The walls were paneled richly in dark wood: The main piece of furniture was a desk beside an inner office door. A broad-shouldered man in a black suit, white shirt, and red tie waited behind the desk. The only thing to distinguish the scene from a high-class legal practice was the submachine gun resting by his right hand.

"Spresh'she de hoh'sprashe?"

"No," said Roland. "Use English, please."

"Okay," said the man with the gun. He looked at Miriam, and she had the disquieting sense that he was photographing her, storing her face in his memory. He had frizzy black hair, swept back from high temples, combined with a nose like a hatchet and a glare like a caged hawk. "I am Matthias. I am the Boss's secretary, which is, his keeper of secrets. That is his office door. You go in there without permission over my dead body. This is not an, um, how would you say it?" He glanced at Roland.

"Metaphor," Roland offered.

"Metaphor." Matthias looked at her again. He wasn't smiling. "The Boss is expecting you. You may enter now."

Miriam looked sidelong at him as Roland marched over to the door and opened it, then waved her forward. Matthias kept his eyes on her—and one hand close to the gun. She found herself involuntarily giving him a wide berth, as she would a rattlesnake. Not that he looked particularly venomous—a polite, clean-shaven man in a pin-striped suit—but there was something about his manner . . . she'd seen it before, in a young DEA agent she had dated for a couple of months before learning better. Mike Fleming had been quietly, calmly, crazy, in a way that made her cut and run before she got dragged too far in with him. He'd been quite prepared to give his life for the cause he believed in—or to make any other sacrifice for that matter: He was utterly unable to see the walls of the box he'd locked himself in. The kind of guy who'd arrest a cripple with multiple sclerosis for smoking a joint to deaden the pain. She suppressed a shudder as she entered the inner office.

The inner office was as excessive as the suite they'd given her, the Mafia special with the locked door and the auction house's ransom in antiques. The floor was tiled in hand-polished hardwood, partially covered by a carpet that was probably worth as much as her house. The walls were paneled in wood blackened with age. There were a couple of discreet oil paintings of big red-faced men in medieval-looking armor or classical robes posed before a castle, and a pair of swords rested on pegs in the wall above the desk. There was a huge walnut desk positioned beside the window bay and two chairs were drawn up before it, positioned so that the owner of the office would be all but invisible from the window.

Roland stopped before the desk, drew himself up to attention, and saluted. "My lord, I have the pleasure of presenting to you . . . Miriam Beckstein."

The presence in the chair inclined his head in acknowledgment. "That is not her real name, but her presence is sufficient. You may be at ease." Miriam squinted, trying to make out his features against the glare. He must have taken her expression for hostility, for he waved a hand: "Please be seated, the both of you. I have no argument with you, ah, Miriam, if that is the name you wish to be known by."

Roland surprised her by pulling a chair out and offering it to her. She startled herself in turn by sitting down, albeit nervously, knees clenched together and back stiffly erect. "Who *are* you people?" she whispered.

Her eyes were becoming accustomed to the light: She could see the man in the high-backed chair smile faintly. He was in late middle age, possibly as old as Morris Beckstein would have been, had he lived. His suit was sober—these people dressed like a company of undertakers—but so well cut that it had to be hand-tailored. His hair was graying, and his face was indistinguished, except for a long scar running up his left cheek.

"I might ask the same question," he murmured. "Roland, be seated, I say!" His tone of voice said he was used to being obeyed. "I am the high Duke Angbard of house Lofstrom, third of that name, trustee of the crown of guilds, defender of the king's honor, freeman of the city of Niejwein, head of security of the Clan Reunified, prince of merchant-princes, owner of this demesne, and holder of many more titles than that—but those are the principal ones." His eyes were the color of lead, a blue so pale she found them hard to see, even when they were focused directly on her. "Also, if I am not very much mistaken, I am your uncle."

Miriam recoiled in shock. *"What?"* Another voice echoed her. She glanced sideways to see Roland staring at her in astonishment. His cool exterior began to crack.

"My father would never—" Roland began.

"Shut *up*," said Angbard, cold steel in his voice. "I was not referring to your father, young man, but to your aunt once removed: Patricia."

"Would you mind explaining just what you're talking about?" Miriam demanded, anger finally getting the better of her. She leaned forward. "Your people have abducted me, ransacked my house, and kidnapped me, just because you think I'm some kind of long-lost relative?"

Angbard nodded thoughtfully. "No. We are *absolutely certain* you're a long-lost relative." He glanced at his nephew. "There is solid evidence."

Roland leaned back in his chair, whistled tunelessly, all military pretense fled. He stared at her out of wide eyes, as if he was seeing a ghost.

"What have *you* got to whistle about?" she demanded.

"You asked for an explanation," Angbard reminded her. "The arrival of an unknown world-walker is always grounds for concern. Since the war . . . suffice to say, your appearance would have been treated drastically in those days. When you stumbled across the old coast trail a week ago, and the patrol shot at you, they had no way of knowing who you were. That became evident only later—I believe you left a pair of pink house-shoes behind?—and triggered an extensive manhunt. However, you are clearly not connected to a traitorious faction, and closer research revealed some interesting facts about you. I believe you were adopted?"

"That's right." Miriam's heart was fluttering in her ribs, shock and unpleasant realization merging. "Are you saying you're my long-lost relatives?"

"Yes." Angbard waited a moment, then slid open one of the drawers in his desk. "This is yours, I believe."

Miriam reached out and picked up the locket. Tarnished with age, slightly battered—an island of familarity. "Yes."

"But not this." Angbard palmed something else, then pushed it across the desk toward her.

"Oh my." Miriam was lost for words. It was the identical twin to her locket, only brightly shining and lacking some scratches. She took it and sprang the catch—

"Ouch!" She glared at Roland, who had knocked it out of her hand. But he was bending down, and after a moment she realized that he was picking it up, very carefully, keeping the open halves facedown until it was upon the duke's blotter.

"We will have to teach you how to handle these things safely," Angbard said mildly. "In the meantime, my sister's is yours to keep."

"Your sister's," she echoed stupidly, wrapping her fingers around the locket.

"My sister went missing thirty-two years ago," Angbard said with careful lack of emphasis. "Her caravan was attacked, her husband slain, and her guard massacred, but her body was never found. Nor was that of her six-week-old daughter. She was on her way to pay attendance to the court of the high king, taking her turn as the Clan's hostage. The wilds around Chesapeake Bay, as it is called on your side, are not heavily populated in this world. We searched for months, but obviously to little effect."

"You found the box of documents," Miriam said. The effort of speaking was vast: She could hear her heart pounding in her ears.

"Yes. They provide impressive supporting evidence—circumstantial but significant. While you were unconscious, blood samples were taken for, ah, DNA profiling. The results will be back tomorrow, but I am in no doubt. You have the family face and the family talent—or did you think world-walking was commonplace?—and your age and the documentary evidence fits perfectly. You are the daughter Helge, born to my elder sister, Patricia Thorold Hjorth, by her husband the western magistrate-prince, Alfredo Wu, and word of your survival is going to set the fox among the Clan chickens with a vengeance when it emerges." He smiled thinly. "Which is why I took the precaution of sending away the junior members of the distaff side, and almost all the servants, before bidding you welcome. It would not have done for the younger members of the Clan to find out about your existence before I looked to your defense. Some of them will be feeling quite anxious about the disruption of the braid succession, your highness."

"*Highness?* What are you talking about?" Miriam could hear her voice rising, out of control, but she couldn't get it under control. "What are you on? Look, I'm a business journalist covering the Masspike corridor, not some kind of feudal noble! I don't know about *any* of this stuff!" She was on her feet in front of the desk. "What's world-walking, and what does it have to do—"

"Your highness," Angbard said firmly, "you *were* a business journalist, on the other side of the wall of worlds. But world-walking is how you came here. It is the defining talent of our Clan, of the families who constitute the Clan. It is in the blood, and you are one of *us*, whether you will it or no. Over here, you are the eldest heir to a countess and a magistrate-prince of the outer kingdom, both senior members of their families, and however much you might wish to walk away from that fact, it *will* follow you around. Even if you go back over there."

He turned to Roland, ignoring her stunned silence. "Earl Roland, you will please escort your first cousin to her chambers. I charge you with her safety and protection until further notice. Your highness, we will dine in my chambers this evening, with one or two trustworthy guests, and I will have more words for you then. Roland will assign servants to see to your comfort and wardrobe. I expect him to deal with your questions. In the meantime, you are both dismissed."

Miriam glared at him, speechless. "I have only your best interests at heart," the duke said mildly. "Roland."

"Sir." Roland took her arm.

"Proceed."

Roland turned and marched from the office, and Miriam hurried to keep up, angry and embarrassed and trying not to show it. *You bastard!* she thought. Out in the corridor: "You're hurting me," she hissed, trying not to trip. "Slow down."

Roland slowed and—mercy of mercies—let go of her arm. He glanced behind, and an invisible tension left his shoulders. "I'm sorry," he said.

"You're sorry?" she replied, disbelievingly. "You nearly twisted my arm out of its socket!" She rubbed her elbow and winced.

"I *said* I'm sorry. Angbard isn't used to being disobeyed. I've never seen *anyone* take such liberties with him and escape punishment!"

"Punishment—" she stopped. "You weren't kidding about him being the head of secret police, were you?"

"He's got many more titles than he told you about. He's responsible for the security of the entire Clan. If you like, think of him as the head of the FBI here. There was a civil war before you or I were born. He's probably ordered more hangings than you or I have had hot dinners."

Miriam stumbled. "Ow, shit!" She leaned against the wall. "That'll teach me to keep my eye on where I'm going." She glanced at him. "So you're telling me I wasn't paying enough attention?"

"You'll be all right," Roland said slowly, "if you can adapt to it. I imagine it must be a great shock, coming into your inheritance so suddenly."

"Is that so?" She looked him up and down carefully, unsure how to interpret the raised eyebrow—*Is he trying to tell me something or just having a joke at my expense?*—then a second thought struck her. "I think I'm missing something here," she said, deliberately casually.

"Nothing around here is what it seems," Roland said with a little shrug. His expression was guarded. "But if the duke is right, if you really *are* Patricia's long-lost heir—"

Miriam recognized the expression in his eyes: It was belief. *He really* believes *I'm some kind of fairy-tale princess,* she realized with dawning horror. *What have I got myself into?*

"You'll have to tell me all about it. In my chambers."

CINDERELLA 2.0

Roland led her back to her suite and followed her into the huge reception room at its heart. He wandered over to the windows and stood there with his hands clasped behind his back. Miriam kicked her heels off and sat down in the huge, enveloping leather sofa opposite the window.

"When did you discover the locket?" he asked.

She watched him curiously. "Less than a week ago."

"And until then you'd grown up in ignorance of your family," he said. "Amazing!" He turned around. His face was set in a faintly wistful expression.

"Are you going to just stand there?" she asked.

"It would be impertinent to sit down without an invitation," he replied. "I know it's the case on the other side, but here, the elders tend to stand on points of etiquette."

"Well—" her eyes narrowed. "Sit down if you want to. You're making me nervous. You look as if you're afraid I'll bite."

"Um." He sat down uneasily on the arm of the big chair opposite her. "Well, it's irregular, to say the least, to be here. You being unwed, that is."

"What's that got to do with it?" she snapped. "I'm divorced. Is that another of the things you people are touchy about?"

" 'Divorced?' " He stared at her hand, as if looking for a ring. "I don't know." Suddenly he looked thoughtful. "Customs here are distinctly different from the other side. This is not a Christ-worshiping land." Another thought struck him. "Are you, uh . . . ?"

"Does Miriam Beckstein sound Christian to you?"

"It's sometimes hard to tell with people from the other side. Christ worship isn't a religion here," he said seriously. "But you are divorced. And a world-walker." He leaned forward. "What that means is you are automatically a Clan shareholder of the first rank, eligible, unwed, and liable to displace a dozen minor distant relatives from their Clan shares, which they thought safe. Your children will displace theirs, too. Do you know, you are probably a great-aunt already?"

To Miriam this was insupportable. "I don't want a huge bunch of feuding cousins and ancestors and children! I'm quite happy on my own."

"It's not as simple as that." A momentary flash of irritation surfaced: "Our personal happiness has nothing to do with the Clan's view of our position in life. *I* don't like it either, but you've got to understand that there are people out there whose plans will be disrupted by the mere knowledge of your existence, and other people who will make plans for you, regardless of your wishes!"

"I—" she stopped. "Look, I don't think we've got this straight. I may be related to your family by genetics, but I'm not one *of* you. I don't know how the hell you think or what your etiquette is like and I don't care about being the orphan of a countess. It doesn't *mean* anything to me." She sighed. "There's been some huge mistake. The sooner we get it over with and I can go back to being a journalist, the better."

"If you want it that way." For almost a minute he brooded, staring at the floor in front of her. Miriam hooked one foot over the other and tried to relax enough to force her shoulders back into the sofa. "You might last six weeks," he said finally.

"Huh?"

He frowned at a parquet tile. "You can ignore your relatives, but they can't ignore you. To them you're an unknown quantity. The Clan shareholders all have the ability to walk the worlds, to cross over and follow you. Over here they're rich and powerful—but your current situation makes them insecure because you're unpredictable. If you do what's expected of you, you merely disrupt several inheritances worth a baron's estate. If you try to leave, they will think you are trying to form a new schismatic family, maybe even lure away family splinters to set up your own Clan to rival ours. How do you think the rich and powerful deal with threats to their existence?" He looked grave. "I'd rather not measure you for a coffin so soon after discovering you. It's not every day I find a new second cousin, especially one who's as educated and intelligent as you seem to be. There's a shortage of good conversation here, you know."

"Oh." Miriam felt deflated, frightened. *What happens to business life when there's no limit to liability and the only people you can work with are your blood relatives?* Instinctively she changed the subject. "What did your uncle mean about tonight? And servants, I mean, *servants*?"

"Ah, that." Roland slipped down into the seat at last, relaxing a little. "We are invited to dine with the head of one of the families in private. The most powerful family in the Clan, at that. It's a formal affair. As for the servants, you're entitled to half a dozen or so ladies-in-waiting, your own guard of honor, and various others. My uncle the duke sent the minor family members away, but in the meantime there are maids from below stairs who will see to you. Really I would have sent them earlier, when I brought you up here, but he stressed the urgent need for secrecy and I thought—"

he paused. "You really did grow up over there, didn't you? In the *middle* classes."

She nodded, unsure just how to deal with his sudden attack of snobbery. Some of the time he seemed open and friendly, then she hit a blind spot and he was Sir Medieval Aristocrat writ large and charmless. "I don't do upper class," she said. "Well, business class, maybe."

"Well, you aren't in America any more. You'll have get used to the way we do things here eventually." He paused. "Did I say something wrong?"

He had, but she didn't know how to explain. Which was why a couple of hours later she was sitting naked in the bathroom, talking to her dictaphone, trying to make sense of the insanity outside—without succumbing to hysteria—by treating it as a work assignment and reporting on it.

"Now I know how Alice felt in looking-glass land," she muttered, holding her dictaphone close to her lips. "They're mad. I don't mean schizophrenic or psychotic or anything like that. They're just not in the same universe as anyone else I know." *The same universe* was a slip: She could feel the hysterical laughter bubbling up inside her. She bit her lower lip, painfully hard. "They're *nuts*. And they insist I join in and play their game by their rules."

There was some bumping and thumping going on in the main room of the suite. That would be the maidservants moving stuff around. Miriam paused the tape for a moment, considering her next words. "Dear Diary. Forty-eight hours ago I was hanging out in the forest, happy as a clam with my photographs of a peasant village that looked like something out of the middle ages. I was exploring, discovering something new, and it was great, I had this puzzle-box reality to crack open, a whole new story. Now I discover that I *own* that village, and a hundred more like it, and I literally have the power of life and death over its inhabitants. I can order soldiers to go in and kill every last one of them, on a whim. Once the Clans recognize me officially, at an annual session,

that is. And assuming—as Roland says—nobody assassi-
nates me. Princess Beckstein, signing off for *The Weatherman,* or maybe *Business 2.0.* Jesus, who'd have thought I'd
end up starring in some kind of twisted remake of *Cinderella*? Or that it would turn out so weird?"

*And I called Craig Venter and Larry Ellison robber
barons in print,* she thought mordantly, keying the "pause"
button again.

"Put that way it sounds funny, but it isn't. First I thought it
was the feds who broke in and grabbed me, and that's pretty
damn scary to begin with. FEMA, secret security courts
with hearings held *in camera.* Then, it could have been the
mob, if the mob looked like FBI agents. But this could actually be worse. These guys wear business suits, but it's only
skin-deep. They're like sheikhs from one of the rich Gulf
Emirates. They don't dress up medieval, they *think* medieval
and buy their clothes from Saks or Savile Row in England."

A thought occurred to her. *I hope Paulette's keeping the
video camera safe. And her head down.* She had an ugly,
frightened feeling that Duke Angbard had seen right through
her. He scared her: She'd met his type before, and they
played hardball—hard enough to make a Mafia don's eyes
water. She was half-terrified she'd wake up tomorrow and
see Paulie's head impaled on a pike outside her bedroom
window. *If only Ma hadn't given me the damned locket—*

A tentative knock on the door. "Mistress? Are you ready
to come out?"

"Ten minutes," Miriam called. She clutched her recorder
and shook her head. Four servants had shown up an hour
ago, and she'd retreated into the bathroom. One of them,
called something like Iona, had tried to follow her. Apparently countesses weren't allowed to use a bathroom without
servants in attendance. That was when Miriam had locked
the door and braced the linen chest against it.

"Damn," she muttered and took a deep breath. Then she
surrendered to the inevitable.

They were waiting for her when she came out. Four
women in severe black dresses and white aprons, their hair

covered by blue scarves. They curtseyed before her as she looked around, confused. "I'm Meg, if it please you, your highness. We is to dress you," the oldest of them said in a soft, vaguely Germanic accent: Middle-aged and motherly, she looked as if she would be more at home in an Amish farm kitchen than a castle.

"Uh, it's only four o'clock," Miriam pointed out.

Meg looked slightly shocked. "But you are to be received at seven!" She pointed out. "How're we to dress you in time?"

"Well." Miriam looked at the other three: All of them stood with downcast eyes. *I don't like this,* she thought. "How about I take something from my wardrobe—yes, they kindly brought all my clothes along—and put it on?"

"M-ma'am," the second oldest ventured: "I've seen your clothes. Begging your pardon, but them's not court clothes. Them's not suitable."

'Court clothes'? More crazy formal shit. "What would you suggest, then?" Miriam asked exasperatedly.

"Old Ma'am Rosein can fit you up with something to measure," said the old one, "should I but give her your sizes." She held up a very modern-looking tape measure. "Your highness?"

"This had better be good," Miriam said, raising her arms. *Why do I never get this kind of service at the Gap?* She wondered.

Three hours later Miriam was readied for dinner, and knew exactly why she never got this kind of service in any chain store—and why Angbard had so many servants. She was hungry, and if the bodice they'd squeezed her into allowed her to eat when she got there she might consider forgiving Angbard for his invitation.

The youngest maidservant was still fussing over her hair—and the feathers and string of pearls she had woven into it, while lamenting its shortness—when the door opened. It was, of course, Roland, accompanied now by a younger fellow, and Miriam began to get an inkling of what a formal dinner involved.

"Dear cousin!" Roland saluted her. Miriam carefully met his eyes and inclined her head as far as she could. "May I present you with your nephew twice removed: Vincenze?" The younger man bowed deeply, his red embroidered jacket tightening across broad shoulders. "You look splendid, my dear."

"Do I?" Miriam shook her head. "I feel like an ornamental flower arrangement," she said with some feeling.

"Charmed, ma'am," said Vincenze with the beginning of a stutter.

"If you would like to accompany me?" Roland offered her his arm, and she took it with alacrity.

"Keep the speed down," she hissed, glancing past him at his younger relative, who appeared to be too young to need to shave regularly.

"By all means, keep the speed down." Roland nodded.

Miriam stepped forward experimentally. Her maidservants had taken over an hour to install her in this outfit: *I feel like I've fallen into a medieval costume drama*, she thought. Roland's high linen collar and pantaloons didn't look too comfortable, either, come to think of it. "What sort of occasion is this outfit customary for?" she asked.

"Oh, any formal event where one of our class might be seen," Roland observed: "except that in public you would have a head covering and an escort. You would normally have much more jewelry, but your inheritance—" he essayed a shrug. "Is mostly in the treasury in Niejwein." Miriam fingered the pearl choker around her neck uncomfortably.

"You wore, um, American clothing today," she reminded him.

"Oh, but so is this, isn't it? But of another period. It reminds us whence our wealth comes."

"Right." She nodded minutely. *Business suits are informal dress for medieval aristocrats*? And formal dress that was like something that belonged in a movie about the Renaissance. *Everything goes into the exterior,* she added to her mental file of notes on family manners.

Roland escorted her up the wide stairs, then at the tall

doors at the top a pair of guards in dark suits and dark glasses announced them and ushered them in.

A long oak table awaited them in a surprisingly small dining room that opened off the duke's reception room. Antique glass globes rising from brass stems in the wall cast a pale light over a table glistening with silver and crystal. A servant in black waited behind each chair. Duke Angbard was already waiting for them, in similarly archaic costume: Miriam recognized a sword hanging at his belt. *Do swords go with male formal dress here?* she wondered. "My dear niece," he intoned, "you look marvelous! Welcome to my table." He waved her to a seat at the right of the head, black wood with a high back and an amazingly intricate design carved into it.

"The pleasure's mine," Miriam summoned up a dry smile, trying to strike the right note. *These goons can kill you as soon as look at you*, she reminded herself. Medieval squalor waited at the gate, and police cells down in the basement: Maybe this wasn't so unusual outside the western world, but it was new to her. She picked up her skirts and sat down gingerly as a servant slid a chair in behind her. The delicacy of its carving said nothing about its comfort—the seat was flat and extremely hard.

"Roland, and young Vincenze! You next, by the Sky Father."

"P-pleased to accept," Vincenze quavered.

The outer door opened again, sparing him further risk of embarrassment, and a footman called out in a low voice: "The Lady Margit, Chatellaine of Praha, and her excellency the Baroness Olga Thorold."

Six women came in, and now Miriam realized that she was probably underdressed, for the two high-born each wore the most voluminous gowns she'd ever seen, with trains that required two maids to carry them and hair so entangled in knots of gold and rubies that they resembled birds' nests. They looked like divas from a Wagner opera: the fat lady and the slim virgin. Margit of Praha was perhaps forty, her hair beginning to turn white and her cheeks sagging slightly. She looked as if she might be merry under other circumstances, but now her expression was grimly set. Olga Thorold, in contrast, was barely out of adolescence, a coltish young girl with a gown of gold and crimson and a neck swathed in gemstones that sparked fire whenever she moved. Olga looked half-amused by Miriam's cool assessing glance.

"Please be seated," said Angbard. Olga smiled demurely and bowed her neck to him. Margit, her chaperone, merely nodded and took a seat. "I believe you have heard tell of the arrival of our returning prodigal," he commented. "Pitr, fetch wine if you please. The Medoc."

"I have heard quite a few strangenesses today," Margit commented in English that bore a strangely clipped accent. "This songbird in your left hand, she is the daughter of your sister, long-lost. Is this true?"

"It is so," Angbard confirmed. A servant placed a cut-crystal glass of wine in front of Miriam. She began to reach toward it, then stopped, noticing that none of the others made such a gesture. "She has proven her heritage—the family trait—and the blood tests received barely an hour ago affirm her. She is of our bloodstock, and we have information substantiating, sadly, the death of her dam, Patricia Thorold Hjorth. I present to you Helge, also known as Miriam, of Thorold Hjorth, eldest heir surviving."

"So charmed!" Olga simpered at Miriam, who managed a wordless nod in reply.

Plates garnished with a starter materialized in front of everybody—roasted fowl of some kind, tiny enough to fit in Miriam's gloved hand. Nobody moved, but Angbard raised his hands. "In the name of the sky father—"

Miriam froze, so utterly startled that she missed the murmured continuation of his prayer, the flick of wine from glass across the tabletop, the answering murmer from Roland and Olga and Margit and the stuttered response from Vincenze. *He* said *this wasn't a Christian country,* she reminded herself, in time to move her lips as if saying something—anything, any response—just to fit in. Completing his brief prayer, Angbard raised his glass. "Eat, drink, and be safe under my roof," he told them, then took a mouthful of wine. After which it appeared to be open season.

Miriam's stomach grumbled. She picked up knife and fork and attacked her plate discreetly.

"One hears the strangest stories, dear." Miriam froze and glanced across the table: Margit was smiling at her sympathetically. "You were lost for so long, it must have been terrible!"

"Probably." Miriam nodded absentmindedly and put her fork down. "And then again, maybe not." She thought for a moment. "What have you heard?"

"Lots," Olga began breathlessly. "You were orphaned by savages and raised in a workhouse as a scrub, isn't that so, nana? Forced to sleep in the fireplace ashes at night! Then Cousin Roland found you and—"

"That's enough, dear," Margit said indulgently, raising a gloved hand. "It's her story, to tell in her own way." She raised an eyebrow at Miriam. Miriam blinked in return, more in startlement at the girl's artlessness than her chaperone's bluntness.

"I would not mind hearing for myself how your upbringing proceeded," Angbard rumbled.

"Oh. Indeed." Miriam glanced down, realizing that her appetizer had been replaced by a bowl of soup—some kind of broth, anyway—while they spoke. "Well. I wouldn't want to disappoint you—" she smiled at Olga—"but I had a perfectly normal upbringing. You know my birth-mother disappeared? When she was found in, uh, the other side, I was taken to a hospital and subsequently adopted by a young childless couple." *Of stone-throwing student radicals who grew up to be academics*, she didn't say. Olga was hanging on her every word, as if she was describing some kind of adventure with pirates and exploits in far-off lands. Either the girl was an idiot or she was so sheltered that all of this sounded exotic to her. Probably the latter.

"A university professor and his wife, a critic and reviewer. I think there was some issue with my—with Patricia's murder, so the adoption agency gave my adoptive parents her personal effects to pass on, but blocked inquiries about me from anywhere else, it being a matter for the police: unsolved murder, unidentified victim, and so on."

"There's only so much you can do to prevent a suicide bomber," Angbard said with deceptive mildness. "But we're not at immediate risk here," he added, smiling at Miriam, an expression clearly intended to reassure her. "I've taken special measures to ensure our safety."

"Your schooling," Olga said. "Did you have a personal tutor?"

Miriam frowned, wondering just what she meant. "No, I went to college, like everybody else," she said. "Premed and history of economics, then med school. Then, well, instead of continuing with med school, I went back to college again to study something else. Medicine didn't get on with me."

"You double-majored?" Roland interrupted.

"Yes, sort of." Miriam put her fork down. She couldn't eat any more, her stomach felt too full and her back ached. She leaned her shoulders against the chair but couldn't relax. "I switched to journalism. Did an MA in it." Her gloved hands felt hot and damp. They reminded her of a long shift on a geriatric ward, a different type of glove she'd ended up wearing for hours on end, cleaning up blockages. *Corn starch,* she thought absentmindedly. *Must get some dusting powder.* "I began on the biotech sector beat but found the IT industry shysters more interesting." She paused. Olga's expression was one of polite incomprehension, as if she'd suddenly begun speaking fluent Japanese. "Yourself?"

"Oh, *I* had a personal tutor!" Olga enthused. "But Daddy didn't want to send me away to school on the other side. We were having a spot of bother and he thought I'd need too many bodyguards."

Angbard smiled again, in a manner that Miriam found disquietingly avuncular. "There has been a threat of rebellion in Hel these past two years," he explained with a nod in Miriam's direction. "Your father needed the troops. Perhaps next year we can send you to Switzer-Land?"

"Oh, yes!" Olga clapped her hands together discreetly. "I'd like that."

"What would you like to study?" Miriam asked politely.

"Oh, everything! Deportment, and etiquette, and management of domestic events—balls and banquets. It's so important to get the little things right, and how are you to supervise everything if you don't know what your steward is doing?" She gave a little squeal. "I do hope they'll let me continue with the violin, though."

Miriam forced herself to keep a straight face. "I can see you're going to make a very good marriage," she said, voice neutral. It all added up to a horribly consistent picture: the older woman as chaperone, the total eagerness for the description of her own upbringing and education, the wistfulness for a place at an expensive finishing school. *This could be a problem*, she thought dispassionately. *If they expect me to behave like* this, *someone is going to be very disappointed. And it won't be me . . .*

"I'm sure she'll marry well," said Margit, venturing an opinion for the first time. Vincenze whispered something to Roland, who forced a knowing chuckle. "She's of the right age." Margit looked at Miriam dubiously. "I expect you'll—" she trailed off.

"Discussions of Countess Helge's eventual disposition are premature," Angbard said coolly. "Doubtless she will want to make a strong alliance to protect herself. I'm sure she has a solid head on her shoulders, and will want to keep it there." He smiled: a thin, humorless expression.

Miriam swallowed. *You old bastard! You're threatening me!* Servants removed her plate and refilled her wine glass. Growing anger threatened to overwhelm her. She took an overhasty mouthful to conceal her expression, leaving a bleeding ring of lip gloss on the crystal. Her heart was pounding and she couldn't seem to get enough air.

"To set your mind at ease, my dear, you are quite safe for the time being," said Angbard. "This is a doppelgängered house, with a secured installation on the other side, as strongly defended there as here—but if you were to venture outside of it you would be in jeopardy. I am concerned about your *other* relatives, such as the family Axl, and your late father's heirs of family Wu, in the far west. A strong alliance would go a long way toward protecting you."

"An alliance," she said thickly. It seemed to be hot in the dining room. She finished her glass, to buy some time. "Y'-know, it seems to me that you're taking a lot for granted. That I'll fit in and adapt to your ways."

"Isn't that how it always works?" asked Olga, confused. A dessert appeared, individual plates of chocolate truffles drizzled in syrup, but Miriam had no room for food. Her meal sat heavily on the top of her stomach.

"Not always, no," Miriam said tightly. She picked up her full wineglass, then frowned, remembering two—three?—refills before it, and put it down again, a little harder than she'd intended. Roland smiled at her indulgently. They *all* seemed to be smiling at her too much this evening, she noticed. As if they expected her to break down in tears and thank them for rescuing her from a life of drudgery. She forced herself to straighten her shoulders, sipped sparingly from her glass, and tried to ignore the growing pains in the small of her back. If she could just get through the remainder of the meal she'd be all right. "But we'll worry about that when we get to it, won't we?" She mustered a pained smile and everyone pretended she hadn't said anything. *The strange cousin's faux pas*, she thought, as Vincenze asked Roland something about cavalry maneuvers.

A few minutes later, Angbard rapped a silver dessert spoon on his glass. "If you have finished eating, by all means let the after-dinner entertainment commence," he said.

Servants wheeled a tall trolley in and Miriam blinked in surprise. A huge thirty-inch Sony flat-panel television faced them, glassy-eyed, blocking the doorway. A black video recorder sat on a shelf below it, trailing cables. A white-gloved footman handed the remote to the duke on a silver plate. He bowed himself out as Angbard picked it up and pointed it at the set.

It was all Miriam could do to keep her jaw from dropping

when a familiar signature tune came welling out of concealed speakers around the dining chamber. A helicopter descended onto a rooftop pad outside a penthouse suite: The famous Stetson-wearing villain stepped out into a sea of family intrigue. Miriam gulped down her wine without choking and reached for the inevitable—invisible—refill, barely tasting it. Her nose was going numb, a warning sign that she normally ignored at her peril, but this was just *too* bizarre to take while remaining sober. *Dallas!* she thought, making it a curse. As a choice of after-dinner videos, it was perfect. She'd been wrong about the ordeal being nearly over: The meal was only the beginning.

Roland tried to say something as they left Angbard's rooms. "Hush," she said, leaning on his arm as they descended the grand staircase. Her back ached and she was wobbling on her heels. "Just get me back to my room."

"I think we need to talk," he said urgently.

"Later." She winced as they reached the corridor. *Take lots of little steps,* she thought. The ache in her back was worst in the region of her kidneys. She felt drunk. "Tomorrow."

He held the door open for her. "Please—"

She looked into his eyes. They were wide and appealing: He was a transparently gallant, well-meaning young man— *Young? He's only a couple of years younger than I am*—with a great ass, and she instinctively distrusted that. "Tomorrow," she said firmly, then winced. "I'm tired. Maybe after breakfast?"

"By all means." He stepped back and Miriam turned to close the door, only to find the head maidservant, Meg, standing ahead of her.

"Ah. Meg." Miriam smiled experimentally. Glanced at the bathroom. "I've had a long day and I'm going to bed shortly. Would you mind leaving?"

"But how is you to undress?" Meg asked, confused. "What if you want something in the night?"

"What's the usual arrangement?" Miriam asked.

"Why, we sleep inside the door here, against your needs."
She dipped her head.

"Oh my." Miriam sighed, and would have slumped but for
her dress, which seemed to be holding her upright. "Oh god."
She took a stride toward the bathroom, then caught herself on
the door frame with one arm. "Well. You can start by undress-
ing me." It took the combined efforts of two maids ten minutes
to strip Miriam down to her underwear. Eventually something
gave way and her ribs could move again. "Oh. Oh!" Miriam
took a breath, then gulped. "'Scuse me." She fled dizzily into
the bathroom, skidding on the tiled floor, and locked the door.
"Shit, shit . . ." she planted herself firmly on the toilet.

After a moment, she breathed a sigh of relief. Her gaze
fell on the dictaphone and she picked it up. "Memo to self,"
she muttered. "At a formal banquet the pain in the small of
your back might be the chair, but on the other hand it might
be your kidneys backing up." Four, no five, glasses of wine.
She shook her head, still wobbly, and took another deep
breath. "And the breathing trouble. Fuck 'em, next time—if
they want formal, they can put up with whatever I can buy
off the rack in Boston. I'm not turning myself into an ortho-
pedic basket case in the name of local fashion."

Miriam took another deep breath. "Right. More notes.
Margit of Praha, middle-aged, looks to be a chaperone for
Olga Thorold, who seems to be senior to her. Olga is a ditz.
Thinks a Swiss finishing school is higher education. Main
ambition is to make a good marriage. I think Angbard may
have been showing her to me as a role model, fuck knows
why—maybe that's what high-born women do around here.
I think Vincenze is just horribly shy. May be some sort of
all-male schooling for menfolk here. Their English is better
than the women's. I wonder if that means they get out more."

She hit the "pause" button, then finished with the toilet.
Standing up, she stripped off, then luxuriated in the sensation of having nothing at all in contact with her skin.

A thought struck her. "I'm going to have a bath," she
called through the door. "Don't wait up for me. I don't need
any help."

It was Miriam's third bath of the day, but it didn't strike her as excessive. Her skin itched. She poured expensive bath salts and perfumed oil into the water without remorse, then slid down into the sea of foam. "Memo: The bath obviously came over from the other side. That means they must have some way of moving heavy items. I need to find out how. If some asshole cousin is going to try killing me because of my name, I'd like to know whether they're likely to use a pistol or a B-52." A thought struck her. "It looks like they're stuck in a development trap, like the Gulf Emirates. The upper class is fabulously rich and can import luxury items to their heart's content, and send their kids for education overseas, but they can't import enough, uh—*stuff*—to develop their population base. Start an industrial revolution. Whatever." She leaned back, feeling her spine unkink. "I wish I knew more about developing world economics. Because if that's what this all boils down to, I'll have to change things."

She put the recorder down and soaped herself all over, trying to scrub away the sweat and stress.

"Personal File: Roland. He's too damn smooth." She paused, biting her upper lip. "Reminds me of the college jocks, same kind of clean-cut hunky outdoors thing, except he's painfully polite and doesn't smell of beer or cigarettes. And he's trying to hide something. Second cousin, which means, um. I have *no* idea what that means in the context of this extended Clan-family structure thing, except he treats me like I'm made of eggshells and soap bubbles. Great class, behaves like a real gentleman, then again, he's probably a gold-plated bastard under the smooth exterior. That, or Uncle Angbard is trying to throw us together for some reason. And *he* is a tough cookie. Right out of *The Godfather*. Trust him as far as you can throw him."

She leaned back farther. "Next Memo: sexual politics. These people are basically medievals in suits. Olga is the giveaway, but the rest of it is pretty hard to miss. Better not talk about Ben or the divorce, or the kid, they might get weird. Maybe I can qualify as an aged spinster aunt who's too important to mess with, and they'll leave me alone. But if they expect me to lie back and act like a, a countess, someone's going to be in trouble." *And it could be me*, she admitted. Stuck in a strange land with weird and stifling customs, under guard the whole time—

"Memo: The locket is not unique. Duke Angbard owns its twin. He gave it to me to keep and talked about a doppelgängered house. And the family trait. Which means they know all about it—and about how it works and how you use them. Hmm. Find out what they know before you start messing."

There was a lot to think about. "Most kids sometimes play make-believe, that they're actually the long-lost prince or princess of a magical kingdom. Not fucking Ruritania with poison-tasters, armed guards, and *Dallas* reruns as the height of sophisticated after-dinner entertainment." She hummed tunelessly. "I wonder where they get the money to pay for the toys?" Something Paulette had said was trying to surface, but she couldn't quite remember what.

The bathtub drained and Miriam caught herself yawning as she toweled herself dry. "Maybe it'll all go away in the morning," she told herself.

ECONOMICS LESSON

Miriam jolted awake with her eyes open and a strong sense of panic. Incoherent but unpleasant dreams dogged her: goggled soldiers looming over her bed, limbs moving through molasses, *too slow, too slow . . .*

The bed was too big, much too big. She groped for the side of it, floundering across cold white sheets like an arctic explorer.

"Aagh." She reached open air, found herself looking down at the floor from an unaccustomed height. Her arm hurt, her mouth tasted horrible—something had obviously died in it the night before, and she ached everywhere but especially in a tight band across her forehead. "Mornings!" The air was distinctly cold. Shivering, she threw the comforter off and sat up, then jumped.

"What are you doing in here!" she squeaked, grabbing the covers.

"Excuse, ma'am—we required to attend?" The maid's accent was thick and hard to make out: English clearly wasn't her first language, and she looked shocked, though whether it was at Miriam's nakedness or her reaction to her presence wasn't clear.

"Well." Miriam held her breath for a moment, trying to get her heart under control. "You can just wait outside the door. I'll be up in a minute."

"But how is you to be dress?" asked the woman, a rising note of unhappiness in her voice.

"I'll take care of that myself." Miriam sat up again, this time holding the bedding around her. "Out. I mean, right out of my chambers, all of you, completely out! You can come back in half an hour. And shut the door."

She stood up as the door clicked shut, her heart still pounding. "How the hell do they manage?" she wondered aloud. "Jesus. *Royalty!*" It came out as a curse. It had never occurred to her to sympathize with the Queen of England before, but the idea of being surrounded by flunkies monitoring her every breath gave her a a sinking feeling in her stomach.

I've got to get away from this for a while, she realized. *Even if I can't avoid them in the long term, they'll drive me mad if I don't get some privacy.* Domestic servants were something that had passed out of the American middle-class lifestyle generations ago. Just the idea of having to deal with them made Miriam feel as if she was about to break out in hives.

Right. I've got to get away for a bit. How? Where? Miriam glanced at the bedside table and saw temporary escape sitting there, next to her dictaphone. *Ah.* A plan! She approached the huge chest of drawers and rummaged through it, hunting clothes. Ten minutes later she was dressed in urban casual—jeans, sneakers, sweater, leather jacket. Someone had helpfully installed some of her bags in the bottom of a cavernous wardrobe, and her small reporter's briefcase was among them, preloaded with a yellow pad, pens, and some spare tapes and batteries.

She poked her nose around the bedroom door cautiously. No, there was nobody lurking in ambush. *It worked!* She told herself. A quick dash to the bathroom and she was ready to activate her plan. Ready, apart from a hollow feeling in the pit of her stomach, anyway. "Damn. I'll need money." She ransacked the reception room in haste, hunting for her personal effects, and found them in a closed bureau of exquisite workmanship—her wallet, driving license, credit cards, and house keys. Either the servants didn't dare tamper with the private possessions of a relative of the duke—or they didn't know what they were. She found some other items in the bureau that shook her—her snub-nosed pistol and a box of ammunition that she didn't remember buying. "What *is* this?" she asked herself before putting the gun in her jacket pocket. She kept her hand around it. If what she was planning didn't work . . . well, she'd jump that hurdle when she reached it.

They're treating me as family, she realized. *Adult, mature, sensible family, not like Olga the ditz. Servants and assassins crawling out of the woodwork, it's a whole different world. Oh my.*

Carefully not thinking too hard about the likely consequences of her actions, Miriam walked to the center of the reception room between sofa and fireplace, snapped open her locket with her left hand, and focused on the design inside.

"Owww!" She stumbled slightly and cradled her forehead. Vision blurred, and everything throbbed. "Shit!" She blinked furiously through the pounding of her abruptly upgraded headache. The room was still there: bureau, chairs, fireplace—

"I wondered how long you'd take," Roland said from behind her.

She whirled, bringing her gun to bear, then stopped. "Jesus, don't *do* that!"

Roland watched her from the sofa, one hand holding a pocket watch, the other stretched out along the cushioned back. He was wearing a sports jacket and chinos with an open-necked shirt, like a stockbroker on casual Friday.

The sofa was identical to the unoccupied one in the suite she'd just left—or so close as to be its twin. But Roland wasn't the only different feature of the room. The quality of light coming in through the window was subtly altered, and some items had appeared on the side table, and the bedroom door was shut. "This isn't the same apartment," she said slowly, past the fog of headache. "It's a doppelgänger, right? And we're on the other side. *My* side."

Roland nodded. "Are you going to shoot me or not?" he asked. "Because if you aren't, you ought to put that away."

"Oops. Sorry." She lowered the pistol carefully and pointed it at the floor. "You startled me."

Roland relaxed visibly. "I think it's safe to say that *you* startled *me*, too. Do you always carry a gun when you explore your house?"

"I hope you'll excuse me," she said carefully, "but after waking up in bed with a stranger leaning over me for the second time in as many days, I tend to overreact a little. And I wasn't sure how the duke would respond to me going walkabout."

"Really?" He raised an eyebrow.

"No shit." She glanced around. The bathroom door was closed—she needed some Tylenol or some other painkiller bad. "Do you keep hot and cold running servants on this side, too?"

"Not many; there's a cook and some occasional cleaning staff, but mostly this is reserved for Covert Operations, and we pay much more attention to secrecy. Over here it's a . . . a safe house, I guess you'd call it, not a palace. I take it you haven't eaten—can I invite you to join me downstairs for breakfast?"

"As long as I don't have to dress for it," she said, checking then pocketing her gun. She picked up her briefcase. "I dug the lecture about not being able to hide, I don't want you to misunderstand me. But there are some things I really need to do around town today. Assuming I'm not under house arrest?"

Roland shrugged. "I don't see why not," he said. "I can answer for your security, in any case. Will you be able to do your stuff if I come along?"

Miriam looked out of the window and took a deep breath. "Well." She looked at him again. "I guess so." *Damn, there goes my chance to warn Paulie.* "Is it really that risky?"

"Breakfast first." He was already heading for the door. He added, over his shoulder, "By now news of your arrival will have leaked out and junior members of at least two of the other families will be desperate, absolutely desperate. But they don't know what you look like so you probably don't need a permanent bodyguard yet. And once your position is secure, they won't be able to touch you."

" 'Breakfast,' " she said, " 'first.' "

There was a kitchen on the ground floor, but there was nothing medieval about it. With its stainless-steel surfaces, huge chest freezer, microwave ovens, and gas range, it could have been the back of a restaurant. The dining room attached to it didn't look anything like Angbard's private apartment, either. It reminded Miriam more of a staff room at an upmarket consultant's office. A couple of guys in dark suits nodded at Roland from a table, but they were finishing up cups of coffee and they cleared out as soon as he offered her a seat. "Tell me, what did you think of, uh, Olga?"

While she tried to puzzle out what he meant by that question, a waitress appeared, notepad poised. "What's on the menu this morning?" Miriam asked.

"Oh, anything you'd like." She smiled breezily. "Coffee, we have a whole range of different types at present. Eggs, bacon, sausages, granola, breakfast cereal, juice—whatever."

"Double espresso for me," said Roland. "Rye sourdough toast, extra-mature thick-peel marmalade, unsalted butter. Two fried eggs, sunny-side up."

"Hmm. A large cappuccino for me, I think," said Miriam. "Can you manage a Spanish omelette?"

"Sure!" Miss Breezy grinned at her. "With you in five minutes."

Miriam blinked at her receding back. "Now *that* is what I call service."

"We take it seriously around here," Roland said drily. "That's why we go through a Human Resources department."

"You run this household like a company." Miriam frowned. "In fact, this is a family business, isn't it? That's what you're in." She paused. "Interuniversal import/export. Right?"

"Right." He nodded.

"And you've been doing it for hundreds of years."

"Right you are," he said encouragingly. "You're figuring it out for yourself."

"It's not that hard." The distinctive noise of a coffee percolator made her raise her head. "How do *you* think last night went?"

"I think—" he watched her examining him. "Do you know you've got a very disquieting stare?"

"Yes." She grinned at him. "I practice in the mirror before I go in to an interview. Sometimes it makes my victims give away more than they intended to. And sometimes it just gives them bad dreams afterward."

"Eeh. I can see you'd be a bad enemy, Miss Beckstein."

"Miz, to you." She paused.

The waitress was back, bearing a tray laden with coffee, milk, and a sugar bowl. "Call if you need anything more," she reassured them, then disappeared again.

Roland's eyes narrowed at he looked at her. "You remind me of when I was at college," he said.

"You were at college?" she asked. "Over here, I mean?"

"Oh, yes." He picked up his espresso and spooned a small quantity of brown sugar crystals into it.

"The girls don't seem to get that treatment," she pointed out sharply.

"Oh, but some of them do," he replied, blowing on his coffee. "At least, these days, this generation. Olga is a throwback—or, rather, her father is. I'm not sure quite what the duke was trying to prove, inviting you to dine with us, but he said something about culture shock earlier. He's a perceptive old coot, gets hold of some very unexpected ideas and refuses to let them go. I'm half-wondering if he was testing you. Seeing if you'd break cover under stress or how you'd hold up in public by using an audience he could silence if the need arose."

"A-ha." She took a first sip of her coffee. "So what did you study?"

"As an undergrad, economics and history. Before Harvard, my parents sent me to Dartmouth," he said quietly. "I think I went a bit crazy in my first couple of years there. It's very different over here. Most of the older generation don't trust the way everything has changed since 1910 or so. Before then, they could kid themselves that the other side, this America, was just different, not better. Like the way things were when our first ancestor accidentally stumbled upon a way to visit a town in New England in 1720 or so. But now they're afraid that if we grew up here or spent too much time we'd never want to come home."

"Sort of like defecting diplomats and athletes from the old Communist Bloc," Miriam prodded.

"Approximately." He nodded. "The Clan's strength is based on manpower. When we go back, you and me, we'll have to carry some bags. Every time we cross over, we carry stuff to and fro. It's the law, and you need a good reason to flout it. There's a post room: You're welcome to come and go at will as long as you visit it each time to carry post bags back and forth."

"A post room," she said.

"Yes, it's in the basement. I'll show you it after—ah, food."

For a few minutes they were both too busy to talk. Miriam had to admit that the omelette she'd ordered was exceptionally good. As she was draining her coffee, Roland took up the conversation again. "I'm over here to run some business errands for the Boss today. I hope you don't mind if I take a few minutes out while you're doing whatever it is you were planning to do?"

"No, I mean, be my guest—" Miriam was nonplussed. "I'm not sure," she added slowly. "There are a few things I needed to do, starting with, well, just seeing that I'm allowed out and about, know what I mean?"

"Did you have any concrete plans?" Roland looked interested.

"Well," she leaned back and thought. "I have—had, before all this landed on me—a commission to write a feature for a magazine. Nothing hard, but I'll need my iMac to write it on. And I *must* write it, if I don't want to vanish off the face of the earth, careerwise." She tried a smile. "Got to keep my options open. I'm a working girl."

Roland nodded. "Okay. And after that?"

"Well. I was thinking about going home. Check my answering machine, make sure everything's okay, reassure the neighbors that I'm all right, that kind of thing." *Make sure they haven't found Paulie's CD-ROM. Try to get a message to her to keep her head down.* "I don't have to stay for long," she added hastily. "I'm not thinking about running away, if that's what you're worried about."

Roland frowned thoughtfully. "Listen, is it just your mail and phone that you need? Because if so, it would be a lot safer just to divert everything. We've got a telephone switch in the subbasement and we can slam your domestic subscriber lines right over. But it would be a good thing if you avoided your home for the next few days. I can send someone around if there's anything you need, but—" he shrugged.

"Why?" she asked.

"Because." He put his butter knife down. "We, uh, when there's a succession crisis or a war within the Clan, things can get very messy, very fast." He paused for a moment, then rushed on: "I wouldn't want to risk anyone getting a clean shot at you."

Miriam sat very still, blood pounding in her ears. "Does that mean what I think it means?" she asked.

"Yes—your house is a target. We have it under surveillance, but accidents can happen, someone can miss something, and you might be walking into a booby trap. Tripwires inside the front door. It won't be secure until we've doppelgängered it, which might take some time because it's way out in the sticks on this side, and we'd need to fortify the area to stop anyone crossing over inside your living room. It took days for us to find you, even with the office chair in the forest as a marker. But you might not be so lucky next time."

"Oh." Miriam nodded to herself, absorbing this new and unwelcome fact. *So you found me by the chair?* "What about my mother?"

Roland looked puzzled. "But your mother's—"

"No, I mean my *adoptive* mother." Miriam gritted her teeth. "You know, the woman who raised me from a baby as her own? Who is now all alone and wheelchair-bound? Is she at risk? Because if so—" she realized that her voice was rising.

"I'll see to it at once," Roland said decisively and pulled out his mobile phone. It obviously hadn't occurred to him that Iris was of any importance.

"Do so," Miriam said tersely. "Or I'll never speak to you again."

"That's uncalled for." Roland looked serious. "Is there anyone else I should know about?" he asked after a moment.

Miriam took a deep breath. *Here goes,* she thought. "My ex-husband is remarried and has a wife and child," she said. "Is he at risk?"

Roland mulled it over for a minute. "He's a commoner," he said finally. "There were no children and you're divorced. So I guess he's out of the frame."

No children. Miriam shook her head. "You'll have to tell me about your inheritance laws," she said carefully. *Oh, what complications!* Someone out there in America was a twelve-year-old girl—Miriam didn't know where, she only knew general details about her adoptive family—who might have inherited Miriam's current problem. *She's too young*, Miriam thought instinctively. *And she has no locket*. But the adoption records were sealed and nobody but Ben and Iris knew about the pregnancy. If the family hadn't found her, then—

"Oh, they're simple enough," said Roland, a slightly bitter note in his voice. "The, um, family talent? It only breeds true among the pure-blooded line. They found that out pretty early. It's what the biologists call a recessive trait. On the other side, um, marriage customs are different—cousin marriages are allowed, for one thing—and for another, children who don't have the talent aren't part of the Clan. But they're kept in the families. They form the outer, nonshareholding part of the Clan, but if two of them marry some of their children may inherit the talent."

Good news mixed with bad news. On the one hand, her daughter—who she hadn't seen since two days after her birth—was safe from the attentions of the family, safe to lead a normal life unless Miriam drew attention to her. As long as the family dug no deeper than they had so far. On the other hand— "You're telling me that my parents were *cousins*?"

"Second cousins once removed, I think," Roland replied. "Yes. By family law and custom marrying out is forbidden. You might want to bear that in mind, by the way, it's the one big taboo." He glanced aside nervously. "But you're probably safe because you did it over here and divorced him before anyone knew." He was staring at the wall, she realized, staring at something that wasn't there in an attempt to avoid her gaze. *Unpleasant memories?* "Otherwise there would be repercussions. Bad ones."

"You're telling me." She noticed her fingers turning white around the rim of her coffee cup. "So presumably Uncle Angbard will make life hard for me if I try to take off and he wants me to marry someone who's a not-too-close family member."

"That's an understatement." Roland's cheek twitched. "It's not as if the council would give him any other options," he muttered.

"What else?" Miriam asked as the silence grew uncomfortable.

"Well!" Roland shook himself and sat up. He began ticking off points on his fingers, his movements precise and economical and tense. "We are expected to abide by the rules. First, when you come over here, you stop by the post room in each direction and carry whatever's waiting there. You get a free pass this time, but not in the future. Second, you check with Security before you go anywhere. They'll probably want you to carry a mobile phone or a pager, or a bodyguard if the security condition is anything but blue—blue for cold. Oh, and third—" he reached into an inner pocket— "the duke anticipated that you might want to go shopping, so he asked me to give you this." He passed her an envelope, the hint of a smile tugging at his lips.

"Hmm." Miriam opened it. There was an unsigned silvery-colored Visa card inside with her name on it. "Hey, what's this?"

"Sign it." He offered her a pen, looking pleased with himself, then watched while she scribbled on the back. "Your estate is in escrow for now, but you should consider this an advance against your assets, which are reasonably large." His grin widened. "There may be problems with the family, but spending money isn't one of them."

"Oh." She slid it into her purse. "Any other messages from the duke?"

"Yes." Roland managed a straight face. "He said, 'Tell her she's got a two-million-dollar credit limit and to try not to spend it all at once.'"

Miriam swore in a distinctly unladylike manner.

He laughed briefly. "It's *your* money, Miriam—Countess Helge. The import/export trade your ancestors pioneered is lucrative, and you can certainly earn your keep through it. Now how about we visit the post room so I can do my business, and then maybe you can do whatever it is that you need to do?"

The post room was a concrete-lined subbasement, with pigeonholes sized to accommodate the big wheeled aluminum suitcases that the family used for "mail." Roland picked a clipboard from the wall and read through it. "Hmm. Just two cases to FedEx today and that's it."

"Suitcases." She looked at them dubiously, imagining all sorts of illegal contraband.

"Yes. Help me. Take that one. Yes, the handle locks into place as the wheels come out."

Struggling slightly, Miriam tugged the big suitcase out of the post room and into the stark cargo elevator next to it. Roland hit the button for the basement, and they lurched upward.

"What's in these things?" she asked after a moment. "Tell me if it's none of my business." *I'm not sure I want to know,* she thought, unable to avoid a flashback to the meeting in Joe's office, the threats on her phone.

"Oh, it's perfectly legal," Roland assured her. "This is all stuff that is cheap enough in Gruinmarkt and Soffmarkt or the other kingdoms of the coast and wants shipping to the Outer Kingdom—that would be California and Oregon—on this side. On the other side, there are no railroads or airports and cargo has to go by mule train across the Great Plains and the Rocky Mountains. Which are full of nomad tribes, so it takes months and is pretty risky. We bring our goods across to this side, heavily padded, and ship them by FedEx. The most valuable items in here are the sealed letters sent by the family post—we charge several times their weight in gold in return for a postal service that crosses the continent in a week. We also move intelligence. Our western Clan members—the Wu family, formerly known as Arnesen, and braided with the eastern families—exchange information with us. By coordinating our efforts, we can protect our traditional shipping on the other side from large bandit tribes like the Apache. It also helps us exert political leverage beyond our numbers. For example, if the Emperor Outside dies and there is a succession struggle, we can loan the Wu family funds with which to ensure a favorable outcome and do so long before news would otherwise reach us across the continental divide."

Miriam's eyes were nearly bulging as she tried to make sense of this. "You mean there's no *telegraph*?" she asked.

"We *are* the telegraph," he told her. "As for the rest of what's in these suitcases, it's mostly stuff that only comes from the east and is expensive in the west. Like, for example, diamonds from India. They're expensive enough in the Gruin-

markt and almost impossible to get in the Outer Kingdom—
it's much cheaper to ship them across the Boreal Ocean by
barque than the western ocean by junk, especially since the
Mongols refuse to trade with the east. Or penicillin. The ability to guarantee that a prince's wife will not die of childbed
fever is worth more than any amount of precious stones."

"And going the other way . . ."

"More messages. More diplomatic intelligence. Spices
and garnets and rubies and gold from the Outer Kingdom's
mines."

Miriam nodded. The elevator doors opened onto the underground garage, and she followed him out into the concrete maze.

Several vehicles were parked there, including a long black
Mercedes limousine—and her own slightly battered Saturn.
Roland headed for the Merc. "Once we've fitted your car
with some extras, you can use it—if you want," he said. "But
you can use any of the other cars here, too."

Miriam shook her head, taking in a sleek Jaguar coupe
parked behind a concrete column. "I'm not sure about that,"
she murmured. *What would it do for my independence?* she
wondered, watching as Roland opened the Mercedes's trunk
and lifted the suitcases into it. The two-million-dollar card
in her purse was much more intoxicating than the wine last
night, but didn't feel as real. *I'll have to try it,* she realized.
But what if I get addicted?

The Mercedes was huge, black, and carried almost a ton of
armor built into its smoothly gleaming bodywork. Miriam
only realized this when she tried to open the passenger side
door—it was heavy, and as it swung open she saw that the
window was almost two inches thick and had a faint greenish tint. She sat down, pulled her seatbelt on, and tugged the
door shut. It thudded into position as solidly as a bank
vault.

"You're serious about being attacked," she said soberly.

"I don't want to alarm you," said Roland, "but the contents of those two suitcases are worth the equivalent of twenty million dollars each on the other side. And there are several hundred active family members that we know of—and possibly ones we don't in hidden cells established by their family elders to gain a competitive edge over their rivals in the Clan. You're unusual in that you're a hidden one who was never intended to be hidden. The families *in camera* could raid us, and unless we took precautions we'd be sitting ducks. A young man like Vincenze—" he shrugged—"maybe a bit more mature. Waiting on a street corner. Can set off a bomb or walk up behind someone and shoot him, then just vanish into thin air. Unless there's a doppelgänger on the other side or maybe a hill where over here there's a cleared area, there's no way of stopping that."

"Twenty million."

"At a very approximate exchange rate," Roland offered, starting the engine. Bright daylight appeared from an electrically operated door at the top of the exit ramp. He put the Mercedes in gear and gently slid forward. "We're fairly safe, though. This car has been customized by the same people that made Eduard Shevardnadze's car. The President of the Republic of Georgia."

"Should that mean something?" asked Miriam.

"Two RPG-7s, an antitank mine, and eighty rounds from a heavy machine gun. The passengers survived."

"I hope we're not going to encounter that sort of treatment," she said with feeling, reaching sideways to squeeze his fingers.

"We aren't." He squeezed back briefly, then accelerated up the ramp. "But there's no harm in taking precautions."

They came up out of the ground near Belmont, and Roland chauffeured them smoothly onto the Cambridge turnpike and then I-95 and the tunnel. They exited the highway near Logan International, and Roland drove toward the freight terminal. Miriam relaxed against the black leather and propped her feet up against the wooden dashboard. It smelled like a very expensive private club, redolent of the stink of money. She'd been in rooms with billionaires before and any number of sharkish venture capitalists, but somehow this was different. Most of the billionaires she knew were manipulative jerks or workaholics, obsessive and insecure about something or other. Roland, in contrast, was "old money"—old and unselfconscious, mature as a vintage wine. So old that he'd never known what it was like to be poor—or even upper-middle class. For a moment, she felt a flash of green-eyed envy—then remembered the two-million-dollar ballast in her purse.

"Roland, how rich am I?" she asked nervously.

"Oh, very," he said casually. He swung the Mercedes into the entrance to a parking lot, where an automatic barrier lifted—also automatically—and then brought them to a halt in front of an anonymous-looking office with a FEDEx sign above it. "I don't know for sure," he added, "but I think your share may run to almost one percent of the Clan's net worth. Certainly many millions."

"Oh, how marvelous," she said sarcastically. Then more thoughtfully, "I could pay all Iris's medical bills out of the petty cash. Couldn't I?"

"Yes. Help me with the suitcases?"

"If you help me sort out Iris's medical bills. Seriously."

" 'Seriously'? Yes, I'll do that." She stood up and stretched, then waited while Roland lifted the heavy cases out of the trunk. She took one and followed him as he rolled the other up to the door, swiped a magnetic card, and entered under the watchful eye of a security camera.

They came to a small office where a middle-aged man in a white shirt and black tie was waiting. "Today's consignment," said Roland. "I'd like to introduce you to Miriam. She might be making runs on her own in future—if things work out. Miriam, this is Jack. He handles dispatch and customs at this end."

"Thank you, sir," said Jack, handing Roland a board with a three-part form ready to sign. "This is just a formality to confirm I've received everything," he added for her benefit. Balding, overweight, and red-faced, Jack was about as homely as anyone she'd seen since she'd been pitched headfirst into this nightmare of aristocracy. Miriam smiled at him.

"There, that's it, then," he said, taking the papers back from Roland. "Have a nice day, now!"

"My best to your wife," Roland replied. "Come on, Miriam. Time to go."

"Okay." She followed him back to the car. He started the engine and eased them back out into the local traffic around the light industrial area. "Where next?"

"Oh, we pick up the cases for the return leg, then we're at liberty," he said. "I thought you wanted to do some shopping? And some other things to see to? How about a couple of hours at Copley Place and messing around Back Bay, then lunch?"

"Sounds good," she agreed.

"Okay." He pulled over, into another parking lot. "Give me a hand again?"

"Sure."

They got out and Miriam followed him into yet another office. The procedure was the same in reverse: Roland signed a couple of forms and this time collected two identical, ribbed aluminium suitcases, each so heavy that Miriam could barely carry hers. "Right, now into town," he said after he lifted them both into the car's trunk. "It's almost ten o'-clock. Think you've got time to hit the shops and be back by five?"

"I'm sure I have." She smiled at him. "There's some stuff I could do with your help for, actually. Want to hang around?"

"Delighted to oblige."

The Copley Place shops weren't exactly ideal, but it was totally covered and had enough stuff in it to keep Miriam occupied for a couple of hours. The platinum card didn't catch fire—it didn't even show signs of overheating when she hit Niemann Marcus and some less obvious shops for a couple of evening outfits and an expensive piece of rolling luggage.

After the first half hour, Roland did what many polite heterosexual men did: zoned out and smiled or nodded whenever she asked him for an opinion. Which was was exactly what Miriam was hoping for, because her real goal wasn't to fill her wardrobe with evening dresses and expensive lingerie (although that was an acceptable side effect) but to pull out a bundle of cash and use some of it to buy certain accessories. Such as a prepaid mobile phone and a very small Sony laptop with a bundle of software ("If I can't go back home, I'll need something to write my articles on," she pointed out to Roland, hoping he wouldn't figure out how big a loss-leader that would make it). She finished her spree in a sports shop, buying some outdoors tools, a pocket GPS compass, and a really neat folding solar panel, guaranteed to charge her laptop up—which she picked up while he was poking around a display of expensive hunting tackle.

She wasn't totally sure what she was going to do with this stuff, but she had some ideas. In particular, the CD-ROMs full of detailed maps of the continental United States and the other bits of software she'd slipped in under his nose ought to come in handy. Even if they didn't, she figured that if Angbard expected her to shop like a dizzy teenager, then she ought to get him used to her shopping like a dizzy teenager. *That way he'll have one less handle on me when I stop*, she thought, a trifle smugly.

Twelve thousand dollars went really fast when she was buying Sony notebooks, and even faster when she switched to Hermes and Escada and less well-known couture. But it felt unreal, like play money. Some of the clothes would have to be altered to fit, and delivered: She took them anyway. "I figure it can be altered on the other side," she murmured to Roland by way of explanation. He nodded enthusiastically and she managed to park him for a few minutes in a bookshop next door to her real target, a secondhand theatrical clothing shop for an old-fashioned long skirt and shirtwaist that could pass for one of the servants. *Theatrical supplier, my ass*, she thought. *The escape committee is in!*

Around two o'clock she took mercy on Roland, who by this time was flagging, checking his watch every ten minutes and following her around like a slightly dejected dog. "It's okay," she said, "I'm about done. How about we catch that lunch you were talking about, then head back to the house? I've got to get some of these clothes altered, which means looking up Ma'am Rosein, and then I need to spend a couple of hours on the computer."

"That's great," Roland said with unconcealed sincerity. "How about some clam chowder for lunch?"

Miriam really didn't go for seafood, but if it kept him happy that was fine by her. "Okay," she said, towing along her designer escape kit. "Let's go eat!"

They ate. Over lunch she watched Roland carefully. *He's about twenty-eight*, she thought. *Dartmouth. Harvard. Real Ivy League territory and then some. Classic profile.* She sized him up carefully. *Shaves well. Looks great. No visible bad habits, painfully good manners. If there wasn't clearly something going on, I'd be drooling. Wouldn't I?* She thought. *In fact, maybe there's something in that? Maybe that's why Angbard is shoving us together. Or not. I need to find out more about the skeletons in the Clan closet and the strange fruit rotting on the family tree.* And there were worse ways of doing that than chatting with Roland over lunch.

"Why is your uncle putting you on my case?" she finally asked over dessert, an exquisite crème brûlée. "I mean, what's *your* background? You said he was thinking one step ahead. Why you?"

"Hrrm." Roland stirred sugar into his coffee, then looked at her with frank blue eyes. "I think your guess is as good as mine."

"You're unmarried." She kicked herself immediately afterward. *Very perceptive, Ms. Holmes.*

"As if that matters." He smiled humorlessly. "I have an attitude problem."

"Oh?" She leaned forward.

"Let's just say, Angbard wants me where he can keep an eye on me. They sent me to college when I was eighteen," he said morosely. "It was—well, it was an eye-opener. I stayed for four years, then applied to Harvard immediately. Economics and history. I thought I might be able to change things back home. Then I decided I didn't want to go back. After my first year or so, I'd figured out that I couldn't stay over here just on the basis of my name—I'd have to work. So I did. I wasn't much of one for the girls during that first degree—" he caught her speculative look— "or the boys."

"So?" *Personal Memo: Find out what they think of sex, as opposed to marriage. The two are not always interchangeable.* "What next?"

"Well." He shrugged uncomfortably. "I wanted to stay over here. I got into a postgrad research, program, studying the history of economic development in the Netherlands. Met a girl named Janice along the way. One thing led to another."

"You wanted to marry her?" asked Miriam.

"Sky father, no!" He looked shocked. "The Clan council would never have stood for it! Even if it was just over here. But I could buy us both a house over here, make believe that—" He stopped, took a sip of coffee, then put his cup down again. All through the process, he avoided Miriam's gaze.

"You didn't want to go back," she stated.

"You can cross over twice in a day, in an hour, if you take beta-blockers," he said quietly. "Speaking of which." He extracted a blisterpack of pills from his inner pocket and passed it across to her. "They do something about the headaches. You can discharge your duty to Clan and family that way, keep the post moving, and live nine-tenths of your life free of . . . of . . . of . . ."

Miriam waited for him to sort his tongue out.

"Jan and I had two years together," he finally said quietly. "Then they broke us up."

"The Clan." Her mouth was dry. She turned the pack of pills over and over, reading the label. "Did they—"

"Indirectly." He interrupted her deliberately, then finished his coffee cup. "Look, she kept asking *questions.* Questions that I couldn't answer. Wasn't allowed to answer. I'd have been required to go home and marry someone of high rank within the Clan sooner or later, just to continue the blood-line, but I'm a man. I'm allowed to spend some time settling down. But eventually . . . if we marry out we go extinct in two, maybe three generations. And the money goes down faster, because our power base is built on positive market ex-ternalities—have you—"

"Yes," she said, mouth dry despite the coffee she'd just swallowed without tasting. "The more of you there are, the more nodes you've got to trade between and the more effec-tively you can run your import/export system, right?"

"Right. We're in a population trap, and it takes special dis-pensation to marry out. Our position is especially tenuous because of the traditional nobility; a lot of them see us as vile upstarts, illegitimate and crude, because we can't trace our ancestry back to one of the hetmen of the Norge fleet that conquered the Gruinmarkt away from the Auslaand tribes about four, five hundred years ago. We find favor with the crown, because we're rich—but even there we are in a cleft stick: It does not do well to become so powerful that the crown itself is threatened. If you get the chance to marry into the royal family—of Gruinmarkt or of one of our neigh-bors—but that's the only way you could marry out without the council coming down on you."

"Huh. Other kingdoms? Where did they come from, any-way? It's, I'd have said medieval—"

"Nearly." Roland nodded. "I did some digging into it. You are aware that in your world the feudal order of western Eu-rope emerged from the wreckage of the Roman Empire, im-posed largely by Norse—Viking—settlers who had assimilated many of the local ways? I am not sure, but I be-lieve much the same origin explains our situation here. On this coast, there are several kingdoms up and down the seaboard. Successive waves of emigration from the old countries of the Holy Empire conquered earlier kingdoms up and down the coast, forced into a militarized hierarchy to defend themselves against the indigenous tribes. Vikings, but Vikings who had assimilated the Roman church—the worship of the divine company of gods—and such learning as the broken wreckage of Europe had to offer. We sent agents across the Atlantic to explore the Rome of this world thirty years or so ago: It lies unquiet beneath the spurs of the Great Khan, but the churches still make burned offerings before the gods. Maybe when there are more of us we will open up trade routes in Europe . . . but not yet."

"Um. Okay." Miriam nodded, reduced to silence by a sudden sense of cultural indigestion. *This is so alien!* "So what about you? The Clan, I mean. Where do you—we—fit into the picture?"

"The Clan families are mostly based in Gruinmarkt, which is roughly where Massachusetts and New York and Maine are over here. But we, the Clan families, were ennobled only in the past six generations or so—the old landholders won't ever let you forget it. The Clan council voted to make children of any royal union full members—that way, the third generation will be royalty, or at least nobility, *and* have the talent. But nobody's married into one of the royal families yet—either in the Gruinmarkt, or north or south for that matter.

"In the Outer Kingdom, to the west, things are different again—there are civil service exams. Again, we've got an edge there. We have schools over here and ways to cheat. But I was talking about the population trap, wasn't I? The council has a long arm. They won't let you go. And it'll take more than just one person on the inside, pushing, to make them change. I've tried. I got a whole huge reform program mapped out that'd break their dependency, begin developing the Gruinmarkt—but the council tore it up and threw it out without even reading it. Only Duke Angbard kept them from going further and declaring me a traitor."

"Let me get this straight," Miriam said, leaning forward. "You lived with Janice until she couldn't put up with you not telling her what you were doing for two hours a day, couldn't put up with not knowing about your background, and until your elders began leaning on you to get married. Right?"

"Wrong," he said. "I told Uncle Angbard where he could

shove his ultimatum." He hunched over, a picture of misery. "But she moved out, anyway. She'd managed to convince herself that I was some kind of gangster, drug smuggler, whatever, up to my ears in no good. I was trying, *trying,* to get permission to go over for good, to try to make it up to her, to make everything all right. But she was killed by a car. A hit-and-run accident, the police said."

He fell silent, story run down.

Well, she thought. Words failed her for a minute. "Were the two things connected? Causally, that is?"

"You mean, did the council have her killed?" he asked harshly. "I don't know. I've refused to investigate the possibility. Thousands of pedestrians are killed by hit-and-run drivers every year. She'd walked out on me, and we might never have got back together. And if I *did* discover that one of my relatives was responsible, I'd have to kill them, wouldn't I? You didn't live through the war. Trust me, you don't want to go there, to having assassins stepping out of thin air behind people and garotting them. Far better to let it lie."

"That doesn't sound like the same man speaking," she speculated.

"Oh, but it does." He smiled lopsidedly. "The half of me that is a cold-blooded import/export consultant, not the half of me that's a misguided romantic reformer who thinks the Gruinmarkt could industrialize and develop in less than half a century if the Clan threw its weight behind the project. I'm hoping the duke is listening . . ."

"Well, he has you where he can keep an eye on you." Miriam paused. "For your own good, to his way of thinking."

"Politics." Roland made it sound like a curse. "I don't *care* about who gets the credit as long as the job gets done!" He shook his head distractedly. "That's the problem. Too many vested interests, too many frightened little people who think any progress that breaks the pattern of Clan business activities is a personal attack on them. And that's before we even get started talking about the old aristocracy, the ones who aren't part of us."

"He's keeping you under his thumb until he can figure out a way to get a hold on you," Miriam suggested. "Some way of tying you down, maybe?"

"That's what I'm afraid of." He looked around, trying to catch the waiter's eye. "I figured you'd understand," he said.

"Yes, I guess I do," she said regretfully. "And if that's what he's got in mind for you, what about me?"

They drove back to the house in the suburbs in companionable silence. From the outside, the doppelgängered mansion looked like a sedate business unit, possibly a software company or an accounting firm. As they rolled onto the down ramp, Roland cued the door remote, and the barrier rolled up into the ceiling. For the first time Miriam realized how thick it was. "That's bombproof, isn't it?"

"Yup." He drove down the ramp without stopping and the shutters were already descending behind them. "We don't have the luxury of a beaten fire zone on this side."

"Oh." She felt a chill. "The threats. It's all real."

"What were you expecting, lies?" He slid them nose-first into a parking spot next to the Jaguar, killed the engine, then systematically looked around before opening the door.

"I don't know." She got out and stretched, looking around. "The garage door. That's what brought it home."

"The only home for the likes of us is a fortress," he said, not without bitterness. "Remember the Lindbergh baby? We've got it a hundred times worse. Never forget. Never relax. Never be normal."

"I don't—" she took a deep breath. "I don't think I can learn to live like that."

"Helge—Miriam—" he stopped and looked at her closely, concerned. "It's not as bad as it sounds."

She shook her head wordlessly.

"Really." He walked around the car to her. "Because you're not alone. You're not the only one going through this."

"It's—" She paused. "Claustrophobic." He was standing

close to her. She stepped close to him and he opened his arms and embraced her stiffly.

"I'll help, any way I can," he murmured. "Any way you want. Just ask, whatever you need." She could feel his back muscles tense.

She hugged him. Wordless thoughts bubbled and seethed in her mind, seeking expression. "Thank you," she whispered, "I needed that." Letting go.

Roland stepped back promptly and turned to the car's trunk as if nothing had happened. "It'll all work out; we'll make sure of it." He opened the car's trunk. "Meanwhile, can you help me with these? My, you've been busy."

"I assume we can get it all back?"

"Whatever you can carry," he said. "Even if it's just for a minute."

"Whatever," she said, bending to take the strain of another of the ubiquitous silvery aluminium wheeled suitcases and her own big case stuffed with shopping.

"Downstairs and across?" he asked.

"Hmm." She shrugged. "Does the duke expect us to dine with him tonight?"

"Not that I've heard."

Well, okay, she mused. "Then we don't need to go back immediately."

"Mm." He opened the lift gates. "I'm afraid we do; we've got to keep the post moving, you see. Two trips a day, five days on and five days off. It's the rules." He waved her into the lift and they stood together as it began to descend.

"Oh, well." She nodded. "I suppose . . ."

"Would you mind very much if I invited you to dine with me?" he asked in a sudden rush. "Not a formal affair, not at all. If you want someone else around, I'm sure Vincenze is at a loose end . . ."

She smiled at him uncertainly, surprised at her own reaction. She bit her lip, trying not to seem overeager. "I'd love to dine with you," she said. "But tonight I'm working. Tomorrow?"

"Okay. If you say so."

At the bottom of the shaft he led her into the post room.
"What's here?" she asked.

"Well." He pointed to a yellow square marked on the
floor, about three feet by three feet. "Stand there, facing that
wall."

"Okay. What now?" she asked.

"Pick up the two cases—yes, I know they're heavy, you
only need to hold them clear of the floor for a minute. Do
you think you can do that? And focus on that cupboard on
the wall. I'll look away and hit this button, and you do what
comes natural, then step out of the square—fast. I'll be
through in a couple of minutes; got an errand to run first."

"And—oh."

She saw the motorized screen roll up; behind it was a
backlit knotlike symbol that made her eyes swim. It was *just
like* the locket. In fact, it was the *same* as the locket, and she
felt as if she was falling into it. Then her head began to ache,
viciously, and she slumped under the weight of the suitcases.
Remembering Roland's instructions, she rolled them forward, noting that the post room looked superficially the
same but the screened cupboard on this side was closed and
there were some scrapes on the wall.

"Hmm." She glanced around. No Roland, as yet. *Well,
well, well*, she thought.

She glanced down at the case she'd carried over, blinked
thoughtfully, then walked over to the wall with the pigeonholes, where another case was waiting. One that hadn't been
prepared for her. She bent down and sprang the catch on it,
laid it flat on its side and lifted the lid. Her breath caught in
her throat. She wasn't sure what she'd been expecting. She'd
been hoping for gold, jewels, scrolls, or maybe antibiotics
and computers. This was what she'd been afraid of. She shut
the case and stood it upright again, then walked back to the
ones she'd brought over and concentrated on quieting her
racing heartbeat and smoothing her face into a welcoming,
slightly coy smile before Roland the brilliant reformer,
Roland the sympathetic friend, Roland the lying bastard
scumbag could bring his own suitcase through.

Who did you think you were kidding? she wondered bitterly. *You knew it was too good to be true.* And indeed it had been clear from the start that there had to be a catch somewhere.

The nature of the catch was obvious and ironic with twenty-twenty hindsight, and when she thought about it she realized that Roland hadn't actually lied to her. She just hadn't asked the right questions.

What supplied the family's vast wealth on her own, the other, the American side of the border? It sure wasn't a fast postal service, not when it took six weeks to cross an untamed wilderness on pack mules beset by savage tribes. No, it was a different type of service—one intended for commodities of high value, low weight, and likely to be interrupted in transit through urban America. Something that the family could ship reliably through their own kingdoms and move back and forth to American soil at their leisure. In America they made their money by shipping goods across the Gruinmarkt fast; in the Gruinmarkt they made their money by moving goods across America slowly but reliably. The suitcase contained almost twenty kilograms of sealed polythene bags, and it didn't take a genius with degrees in journalism and medicine to figure out that they'd be full of Bolivian nose candy.

She thought about the investigation she'd been running with Paulie, and she didn't know whether to laugh or cry. Instead she began whistling a song by Brecht—*Supply and Demand*—as she picked up her own suitcase and headed for the elevator to her suite.

My long-lost medievalist world-walking family are drug import/ export barons, she realized. *What the hell does that make* me?

IN THE FAMILY WAY

A lone in her apartment with the door locked, Miriam began to unpack her suitcase full of purchases. She'd arrived to find the maids in a state of near panic: "Mistress, the duke, he wants to see you tomorrow lunchtime!" In the end she'd dismissed them all except for Meg, the oldest, who she sat down with for a quiet talk.

"I'm not used to having you around all the time," she said bluntly. "I know you're not going to go away, but I want you to make yourselves scarce. Ask one of the electricians to put a bell in, so I can call you when I need you. I don't mind people coming in to tidy up when I'm out of my rooms, but I don't want to be surrounded all the time. Can you do that?" Meg had nodded, but looked puzzled. "Any questions?" Miriam asked.

"No, ma'am," Meg had replied. But her expression said that she thought Miriam's behavior was distinctly strange.

Miriam sighed and pointed at the door. *Maybe if I act like they're hotel staff . . .* "I'll want someone to come up in about three hours with some food—a tray of cold stuff will do—and a pot of tea. Apart from that, I don't expect to see anyone tonight and I don't want to be disturbed. Is that okay?"

"Yes'm." Meg ducked her head and fled. "Okay, so that works," Miriam said thoughtfully. Which was good because now she had some space to work in, unobserved.

Fifteen minutes later the luggage was stowed where Miriam wanted it. Her new laptop was sitting on the dresser, plugged in to charge next to a stack of unopened software boxes. Her new wardrobe was hung up, awaiting the attentions of a seamstress whenever Miriam had time for a fitting. And the escape kit, as she was already thinking of it, was stashed in the suitcase at the back of the wardrobe.

"Memo." She picked up her dictaphone and strolled through into the bathroom. It was the place she found it easiest to think. Cool white tiles, fine marble, nothing to aggravate the pounding headache she'd been plagued by for so much of the past week. Plus, it had a shower—which she turned on, just for the noise. "Need to look for a bug-sweeping kit next time I get time on the other side. Must try the beta-blockers too, once I've looked up their side effects. Wonder if they've got a trained doctor over here? Or a clinic of some kind? Anyway."

She swallowed. "New memo. Must get the dictation software installed on the laptop, so I can transcribe this diary. Um. Roland and the family business bear some thought." *That's the understatement of the century,* she told herself. "They're . . . oh hell. They're not the Medelin cartel, but they probably ship a good quantity of their produce. It's a family business, or rather a whole bunch of families who intermarry because of the hereditary factor, with the Clan as a business arrangement that organizes everything. I suppose they probably smuggled jewels or gold or something before the drugs thing. The whole nine yards about not marrying out—whether the ability is a recessive gene or not doesn't matter—they've got *omerta*, the law of silence, as a side effect of their social setup. In this world, they're upwardly mobile nobles, merchant-princes trying to marry into the royal family. In *my* world, they're gangsters. Mafia families without the Sicilian in-laws."

She hit the "pause" button for a moment.

"So I'm a Mafia princess. Talk about not getting involved with goodfellas! What do I make of it?"

She paused again and noticed that she was pacing back and forth distractedly. "It's blood money. Or is it? If these people *are* the government here, and they say it's legal to smuggle cocaine or heroin, does that make it okay? This is one huge can of worms. Even if you leave ethics out of the question, even if you think the whole war on drugs is a bad idea like prohibition in the twenties, it's still a huge headache." She massaged her throbbing forehead. "I really need to talk to Iris. She'd set me straight."

She leaned her forehead against the cool tiles beside the mirror over the sink. "Problem is, I *can't* walk away from them. I can't just leave, walk out, and go back to life in Cambridge. It's not just the government who'd want to bury me so deep the sun would never find me. The Clan can't risk me talking. Now that I think about it, it's weird that they let Roland get as far as he did. Only. If he's telling the truth, Angbard is keeping him on a short leash. What does that suggest they've got in mind for me? A short leash and a choke collar?"

She could see it in her mind's eye, the chain of events that would unfold if she were to walk into an FBI office and prove what she could do—maybe with the aid of a sack of cocaine, maybe not. *Maybe with Paulie's CD full of research, too,* she realized, sitting up. "Shit." A dawning supposition: Drug-smuggling rings needed to sanitize their revenue stream, didn't they? And the business with Biphase and Proteome was in the right part of the world, and the Clan was certainly sophisticated enough . . . if her hunch was right, then it was, in fact, her long-lost family's investments that Paulie was holding the key to.

In the FBI office first there'd be disbelief. Then the growing realization that a journalist was handing them the drugs case of the century. Followed by the hasty escalation, the witness protection program offers—then their reaction to her demonstrated ability to walk through walls. The secondary scenarios as the FBI realize that they can't protect her, can't even protect themselves against assassins from another world. Then blind panic and bad decisions.

"If the families decided to attack the United States at home, they could make al Qaida look like amateurs," she muttered into her dictaphone, stricken. "They have the resources of a government at their disposal, because over here they're running things. Does that make them a government? Or so close it makes no difference? They're rich and powerful on the other side, too. Another generation and they'll probably be getting their fingers into the pie in D.C. I wonder. They make their money from smuggling, and they're personally immune to attempts to imprison them. The only thing that could hurt them would be if Congress decriminalized all drugs, so the price crashed and they could be shipped legally. Maybe the families are actually *pushing* the war on drugs? Paying politicians to call for tougher sanctions, border patrols against ordinary smugglers? Breaking the competition and driving the price up because of the law of supply and demand. *Damn*."

She flicked the "stop" button on her dictaphone and put it down, shuddering. It made a frightening amount of sense. *I am sitting on a news story that makes the attack on the World Trade Center look like a five-minute wonder*, she realized with a sinking feeling. *No, I am sitting in the* middle *of the story. What am I going to do?*

At that exact moment the telephone out in her reception room rang.

Old habits died hard, and Miriam was out of the bathroom in seconds with the finely honed reflexes of a journalist with an editor on the line. She picked the phone up before she realized there were no buttons, nothing to indicate it could dial an outside line. "Yes?"

"Miriam?"

She froze, heart sinking. "Roland," she said distantly.

"You locked your door and sent your maids away. I wanted to make sure you're all right."

" 'All right.' " She considered her next words carefully. "I'm not all right, Roland. I looked in the suitcase. The other one, the one waiting in the post room." Her chest felt tight. He'd lied to her: but on the other hand, she'd been holding more than a little back herself—

A pause. "I know. It was a test. The only question was which one you'd open. I don't know if it makes any difference, but I was ordered to give you the opportunity. To figure it all out for yourself. 'Give her enough rope' were his exact words. So now you know."

"Know what?" she said flatly. "That he's an extremely devious conspirator or about the family's dirty little secret?"

"Both." Roland waited for her to reply.

"I feel used," she said calmly. "I am also extremely pissed off. In fact, I'm still working out how I feel about everything. It's not the drugs, exactly: I don't think I've got any illusions about that side of things. I studied enough pharmacology to know the difference between propaganda and reality, and I saw enough shit in med school from ODs and drunk drivers and people coughing up lung cancers to know you get the same results whether the drug's illegal or not. But the manipulative side of it—there's a movie on the other side called *The Godfather*. Have you ever seen it?"

"Yes. That's it, exactly." He sounded dryly amused. "By the way, Don Corleone asked me to tell you that he expects to see you in his office tomorrow at ten o'clock sharp." His voice changed, abruptly serious. "Please don't shout at him. I think it's another test, but I'm not sure what kind— whichever, it could be very dangerous. I don't want to see you get hurt, Miriam. Or Helge, as he'll call you. But you're Miriam to me. Listen, for your own good, whatever he says, *don't refuse a direct order*. He is *much* more dangerous than he looks, and if he thinks you'll bite him, he may put family loyalty aside, because his *real* loyalty is to the Clan as a whole. You're a close family member, but the Clan, by the law of families, comes first. Just sit tight and remember that you've got more leverage than you realize. He will want you to make a secure alliance, both to keep you safe—for the memory of his stepsister—and to shore up his own position. Failing that, he'll be able to pretend to ignore you as long as you don't disobey a direct order. Do you hear what I'm saying?"

"Yes." Her heart pounded. "So it's going to happen."

"What?"

"Fucking Cinderella. Never mind. Roland, I am not stupid. I need some time to myself to think, that's all. I'm angry with you in the abstract, not the particular. I don't like being made to jump through hoops. I hear what you're saying. Do you hear *me?*"

"Yes." A pause. "I think I do. I'm angry too."

"Oh, really?" she asked, half-sarcastically.

"Yes." This time, a longer pause. "I like your sense of humor, but it's going to get you into deep trouble if you don't keep it under control. There are people here who will respond to sarcasm with a garotte. Trying to change the way the Clan works from the inside is *hard.*"

"Good-bye." She hung up hastily and stood next to the phone for a long minute, heart thudding at her ribs, head throbbing in time to it. The smell of leather car seats was strong in her nose, the echo of his smile over lunch fixed in her mind's eye. *Duke's orders*, she thought. *Well, he* would *say that, wouldn't he?*

She managed to pull herself away from the telephone and walked back into her bedroom, to the dresser with the tiny Picturebook computer perched next to the stack of disks and the external DVD-ROM drive. She had software to install. She riffled through disks containing relief maps of North America, an electronic pharmacopoeia, and a multimedia history of the Medici families. She put them down next to the encyclopedia of medieval history and other textbooks that had seemed relevant.

Once she'd made her first notes for the article Steve had commissioned, she'd start installing the software. Then she had a long night of cramming ahead, reading up on the great medieval merchant princes and their dynasties. The sooner she got a handle on this situation, the better . . .

Another morning dawned—a Sunday, bright and cold. Miriam blinked tiredly and threw back her bed clothes to let the cold air in. *I may be getting used to this,* she thought blearily. *Oh dear.* She looked at her watch and saw that the ten o'clock interview with Duke Angbard was worryingly close. "Shit," she said aloud, but was gratified to note that the word brought no maidservants scurrying out of the woodwork. Even better, the outer suite was empty except for a steaming jug of strong coffee and a tray piled with croissants, just as she'd requested. "I could get used to this level of room service," she muttered under her breath as she dashed into the bathroom. The computer was still running from last night, a screensaver showing.

She laid out her clothes for the meeting with the duke. After a moment's thought, she dressed conservatively, choosing a suit with a collarless jacket that buttoned to her throat. "Think medieval," she told herself. "Think demure, feminine, unprovocative." For a touch of color, she tied a bright silk scarf round her throat. "Think camouflage." *And remember what Roland said about not defying the old bastard openly. At least, not yet.* How and where to get the leverage was the sixty-four-thousand-dollar question, of course, to be followed by the bonus question of when and how to use it to shaft him, but she doubted she'd find such tools conveniently lying around while she lived as a guest—or valued prisoner—in his house. This whole business of being beholden to a powerful man left a nasty taste in her mouth.

However, there was one thing she could carry to even up the odds—a very potent equalizer. To complete her ensemble, Miriam chose a small black makeup bag, clearly too small to hold a gun or anything threatening. She didn't load it down with much: just a tube of lipstick, some tissues, and a running dictaphone.

The door to her suite was cooperating today, she noted as she pushed into the corridor outside. She remembered the way to the duke's suite and made her way quietly past a pair of diligent maidservants who were busy polishing the brasswork on one of the doors and a footman who appeared to be replacing the flowers on one of the ornamental side tables. They bowed out of her way and she nodded, passing them hastily. The whole palace appeared to be coming awake, as if occupants who had been sleeping were coming out of the woodwork to resume their life.

She reached the duke's outer office door and paused. Big double doors, closed, with a room on the other side. She took a deep breath and pushed the button set beside the door.

"Wer ish?" His voice crackled tinnily: a loose wire somewhere.

"It's Miriam—Helge. I believe the duke wanted to talk to me," she replied to the speaker.

"Enter." The lock clicked discreetly and Miriam pushed the door inward. It was astonishingly heavy, as if lined with steel, and it drifted shut behind her.

Matthias, the frightening secretary, was waiting behind the big desk in shirtsleeves, his jacket slung over the back of his chair. This time she noted the pile of papers in front of him. Some of them looked like FedEx waybills, and some of them looked like letters.

"Helge. Miriam." Matthias nodded to her, almost friendly.

"Yes." *Why does he make me so nervous?* She wondered. Was it just the shoulder holster he wore so conspicuously? Or the way he avoided eye contact but scanned across and around her all the while?

"You have an appointment," he said. "But you should call first, before setting out. So that we can send an escort for you."

" 'An escort'?" She asked. "Why would I want an escort?"

He raised an eyebrow. "Why wouldn't you? You are a lady of status, you deserve an escort. To be seen without one is a slight to your honor. Besides, someone might seek to take advantage of the deficiency in order to approach you."

"Uh-huh. I'll think about it." She nodded at the inner door. "Is he ready?"

"One moment." Matthias stood, then knocked on the door. A muttered exchange followed. Matthias pulled the door ajar, then held it for her. "You may enter," he said, his expression unreadable. As she passed his desk, he moved to place his body in front of the papers there.

Miriam pretended not to notice as she entered the lion's den. As before, Duke Angbard was seated at his writing desk, back to the window, so that she had to squint into the light to see him. But this time there was nobody else present, and he rose to welcome her into his study.

"Ah, Miriam, my dear niece. Please come in."

He was trying for the kindly uncle role, she decided, so she smiled warmly in return as she approached the desk. "Uncle. Uh, I'm unfamiliar with the proper form of address. I hope you don't mind if I call you Angbard?"

"Not in private." He smiled benevolently down at her. "In public, it would be best to call me 'your excellency' or 'uncle,' depending on context—official or familial. Please have a seat."

"Thanks." She sat down opposite him, and he sat down in turn. He was wearing another exquisitely tailored suit of conservative cut with, she couldn't help noticing, a sword. It was curved: a saber, perhaps, but she couldn't be sure—the blades with which she was most familiar were scalpels. "Is there anything in particular you wanted to talk to me about?"

"Oh, many things." His broad wave took in half the world. "It isn't customary here to introduce conversations with business, but I gather you are accustomed to a life conducted at a brisker pace." He leaned back in his chair, face shadowed. "Roland tells me you opened the second case," he said briskly. "What have you to say for yourself?"

Ah, the moment of truth. Miriam leaned back, consciously mirroring his posture. "Well, I'd have to say that only an idiot lets themselves be sucked into any business arrangement without a full awareness of what it involves," she said slowly. "And nobody had ordered me *not* to peek. You should also note that I'm here to discuss it with you, and the only other person who knows about it is Roland. What do you think?"

"I think that shows a necessary level of discretion," he replied after a moment. "Now. What is your opinion of the business? And of your own relationship to it?"

"It makes a lot of sense for a group of families in the position that ours so clearly occupies," she said, carefully trying to avoid giving the wrong impression. "I can see why you might want to test a new, ah, family member. As businesses go it is neatly orchestrated and appears to be efficiently run." She shrugged, biting back the urge to add: *for an eighteenth-century family concern. As business organizations go, it's still in the dark ages . ...* "And it's hardly appropriate for me to comment on where that platinum credit card came from, is it?"

"Indeed not," he said acerbically. "But you seem to be clear on your position." A sudden tightening of the skin around his eyes. "Are you a drug user?" he asked.

"Me?" She laughed, mentally crossing her fingers. "No! Never." *At least, not heroin or crack. Please don't let him ask about anything else.* Like many students, she'd acquired a passing familiarity with marijuana, but had mostly given it up some time ago. And she didn't think he was the type to count coffee, cigars, or whiskey as drugs.

"That's good," he said seriously. "Most users are indiscreet. Can't keep secrets. Bad for business."

"Sobriety is next to godliness," she agreed, nodding enthusiastically, then wondered if she'd overdone it when he fixed her with a slightly jaundiced stare. *Oops, five glasses of wine*, she remembered—and shrugged self-deprecatingly. His glare slowly faded.

"You have your mother's sly tongue," he commented. "But I didn't call you here to ask you questions about your opinion of our business. I gather that Roland has been filling in a few of the gaps in your education—some of them, like a working knowledge of hightongue, will take a long time to remedy—but I dare say he has not been forthcoming in full with the details of your position in the Clan. Is that the case?"

Miriam could feel her forehead wrinkle. "He said I was rich and of very high position. But he didn't explain in detail, no. Why?"

"Well, then," said the duke, "perhaps I had better hasten to explain. You see, you are in a unique position—two unique positions."

"Really? What kind?" she asked brightly. *Missionary or. . . .*

"You know that there are five families in the Clan," Angbard began. "These are Lofstrom—the senior family—Thorold, Hjorth, Wu, Arnesen, and Hjalmar. Yes, I know that's six. The familial name does not necessarily correspond to a lineage. Our families are the descendants of the children of the founder, Angmar Lofstrom. He had many children, but the blood ran thin—only when their children married and the great-grandchildren showed the family trait were we able to come together to form the Clan."

He cleared his throat. "Wu is not the name of one of our original ancestors; it is a name that the second son of line Arnesen took upon emigrating to the Outer Kingdom, two thousand miles to the west, perhaps a hundred and twenty years ago. The idea was that family Wu would become our western arm, trading with us by way of the Union Pacific Railroad, to mutual benefit. That wasn't the first attempt, by the way. Angmar the elder's youngest son, Marc, tried to cross the wilderness far earlier, but the attempt came to nothing and Marc was lost. So, we have branches on both sides of the Continental Divide. And a history of other families. Once there were seven lineages—but I digress."

"But how does it all work?" Miriam asked. "How does the Clan come out of all this?"

"The Clan is not what you'd call a limited liability company—it is a partnership. A family firm, if you like. You see, we hold our lands and riches and titles in common trust for the Clan, which operates in concert and receives the profits from all our ventures. The Clan makes use of all who have the world-walking talent—the members of the inner families—and arranges or authorizes marriages that braid the families together across generations, avoiding both outbreeding and too many close kin marriages. It also controls the outer family—those who lack the talent, but whose children might possess it if they marry like with like—and finds jobs for them over here. For example, Matthias cannot ever visit Boston on his own—but he has a talent for security, and makes a most excellent mailed fist. We number almost five hundred world-walkers now, and with two thousand in the outer families the pickings at the lower ranks are slim."

He coughed. "One iron rule is that family members are required to marry into another family lineage—otherwise the blood runs thin within a generation. The only exceptions are by prior dispensation of the council, to permit an alliance outside the Clan, such as adoption into the nobility. The second iron rule is that inheritance follows Clan shareholdings, not lineage or family. If you die, your children inherit whatever the Clan allocates to them—you hold your estates from the Clan, they don't belong to you because without the Clan you would be nothing. The system is supposed to encourage cooperation and it usually succeeds, but there are exceptions. Sixty years ago, a war broke out within the Clan, between families—Wu and Hjorth on one side, Thorold, Lofstrom, Arnesen, and Hjalmar on the other. Nobody is certain what started it any more—those who knew died early on—but my personal supposition is that the Wu family, in their ambition to climb into the eternal palace itself, exposed themselves to court intrigue and were turned into a weapon against us by the palace of the Outer Kingdom, which considered the Wu lineage to be a threat. In any event, it was a bloody period in our history. During the war years, our numbers fell from perhaps a thousand of the true blood to fewer than two hundred. The war ended thirty-five years ago with a treaty, solemnized by the marriage of Patricia Lofstrom Thorold to Alfredo Wu. Patricia was my half-sister, and I inherited custody of the Lofstrom estates."

He paused to clear his throat. "Your mother's death is now

confirmed, although neither her nor Alfredo's body was recovered. Since then, there has been no pretender to the estates of the Thorold–Hjorth shareholding, which were therefore administered as a trusteeship under the order of the high crown."

" 'The high crown?' "

"Yes, the royal family," he said irritably. "You don't have one, I know. We have to put up with them, and they can be a blithering nuisance!"

"Ah, I think I begin to see." She crossed her ankles. "So. There's a big shareholding in the Clan enterprise, under the control of an external party who knows who and what you are. Then I come along and offer you a lever to take it back under the family's control. Is that right?"

"Yes. As long as nobody kills you first," he said.

"Now, wait a minute!" She leaned forward. "Who would do that? And why?"

"Oh, several parties," Angbard said with what Miriam found a distinctly unnerving tone of relish. "The crown, to maintain their grip on almost a tenth of our properties and revenues without forcing an outright war with their most powerful nobles. Whoever killed Patricia, for the same reason. Any of the younger generations of lineages Hjorth and Thorold, who must be hoping that the shares will escheat to them in due course should no pretender emerge and should those families re-create the braid of inheritance. And finally, the Drug Enforcement Agency."

"What are *they* doing here?"

"They aren't, I merely name them as another party who would take an instant dislike to you were they to become appraised of your existence." He smiled humorlessly. "Think of it as a test, if you like."

"Ri-i-ight," she drawled. *I already figured that much out for myself, thanks*. "I believe I see where you're coming from, Uncle. One question?"

"Ask away, by all means."

"Roland. Does *he* have a motive?"

Angbard startled her by laughing loudly. "Roland the

dreaming runaway?" He leaned back in his chair. "Roland, who tried to convince us all to sign away our lands to the peasantry and set up a banking system to loan them money? Roland the *rebel*? He's squandered all the credibility he might have built by refusing to play the game over here. I think Roland Lofstrom will make a suitable husband for Olga Thorold. And she should make him an excellent wife—she'll slow him down and that's necessary, he has disruptive tendencies. Once he's yoked to the Clan, it might be time to revisit some of his ideas, but as things stand the council can't afford to be seen taking him seriously—by rebelling in his youth he has automatically tainted any valid reformist ideas he may present. Which is a shame. Meanwhile, you are my direct niece. Patricia, your mother, was the daughter of my father's first wife. Roland, in contrast, is the son of my half-brother, by my father's third wife. He's not a blood relative of yours—at least, not within four generations. Three wives, three children, three scandals! My father lent our affairs much complexity . . .

"Anyway, Roland will create another Thorold–Lofstrom braid, which will be of considerable use to my successor, whoever he is. But he's not important and he has no stake in your disarray. In fact, that is why it was safe for him to know of your existence so early."

Miriam shook her head. The family intricacies confused her, and she was left with nothing but a vague impression of plaited families and arranged marriages. "Have you asked Olga's opinion about this?" she asked.

"Why would I? She'll do as she's told for the good of the Clan. She's a sweet child."

"Oh, that's all right then," Miriam said, nodding slightly and biting her cheek to keep a straight face.

"Which brings me to you, again," Angbard nodded. "Obviously, you are *not* a sweet child. You're an experienced dowager, I would say, and sharp as a razor. I approve of that. But I hope I have made it clear to you that your future is inextricably tied to the Clan. You can't possibly go back into obscurity on the other side—your enemies would seek you out, whether you will it or no. Nor can you afford not to take sides and find a protector."

"I see," she stated, biting the words out sharply.

"I think it would be best for you to see something of the other families before we discuss this further," Angbard continued, ignoring her coolness. "As it happens, Olga is summoned to pay attendance upon the person of the king for the next three months, who as it also happens is not one of us— it would be a good thing at this juncture for you to make your debut before the royal court and that part of the Clan that is in residence in the capital in her company. Your presence should lure certain lice out of the bedding in, ah, a controlled manner. Meanwhile you will not entirely be at a loose end, or without support, when you make the rounds of the eligible nobility before the annual grand meeting at Beltaigne, seven months hence. Olga can advise you on bloodlines and shareholdings and etiquette, and begin language lessons. I place no obligation upon you to make a hasty alliance, just so long as you understand your situation."

"Right. So I'm to go looking for an alliance—a husband who meets with your approval—at court. When do you expect me to do this?" Miriam asked, with a forced brightness that concealed her slowly gathering anger. "I assume you're planning on exhibiting me widely?"

"Olga departs tomorrow morning by stage," Angbard announced. "You shall travel with her, and on arrival at court in Niejwein she will help you select your ladies-in-waiting— of low but family rank, not base servants such as you have had here. Your maids are already packing your bags, by the way." He fixed her with a coldly unamused smile. "Think of it as a test, if you like. You do see this is for your own long-term good, don't you?" he asked.

"Oh, I see, all right," Miriam said and smiled at him, as sweet as cyanide-laced marzipan. "Yes, I see everything very clearly indeed."

Miriam politely declined the duke's invitation to lunch and returned to her apartment in a state of barely controlled fury. Her temper was not made better by the discovery that her maids had packed most of her clothes in heavy wooden trunks.

"Fuck!" She spat at the bathroom mirror. "You *will* be good, won't you," she muttered under her breath. "Patronizing bastard, *my dear.*"

Murderous bastard, a still small voice reminded her from inside. Duke Angbard was quite capable of killing people, Roland had said. Paulie's words came back to haunt her: '*If you back down, they own you; it's as simple as that.*' And what the hell was that crack about luring lice out of the bedding meant to mean? She sobered up fast. *I need advice,* she decided. And then a thought struck her—a thought simultaneously wicked and so delicious that it brought a smile to her lips. A *perfect* scheme, really, one that would gain her exactly what she needed, while simultaneously sending an unequivocal message to the duke, if she went all the way through with it. She raised one middle digit: "Sit and swivel!" she whispered triumphantly. *Yeah,* that *will work!*

She headed back into the suite, chased her maids out, shut the door, and picked up the phone. "Put me through to Earl Roland," she demanded in her most imperious voice.

"Yes, ma'am," the operator confirmed. "One moment."

"Roland?" she said, suddenly much less confident. '*Roland the dreamer,*' his uncle called him. Roland the disruptive influence, who looked too good to be true. Did she go through with this? Just picking up the phone made her feel obscurely guilty. It also gave her a thrill of illicit anticipation.

"Miriam! What can I do for you?"

"Listen," she said, licking her suddenly dry lower lip. "About yesterday. You invited me to . . . dinner? Does that invitation still stand?"

"You've seen the old man?" he asked.

"Yes." She waited.

"Oh. Well, yes, the invitation still stands. Would you like to come?"

"As long as it's just you and me. No servants, no company, no nothing."

"Oh!" He sounded amused. "Miriam, have you any idea how fast word of that would get around, now that the palace is fully staffed again? That sort of thing just doesn't happen you know. Not with servants."

"It's not like that: I need confidential advice," she said. Lowering her voice, "They must know I've spent over thirty years on the other side. Can I catch a couple of hours with you, without anyone snooping?"

"Hmm." He paused for a bit. "Only if you can manage to become invisible. Listen, I am in the suite on the floor above you, second along. I'll have dinner laid out at six, then send the servants away. Still, it'll be best if nobody sees you. It would cause tongues to wag—and give your enemies words to throw back at you."

"I'll think of a way," she promised. "Lay on the wine and dress for dinner. I'll be seeing you."

PART 3

hothouse

flowers

REVENGE OF
THE INVISIBLE WOMAN

The small town of Svarlberg squatted at the mouth of the Fall River on the coast, a day's ride south of Fort Lofstrom. Overlooked by a crumbling but huge stone fortress built in the romans model, brought to the western lands by survivors of the Roman Gothic war against the Turkic occupiers of Constantinople and now used as a bulwark against threat of invasion by sea, Svarlberg was home to a thriving fishing community and a harbor much used by coast-hugging merchants.

Not that many merchants would put into this harbor so late in the year. A few late stragglers coming down the coast from the icy trapping settlements up north, and perhaps an overdue ship braving the North Atlantic winter to make the last leap from the Ice Isles to western civilization—but winter was beginning to bite, and only rich fools or the truly desperate would brave the boreal gales this late in the year.

When the horseman reined in his tired mount outside the port-side inn, wearily slid out of the saddle, and banged on the door, it took a minute for the owner to open the hole and look out. "What are you wanting?" he asked brusquely.

"Board, beer, and stable." The rider held up a coin so the innkeeper could see it. "Or are you already asleep for the winter, like a bear fattened on salmon since I was here last, Andru?"

"Ah, come you in." Andru the innkeeper unbarred the heavy door and yelled over his shoulder: "Markus! Markus! Where is the boy?" A freezing draft set him to shivering. "It's perishing cold out. Will you be staying long this time, sir?"

A thin boy came rushing out of the kitchens. "Ma said I was to—" he began.

"Horse," said Andru. "Stable. Brush. Oats. You know what to do."

"Yes, master." The boy half-bowed cringingly, then waited while the rider unstrapped one saddle bag before leading the gelding around the side of the inn.

"Layabout would rather stay in the warmth," Andru said, shaking his head and glancing along the street in the vain hope of some more passing trade, but it was twilight, and everyone with any sense was already abed. He stepped aside to let his customer in, then pulled the door shut. "What'll it be first, sir?"

"Whatever you've got." The rider bared his teeth in a smile half-concealed by a heavy scarf. "I'm expecting a visitor tonight or tomorrow. If you've got a private room and a pipe, I'll take it."

"Be at your ease sir, and I'll sort it out immediately." The innkeeper hurried off, calling: "Raya! Raya! Is the wake room fit for a king's man?"

The inn was half-empty, dead as a doornail by virtue of the time of day and the season of year. A drunken sailor lay in one corner, snoring quietly, and a public scribe sat at one end of a table, mumbling over a mug of mulled wine and a collection of fresh quills as he cut and tied them for the next week's business. It was definitely anything but a thriving scene. Which suited the horseman fine, because the fewer people who saw him here, the better.

A moment later, the innkeeper bustled up—"This way, this way please, kind sir!"—and herded the rider through a side door. "We've laid out the wake room for you, sir, and if you will sit for it a selection of cold cuts and a bottle of the southern wine: Will that be sufficient? It's late in the season but we will be roasting a lamb tomorrow if you should be staying—"

"Yes, yes—" the inkeeper hurried out again and the rider settled himself in the armchair beside the table and stretched out his legs, snarling quietly when the kitchen girl didn't hurry to remove his boots fast enough.

Two hours later he was nodding over his second cup of wine—the room was passably warm, and a couple of large chunks of sausage and pickled tongue had filled his belly comfortably—when there was a discreet tap on the door. He was on his feet instantly, gun at the ready. "Who is it?" he asked quietly.

"When the dragon of the north wind blows—shit, is that you, Jacob?"

"Hello, Esau." Jacob dragged the door open one-handed. The revolver vanished.

"It's *freezing* out there." The man called Esau blew on his fingers, shook his head, then began to peel his gloves off.

Jacob kicked the door shut. "You really need to observe proper security discipline," he said.

"Yeah well, and how many times have we done this?" Esau shrugged. "Stupid christ-cultist names from the far-side, dumb pass-phrases and secret handshakes—"

"If I was ill and sent a proxy, the dumb pass-phrases would be the only thing that could tell you who they were," Jacob pointed out.

"If you were ill, you'd have radio'd ahead to call off the meeting. Is that a bottle of the local emetic? I'll have a drop."

"Here. Settle down." Jacob poured. "What have you got for me?"

Esau shrugged. "This." A leather purse appeared, as magically as Jacob's pistol. "Pharmaceutical-grade, half a kilo."

"That'll do." Jacob transferred it to his belt pouch without expression. "Anything else?"

"Well." Esau settled down and picked up the full glass. "Certain feathers have been—ruffled, shall we say—by the news of those pink slippers. That account was supposed to have been settled a very long time ago. Do you have an update for me?"

"Yes." Jacob nodded, then picked up his own glass. "Nothing good. A couple more sightings and then a search and sweep found a very wet chair in the woods near Fort Lofstrom. It was from the other side. Need I say any more? It was too obvious to cover up, so the old man sent a snatch squad through and they pulled in a woman. Age thirty-two, professional journalist, and clearly a long-lost cousin."

"A woman journalist? Things are passing strange over there."

"You're telling me. Sometimes I get to visit on business. It's even weirder than those sheep-shagging slant-eyes on the west coast." Jacob put the empty glass down—hard—on the table. "Why does this shit always happen when I'm in charge?"

"Because you're good," soothed Esau. "Don't worry, we'll get it sorted out and I'm pretty sure the—control—will authorize a reward for this. It's exactly what we've been looking out for all these years." He smiled at Jacob and raised his glass. "To your success."

"Huh." But Jacob raised his (empty) glass right back, then refilled both of them. "Well. The old asshole put the runaway on her case, but she's turning out to be a bit hot. She's the grand dowager's granddaughter, you know? And a tearaway. All too common in women from over there, you know. She's poking her nose into all sorts of corners. If the old bat recognizes her formally, seven shades of shit will hit the Clan council balance of power, but I have a plan that I think will cover the possibility. She could be very useful if I can coopt her."

"What about her mother?" Esau leaned forward.

"Dead." Jacob shrugged. "The baby was adopted on the other side. That's why she was missing for so long. We've got the foster mother under surveillance, but . . ." he shook his head. "It's a thirty-two-year-old trail. What do you expect?"

"I expect her to—" Esau frowned. "Look, I'm going to have to break cover on this and go get instructions from my superiors. There may be preexisting orders in effect for just this situation, but if not it would be as well for you to proceed as you see fit. Anything that keeps the Clan from asking awkward questions is all right by us, I think. And I don't want to risk using one of your magical radio thingies in case they've got a black chamber somewhere listening in. Are you going to be here overnight?"

"I will be." Jacob nodded. "I was planning to leave in the morning, though."

"That's all right. I'll cross over and ask for directions. If anyone knows anything, I'll pass on your instructions before you leave." He rubbed his forehead in anticipation, missing Jacob's flash of envy, which was in any case quickly masked. "If I don't show, well, use your imagination. We don't need the Clan raking over the evidence . . ."

"Evidence that might point to your faction's existence."

"Exactly."

Servants were invisible, Miriam realized, as she hurried through the narrow rough-walled corridor below stairs. Take this particular servant, for example. She was wearing the long black skirt, white blouse, and starched apron of a parlor maid, hurrying along beneath a tray with a pot of coffee on it. Nobody paid her a second glance. Maybe they should have, she decided, carefully putting one foot in front of another. The servant outfit was inauthentic, machine-woven, obviously wrong if anyone had looked closely, and bulked up from hiding something underneath. But the house was still in upheaval, individual servants were mostly beneath notice to the noble occupants, and the staff was large enough that she didn't expect to be noticed by the real maids. *This i going to be really useful*, Miriam decided, balancing the tra carefully as she mounted the staircase.

The tight spiral steps were a trial, but she managed not t tread on her hem as she wound her way up to the floor above Once she squeezed against the wall to let an equerry by: H glanced at her in mild disgust and continued on. *Score one t the invisible woman*, she told herself. She stalked along th corridor, edgy with anticipation. Planning this move in col blood was all very well, but she wouldn't be able to go throug with it if the idea of an illicit assignation with Roland didn' set her pulse racing. And now she came to the final passage she found her blood wasn't cool at all.

She found the right door and entered without knocking. I was another private apartment, seemingly empty. She pu the tray down on the sideboard beside the door, then looke around. One of the side doors opened: "I didn't order—oh."

"We meet again." She grinned nervously at him, the dropped the latch on the door. "Just in case," she said.

Roland looked her up and down in mild disbelief. "The mistress of disguise? It's a good thing I swept the room ear- lier. For bugs," he added, catching her raised eyebrow.

"Well, that was prudent. You look great, too." He'd dressed in a black tuxedo, she noted with relief. He'd taken her seri- ously; she'd been a little worried. "Where's the bathroom?"

"Through there." He looked doubtful.

"Back in a minute," she said, ducking inside.

She closed the door, hastily untied her servant's apron, shook her hair out of the borrowed mob cap, then spent a minute fumbling with her waistband. She stripped off the servant's outerwear, then paused to look in a mirror. "Go kill him, girl," she told herself. She deftly rolled on a coat of lip gloss, installed earrings and a single string of pearls. Finally she pulled on her black evening gloves, did an ex- perimental twirl that set two thousand dollars' worth of eve- ning dress swirling, blew herself a kiss in the mirror, and stepped out.

Roland was waiting outside, holding a goblet of wine out

toward her: He nearly dropped it when he saw her. "You look absolutely spectacular," he said, finally. "How did you do it?"

"Oh, it wasn't hard." She shrugged her shoulders, which were bare. "You could conceal an arsenal under one of those maids' uniforms." *I know. I did.* She took the glass from him, then took his hand, led him to the sofa. "Sit." She sat herself, then patted the leather seat next to her. "We need to talk."

"Sure." He followed her, looking slightly dazzled.

She felt a stab of tenderness mixed with regret, unsettling and unexpected. *What am I really doing here?* she half-wondered, then shoved the thought aside. "Come on. Sit down." He sat in the opposite corner of the huge leather sofa, one arm over the back, the other cradling his glass in front of him, almost hiding behind it. "I had my chat with Angbard today."

"Ah." He looked defensive.

She took a sip from the glass and smiled at him. The wine was more than good, it was excellent, a rich, fruity vintage with a subtle aftertaste that reminded her of strawberries and freshly mowed lawns. She fired another smile at him, and he cracked, took a mouthful, and tried to smile back.

"Roland, I think the duke may be lying to us—separately. Or merely being economical with the truth."

"Ah, 'lying'?" He looked cautiously defensive.

"Lying." She sighed, then looked at him sidelong. "I'm going to tell you what he told me, then you can tell me if that's what he told you. Do you think you can do that? No need to reveal any secrets . . ."

" 'Secrets,' " he echoed. A shadow flickered across his face. "Miriam, there are things I'm not allowed to tell you, and I don't like it, but it's possible that—well, some of them may be seeds."

" 'Seeds'?"

"Tests, for me, to see if I can keep secrets." He took a mouthful of the Cabernet. "Stuff that, if I tell you, will probably make you do something predictable, so that he'll know I told you. Do you understand? I'm not considered trustwor-

thy. I came back with ideas about, well, about trying t[
change the way things are done. Ideas that upset a lot of people. The duke seems to like me—or at least think some of
my ideas could be useful—but he certainly doesn't trust me.
That's why he keeps me so close at hand."

"Yes." She nodded thoughtfully. Her opinion of him rose
yet again: *He doesn't lie to himself*. "I guessed that. Which is
why I'm going to tell you what he told me and you're just
going to decide whether to confirm it if it's true."

"Uh, okay." He was intensely focused on her. *Good*, she
thought, feeling a little thrill. She slid one leg over the other,
let a calf encased in sheer black stocking sneak out. *The
game's afoot*, she thought to herself, then noticed his response and felt her breath catch in her throat. *Then again,
maybe it's not all a game.*

"Okay, this is what he told me. He says I'm in an exposed
position and liable to be attacked, maybe murdered, if I
don't dig myself inextricably into the Clan power structure
as soon as possible. He says I have some discretion, but I
ought to marry within the families and do it soon. Which I
think is bullshit, but I let him lead me on. So he's sending me
to the royal court with Olga, for a formal presentation and
coming-out. We leave tomorrow." When she said *tomorrow*
he frowned.

"There's more." She paused to drink, then put her empty
glass down. Her stomach felt warm, relaxed. She met his
eyes. "Is what he told me about expecting me to find a husband among the families what you heard?"

"Yes." Roland nodded. "I didn't know you were to leave
tomorrow, though," he said, sounding a little disappointed.

Miriam straightened up and leaned toward him. "Yes,
well, he also discussed *you*," she said. "He said he's going to
marry you off to Olga."

"Bastard—" Roland's raised his glass to hide his expression, then drank its contents straight down.

"What, no comment?" Miriam asked, her heart pounding.
This was the critical moment—

"I'm sorry. Not your fault," he said hoarsely. "I'd guessed

he was going to try something to tie me down, but not that crude." He shook his head frustratedly. *"Stupid."* He took a deep breath, visibly struggling for control.

"I take it that's a no."

He put his glass down on the low table beside the sofa. As he straightened up, Miriam laid one hand on his arm. "What you told me the other day—he wants you nailed to a perch, just an obedient little branch on the family tree," she said urgently. "Angbard wants you to make an appropriate marriage and breed lots of little Thorold– Lofstroms to look after him in his old age. With Olga."

"Yes." Roland shook his head. He didn't seem to notice her hand on his arm. "I thought he was at least still interested in— shit. Olga's loyal. It means he's been stringing me along with his warnings to shut up and play the political game—all along, all the time." He stood up and paced across the room agitatedly. "He's been keeping me here on ice to stop me getting my point across." He reached the fireplace and paused, thumping the heel of his right hand into his left palm. *"Bastard."*

"So Uncle Angbard has been messing you around?"

" 'Uncle'—" he shook his head. "He's much more your uncle than mine. You know how the family braids work? There are several deaths and remarriages in the tree."

Miriam stood up. *Don't let him get distracted now. This is the point of no return*, she realized. *Do I want to go through with this?* Well, the answer that came to mind wasn't "no." She screwed up her courage and walked over to him. "Olga would lock you in and throw away the key."

"She'd—no, not deliberately. But the effect would be the same." He didn't seem to notice her standing a few inches in front of him, close enough to feel her breath on his cheek. *Is he completely blind—or just too distracted to notice what his eyeballs are seeing?* Miriam wondered, half-turning to face him and pushing her chest up as far as she could without being blatant about it—which was difficult, given what she was wearing. "He wants to tie me in with children, a family. I'd have to protect them."

On second thoughts . . . he was looking her in the eyes,

now, and he'd noticed her, all right. "That's not the only option," she murmured. "You don't have to surrender to Angbard."

"I don't—" He trailed off.

She leaned forward and wrapped her arms around his waist. "What you said earlier," she tried to explain. "You offered to help." She looked up at him, still maintaining eye contact. "How serious are you?" she asked, her voice a whisper.

He blinked slowly, his expression thoughtful, then she saw him focusing on her properly, and it did something odd to her. She felt suddenly embarrassed, as if she'd made some horrible faux pas in public. "It wouldn't be sensible," he said slowly. Then he embraced her, hugging her tightly. "Are you sure it's what you want?"

And now she *really* felt something, and it wasn't what she'd expected when the idea of compromising Angbard's plans for Olga stole into her mind. "The door's locked. Who's going to know? A serving girl goes in, a serving girl goes out, I'm in my bedroom working, it's all deniable." She pressed her chin into his shoulder. "I want you to pick me up, carry me into your bedroom, and take my clothes off—slowly," she whispered into his ear.

"Okay," he said.

She turned her head and laid her lips alongside his. He'd shaved. After a moment she felt his jaws loosen, exploration begin. Her whole weight fell against him and he lifted her, then put her down on her feet.

"Over here," he said, arm dropping to her waist, half-leading her.

The bedroom furnishings were different. A big oak four-poster with a red- and gold-tapestried canopy dominated the room, and the secondary items were different. She pulled him toward the bed, then paused in front of it. "Kiss me," she said.

He leaned over her and she sank into him, reaching down to his trousers with one hand to fumble at unfamiliar catches. He groaned softly as she caressed him. Then his jacket was on the floor, his bow tie dangling, his trousers loose. A shocking sense of urgency filled her.

Hours passed. They were both naked now: She lay with her back to Roland, his arms curled protectively around her. *This is unexpected*, she thought dizzily. A little tremor surged through her. *Wow*. Well, her plan had worked: pull him into bed and annoy the hell out of Angbard by being a loose cannon. Except that wasn't how it had turned out. She liked Roland a lot, and that wasn't in the script.

"This is so wrong," he mumbled into her hair.

She tensed. "What is?" she asked.

"Your uncle. He'll kill me if he suspects."

"He'll—" Her blood ran cold for a moment. "You're sure?"

"You're immune," he said in a tone of forced calm. "You've got huge leverage, and he doesn't have specific plans for you. I'm meant to marry Olga, though, and that's an end of it. Open defiance is *bad*. He's probably been planning the marriage for years."

"Surely I'm an, uh, acceptable substitute?" she asked, surprising herself. It hadn't been in the plan when she came upstairs, unless her subconscious had been working overtime on strategies for spiking Angbard's plans.

"That's not the point. It's not just about producing offspring with the ability, you know? You're about the most unsuitable replacement for Olga it's possible to imagine. Making me marry Olga would buy Angbard influence with her father's braid and tie me down with a family. But an alliance with you wouldn't do that—in fact, he'd risk losing influence over both of us, to no gain for himself." He paused for breath. "Aside from marrying out, one of the council's worst fears is fragmentation—world-walkers leaving and setting up as rivals. We're both classic fragmentation risks, disaffected rebellious adults with independent backgrounds. My plans . . . reform has to come from within or it's seen as a threat. That's why I was hoping he might still be listening to me. There's nothing personal about Clan alliances, Miriam. Even if Angbard the kindly uncle wanted to let you and me stay together, Angbard the duke would be seen as weak by the council, which would open him up to challenge . . . he can't take that risk, he'd have to split us up."

"I didn't know about the competition angle," she murmured. "What a mess." *I don't want to think about it.*

"This is a—it isn't a . . . a one-night stand?" he asked.

"I hope not." She nuzzled back deeper into his arms. "What about you? What do you want?"

"What I want seldom has anything to do with what I get," he said, a trifle bitterly. "Although—" he stroked her flank silently.

"We have a problem," Miriam whispered. "Tomorrow they're going to put me in a stagecoach with Olga and send us both to the royal court. Herself to pay respects to the king, me to be exhibited like some kind of prize cow. You're going to be staying here, under his eye. That right?"

She felt his nod: It sent a shiver through her spine. "It's a test," he murmured. "He's testing you to see what you're made of—also to see if your presence lures certain disaffected elements into the open."

"We can try for a different outcome. Olga can be taken out of the picture by, well, anything."

He tensed. "Do you mean what I think—"

"No." She felt him relax. "I'm *not* going to start murdering women in order to steal their husbands." She stifled a laugh—if it came out, it would have been more than slightly hysterical. "But we've got a couple of months, the whole of winter if I understand it, before anything happens. She doesn't need to know anything. I bought a prepaid phone, right under your nose. I'll leave you the number and try to arrange to talk to you when we're both on the other side. Hell, the horse might even learn to sing."

"Huh?"

"There might be a plague of smallpox. Or the crown prince might fall truly, madly, deeply in love with a shallow eighteen-year-old ditz whose one redeeming feature is that she plays the violin, getting you off the hook."

"Right." He sounded more certain. "I need that number."

"Or my uncle might fall down a staircase," she added.

"Right." He paused.

"A thought?" she asked.

"Only this." She felt lips touch the top of her spine. "You'd better be sneaking back to your apartment soon, because it's three in the morning and we can't afford to be compromised—either of us. But I want you to know one thing. Something I kept meaning to tell Janice, but never got a chance to—and now it's too late."

"What's that?" she asked sleepily.

"I know this is crazy and dangerous, but I think I'm falling in love with you."

Somehow Miriam made it back to her rooms without attracting any notice—possibly the sight of disheveled and half-drunk maids stumbling out of an earl's rooms and through the corridors at night was not one to arouse undue interest. She undressed and folded her clothing carelessly, stuffing cheap theatrical maid's costume and designer gown alike into her suitcase. She freshened up in the bathroom, as much as she could without making the plumbing gurgle. Then, completely naked, she sat down in front of her laptop. *Better check it before bed*, she thought muzzily. Clicking on the photo utility, she spooled back through the day's footage, back to her own exit—neatly packaged in a gray suit—en route to her appointment with the duke.

The camera was set to grab one frame per second. She fast-forwarded through it at thirty FPS, two seconds to the minute, two minutes to the hour. After ninety seconds, she saw the door open. Pausing, she backed up then single-stepped through the footage. Someone, an indistinct blur, moved from the main door to her bedroom. Then a gray blur in front of the laptop itself, then nothing. She had a vague

impression of a dark suit, a man's build. But it wasn'
Roland, and she felt a moment of fear at the realization.

But she'd gone into the bedroom safely. Nobody had tam-
pered with her aluminium suitcase, and her chests of clothing were already stashed in the main room. So before darin
to go to bed, Miriam spent a fruitless half-hour searchin
her bedroom from top to bottom, peering under the bed an
lifting mattresses, checking behind the curtains.

Nothing. Which left a couple of disturbing possibilities i
mind. *Don't try world-walking in your bedroom,* she sternl
warned herself, *and check the computer for back doors in th
morning.* She packed the computer and its extras—and th
gun—in her suitcase. Then she lay down and drifted int
sleep disturbed by surprisingly explicit, erotic phantoms tha
left her aching and sore for something she couldn't have.

She was awakened in the dim predawn light by a clatter
ing of serving maids. "What's going on?" she mumbled, lift
ing her head and wincing at her hangover. "I thought
said—"

"Duke's orders, ma'am," Meg apologized. "We've t
dress you for travel."

"Oh hell." Miriam groaned. "He said that?"

He had. So Miriam did her waking up that morning wit
three other women fussing over her, haphazardly crammin
her into a business suit—about the most inappropriate trave
garb she could think of—and then from somewhere the
produced a voluminous greatcoat that threatened her wit
heat stroke while she already felt like death warmed over.

"This," she said through gritted teeth, "is excessive."

"It's cold outside, ma'am," Meg said firmly. "You'll nee
it before the day is out." She held out a hat to Miriam
Miriam looked at it in disbelief, then tried to balance it o
her head. "It goes like this," said Meg, and seconds later i
did. With a scarf to hold it in place, Miriam felt cut off fron
the world almost completely. *Are they trying to hide me?* sh
wondered, anxious about what that could mean.

They led her downstairs, with a trail of grunting porters

hefting her trunks—and incongruous metal suitcase—and then out through a pair of high double doors. Meg was right. Her breath hung steaming in the air before her face. In the past week, autumn had turned wintry with the first breath of air rushing down from the Arctic. A huge black wooden coach balanced on wheels taller than Miriam stood waiting, eight horses harnessed before it. A mounting block led up to the open door, and she was startled to see the duke standing beside it, wearing a quite incongruous Burberry overcoat.

"My dear!" he greeted her. "A final word, if I may, before you depart."

She nodded, then glanced up as the porters hoisted her trunks onto the roof and a small platform at the back of the carriage.

"You may think my sending you to court is premature," he said quietly, "but my agents have intercepted messages about an attempt on your life. You need to leave here, and I think it best that you be among your peers. You'll be staying at the Thorold Palace, which is maintained as a common residence in the capital by the heads of the families; it's doppelgängered and quite safe, I assure you. It will be possible for you to return later."

"Well, *that's* a relief," she said sarcastically.

"Indeed." He looked at her oddly. "Well, I must say you look fine. I do commend Olga to you; she is not as stupid as she appears and you *will* need to learn the high speech sooner rather than later—English is only spoken among the aristocracy."

"Well, uh, okay." She shuffled nervously. "I'll try not to trip over any assassins, and I may even meet an appropriate husband." She glanced at the coach as one of the horses snorted and shook its harness. She felt even more peculiar when she realized that she was not entirely lying. If marrying Roland—even having another child with him—would get him into her bed on a regular basis, she was willing to at least contemplate the possibility. She needed an ally—and friend—here, and he had the potential to be more than that.

"Indeed." He nodded at her, and for the first time she noticed that there was a certain translucency to his skin, as if
he wasn't entirely well. "Good hunting." And then he turned
and strode away, leaving her to climb into the carriage and
wait for departure.

COURT APPEARANCE

Miriam's first unpleasant surprise—after finding that the Tylenol was all packed in her trunks and inaccessible—was that the carriage was unheated and the leather seats hard. Her second, as she shivered and tried to huddle into one corner under a thick blanket, came as Olga swept up the steps and into the seat opposite her. Olga's blonde hair was gathered up under a scarf and hat, and she wore a wool coat over a suit that made her look like a brokerage house yuppie. "Isn't this *wonderful?*" she cooed as plump Lady Margit, in twinset and pearls by day, huffed and puffed up and into the seat next to Miriam, expanding to flow over two-thirds of it.

"It's wonderful." Miriam smiled weakly as the coachman cracked his whip overhead and released the hand brake. The noise and vibration of wooden wheels turning on cobblestones shuddered through her hangover as the coach creaked and swayed forward.

Olga leaned toward her. "Oh dear, you look unwell!" she

insisted, peering into Miriam's eyes at close range. "Wh.
could it be?"

"Something I drank, I think," Miriam mumbled, turnin
away. Her stomach was distinctly rough, her head poundec
and she felt too hot. "How long will we be on the road?"

"Oh, not long!" Olga clapped her hands briskly an
rubbed them together against the cold. "We can use th
duke's holdings to change teams regularly. If we make goo
time today and keep driving until dusk, we could be at Ode
mark tomorrow evening and Niejwein the next afternoon
All of two hundred miles in three days!" She glanced a
Miriam slyly. "I hear over on the other side you have magical carriages that can travel such a distance much faster?"

"Oh, *Olga*," muttered Margit, a trifle peevishly.

"Um." Miriam nodded, pained. *Two hundred miles in
three days*, she thought. *Even Amtrak can do better than
that!* "Yes, but I don't think they'd work too well over *here*,"
she whuffed out, as a particularly bad rut in the road threw
her against the padded side of the carriage.

"What a shame," Olga replied brightly. "That means we'll
just have to take a little longer." She pointed out of the carriage door's open window. "Oh, look! A squirrel! On that
elm!"

It was at this point that Miriam realized, with a sickly
sinking feeling, that taking a carriage to the capital in this
world might be how the aristocracy traveled, but in comfort
terms it was the equivalent of an economy-class airline
ticket to New Zealand—in an ancient turboprop with mal-
functioning air-conditioning. And she'd set off with a hangover and a chatterbox for a fellow traveler, without
remembering to pack the usual hand luggage. "Oh god," she
moaned faintly to herself.

"Oh, that reminds me!" Olga sat upright. "I nearly forgot!" From some hidden pocket she pulled out a small,
neatly wrapped paper parcel. She opened it and removed a
pinch of some powdery substance, then cast it from the window. "Im nama des'Hummelvat sen da' Blishkin un' da

ɡeshes des'reeshes, dis expedition an' all, the mifim ɛeesh'n," she murmured. Then Olga noticed Miriam looking at her blankly. "Don't you pray?" she asked.

"Pray?" Miriam shook her head. "I don't understand—"

"Prayers! Oh, yes, I forgot. Didn't dear Roland say that on the other side everybody is pagan? You all worship some dead god on a stick, impaled or something disgusting, and pray in *English*," she said with relish.

"Olga," Margit said warningly. "You've never been there. Roland's probably telling fibs to confuse you."

"It's all right," Miriam replied. *What, Margit isn't a world-walker?* she wondered. *Well, that would explain why she's stuck chaperoning Olga around.* "We don't speak, um, what is the language called again?"

"Hoh'sprashe?" said Olga.

"Yes, that's it. And the other side is similar to this side geographically, but the people and how they dress and act and talk are different," she said, trying to think of something it would be safe to talk about.

"I'd heard that," said Olga. She leaned back against her bench, thoughtfully. "You mean they don't know about the Sky Father?"

"Um." Miriam's evident perplexity must have told its own story, because Olga beamed brightly at her.

"Oh, I see! I'll have to tell you all about the Sky Father and the Church!" Olga leaned forward. "You don't believe, do you?" she said very quietly.

Miriam sat up. *Wha-a-at?* she thought, suddenly surprised. "What do you mean?" she asked.

"Sky Father." Olga glanced sideways at Margit, who appeared to be dozing. "*I* don't believe in him," she said, quietly defiant. "I figured that much out when I was twelve. But you mustn't ever—ever—act as if you don't. At least, in public."

"Hmm." Miriam tried to think straight, but her headache was militating against coherency. "What's the problem? Where I come from, I was raised by unobservant Jews—

Jews are, like, a minority religion—but I wasn't Jewish, either, I wasn't their child and it passes down by birth." *Le's
leave what I actually believe out of this or we'll be here a
day.* "Is there . . . what's the Church like? I haven't seen an
sign of it at the duke's palace."

"You didn't see the chapel because he told us you weren't
ready," Olga said quietly, pitching her voice just above the
level of the road noise. "But he told me you'd need to know
before court. So you don't give your enemies anything to use
against you."

"Oh." Miriam looked at Olga with something approach-
ing respect. *The ditz is a self-made atheist? And the families
are religious?* "Yes, I think he was right," she said evenly.
"Just how influential is the Church?" She asked, steeling
herself for bad news.

"Very!" Olga began with forced enthusiasm. "Mass is
held every day, to bring the blessing of Sky Father and
Lightning Child down upon us. They both have their priests,
as does Crone Wife, and the monastic orders, all organized
under the Church of Rome by the Emperor-in-God, who
rules the Church in the name of Sky Father and interprets
Sky Father's wishes. Not that we hear much from Rome—it
has been under the reign of the Great Khan these past decades, and the ocean crossing is perilous and difficult. Next
month is Julfmass, when we celebrate Lightning Child driving out the ice wolf of the north who eats the sun; there'll be
big feasts and public entertainments, that's when betrothals
and further knots in the braids are formally announced! It's
so exciting. They're cemented at Beltaigne, as spring turns
toward summer, right after the Clan meets—"

"Tell me about Julfmass," Miriam suggested. "What happens? What's it supposed to be about, and what do I need to
know?"

Ten miles down the road they were joined by a mounted escort. Rough-looking men on big horses, they wore metal armor over leather. Most of them carried swords and lances,

ut two—Miriam peeped out at the leaders—had discreetly
olstered M-16s, identifying them beyond a shadow of a
oubt as family troopers.

"Halle sum faggon," the sergeant called out, and the coach-
nan replied, "Fallen she in'an seien Sie welcom, mif'nsh."

Miriam shook her head. Riders ahead and riders behind.
They're friendly?" she asked Olga over Margit's open-
nouthed snores.

"Oh yes!" Olga simpered her patented dumb-schoolgirl
imper, and Miriam waited for her to get over it. *She's been
aised wholly apart from men, unless I am very much mis-
aken*, she reasoned. *No wonder she goes strange whenever
inything that needs to shave passes through the area.*
'Your uncle's border guards," she added. "Aren't they hand-
ome?"

"Mmmph." Miriam blinked slowly. *Handsome.* She had a
udden hot flashover to the night before, Roland's hands gen-
ly teasing her legs apart during a long-drawn-out game that
:nded with them both spent, damp, and woozy—then she
ook in Olga's innocent, happy face and felt abruptly down-
nearted, as if she'd stolen a child's toy. *This wasn't part of
'he plan*, she thought dispiritedly. "They're guards," she said
:iredly. "Seen one set of guards, seen 'em all. I just wish I
:ould get at my suitcase." She'd stashed her pistol in it last
night, along with her notebook computer and the rest of her
:scape kit.

"Why is that?" asked Olga.

"Well." Miriam paused. How to put it diplomatically?
"What if they wanted to take advantage of us?" she asked,
fumbling for an alternative to suggesting that Angbard's
guards might not be effective.

"Oh, that's all right," Olga said brightly. She fumbled
with something under her blanket, then showed it to Miriam,
who blinked again, several times.

"Be careful where you wave that," she suggested.

"Oh, I'll be all right! I've been training with guns since I
was *this* high," she said, lowering the machine pistol. "Don't
you do it over there?"

"Ah." Miriam looked at her faintly. "No, but I suppo[se] conditions are different there."

"Oh." Olga looked slightly puzzled. "Aren't you allow[ed] to defend yourselves?"

"We've got this thing called a government," Miriam sa[id] dryly. "It does the defending for us. At least in theory."

"Hah. There was nobody to do that for our grandmoth[er] when the civil war began. Many of them died before . [..] well, even Daddy said I needed to learn to shoot, and he'[s a] terrible backwoodsman! There aren't enough of us with [the] talent, you know, we all have to muck in like common[er] these days. I may even have to join the family *trade* afte[r I] marry, can you believe it?"

"The, ah, thought hadn't occurred to me." Miriam tried [to] sound noncommittal; the idea of Olga running around Ca[m]bridge with a machine pistol, a platinum credit card, and [a] suitcase full of cocaine would have been funny if it had[n't] been so frightening.

"I really hope it happens," Olga said, slightly mo[re] thoughtfully. "I'd like to see . . . over there." She sat up. "B[ut] you asked about bandits! We are unlikely to meet any unle[ss] we travel in the spring thaw. They know too well what w[ill] happen if they try the Clan's post, but after a harsh win[ter] some of them may no longer care."

"I see." Miriam tried not to show any outward sign of b[e]ing disturbed, but for a moment she felt a chill of absolu[te] fear at this naïve, enthusiastic, emotional—but not stupid-child. She shuffled her legs together, trying to pinch out t[he] draft. It would be a long day, without any distractions. "T[ell] me about the Church again . . ."

Two extremely uncomfortable days passed in chilly bor[e]dom. They stopped at a coaching house the first night an[d] Miriam insisted on unloading a suitcase and trunk. The ne[xt] day she scandalized Margit by wearing jeans, fleece, an[d] hiking boots, and Olga by spending the afternoon engrosse[d] n a book. "You'd best not wear that tomorrow," Margit said disapprovingly when they stopped that evening at another post house. "It is for us to make a smart entrance, to pay our respects at court as soon as we arrive, do you see? Did you bring anything suitable?"

"Oh hell," replied Miriam, confusing her somewhat (for Hel was a province administered by Olga's father). "If you could help me find something?"

Expensive western formal costume—Armani suits, Givenchy dresses, and their equivalents—appeared to be de rigueur among the Clan in private. But in public in the Gruinmarkt, they wore the finery of high nobility. Their peculiarities were kept behind closed doors.

The duke's resident seamstress had packed one of Miriam's trunks with gowns fitted to her measurements, and at dawn on the third day Margit shoehorned her into one deemed suitable for a court debut. It was even more elaborate than the gown they'd fitted her for dinner with the duke; it had hooped underskirts, profusions of lace exploding at wrist and throat, and slashed sleeves layered over skin-tight inner layers. Miriam hated everything it said about the status of women in this society. But Olga wore something similar, even more excessively wasp-waisted, with an exaggerated pink bustle behind that suggested to Miriam nothing so much as a female baboon in heat. Margit declared Miriam's presentation satisfactory. "That's most fittingly elegant!" she pronounced. "Let no time be lost, now, lest we be undone by our lateness."

"Mmph," said Miriam, holding her skirts out of the courtyard dampness and trying to avoid tripping over them on her way over to the coach. *Really*, she thought. *This is crazy! I should have just crossed over and caught the train.* But Angbard had insisted—and she could second-guess his reasoning. *'Avoid transport bottlenecks where somebody might intercept her—also, see if she breaks.'* After three days on the road she was feeling ripe, long overdue for a shower. The last thing she needed was a new dress, let alone one as intri-

cately excessive as this. Only a grim determination not
play her hand too early made her put up with it. She settl
into her accustomed corner in a rustling heap of bottle-gre
velvet and tried to get comfortable, but her back was sti
the dress vast and uncontrollable, and parts of her we
sweating while other bits froze. Plus, Olga was looking
her triumphantly.

"You look marvelous," Olga assured her, leaning forwar
and resting a hand in the vicinity of Miriam's knee. "I'
sure you'll make a great entry at court! You'll be surrounde
by suitors before you've been there a moment—despite you
age!"

"I'm sure," Miriam said weakly. *Give me patience,* sh
prayed to the goddess of suffering in the name of beaut
and/or social conformity. *Otherwise I swear I'll strangl
someone . . .*

Before they moved off, Margit insisted on dropping th
blinds. It reduced the draft, but in the closeness of the car
riage Miriam began to feel claustrophobic. Olga insisted or
painting Miriam's cheeks and eyebrows and lips, redoing the
procedure while the carriage swayed and bumped along an
increasingly well-maintained stone-cobbled street. Other
carriages and traffic rattled past, and presently they heard
people calling greetings and warnings. "The gates," Olga
said, breathlessly. "The gates!"

Miriam sneaked a peek through the blinds before Margit
noticed and scolded her. The gate house was made of stone,
perhaps four stories high. She'd seen similar on a vacation in
England many years ago. The walls themselves were of
stone, but banked with masses of rammed earth in front and
huge mounds of mud beyond the ditch. *Isn't that something
to do with artillery?* she thought, puzzled by memories of an
old History Channel documentary.

"Put that down at once, I say!" Margit insisted. "Do you
want *everyone* to see you?"

Miriam dropped the window blind. "Shouldn't they?" she
asked.

"Absolutely not!" Margit looked scandalized. "Why, it would be the talk of society for months!"

"Ah," Miriam said neutrally. Olga *winked* at her. *So this is how it works,* she realized. *Enforcement through peer pressure. If they get the idea that I'm not going to conform, I'm never going to hear the end of it,* she realized. Olga, far from being her biggest problem, was beginning to look like a potential ally.

Their first call was at the Thorold Palace, a huge rambling stone pile at the end of the Avenue of Rome, a broad stone street fronted by mansions. The carriage drew right up to the front entrance, their escort of guards strung out behind it as servants emerged with a mounting box, which they shoved into place before holding the door open. Margit was the first to leave, followed by Olga, who squeezed through the door with a shake of her behind; Miriam emerged last, blinking in the daylight like a prisoner released from some oubliette.

A butler in some sort of intricate house uniform—a tunic over knee breeches and floppy boots—read from a letter in a loud voice to the assembled gaggle of onlookers. "His excellency the high Duke Angbard of house Lofstrom is pleased to consign to your care the Lady Margit, Chatellaine of Praha, her excellency the Baroness Olga Thorold, and her excellency the Countess Helga Thorold Hjorth, daughter of Patricia of that braid." He bowed deeply, then gave way to a man standing behind him. "Your excellency."

"I bid you welcome to the house in my custody, and urge you to accept my hospitality," said the man.

"Earl Oliver Hjorth," Olga stage-whispered at Miriam. Miriam managed a fixed, glassy-eyed smile then followed Olga's lead by picking up her skirts and dipping. "I thank you, my lord," Olga replied loudly and clearly, "and accept your protection."

Miriam echoed him. English, it seemed, was still the general language of nobility here. Her hoh'sprashe was still restricted to a couple of polite nothings.

"Delighted, my beaux," said the earl, not cracking a smile. He was tall and thin, almost cadaverous, his most striking feature a pair of striking black-rimmed spectacles that he wore balanced on the tip of his bony nose; dusty black trousers and a flared red coat worn over a lace-throated shirt completed his outfit. There was something threadbare about him, and Miriam noticed that he didn't wear a sword. "If you will allow Bortis to show you to your rooms, I believe you are expected at court in two hours."

He turned and stalked away grimly, without further comment.

"Why, the effrontery!" Olga gripped Miriam's hand tightly.

"Huh?"

"He's snubbing you," Olga hissed angrily, "and me, to get at you! How peculiarly rude! Oh, come on, let the servant show us to our rooms—and yours. We still need to finish you for the royal court."

An hour later Miriam had two ladies-in-waiting, an acute attack of dizziness, growing concerns about the amenities of this ghastly stone pile—which appeared to lack such essentials as running water and electricity—and a stiff neck from all the necklaces they'd hung on her. The ladies-in-waiting were, like Margit, family members who lacked the fully expressed trait that allowed them to world-walk. The Misses Brilliana of Ost and Kara of Praha—one blonde, the other brunette—looked like meek young things waiting their turn for the marriage market, but after spending a couple of days with Olga, Miriam took that with a pinch of salt. "Were you really raised on the other side?" Kara asked, wide-eyed.

"I was." Miriam nodded. "But I've never been presented at court before."

"We'll see to that," the other one, Brilliana, said confidently. "You look splendid! I'm sure it will all go perfectly."

"When do we need to leave?" asked Miriam.

"Oh, any time, I suppose," Brilliana said carelessly.

The coach was even more claustrophobic with six over-dressed women jammed into it. It jarred and bumped through the streets and Brilliana and Kara made excited small talk with Olga's companions, Sfetlana and Aris. Olga, sandwiched between the two, caught Miriam's eye and winked. Miriam would have shrugged, but she was hemmed in so tightly that she could barely breathe, let alone move. *It's a good thing I'm not claustrophobic*, she thought, mor-dantly trying to find something good about the situation.

After what felt like an hour of juddering progress, the car-riage turned into a long drive. As it drew to a halt, Miriam heard a tinkle of glassware, laughter, strains of string music from outside. Olga twitched. "Hear, violins!" she said.

"Sounds like it to me." The door opened and steps ap-peared, as did two footmen, their gold-encrusted livery as pompous and excessive as the women's dresses. They hov-ered anxiously as the occupants descended.

"Thank you," Miriam commented, surprising the footman who'd offered her his hand. She looked around. They stood before the wide-flung doors of a gigantic palace, a flood of light spilling out through the glass windows onto the lawn. Within, men in coats cut away over ballooning knee breeches mingled with women in elaborate gowns: The room was so huge that the orchestra played from a balcony, above the heads of the court.

Miriam went into a state of acute culture shock almost im-mediately, allowing the Misses Kara and Brilliana to steer her like a galleon under full sail. Someone bellowed out her name—or the parcel of strange titles by which she was known here. She shook herself for a moment when she saw heads turn to stare at her—some inquisitive, some surprised, others supercilious, and some hostile—the names meant nothing to her. All she could think of was trying not to trip over her aching toes and keeping the glassy-eyed shit-eating grin steady on her rouged and strained face. *This isn't me*, she thought vaguely, being presented to a whirl of titled pompous idiots and simpering women swathed in silk and furs. *This is a bad dream*, she repeated to herself. She shied away from the idea that these people were her family, that she might had to spend the rest of her life attending this sort of event.

Miriam had done formal dinners and award ceremonies before, dinner parties and cocktail evenings, but nothing that came close to this. Even though—from Olga's vague but enthusiastic description of the territories—Niejwein was a small kingdom, not much larger than Massachusetts and so dirt-poor that most of the population lived on subsistence farming, its ruling royalty lived in a casual splendor far beyond any ceremonial that the head of a democratic nation would expect. It was an imperial reception, the prototype that the high school prom or its upmarket cousin, the coming-out ball, aped. Someone clapped a glass into her gloved hand—it turned out to be a disgustingly sweet fruit wine—and she politely but firmly turned down so many invitations to dance that she began to lose track. *Please, make it all go away*, she whimpered to herself, as Kara–Brilliana steered her into a queue running along a suspiciously red carpet toward a short guy swathed in a white fur cloak that looked preposterously hot.

"Her excellency Helge Thorold Hjorth, daughter and heir of Patricia of Thorold, returned from exile to pay tribute at the court of his high majesty, Alexis Nicholau III, ruler in the name of the Sky Father, blessed and awful be he, of all of the Gruinmarkt and territories!"

Miriam managed a deep curtsy without falling off her heels, biting her lip to keep from saying anything inappropriate or incriminating.

"Charmed, charmed, I say!" said Alexis Nicholau III, ruler and et cetera of the Gruinmarkt (by willing concession of the Clan). "My dear, reports of your beauty do not do you justice at all! Such elegant deportment! A new face at court, I say, how charming. Remind me to introduce you to my sons later." He swayed slightly on his raised platform, and Miriam spotted the empty glass in his hand. He was a slightly built man with a straggly red beard fringing his chin and hair going prematurely bald on top. He wore no crown, but a chain of office so intimidatingly golden that it looked as if his spine would buckle at any moment. She felt a stab of sympathy for him as she recognized the symptoms of a fellow sufferer.

"I'm delighted to meet you," she told the discreetly drunken monarch with surprising sincerity. Then she felt an equally discreet tug as Kara–Brilliana steered her aside with minute curtsys and simpering expressions of delight at the royal presence.

Miriam took a mouthful from her glass, forced herself to swallow it, then took another. Perhaps the king had the right idea, she thought. Kara–Brilliana drifted to a halt not far from the dais. "Isn't he *cute?*" Kara squealed quietly.

"Who?" Miriam asked distractedly.

"Egon, of course!"

"Egon—" Miriam fumbled for a diplomatic phrasing.

"Oh, that's right. You weren't raised here," said Brilliana, practicality personified. Quietly, in Miriam's ear, she continued, "See the two youngsters behind his majesty? The taller is Egon. He's the first prince, the likely successor should the council of electors renew the dynasty whenever his majesty, long may he live, goes to join his ancestors. The short one with the squint is Creon, the second son. Both are unmarried, and Creon will probably stay that way. If not, pity the maiden."

"Why pity her, if it's not rude to ask?"

"He's addled," Brilliana said matter-of-factly. "Too stupid to—" she noticed Miriam's empty glass and turned to fetch a replacement.

"Something a bit less sweet, please," Miriam implored. The heat was getting to her. "How long must we stay here?" she asked.

"Oh, as long as you want!" Kara said happily. "The revelry continues from dusk till dawn." Brilliana pressed a glass into Miriam's hand. "Isn't it wonderful?" Kara added.

"I think my lady looks a little tired," Brilliana said diplomatically. "She's spent three days on the road, Kara."

Miriam wobbled. Her back was beginning to seize up

again, her kidneys were aching, and in addition her toes felt pinched and she was becoming breathless. "M'exhausted," she whispered. "Need to get some sleep. 'F you take me home, you can come back to enjoy yourselves. Promise. Just don't expect me to stay upright much longer."

"Hmm." Brilliana looked at her speculatively. "Kara, if it pleases you, be so good as to ask someone to summon our coach. I'll help our lady here to make a dignified exit. My lady, there are a few names you must be presented to before taking your leave—to fail would be to give offense—but there'll be another reception the day after tomorrow; there is no need to converse at length with your peers tonight if you are tired. I'm sure we can spend the time between now and then getting to know our new mistress better." She smiled at Miriam. "A last glass of wine, my lady?"

WAIT TRAINING

Light.

Miriam blinked and twitched into vague wakefulness from a dream of painful desire and frustrated eroticism. Someone sighed and moved against her back, and she jerked away, suddenly remembering where she was with a fit of panic: *Wearing a nightdress? In a huge cold bed? What is going on?*

She rolled over and came up against heavy drapes. Turning around, she saw Kara asleep in the huge four-poster bed behind her, face a composed picture of tranquillity. Miriam cringed, racking her brain. *What did I get up to last night?* she wondered, aghast. Then she looked past Kara and saw another sleeping body—and an empty bottle of wine. Opening the curtain and looking on the floor, she saw three glasses and a second bottle, lying on its side, empty. She vaguely remembered talking in the cavernous stone aircraft hangar that passed for a countess's bedroom. It had been freezing cold in the drafty stone pile, and Kara had suggested they continue talking in the four-poster bed, which filled the room like a small pavilion. Miriam looked closer and saw that Kara was still wearing her full underdress. And Brilliana hadn't even removed her stays.

A slumber party, she figured. She hadn't been in one of those since college. *Poor kids. I took them away from their disco and they just couldn't call it a night.* Kara was only seventeen—and Brilliana an old maid of twenty-two. She felt relieved—and a bit sorry for them.

This would never do. She slipped out of the bed and shivered in the freezing cold air. *I'm adrift,* she thought. Turning, she looked back. The bed was as big as her entire room, back home. *I need to get my perspective back.*

Acutely aware of her bare feet on the heat-sucking stone flags, she tiptoed across to the curtain that concealed the door to the toilet. There were no modern conveniences here, just a pot full of dry leaves, and a latrine with a ten-foot drop over the curtain wall. What you saw was what you got—without servants to help. Living conditions in the big city, even for nobility, were distinctly primitive.

After freezing her ass for the minute it took to get rid of last night's wine, Miriam reentered her main chamber and began hunting through the chests that had been deposited there the afternoon before. One of them—*Ah, yes,* she decided. *This'll do.*

She dressed quickly and in silence, pulling on jeans and a sweater and fleece suited to the other side. There was no thought of waking the two ladies-in-waiting, for she couldn't begin to guess how they'd react and she wanted to move fast. Her shoulder bag was packed in the suitcase. It her took a moment to locate it, along with the Sony notebook, the phone, and the GPS compass. She spent a minute scanning the room with the notebook's built-in camera, then she pulled out a paper reporter's pad and wrote a quick note in ballpoint:

My dear K & B,
Gone over to the other side. Back before nightfall.
Please see to storing my articles and arrange a dinner
for the three of us when I get back, two hours after
dark. Best, Miriam

She left it on the pillow next to Kara's head, pulled out her
locket, and crossed over into the doppelgänger building on
the other side.

Miriam's eyes blurred and her headache redoubled as she
looked around. The space corresponding to her room in the
palace or castle or whatever in Neijwein wasn't a palace in
her own world. Two hundred miles southwest of Boston—
New York! she thought with a jolt of excitement. It was dim
in here, very dim, really nothing but emergency lights. There
was a strong smell of sawdust, and it was bitingly cold. She
stood on top of metal scaffolding, with yellow painted lines
on the floor. *That'll be the layout of the castle back in the
other world,* she realized. *I'd better get out of here before
someone notices me.*

She switched on the GPS compass, waited for it to come
up, then told it to memorize her location. Then she went
down the metal stairs two at a time. She was on the ground
floor of an elderly warehouse. Wooden crates stood between
yellow alleyways—evidently blocking out the walls of the
castle. She headed toward the grand staircase and the main
entrance hall, found it open and a trailer sitting on some concrete blocks installed as a site office. The yellow light was
coming from the trailer windows.

Hmm. Miriam put her hand in her jacket pocket and took
a grip on her pistol. Her head was pounding, as cold air hit
hangover-inflamed sinuses. *I need to dry out for a couple of
days,* she thought abstractedly. Then she knocked on the
door with her left hand.

"Who's there?"

The door swung open and an old man grimaced at her.

"I'm Miriam. From the Cambridge office," she said. "I'l be going in and out of here over the next few days. Inspecting things."

"Marian something?" He blinked, looking annoyed.

"No, Miriam," she said patiently. "Do you have a list of people who're allowed in and out here?"

"Oh, yeah," he said vacantly. He shuffled inside and surfaced with a dirty clipboard. The cabin smelled of stale smoke and boiled cabbage. "Miriam Beckstein," she said patiently and spelled her name. "From Cambridge, Mass."

"Your name isn't down here." He looked puzzled.

"I work for Angbard Lofstrom," she said curtly.

Evidently this was the right thing to say because he jolted upright. "Yes, ma'am! That's fine, everything's fine. How do you spell your name?"

Miriam told him. "Where are we on the street map, and what's the protocol for getting in and out of here?" she asked.

"'Protocol'?" He looked puzzled. "Just come in and knock. This is just a lockup. Nothing important here. Nothing worth stealing, leastways."

"Okay." She nodded, turned, and walked toward the front door and freedom. As she did so, her phone beeped three times, acquiring coverage and notifying her that she had messages.

Once outside, she found herself in a dingy alleyway hemmed in by fire escapes. She walked to the end, then looked around. It was most peculiar, she thought. Security on the warehouse wasn't what she'd have expected, not at all. It was too easy to get in or out. Was she stuck in some kind of low-security zone? She came to a main road, with light traffic and shops on either side. Making a note of the street name, she waved down the first yellow cab to come past.

"Where to?" asked the driver, in an almost-comprehensible accent.

"Penn Station," she said, hoping that he'd been on the job

long enough to have a clue where he was. He seemed to be okay: He nodded a couple of times, then swung his car through a circle and hit the gas.

Miriam lay back and watched the real world go by in a happy daze only slightly tempered by her throbbing head. *Wow, I'm really here!* she thought, feeling the gentle sway of pneumatic tires on asphalt and the warm breeze from the heater on her feet. *Isn't it great?* She wanted the cab ride to last forever, she realized, with a warm glow of nostalgia. Lights and familiar advertisements and people who didn't look like extras from an historical movie flowed past to either side of her heated cocoon. This was her world, a homely urban reality where real people wore comfortable clothes, made thoughtless use of conveniences like electricity and tap water, and didn't weave lethal dynastic games around the future lives of children she didn't want to have.

Wait till I tell Ma, she thought. *Then Paulie.* Followed moments later by: *Damn, first I have to figure out what I can tell them.* Then: *Hey, at least I can talk to Roland . . .*

She looked at her phone. YOU HAVE VOICE MAIL, it said, so she dialed her mailbox.

"Miriam?" His voice was distant and scratchy and her heart skipped a beat. "I hope you get this message. Listen, I come across on a courier run every two days, between ten and four. I think your uncle may suspect something, he's put Matthias on me as an escort. Last night he sent news that you'd arrived at the capital. How are you enjoying life there? Oh, by the way, don't trust anyone called Hjorth; they've got a lot to lose. And watch out for Prince Egon: He's been known to not take no for an answer. Call me when you get a chance."

Her vision had misted at the sound of his voice. *Damn, I didn't plan this.* The taxi drifted in stop-and-go traffic, the driver thumping the steering column in tune with the radio.

At the station Miriam's first act was to hunt down an ATM and try her card. It worked. She pulled out five hundred dollars in crisp green notes and stuffed them in her pocket. *That shouldn't tell them much beyond where I was,* she decided.

Then she hit the ticket desk for a return ticket to Boston on the next Accela service. It took a wad, but once she found the train and settled into the seat, she was pleased with herself for spending it. It would take only three hours, meaning she'd have maybe four hours in Boston before she'd have to go back again.

Miriam settled back in her seat, notebook computer opened in front of her and phone beside it. *Do I have to go back there?* she asked herself morosely. She'd just spent a week on the other side—and that week had been enough to last her a lifetime. She felt the stiff edges of the platinum credit card digging into her conscience. It was blood money, and their damn blood-is-thicker-than-water creed would drag her back—every time. *It didn't drag my birth-mother back,* she thought. *It killed her instead.* Which was even worse, and likelier than not what would happen to her if she ran now—because if she ran, they'd know she was untrustworthy. She wouldn't get another chance. Darker possibilities occurred to her. Even if they didn't want to kill her and reduce their precious gene pool, they could immobilize her permanently by blinding her. She doubted it was a common tactic—even given the Clan's ruthlessness, it would rapidly provoke fear and loathing, a catalyst for conflict—but they might use it as a special measure if they suspected treason, and the possibility filled her with horror.

On the other hand, the thought of voluntarily going back to the drafty castle and the insane family politics was depressing. So she picked up the phone and dialed Roland's number instead.

"Hello?" He answered on the first ring and she cheered up instantly.

"It's me," she said quietly. "Can you talk?"

"Yes." A pause. "He's not around right now, but he's never far away."

"Are they still watching my house?" she asked.

"Yeah, I think so. Where are you?"

"On a train halfway between New York and Boston."

"Don't tell me you're running—"

"No," she said too hastily, "but I've got unfinished business. Not just you—other stuff too. I want to see my mother, and I want to see some other people. Okay? Better not ask too many questions. I'm not going to do anything rash, but I have a feeling I don't want to draw any attention to people I know. But look, are you able to get away for a day? Say, to New York?"

"They've got you in that stone pile?" he asked.

"Yeah. Do you know what it's like?"

"You survived three days with Olga?" His tone was one of hopeful disbelief.

"The facilities are, uh, open plan, and I get to sit cheek by jowl with two of Olga's less enlightened coworkers," she said, eyes swiveling to track down the nearest passengers. She was clear—nobody within two seats of her. Quietly she added, "The ladies-in-waiting are like jail guards, only prettier, if you follow me. They stick like glue. I woke up and they were in my goddamn *bed* with me. You'd think Angbard had set them on me as minders. Honestly, I'm at my wit's end. I'm going to go back this evening, but if you don't come and rescue me soon, I swear I'll kill someone. And I *still* haven't filed copy on that dot-com busted flush feature I'm supposed to be writing for Andy."

"My poor sweetheart." He laughed, a little sadly. "You're not having a good time. Maybe we should form a club?"

"Culture-shocked and brain-damaged?"

"That's right." A pause. "Going back after eight years away, that was the hardest thing. Miriam. You *will* go back to them?"

"Yes," she said quietly. "If I don't, I'll never see you again, will I?"

"Not today. I'll be over again the day after tomorrow," he said. "New York, is it?"

"Yes." She thought for a moment. "Rent a double room at the Marriott Marquis in Times Square. It's anonymous and bland, but I think you've got more travel time than I have. Leave voice mail with the room number and the name you're using and I'll show up as early as possible." She shivered at the thought, shuffling uncomfortably in her seat.

"I'll be there. Promise."

"Bring a couple of new prepaid phones, bought for cas as anonymous as you can. We'll need them. I miss you," sh added very quietly and hung up.

Forty-eight hours to go. It had already been four day since she'd last seen him.

The conductor came around, and she glanced aroun again to confirm how much space she had. The carriage wa half-empty, she'd missed the rush hour crush. Now she di aled another number, one she'd committed to memory be cause she was afraid to program it into the phone.

"Hi, you've reached the answering machine of Paulette Milan. I'm sorry I can't come to the phone right now, but—'

"Paulie, cut the crap and pick up the phone *right now*."

The line clicked. "Miriam! What the fuck are you playing at, sweetie?"

" 'Playing at'? What do you mean?"

"Skipping out like that! Jesus, I've been so worried!"

"You think *you've* been worried? You haven't phoned my house, have you?" Miriam interrupted hastily.

"Oh yeah, but when you didn't answer I left a message about the bridge club. Something I made up on the spur of the moment. I've been so worried—"

"Paulie, you didn't mention the other stuff, did you? Or go around in person?"

"I'm not stupid," Paulette said quietly, all ebullience gone.

"Good—uh, I'm sorry. Let me try again." Miriam closed her eyes. "Hi, I'm Miriam Beckstein, and I have just discovered the hard way that my long-lost family have got very long memories and longer arms, and they invited me to spend some time with them. It turns out that they're in the import/export trade, and they're so big that the story we were working on probably covers some of their turf. Hopefully they don't think you're anything other than a ditzy broad who plays bridge with me, because if they did you might not enjoy their company. *Capisce?*"

"Oh, oh shit! Miriam, I am so sorry! Listen, are you all right?"

"Yeah. Not only am I all right, I'm on a train that gets into Back Bay Station in—" she checked her watch— "about an hour and a half. I don't have long, this is a day trip, and I have to be on the four o'clock return train. But if you can meet me at the station I'll drag you out to lunch and fill you in on everything, and I mean *everything*. Okay?"

"Okay." Paulette sounded a little less upset. "Miriam?"

"Yes?"

"What are they like? What are they *doing* to you?"

Miriam closed her eyes. "Did you ever see the movie *Married to the Mob*?"

"No way! What about your locket? You mean they're—"

"Lets just say, it would be a bad idea for you to phone my house, visit it in person, talk to or visit my mother, or do *anything* that is in any way out of character for a dumb out-of-work research geek who vaguely knows me from work. At least, where they can see you. Which is why I'm phoning on a number you've never seen and probably won't ever see again. Meet me at noon inside the station, near the south entrance?"

"Okay, I'll be there. Better have a good story!"

Paulette hung up, and Miriam settled back to watch the countryside roll by.

When she hit the station, Miriam immediately left it. There was an ATM in the mall across the street, and she pulled another two thousand in cash out of it. There seemed to be no end to the amount she could draw, as long as she didn't mind leaving an audit trail. This time she wanted to. Putting a time stamp on Boston would tell Duke Angbard where she'd been. She planned on telling him first. Let him think she was being open and truthful about everything.

She headed back into the station in the same state she'd been in in the taxi. This was home, a place she'd been before, intimately familiar at the same time that it was anonymous and impersonal. She was shaken by how relieved she was to be back. Suddenly being jobless in a recession with her former employer threatening to blacken her name didn't

seem so bad, all things considered. She almost walked righ
past Paulette, as unnoticed as any other commuter in a rain
coat, but she swerved at the last moment, blinking the daz
away.

"Paulie!"

"Miriam!" Paulette grabbed her in a hug, then held her a
arm's length, inspecting her face anxiously. "You look thin
ner. Was it bad, babe?"

"Was it *bad*?" Miriam shook her head, unsure where to
begin. "Jesus, it was *weird*, and bits of it were very bad and
bits of it were, um, less bad. Not bad at all. But it's not over.
Listen, let's go find something to eat—I haven't had any
breakfast—and I'll tell you all about it."

They found a booth in a not unbearable pizza joint in the
mall, where the background noise loaned them a veneer of
privacy, and Miriam wolfed down a weird Californian pizza
with a topping of chicken tikka on a honeyed sourdough
base. Between bites, she gave Paulette a brief run-down.
"They kidnapped me right out of my house after you left, a
whole damn SWAT team. But then they put me up in this
stately house, a palace really, and introduced me to a real
honest-to-god duke. You know the medieval shit I came back
with? It's real. What I didn't figure on was that my family,
my real family, I mean, are, like, the aristocracy who run it."

"They rule it." Paulette's fork paused halfway to her
mouth. "You're not shitting me. I mean, they're kings and
stuff?"

"No, they're just an extended trading Clan that happens to
be an umbrella for about a third of the nobility that runs the
eastern seaboard—the *nouveau riche* crowd, not long established and deeply paranoid. They're like the Medicis. There
are several countries over there, squabbling feudal kingdoms.
The one hereabouts is called the Gruinmarkt, and they don't
speak English—or rather, the ruling class do, the way the nobles in England spoke French during the middle ages. But
anyway. The high king rules the Gruinmarkt, but the Clan—
the Clan of the families who can walk between worlds—they

own everything. I mean, the king wants to marry one of his sons *into* the Clan to tighten his grip on power."

Miriam paused to finish her pizza, aware that Paulette was staring at her thoughtfully.

"Where do *you* fit in all this?" she asked.

"Oh." Miriam put her fork down. "I'm the long-lost daughter of a noblewoman whose coach was ambushed by bandits. Or assassins—there was a war on at the time, between branches of the Clan. She escaped, ran away to our world, but died before she could get help." Miriam looked Paulette in the eye. "When you were a kid, did you ever fantasize about maybe you were switched with another baby in the hospital, and your real parents were rich and powerful, or something?"

"Why?" Paulette asked brightly. "Isn't that every little girl's daydream? Didn't Mattel build a whole multinational on top of it?"

"Well, when you're thirty-two and divorced and have a life, and long-lost relatives from your newly discovered family show up and tell you that actually you're a countess, it might put a bit of a different spin on things, huh?"

Paulette looked slightly puzzled. "How do you mean—"

"Like, they insist that you marry someone suitable, because they can't have independent women running around. You've got a choice between living in a drafty castle with no electricity and running water, oh, and having lots of children by the husband they've chosen for you, a choice between that and, well, there is no choice marked 'B.' Resistance is futile; you will be assimilated. Got it, already?"

"Oh sweet Jesus. No wonder you look fried!" Paulette shook her head slowly.

"Yeah, well, I was afraid I was going to go crazy if I didn't get away after the last week. What makes it really bad is that, well . . ." Miriam chewed her lower lip for a while before continuing. "Your guesses about where they could make money were right on the nail. I don't know if they're into Proteome Dynamics and Biphase Technologies, but they're sure into everything else under the sun. They gave me a debit card and said, 'Here's a two-million-dollar credit limit try not to overload it.' There is no way in *hell* that they wil let me walk away from them. And the thing that frightens me most is that I'm not, like, one hundred percent sure I entirely *want* to."

Paulie was studying her intently. "Is there something else?" she asked.

"Oh yes, oh yes." Miriam fell silent. "But I don't want to talk about him just now."

"Is he bad? Did he—"

"I *said* I didn't want to talk about it!" she snapped. A moment later, she added, "I'm sorry. No, he isn't bad. You know, it's just you've never been able to resist ragging me about men, and I don't need that right now. It's messy, very messy, and things are bad enough without adding that kind of complication."

"Lovely." Paulette pulled a face. "Okay, so I won't ask you about your mystery boyfriend. Let me see if I've got this straight? It turns out your family think you're a little lost heiress. They want to treat you like one, which is to say, not a hell of a lot like the way it works out in the fairy tales. You'd maybe tell them to screw off, but first they won't, and second they've got lots of money. Third, you've met a man who didn't want to strangle you after five minutes—"

"—*Paulie*—"

"—*sorry,* and he's mixed up in all of it. Is that a fair summary?"

"Pretty much." Miriam waved for the check. "Which is why I had to get away from it all for the day. I'm not a, a prisoner. I'm just considered valuable. Or something." She frowned. "It's absolutely crazy. Even their business operations! It's like something out of the middle ages. They're about three centuries overdue for modernization, and I'm not just talking about the cultural crap. Pure zero-sum mercantilism, red in tooth and nail, in an environment where they have barely invented banking, never mind the limited liability company. Deeply fucking primitive, not to say wasteful of resources, but

hey're set in their ways. I've seen companies like that before;
ooner or later someone else comes along and eats their lunch.
There ought to be something smarter they could be doing, if
only I could think of it . . ."

"O-k-a-y. You do that, Miriam."

The bill arrived and Miriam stuck down a fifty before
Paulette could protest. "Come on." She stood up; Paulette
hurried after.

"Did I just *see* that? Did I? Miriam Beckstein putting
down a thirty percent tip? What the hell is happening to my
eyes?"

"I want out of this restaurant," Miriam said flatly. Continuing on the hoof: "Money doesn't mean anything any more,
Paulie, didn't you catch that bit? I'm so rich I could buy *The
Weatherman* if I wanted to—only it won't do me a blind bit
of good because my problems aren't money-related. There
are factions among the families. One of them wants me
dead. They had a nice little number going with my mother's
shareholding in the Clan; now that I've shown up, I've disrupt a load of plans. Another faction wants me married off.
The king, his number-two prince is a retard, Paulie, and you
know what? I think my old goat of an uncle is going to try to
marry me off to him."

"Oh, you poor baby. Don't they have an equal rights
amendment?"

"Oh, poor-baby me, these guys don't even have a *consti-
tution*," Miriam said with feeling. "It's a whole other world,
and women like me get the . . . get the—hell, think about the
Arabs. The Saudi royal family. They come over here in expensive suits and limousines and buy big properties and lots
of toys, but they don't think like us, and when they go back
home they go straight back to the middle ages. How would
you feel if you woke up one morning and discovered you
were a Saudi princess?"

"Not very likely," Paulette pointed out, "seeing as how I
am half-Italian and half-Armenian and one hundred percent
peasant stock, and damn happy to live here in the U.S. of A.,
where even peasants are middle class and get to be para-

legals and managers. But yeah, I think I see where you coming from." Paulette looked at her grimly. "You got pro lems," she said. "I'd worry about the bunch who want ye out of the way before worrying about the risk of being ma ried off to Prince Charming, though. At least they've g money." She pulled a face. "If *I* found I had a long-lost fan ily, knowing my luck, the first thing they'd do is ask to bo row a hundred bucks until payday. *Then* they'd start with th death threats."

"Well, you might want to think back to what you sai about smuggling," Miriam pointed out. "I don't want to b involved in that shit. And I'm worried as hell about the strin we were pulling on the other week. Have you had any othe incidents?"

" 'Incidents'?" Paulie looked angry. "I don't know i you'd call it that. Somebody burgled my apartment the da before yesterday."

"Oh shit." Miriam stopped dead. "I'm so sorry. Was it bad?"

"It could have been," Paulette said tightly. "I was out a the time. The sergeant said it looked very professional. They cut the phone line and drilled the lock out on the landing, then went in and turned the whole place over. Took my com- puter and every disk they could find. Ransacked the book- cases, went through my underwear—and left my spare credit card and emergency bankroll alone. They weren't after money, Miriam. What do *you* think?"

"What do *I* think?" Miriam stopped in the middle of the sidewalk. Paulette waited for her. "Well, you're still alive," she said slowly.

"Alive—" Paulette stared at her.

"Paulie, these guys play hardball. They leave booby traps. You go into a place they've black-bagged and you open the door and it blows up in your face—or there's a guy waiting for you with a gun and he can leave the scene just by looking at a wrist tattoo. I figure either I'm wrong and the shit Joe Dixon's involved in isn't to do with the Clan or they don't rate you as a threat—just sent some hired muscle to frighten you, rather than the real thing."

"I am *so* relieved. Not."

"Do be. I mean that seriously. If you're still alive, it means they don't think you're a threat. They didn't find the disk, so that's probably an end of it. If you want to get the hell out of this now, just say. I'll find the CD and burn it and you're out of the frame."

Paulette began walking again. "Don't tempt me," she said tightly. Then she stopped and turned to face Miriam. "What are *you* going to do?" she asked bluntly.

"I was hoping you could help me." Miriam paused for a moment, then continued: "Did you get the job?"

"As a paralegal?" Paulette shrugged. "I didn't get that one, but I've got another interview this afternoon," she added self-consciously.

"Well." Miriam paused. "How would you like another job? Starting today?"

"Doing what?" Paulette asked cautiously.

"As my self-propelled totally legal insurance policy," said Miriam. "I need an agent, someone who can work for me on this side when I'm locked up being Princess Buttercup in a palace with toilets consisting of a drafty hole in the wall. You're clean, they didn't pin anything on you, and now that we know who the hell we're up against, we can make sure that you stay that way. What I've got in mind for the job will mostly involve handling nonstolen, nonillegal goods that I want to sell, keeping records, paying taxes, and making like a legitimate import/export business. But it'll also involve planting some records, very *explicit* records, in places where the families can't get their hands on them—without getting caught." Miriam stopped again, thinking. "I can pay," she added. "I'm supposed to be very rich now."

Paulette grinned. "This wouldn't have something to do with you bearing a grudge against the asshole who fired us both, would it?"

"Could be." Miriam thrust her hands deep in her pockets and tried to look innocent.

"When does it start and what does it pay?"

"It starts fifteen minutes ago, and if you want to discuss

pay and conditions, let's go find a Starbucks and talk about
over a coffee . . ."

Miriam became increasingly depressed on the train back
New York. It was late in the year, and darkness was alread
falling as the train raced through the bleak New Englan
countryside. Soon the snow would be falling thick and deep
burying the bare branches beneath a layer of deadenin
numbness. She popped out one of the Atenolol tablets tha
Roland had given her and a couple of Tylenol, swallowin
them with the aid of a Coke from the bar. She felt like au
tumn, too: The train was carrying her south toward a bleal
world where she'd be enveloped in the snow of—well
maybe it was stretching the metaphor past breaking point
Only forty-four hours, and I'll be seeing Roland again, she
thought. Forty-four hours? She brightened for a moment
then lapsed into even deeper gloom. Forty-four hours, forty
of which would be spent in the company of . . . of . . .

She hailed a taxi from the station concourse, feeling
slightly light-headed and numb, as if she hadn't eaten. It
took her to the block near Chinatown where she'd found the
door. It looked a whole hell of a lot less welcoming after
dark and closing time, and she hunched her shoulders as she
stalked down the street, homing in on the alleyway by means
of the green-lit display of her GPS compass.

When she reached the alley, she balked—it was black and
threatening, like a Central Station for muggers and rapists.
But then, remembering who and what she was, she reached
into her pocket and wrapped her right hand around the snub-
nosed pistol she'd carried all day. *They can arrest you, but
they can't hold you,* she reminded herself with a flicker of
reckless glee. What must it be like to grow up with the talent
on the other side, then to come over to this world and realize
that you could do absolutely anything at all and melt away
into the night, undetected? She shivered.

As it happened the alleyway was empty, a faint glow leaking from under the warehouse doorway. She opened it and

walked past the cabin. Nobody hailed her. She followed the GPS compass until its coordinates went to zero and she saw the metal emergency staircase.

At the top of the steps she took a moment to look around. There was no sign of any burglar alarms, nothing to stop anyone coming in off the street. *Hmm. I don't like the look of this,* she thought. Thirty feet farther on there was a sturdy brick wall. *I can't be sure, but it looks like most of the palace would be on the other side of that. Right?* It was weird, but she didn't have time to examine it right now. Putting her GPS compass away, she hauled out the locket from the chair around her neck that she wore under her sweater. She focused on the image and felt—

"Mistress! Oh my—" she stumbled, black shadows pulling at the edges of her vision, and felt hands on her day pack, her shoulders, pulling her toward a richly cushioned ottoman— "you startled us! What *is* that you're wearing? Oh, you're so cold!"

The black shadows began to fade, and she had a feeling like a headache starting a long way away. The huge fireplace in one side of the main room—a fireplace big enough to park her car in—was blazing with flames and light, pumping out heat. Kara helped her stand upright, a hand under one shoulder. "You gave us such a fright!" she scolded.

"I'm back now." Miriam smiled tiredly. "Is there anything to drink? Without alcohol in it?"

"I'll get it," said Brilliana, the more practical of the two. "Would my lady care for a pot of tea?"

"That would be fine." Miriam felt herself closer to fainting than throwing up. *Yes, the beta-blockers seem to work,* she thought. "Drop the 'my lady'—just call me Miriam. You didn't tell anybody to search for me, did you?"

"No, my-Miriam." This from Kara. "I wanted to, but—"

"It's all right." Miriam closed her eyes, then opened them again, to be confronted by a teenager with braided brown hair and a worried expression wearing a brown Dior suit and a blouse the color of old amber. "Nothing to worry about," she said, trying to exude confidence. "I'll be fine when I've had some tea. This always happens. Did anything unusua happen while I was gone?"

"We've been busy making the servants unpack you wardrobe and traveling possessions!" Kara said enthusiasti cally. "And Lady Olga sent you an invitation to walk with her in the orangery, tomorrow morning! Nobody is enter taining tonight, but there's another public reception in Prince Creon's name tomorrow and you have been invited!" Miriam nodded wearily, wishing she wouldn't end every sentence with an exclamation. She half-expected Kara to break out in squeals of excitement. "And Sfetlana has been so excited!"

"About what?" Miriam asked unenthusiastically.

"She's had a proposal of marriage! Delivered by proxy, of course! Lady Olga bore it! Isn't that exciting?"

"What *is* that you're wearing?" asked Brilliana, returning from the fireplace with a silver teapot held carefully in her hands; for the first time Miriam noticed the spindly table beside the ottoman, the chairs positioned around it, the cups and saucers of expensive china. It appeared that ladies-in-waiting led a higher-maintenance lifestyle than servants.

"Something suited to the weather," Miriam muttered. Brilliana was wearing a black dress that would have passed unnoticed at any cocktail party from the 1960s through the 1990s. In the setting of a cold, sparsely furnished castle, there was something unbelievably surreal about it. "Listen, that's a fire and a half." Her skin crawled. "Is there any chance of using it to heat a *lot* of water? Like, enough for a bath? I want to get clean, then find something to eat." She thought for a moment. "Afterward you can choose something for me to wear tomorrow when I go to talk with Lady Olga. And for the reception in the evening as well, I suppose. But right now, I'd kill for a chance to wash my hair."

FIRE WALL

I t turned out that there was a bathtub in her suite. The huge claw-footed cast-iron behemoth lived in a room she hadn't seen before, on the far side of the huge fireplace. There were even servants to fill it: three maids and a grumpy squint-eyed lad who seemed to have only half his wits about him. His job seemed to be to lurk in corners whenever anybody forgot to send him packing for another load of Pennsylvania coal.

Readying the bath involved a lot of running around and boiling coppers on the fireplace. While everybody else was occupied, Miriam pulled on her overcoat and went exploring, picking up Brilliana as a combination of tour guide and chaperone. She'd been half-asleep from exhaustion when she first arrived—and even more dead to the world after the reception at the palace. Only now was she able to take in her surroundings fully. She didn't much like what she was seeing.

"This palace," she said, "tell me about it."

"This wing? This is the New Tower." Brilliana followed a

pace behind her. "It's only two hundred and eighty years old."

Miriam looked up at the roof of the reception room they'd walked into. The plasterwork formed a dizzyingly intricate layering of scalloped borders and sculpted bouquets of fruit and flowers, leaping over hidden beams and twisting playfully around the huge hook from which a giant chandelier hung. The doors and window casements were not built to a human scale, and the benches positioned against each wall looked lost and lonely.

"Who does it belong to?" asked Miriam.

"Why, the Clan." Brilliana looked at her oddly. "Oh, that's right." She nodded. "The families and the braids. You understand them?"

"Not entirely," Miriam admitted.

"Hmm, I had thought as much." Brilliana paced toward the far door, then paused. "Have you seen the morning room yet?"

"No." Miriam followed her.

"Our ancestor Angbard the Sly walked the worlds and accrued a huge fortune. His children lacked the ability, and there were five sons, sons who married and had families, and another six daughters. In that generation some kin married their cousins directly, as was done in those days to forestall dower loss, and the talent was rediscovered. Which was a good thing, because they had fallen upon hard times and were reduced to common merchants. Since then we have kept the bloodline alive by marrying first cousins across alternate generations: Three families are tied together in a braid, two in each generation, to ensure the alliances are kept close. The kin with the talent are shareholders in the Clan, to which all belong. Those who lack the talent but whose children or grandchildren might have it are also members, but without the shares." She waited at the door for Miriam, then lifted the heavy bolt with two hands and pulled it open.

"That's amazing," Miriam said, peering into the vast gloomy recess.

"It is, isn't it?" replied Brilliana, squeezing through the

half-open doorway as Miriam held it open for her. Miriam followed. "These murals were painted by The Eye himself, it is said." Miriam blinked at dusty splendor, a red wool carpet and walls forming scenes disturbingly similar to—and yet different from—the traditional devotional paintings of the great houses of Europe. (Here a one-eyed god hung from a tree, his hands outstretched to give the benefit of his wisdom to the kneeling child-kings of Rome. There a prophet posed before a cave mouth within which lurked something unspeakable.) "The palace is held by the Clan in common trust. It is used by those family members who do not have houses in the capital. Each family owns one fifth of it—one tower— and Baron Oliver Hjorth occupies the High Tower, presiding over all, responsible for maintainance. I think he's angry because the High Tower was burned to a shell eight years ago, and the cost of rebuilding it has proven ruinous," she added thoughtfully.

"Very interesting," murmured Miriam. Thinking: *Yes, it's about fifty feet long*. This part of the palace was clearly doppelgängered, if the wall she'd seen in the warehouse was where she thought it was. Which meant that her own corner was far less secure than Angbard had implied. "Why was I accommodated here?"

"Why, because Baron Oliver refused you as a guest!" Brilliana said, a tight little smile on her face. Miriam puzzled for a moment, then recognized it as the nearest thing to anger she'd seen from the girl. "It is unconscionable of him, vindictive!"

"I'm getting used to it," Miriam said dryly. She looked around the huge, dusty audience chamber then shivered from the chill leaching through its stones. The shutters were closed and oil lamps burned dimly in the chandelier, but despite all that it was as cold as a refrigerator. "What does he have against me, again?"

"Your braid. Your mother married his elder brother. You should inherit the Thorold Hjorth shares. You should, in fact, inherit the tower he has spent so long restoring. Duke Angbard has made it a personal project to bring Oliver to his knees for many years, and perhaps he thinks to use you to provoke the baron into an unforgivable display of disloyalty."

"Oh shi—" Miriam turned to face the younger woman. "And *you?*" she demanded.

"Me?" Brilliana raised a slim hand to cover her mouth, as if concealing a laugh. "I'm in disgrace, most recently for calling Padrig, Baron Oliver's youngest, a pimple-faced toad!" She shrugged uncomfortably. "My mother sent me away, first to the duke, then to the baron's table, thinking his would be a good household for a young maid to grow up in." For a moment, a flicker of nearly revealed anger lit up her face like lightning. "Hoping he'd take a horsewhip to me, more like."

"Aha." Miriam nodded. "And so, when I arrived . . ."

"You're a *countess!*" Brilliana insisted. "Traveling without companions! It's a joke, a position of contempt! Ser Hjorth sent me to dwell with you in this drafty decaying pile with a leaking roof—as a punishment to me and an insult to you. He thinks himself a most funny man, to lay the glove against a cheek that does not even understand the intent behind the insult."

"Let's carry on." Miriam surprised herself by reaching out and taking Brilliana's arm, but the younger woman merely smiled and walked by her side as she headed toward a small undecorated side door. "What did you do to offend the Baron?"

"I wanted to go across to the other side," Brilliana said matter-of-factly. "I've seen the education and polish and the source of everything bright in the world. I know I have not the talent myself, but surely someone can take me there? Is that too much to ask? I've a mother who saw miracles in her youth: carriages that fly and ships that sail against the wind, roads as wide as the Royal Mile and as long as a country, cabinets that show you events from afar. Why should I not have this, but for an accident of birth?" The anger was running close to the surface, and Miriam could feel it through her arm.

She paused next to the small door and looked Brilliana in

the eye. "Believe me, if I could gift you with my talent I would, and thank you for taking it from me," she said.

"Oh! But that's not what I meant—" Brilliana's cheeks colored.

Miriam smiled crookedly. "Did your mother by any chance send you away because you pestered her to take you over to the other side one time too often? And did Oliver banish you here for the same reason?"

"Yes," Brilliana nodded reluctantly. "A lady is someone who never knowingly causes pain to others," she said quietly. "But what about causing pain to one's self?"

"I think—" Miriam looked at her, as if for the first time: twenty-two years old, skin like milk and blonde hair, blue eyes, a puzzled, slightly angry expression, a couple of small craterlike scars marring the line of her otherwise perfect jaw. Wearing a slim black dress and a scarf around her hair, a silver necklace set with pearls around her neck, she looked too—*tense* was the word Miriam was looking for—to fit in here. But give her a jacket and briefcase and nobody would look twice at her in a busy downtown rush hour. "I think you have too low an opinion of yourself, Brill," she said slowly. "What's through this door, do you know?"

"It'll be the way up to the roof." She frowned, puzzled. "Locked, of course."

"Of course." This door had a more modern keyhole and lock. But when Miriam twisted the handle and tugged, it opened, admitting a frigid blast of damp air. "I think you're right about it leading to the roof," Miriam added, "but I'd like to know just where the unlocked doors lead, do you follow me?"

"Brr." Brilliana shivered. She really wasn't dressed for this, Miriam noted.

"Wait here," Miriam instructed. Without pause she entered the doorway. Stone steps spiraled tightly up into blackness. She ascended, guided by touch as much as by vision. *This must be higher than the doppelgänger warehouse's roof*, she guessed. Cold wind smacked her in the face at the top. She turned and looked out across the steeply pitched roof, past machicolations, across gardens spread far below. And then the town, narrow streets and pitched roofs utterly unlike anything she'd see back home stretching away on all sides, dimly lit by lamplight. *What do they burn?* she wondered. Above the entire scene, riding high atop a tattered carpet of fast-moving white clouds, hung the gibbous moon. *Someone has been up here recently*, she thought and shivered. It was freezing cold, wet, and dark. Clambering about on the roof held no appeal, so she turned and carefully descended back into the relative warmth of the moth-eaten outer reception room.

Brilliana jumped as she emerged. "Oh! By my soul, you gave me a fright, my lady. I was so worried for you!"

"I think I gave me a fright too," Miriam commented shakily. She shut the door. "We're going back to the heated quarters now," she said. "And we're going to bolt the door—on the inside. Come on. I wonder if that bath will be ready."

The bath was indeed ready, although Miriam had to ransack her luggage for toiletries and chase two ladies-in-waiting and three servants out of the room before she could strip off and get in the tub. In any event, it grew cold too fast for her to soak in it for long. Baths hereabouts were a major chore, it seemed, and if she didn't get across to the other side regularly, she'd have to get used to making it a weekly event. At least she didn't have to put up with the local substitute for soap, which was ghastly beyond belief.

Drying herself with her feet up against the back side of the fireplace—which for a miracle had warmed right through the stonework—she reflected on the progress she'd made. *Brilliana is going to be okay*, she mused. *Maybe I could give her to Paulie as a gofer?* If she survived the culture shock. *It's no joke*, she chided herself. She'd grown up with museums and films about the past—how much harder would she have it if she'd found herself catapulted into the equivalent of the twenty-sixth century, without any means of going home? She'd be helpless. Had Brilliana ever seen a light switch? Or a telephone? Perhaps—and then again, perhaps not. *I keep forgetting that clothes* don't *make the man— or woman,* she prodded herself. *You could go really badly wrong if you make that mistake here.*

She pulled on her jeans and sweater again, frowning— *Should have asked Kara to get something out for me*—then went back into the main room. The servants had pulled out a small dining table from somewhere, and it was set with silverware and a huge candelabra. "Wonderful!" she said. Kara and Brill were standing beside it, and Kara grinned uncontrollably. "Okay, sit down. Did anyone order any wine?"

Brill had, and the food, which she'd ordered up from the cavernous kitchens far below, was still edible. By the time they'd drained two bottles of a most passable red, Miriam was feeling distinctly tired and even Kara had lost her tendency to squeal, bounce, and end every sentence on an exclamation point. "Bedtime, I think," she said, pointedly dismissing everyone from her chamber before pulling back the curtain on her bed, pulling out the warming pan, and burrowing inside.

The next morning Miriam awakened rapidly and—for a miracle—without any trace of a hangover. *I feel fine,* she realized, surprised. Pulling back the curtain, she sat up to find a maid sitting with downturned face beside her bed. *Oh. I did feel fine,* she amended. "You can send them in," she said, trying to keep the tone of resignation out of her voice. "I'm ready to dress now."

Kara bounded in. "It's your walk with Lady Olga today!" she enthused. "Look what I found for you?"

Miriam looked—and stifled a groan. Kara had zeroed in on one of her work suits, along with a silvery top. "No," she said, levering herself off the bed. "Bring me what I was wearing yesterday. I think it's clean enough to do. Then pass me my underwear and get out."

"But! But—"

"I am thirty-two years old, and I have been putting on my own clothes for twenty-eight of those years," Miriam explained, one gentle hand on Kara's back, propelling her gently toward the door. "When I need help, I'll let you know." Alone, she leaned against the cold wall for a moment and closed her eyes. *Youth and enthusiasm!* She made a curse of the phrase.

Miriam dressed quickly and efficiently, then exited her bedroom to find Kara and a couple of servants waiting by the dining table, on which was laid a single breakfast setting. She was about to protest when she took one look at Kara and bit her tongue. Instead, she sat down. "Coffee or tea, whatever's available," she said to the maid. "Kara. Come here. Sit down with me. Cough it up."

"I'm meant to dress you," she said miserably. "It's my job."

"Fine, fine." Miriam rolled her eyes. "You *do* know I come from the other side?" Kara nodded. "If it makes you feel better, tell yourself I'm a crazy old bat who'll be sorry she ignored you later." She grinned at Kara's expression of surprise. "Listen, there's something you need to know about me: I don't play head games."

"Games? With *heads*?"

Ye gods! "If I think someone has made a mistake, I tell them. It doesn't mean I secretly hate them or that I've decided to make their life unpleasant. I don't do that because I've got other things to worry about, and screwing around like that—" she saw Kara's eyes widen—*Don't tell me swearing isn't allowed?*— "is a waste of time. Do you understand?"

Kara shook her head, mutely.

"Don't worry about it, then. I'm not angry with you. Drink your tea." Miriam patted her hand. "It's going to be all right. You said there's a reception this evening. You said we were invited. You want to go?"

Kara nodded, slowly, watching Miriam.

"Fine. You're coming, then. If you didn't want to go, I wouldn't make you. Do you understand? As long as you do your job properly when you're needed, as far as I'm concerned you're free to do whatever you like with the rest of your time. I am not your mother. Do you understand?"

Kara nodded again, but her entire posture was one of mute denial and her eyes were wide. *Shit, I'm not getting through to her,* Miriam thought to herself. She sighed. "Okay. Breakfast first." The toast was getting cold. "Is Brill going to the party?"

"Yes, mistress." Kara seemed to have found her tongue again, but she sounded a bit shaky. *She's about seventeen,* Miriam reminded herself. *A teenager. Whatever happened to teenage rebellion here? Do they beat it out of them or something?*

"Good. Listen, when you've finished, go find her. I need someone to walk with me to Lady Olga's apartment. When Brill gets back, the two of you are to sort out whatever I'm wearing tonight. When *I* get back I'll need you both to dress me and tell me who everybody is, where the bodies are buried, and what topics of conversation to avoid. Plus a quick course in court etiquette to make sure I know how to greet someone without insulting them. Think you can manage that?"

Kara nodded, a quick flick of the chin. "Yes, I can do that." She was about to say something else, but she swallowed it. "By your leave." She stood.

"Sure. Be off with you."

Kara turned and scurried out of the room, back stiff. "I don't think I understand that girl," Miriam muttered to herself. *Brill I think I've got a handle on, but Kara—* She shook her head, acutely aware of how much she didn't know and, by implication, of how much potential for damage this touchy teenager contained within her mood swings.

Brilliana turned up as Miriam finished her coffee, dressed for an outdoor hike. *Hey, have I started a fashion for trousers?* Miriam rose. "Good morning!" She grinned. "Sleep well after last night?"

"Oh." Brilliana rubbed her forehead. "You plied us with wine like a swain with his—well, I *think* it's still there." She waited for Miriam to stand up. "Would you like to go straight to Lady Olga? Her Aris says she would receive you in the orangery, then take tea with you in her rooms."

"I think, hmm." Miriam raised an eyebrow, then nodded when she saw Brilliana's expression. *No newspapers, no telephones, no electricity. Visiting each other is probably the nearest thing to entertainment they get around here when none of the big nobs are throwing parties.* "Whatever you think is the right thing to do," she said. "Where's my coat . . ."

Brilliana led her through the vast empty reception chamber of the night before, now illuminated with the clear white light of a snow-blanketed day. They turned down a broad stone-flagged corridor. It was empty save for darkened oil paintings of former inhabitants, and an elderly servant slowly polishing a suit of armor that looked strangely wrong to Miriam's untrained eye: The plates and joints not quite angled like anything she'd seen in a museum back home.

"Lady Aris said that her excellency is in a foul mood this morning," Brilliana said quietly. "She doesn't know why."

"Hmmph." Miriam had some thoughts on the subject. "I spent a long time talking to Olga on the way here. She's . . . let's just say that being one of the inner Clan and fully possessed of the talent doesn't solve all problems."

"Really?" Brilliana looked slightly disappointed. She pointed Miriam down a wide staircase, carpeted in blue. Two footmen in crimson livery stood guard at the bottom, backs straight, never blinking at the two women as they passed. Their brightly polished swords looked less out of place to Miriam's eye than the submachine guns slung discreetly behind their shoulders. Any mob who tried to storm the Clan's holding would get more than they bargained for.

They walked along another corridor. A small crocodile of maids and dubious-looking servants, cleaning staff, shuffled out of their way as they passed. This time Miriam felt eyes tracking them. "Olga has issues," she said quietly. "Do you know Duke Lofstrom?"

"I've never been presented to him." Brilliana's eyes widened. "Isn't he your uncle?"

"He's trying to marry Olga off," Miriam murmured.

"Funny thing is, now I think about it, not once during three days in a carriage with her did I hear Olga say anything positive about her husband-to-be."

"My lady?"

They came to another staircase, this time leading down into a different wing of this preposterously huge mansion. They passed more guards, this time in the same colors as Oliver Hjorth's butler. Miriam didn't let herself blink, but she was aware of their stares, hostile and unwelcoming, drilling into her back.

"Is it my imagination or . . . ?" Miriam muttered as they turned down a final corridor.

"They may have been shown miniatures of you," Brilliana said. She shivered, glanced askance at Miriam. "I wouldn't come this way without a companion, my lady. If I was mistrustful."

"Why? How bad could it be?"

Brilliana looked unhappy. "People with enemies have been known to find the staircases very slippery. Not recently, but it *has* happened. In turbulent times."

Miriam shuddered. "Well, I take your point, then. Thank you for that charming thought."

A huge pair of oak doors gaped ahead of them, a curtain blocking the vestibule. Chilly air sent fingers past it. Brilliana held it aside for Miriam, who found herself in a shielded cloister, walled on four sides. The middle was a sea of white snow as far as the frozen fountain. All sound was damped by winter's natural muffler. Miriam suddenly wished she'd brought her gloves.

"Whew! It's cold!" Brill was behind her. Miriam turned to catch her eye. "Which way?" she asked.

"There."

Miriam trudged across the snow, noting the tracks through it that were already beginning to fill in. Occasional huge flakes drifted out of a sky the color of cotton wool.

"Is that the orangery?" she asked, pausing at the door in the far wall.

"Yes." Brilliana opened the door, held it for her. "It's this way," she offered, leading Miriam toward an indistinct gray wall looming from the snow.

There was a door at the foot of the hump. Brilliana opened it, and hot air steamed out. "It's heated," she said.

"Heated?" Miriam ducked in. "Oh!"

On the other side of the wall, she found herself in a hothouse that must have been one of the miracles of the Gruinmarkt. Slender cast-iron pillars climbed toward a ceiling twenty feet overhead. It was roofed with a fortune in plateglass sheets held between iron frames, very slightly greened by algae. It smelled of citrus, unsurprisingly, for on every side were planters from which sprouted trees of not inconsiderable dimensions. Brilliana ducked in out of the cold behind her and pulled the door to. "This is amazing!" said Miriam.

"It is, isn't it?" said Brilliana. "Baron Hjorth's grandfather built it. Every plate of glass had to be carried between the worlds—nobody has yet learned how to make it here in such large sheets."

"Oh, yes, I can see that." Miriam nodded. The effect was overpowering. At the far end of this aisle there was a drop of three feet or so to a lower corridor, and she saw a bench there. "Where do you think Lady Olga will be?"

"She just said she'd be here," said Brilliana, a frown wrinkling her brow. "I wonder if she's near the boiler room? That's where things are warmest. Someone told me that the artisans have built a sauna hut there, but I wouldn't know about such things. I've never been here on my own before," she added a little wistfully.

"Well." Miriam walked toward the benches. "If you want to wait here, or look around? I'll call you when we're ready to leave."

When she reached the cast-iron bench, Miriam turned and stared back along the avenue of orange trees. Brill hadn't answered because she'd evidently found something to busy herself with. *Well, that makes things easier,* she thought lightly. Whitewashed brick steps led down through an open doorway to a lower level, past water tanks the size of crypts. The ceiling dipped, then continued—another green-lined aisle smelling of oranges and lemons, flakes of rust gently dripping from the pillars to the stone-flagged floor. Here and there Miriam caught a glimpse of the fat steam pipes, running along the inside of the walls. The trees almost closed branches overhead, forming a dark green tunnel.

At the end, there was another bench. Someone was seated there, contemplating something on the ground. Miriam walked forward lightly. "Olga?" she called.

Olga sat up when she was about twenty feet away. She was wearing a black all-enveloping cloak. Her hair was untidy, her eyes reddened.

"Olga! What's wrong?" Miriam asked, alarmed.

Olga stood up. "Don't come any closer," she said. She sounded strained.

"What's the matter?" Miriam asked uncertainly.

Olga brought her hands out from beneath the cloak. Very deliberately, she pointed the boxy machine pistol at Miriam's face. "You are," she said, her voice shaking with emotion. "If you have any last lies to whisper before I kill you, say them now and be done with it, *whore*."

PART 4

KILLER STORY

ʰᴏꜱᴛɪʟᴇ ᴛᴀᴋᴇᴏᴠᴇʀ

The interview room was painted pale green except for the floor, which was unvarnished wood. The single window, set high up in one wall, admitted a trickle of wan winter daylight that barely helped the glimmering of the electrical bulb dangling overhead. The single table had two chairs on either side of it. All three pieces of furniture were bolted to the floor, and the door was soundproofed and locked from the outside.

"Would you care for some more tea, Mr. Burgeson?" asked the plainclothes inspector, holding his cup delicately between finger and thumb. He loomed across the table, overshadowing Burgeson's frail form: they were alone in the room, the inspector evidently not feeling the need for a stout sergeant to assist him as warm-up man.

"Don't mind if I do," said Burgeson. He coughed damply into a wadded handkerchief. " 'Scuse me . . ."

"No need for excuses," the inspector said, as warmly as an

artist inspecting his handiwork. He smiled like a mantra "Terrible winters up there in Nova Scotia, aren't they?"

"Character-building," Burgeson managed, before break ing out in another wracking cough. Finally he managed stop and sat up in his chair, leaning against the back with h face pointed at the window.

"That was how the minister of penal affairs described it i parliament, wasn't it?" The inspector nodded sympatheti cally. "It would be a terrible shame to subject you to tha kind of character-building experience again at your age wouldn't it, Mr. Burgeson?"

Burgeson cocked his head on one side. So far the inspec tor had been polite. He hadn't used so much as a fist in the face, much less a knee in the bollocks, relying instead on tea and sympathy and veiled threats to win Burgeson to his side It was remarkably liberal for an HSB man, and Burgeson had been waiting for the other shoe to drop—or to kick him between the legs—for the past ten minutes. "What can I do for you, Inspector?" he asked, clutching at any faint hope of fending off the inevitable.

"I shall get to the point presently." The inspector picked up the teapot and turned it around slowly between his huge callused hands. He didn't seem to feel the heat as he poured a stream of brown liquid into Burgeson's cup, then put the pot down and dribbled in a carefully measured quantity of milk. "You're an old man, Mr. Burgeson, you've seen lots of water flow under the bridge. You know what 'appens in rooms like this, and you don't want it to 'appen to you again. You're not a young hothead who's going to get his self into trouble with the law any more, are you? And you're not in the pay of the Frogs, either, else we'd have scragged you long ago. You're a *careful* man. I like that. Careful men you can do business with." He cradled the round teapot between his hands gently. "And I much prefer doing business to breaking skulls." He put the teapot down. It wobbled on its base like a decapitated head.

Burgeson swallowed. "I haven't done anything to warrant the attention of the Homeland Security Bureau," he pointed t, a faint whine in his voice. "I've been keeping my nose ean. I'll help you any way I can, but I'm not sure how I can e of use—"

"Drink your tea," said the inspector.

Burgeson did as he was told.

"'Bout six months ago a Joe called Lester Brown sold ou his dear old mother's dressing table, didn't he?" said the nspector.

Burgeson nodded cautiously. "It was a bit battered—"

"And four weeks after that, a woman called Helen Blue ame and bought it off you, din't she?"

"Uh." Burgeson's mouth went dry. "Yes? Why ask me all his? It's in my books, you know. I keep records, as the law equires."

The inspector smiled, as if Burgeson had just said something extremely funny. "A Mr. Brown sells a dressing table to a Mrs. Blue by way of a pawnbroker who Mr. *Green* says is known as Dr. *Red*. In't that colorful, Mr. Burgeson? If we collected the other four, why, we could give the hangman a rainbow!"

"I don't know what you're talking about," Burgeson said tensely. "What's all this nonsense about? Who are these Greens and Reds you're bringing up?"

"Seven years in one of His Majesty's penal colonies for sedition back in seventy-eight and you still don't have a fucking clue." The inspector shook his head slowly. "*Levelers*, Mr. Burgeson." He leaned forward until his face was inches away from Burgeson's. "That dressing table happened to have a hollow compartment above the top drawer and there were some most *interesting* papers folded up inside it. You wouldn't have been dealing in proscribed books again, would ye?"

"Huh?" The last question caught Burgeson off-guard, but he was saved by another coughing spasm that wrinkled his face up into a painful knot before it could betray him.

The inspector waited for it to subside. "I'll put it to you like this," he said. "You've got bad friends, Erasmus. They're no good for yer old age. A bit o' paper I can't put me finger

on is one thing. But if I was to catch 'em, this Mrs. Blue
Mr. Brown, they'd sing for their supper sooner than put th
necks in a noose, wouldn't they? And you'd be right back
to Camp Frederick before your feet touch the ground, o
one-way stretch. Which in your case would be approximat
two weeks before the consumption carried you away for go
an' all and Old Nick gets to toast you by the fires of hell.

"All that Godwinite shit and old-time Egalitarianism w
get you is a stretched neck or a cold grave. And you are t
old for the revolution. They could hold it tomorrow and
wouldn't do you any good. What's that slogan— 'Don't tru
anyone who's over thirty or owns a slave'? Do you *real*
think your young friends are going to help you?"

Burgeson met the inspector's gaze head-on. "I have
Leveler friends," he said evenly. "I am not a republican re
olutionary. I admit that in the past I made certain mistake
but as you yourself agree, I was punished for them. My tari
is spent. I cooperate fully with your office. I don't see wha
else I can do to prevent people who I don't know and hav
never heard of from using my shop as a laundry. Do we nee
to continue this conversation?"

"Probably not." The inspector nodded thoughtfully. "Bu
if I was you, I'd stay in touch." A business card appeared be
tween his fingers. "Take it."

Burgeson reached out and reluctantly took the card.

"I've got my eye on you," said the inspector. "You don'
need to know how. If you see anything that might interest me
passing through your shop, I'll trust you to let me know.
Maybe it'll be news to me—and then again, I'll know about
it before you do. If you turn a blind eye, well—" he looked
sad—"you obviously won't be able to see all the titles of the
books in your shop. And it'd be a crying shame to send a
blind man back to the camps for owning seditious tracts,
wouldn't it?"

Two women stood ten feet apart, one shaking with rage, the
other frightened into immobility. Around them, orange trees

oistered in an unseasonable climate perfumed the warm air.

"I don't understand." Miriam's face was blank as she ared down the barrel of Olga's gun. Her heart pounded. *uy time!* "What are you talking about?" she asked, faint ith the certainty that her assignation with Roland had been verseen and someone had told Olga.

"You know very well what I'm talking about!" Olga narled. "I'm talking about my honor!" The gun muzzle idn't deviate from Miriam's face. "It's not enough for you o poison Baron Hjorth against me or to mock me behind my back. I can ignore those slights—but the infamy! To do what you did! It's unforgivable."

Miriam shook her head very slowly. "I'm sorry," she said. 'But I didn't know at the time it started between us, I mean. About your planned marriage."

A faint look of uncertainty flickered across Olga's face. "My betrothal has no bearing on the matter!" She snapped.

"Huh? You mean this *isn't* about Roland?" Miriam asked, feeling stupid and frightened.

"Roland—" Olga stared at her. Suddenly the look of uncertainty was back. "Roland can have nothing to do with this," she claimed haughtily.

"Then I haven't got a clue what the *it* you're talking about is," Miriam said heavily. Fear would only stretch so far, and as she stared at Olga's eyes all she felt was a deep wellspring of resignation, at the sheer total stupidity of all the events that had brought her to this point.

"But you—" Olga began to look puzzled, but still angry. "What *about* Roland? What have you been up to?"

"Fucking," Miriam said bluntly. "We only had the one night together but, well, I really care about him. I'm fairly sure he feels the same way about me, too. And before you pull that trigger, I'd like you ask yourself what will happen and who will be harmed if you shoot me." She closed her eyes, terrified and amazed at what she'd just heard herself say. After a few seconds, she thought, *Funny, I'm still alive.*

"I don't believe it," said Olga. Miriam opened her eyes.

The other woman looked stunned. However, her gun was longer pointing directly at Miriam's face.

"I just told you, dammit!" Miriam insisted. "Look, you going to point that thing somewhere safe or—"

"You and Roland?" Olga asked incredulously.

A moment's pause. Miriam nodded. "Yes," she said, h mouth dry.

"You went to bed with that dried-up prematurely middl aged sack of mannered stupidity? You care about him? don't believe it!"

"Why are you pointing that gun at me, then?"

For a moment, they stood staring at each other; then Olg lowered the machine pistol and slid her finger out of the trig ger guard.

"You don't know?" she asked plaintively.

"Know *what?*" Miriam staggered slightly, dizzy from th adrenaline rush of facing Olga's rage. "What on earth ar you talking about, woman? Jesus fucking Christ, I've jus admitted I'm having an affair with the man you're suppose to be marrying and that *isn't* why you're threatening to kil me over some matter of honor?"

"Oh, this is insupportable!" Olga stared at her. She looke very uncertain all of a sudden. "But you sent your man las night."

"What man?"

Their eyes met in mutual incomprehension.

"You mean you don't know? Really?"

"Know *what?*"

"A man broke into my bedroom last night," Olga said calmly. "He had a knife and he threatened me and ordered me to disrobe. So I shot him dead. He wasn't expecting that."

"You. Shot. A, a rapist. Is that it?"

"Well, that and he had a letter of instruction bearing the seal of your braid."

"I don't understand." Miriam shook her head. "What seal? What kind of instructions?"

"My maidenhead," Olga said calmly. "The instructions

ere very explicit. What is the law where you come from?
bout noble marriage?"

"About—what? Huh. You meet someone, one of you pro-
oses, usually the man, and you arrange a wedding. End of
tory. Are things that different here?"

"But the ownership of title! The forfeiture. What of it?"

"What 'forfeiture'?" Miriam must have looked puzzled
because Olga frowned.

"If a man, unwed, lies with a maid, also unwed, then it is
for him to marry her if he can afford to pay the maiden-price
to her guardian. And all her property and titles escheat to
him as her head. She has no say in the matter should he reach
agreement with her guardian, who while I am in his care here
would for me be Baron Hjorth. In my event, as a full-blood
of the Clan, my Clan shares would be his. This *commoner*—"
she pronounced the word with venomous diction—"invaded
my chamber with rape in mind and a purse full of coin sufficient to pay his way out of the baron's noose."

"And a letter," Miriam said in tones of deep foreboding.
"A letter sealed with . . . what? Ink? Wax? Something like
that, some kind of seal ring?"

"No, sealed with the stamps of Thorold and Hjorth. It is a
disgusting trick."

"I'll say." Miriam whistled tunelessly. "Would you believe
me if I said that I don't have—and have never seen—any
such stamp? I don't even know who my braid *are,* and I really ought to, because they're not going to be happy if I—"
she stopped. "Oh, of course."

" 'Of course,' what?"

"Listen, was there an open door to the roof in your apartment last night? After you killed him? I mean, a door he
came in through?"

Olga's eyes narrowed. "What if there was?"

"Yesterday I world-walked from my room to the other
side," said Miriam. "This house is supposed to be doppelgängered, but there is no security on the other side of my quarters. Anyone who can world-walk could come in. Later,

Brilliana and I found an open door leading to the roof."

"Ah." Olga glanced around, taking in whatever was be-hind Miriam. "Let's walk," she said. "Perhaps I should apol-ogize to you. You have further thoughts on the matter?"

"Yes." Miriam followed Olga, still apprehensive, knee-weak with relief. "My question is: Who profits? I don't have a braid seal, I didn't even know such a thing existed until you told me, but it seems clear that others in my braid would benefit if you killed me. Or if that failed, if I was deprived of a friend in circumstances bound to create a scandal of mon-strous proportions around me, it certainly wouldn't harm them. If you can think of someone who would *also* benefit if you were split apart from your impending alliance—" She bit her tongue, but it was too late.

"About Roland," Olga said quietly.

"Uh. Yes."

"Do you really love him?" she asked.

"Um." Tongue-tied, Miriam tried to muster her shredded integrity. "I think so."

"Well, then!" Olga smiled brightly. "If the two of you would *please* conspire to convince your uncle to amend his plans for me, it would simplify my life considerably." She shook her head. "I'd rather marry a rock. Is he good in bed?"

Miriam coughed violently into her fist. "What would you know about—"

"Do you think I'm completely stupid?" Olga shook her head. "I know you are a dowager, you have no guardian, and you are competent in law. You have nothing to lose by such intrigues. It would be naïve to expect you to abstain. But the situation is different for me. I have not my majority until marriage, and upon marriage I lose my independence. Isn't that an unpleasant paradox?"

"I don't understand you people," Miriam muttered, "but I figure your inheritance and marriage law is seriously screwed. Rape as a tool of financial intrigue—it's disgusting!"

"So we agree on one thing." Olga nodded. "What do you think could be behind this?"

"Well. Someone who doesn't like me—obviously." She

began ticking off points on her fingers. "Someone who holds you in contempt, too, or who actively wants you out of the way. By the way, what would have happened to you if you had shot me?"

"What?" Olga shrugged carelessly. "Oh, they'd have hanged me, I suppose," she said. "Why?"

"Let's see. We have Item Two: someone who has it in for you as well as me. We all center around—" something nagged at her for attention— "No, it's not there yet. Well, Item Three is my unsecured apartment. *That* we can blame on Baron Oliver, huh? Someone took advantage of it to get their cat's-paw into place by way of the roof, I think that's clear enough. I got Brilliana to lock and bolt the inner apartment—which is doppelgängered—last night, when I realized the roof door was open onto areas that aren't secured on the other side. Maybe their first objective was to shoot me in my sleep, and they turned to you as a second target when that failed. By attacking you they could either convince you that I was to blame—you shoot me, they win—or they could deprive me of an ally—you—and perhaps turn others against me. Do you think they believe Roland would think I'd do such a thing to you?"

Olga clutched her arm. "That's it," she said calmly. "If they didn't know about you and Roland, they would believe him to be set on me as his prize. It would be a most normal reaction to be enraged at anyone who ordered his bride-to-be raped away by night. Out of such actions blood feuds are born." Her fingers dug into Miriam's arm. "You would swear to me you had no hand in it?"

"Olga. Do you *really* believe I'd pay some man to rape my worst enemy? As opposed to simply shooting her and having done with the matter?"

Olga slowly relaxed. "If you were not raised *over there*, I might think so. But your ways are so charmingly informal that I find it hard to believe you would be so cruel. Or devious."

"I don't know. The longer I spend here, the more paranoid I become." Miriam shuddered. "Is there any risk of some asshole trying to rape *me* for my presumed riches?"

"Not if you're a guest of someone who cares what hap-

pens on their estate, such as the duke. Even at other time
you are only at risk if your guards fail you, and yo
guardian is willing to accept maidenprice," said Olga. "A
you are of age and able to act as your own guardian, I don
think that situation is likely to arise—an adventurer wh
took you against your will could expect to go to the gallow:
But you *do* have guards, don't you, just in case?" She looke
anxious. "They're very discreet, wherever they're hiding!" *
frown crossed her face. "Assuming the Baron hasn't man
aged to make sure the orders assigning a detachment to you
household haven't been lost . . ."

"No shit," Miriam said shakily as they climbed the steps
toward the entrance, looking around at the same time for
signs of Brilliana. "I must congratulate them on their
scarcity. When I find out who they are and where they live."

The snow was falling thick and fast outside, from a sky the
color of leaden tiles. The temperature was dropping, a blizzard in the making. "You must come up to my receiving
room for tea," Olga insisted, and Miriam found herself unable to decline. Brilliana hurried alongside them as they
reentered the barely heated corridors of the palace, ascend-
ing through a bewildering maze of passages and stairs to
reach Olga's private rooms.

Olga had left her guards behind. *She wanted no witnesses
to our little contretemps,* Miriam thought with a cold chill.
Now she berated them as she entered her outer reception
room, four strapping tall men in household livery worn with
cuirasses, swords, and automatic weapons. "Come in, be
welcome, sit you down," Olga insisted, gesturing toward a
circle of sofas being moved hastily into place by a bevy of
servants. Miriam accepted gratefully, placing Brilliana at
her left, and presently Olga's own ladies-in-waiting shepherded in a small company of servants bearing side tables, a
silver samovar, and sweetmeats on trays. With the blazing
fireplace, it was almost possible to forget the gathering
storm outside.

Now that Olga's fury at Miriam had been diverted toward a different target, she overcompensated, attempting to prove herself a charming hostess by heaping every consideration upon Miriam in a way that Miriam found more than a bit creepy after her earlier rage. Maybe it was just a guilt reaction, Miriam speculated, but it left her feeling very relieved that Olga didn't share her interest in Roland. They were well into a second pot of tea, with Miriam eavesdropping on the Lady Aris's snide comments about the members of this or that social set at court, when there was a polite announcement at the door. "Courier for madame Thorold," announced Olga's steward, poking his head in. "Shall I admit him?"

"By all means." Olga sat up straight as the messenger—dripping wet and looking chilled to the bone—entered. "My good man! What do you have for me?"

"Milady, I have been charged to deliver this into you hands," he said, dropping to one knee and presenting a sealed envelope from a shoulder bag. Olga accepted it, slit the wrapping, and read. She frowned. "Very well. You may tell your master I received word and passed it on to all present here. Feel free to leave immediately."

The messenger backed out, bowing. Olga returned to her chaise, looking distracted. "How unfortunate," she said.

" 'Unfortunate'?" Miriam raised an eyebrow.

"Tonight's reception is postponed," Olga read, "by virtue of the unusually foul weather. It shall in any event be held tomorrow, once arrangements have been made for additional shelter from the elements." She glanced at the shuttered window. "Well, I can't say I am surprised. This may be the season for storms, but this one appears to be setting in hard." Wind howled around the shutters outside.

"Is this normal?" Miriam asked. "To postpone events?"

"By your leave, it's not *normal*, my lady, but it's not un-heralded." Brilliana looked unhappy. "They may need time to move the lifeguard cavalry to other stables, to accommodate the coaches of the visitors. Or a roof may have caved in unexpectedly. This being the first real storm of winter, they may be hoping it will blow itself out overnight."

"Hmm." Miriam drained her teacup. "So it'll be tomorrow night instead?"

"Almost certainly," Olga said confidently. "It's a shame to postpone once, twice is an embarrassment. Especially when the occasion is the return to court of his majesty's winter sessions. And his opening of the sessions and levy of taxes follows the next day, to be followed by a hanging-holiday."

"Well, then." Miriam nodded to herself. "Is anything at all of consequence due to happen then?"

"Oh, a lot of drinking, and not a little eating and making merry," Olga assured her. "It's not a greatly important event for the likes of us. *Our* great sessions fall in six months, near upon Beltaigne, when alliances are discussed and braids rededicated, and the court of families-in-Clan hear grievances and settle treaties."

"Hmm. Well, I suppose I'd better make sure I'm around for that, too," said Miriam, waiting for a servant to refill her cup.

Olga winked at her. "I expect you will be—if we find you some reliable bodyguards."

Late in the afternoon, Miriam returned to her apartment—briefly.

Dismissing the servants, she called Brilliana and Kara into her bedroom. "I'm in trouble," she said tersely.

" 'Trouble,' my lady?" asked Kara, eyes glinting.

"Someone tried to force themselves upon Lady Olga last night. Someone with gold in their pocket and a commission bearing the seal of my braid. Which I have never seen, so I have to take Olga's word for it." She sat down on a chest and waited for Kara's declarations of shock to die down. Brilliana just nodded thoughtfully.

"This room—and other parts of this suite—are not doppelgängered properly," she continued. "On the other side, security is virtually nonexistent—until you go fifty feet that way." She gestured at the wall. "I don't think that's an accident. Nor was that open door last night," she added to Brilliana's questioning look.

"What are we going to *do?*" asked Kara, looking frightened and younger than ever.

"What *you* are going to do—both of you—is tell the servants we're going to have a quiet supper: cold cuts or a pie or something plain and simple. Then we're going to dismiss the servants and go to bed early so we are well rested for the morrow. After they bring our meal up and stoke the fireplace, they can leave." She stood up and paced. "What's really going to happen, once the servants have left is that two of Lady Olga's guards—the guards Baron Hjorth hasn't assigned to me—are going to enter the near audience chamber through the side door."

She grinned at Brilliana's surprise. "You will put on your cloaks and go where they lead you, which will be straight to Lady Olga's rooms, where you will be able to sleep safe and warm until it's time to come back here, in the morning."

"And you, my lady?" asked Kara, searching her face. "You can't spend the night alone here!"

"She doesn't intend to," Brill said tersely. "Do you?"

"Correct." Miriam waited.

"You're going to go over *there*," Brilliana added. "How I'd like to follow you!"

"You can't, yet," Miriam said bluntly. "Someone is conspiring against me. I am going to have to move fast and be inconspicuous. On the other side, there is a teeming city with many people and strange customs. I can't risk you attracting attention while I'm on the run." She raised a finger to anticipate Brilliana's objection. "I'll take you along *later*, I promise. But not this time. Do you understand?"

"Yes." Brill muttered something under her breath. Miriam pretended not to notice.

"That's it, then. If someone comes calling in the night, all they'll find are beds stuffed with pillows: You'll be elsewhere. On the other side, the fewer people who know where I'm going, the safer I'll be. I'll meet you back here tomorrow afternoon, and we'll decide what to do then, depending on whether the opening of the court of winter sessions is going ahead or not. Any last questions?"

It was snowing in New York, too, but nothing like the blizzard that had dumped two feet of snow on Neijwein in a day Miriam met nobody in the warehouse. At the top of the stairs she paused. *What was that trick?* She wondered, racking her brains. A flashback to the training course, years ago: It had been a giggle at the time, spy tradecraft stuff for journalists who were afraid of having their hotel rooms burgled in Krygistan or wherever. But now it came back to her. Kneeling, she tied a piece of black cotton sewing thread from the wall to the handrail, secured with a needle. It was invisible in the twilight. If it was gone when she returned, that would tell her something.

On this trip, she wore her hiking gear and towed her suitcase. With street map in hand, she wanted to give the impression of being a tourist from out of state who'd wandered into the wrong part of town. Maybe that was why a taxi pulled up almost as soon as she emerged from the back street, while her phone was still chirping its voice mail alert.

"The Marriott Marquis, Times Square," she told the driver. Head pounding, she hit the "mail" button and clamped the phone to her ear.

"Marriott Marquis, room 2412, continuously booked for the whole week in the name of Mr. and Mrs. Roland Dorchester. Just ask at the front desk and they'll give you a key."

Thank you, she thought, pocketing the phone and blinking back tears of relief.

The taxi took her straight to the main entrance and a bellboy was on hand to help her with her suitcase. She headed straight to the front desk.

"Mrs. Dorchester? Yes, ma'am, I have your card-key here. If you'd like to sign . . ."

Miriam did a little double-take, then scrawled something that she hoped she'd be able to replicate on demand. Then she took the keys and headed for the elevator bank.

She was inside the glass-walled express elevator, and it was surging up from the third floor in a long glide toward the

ɔp, when a horrible thought occurred to her. *What if they've
ɔt to Roland?* she wondered. *After he booked the hotel.
'hey could be waiting for me.*

It was a frightening thought, and Miriam instinctively
eached toward her pocket. *How the hell do you do this?* Sud-
lenly it occurred to her that the little revolver was as much
ɔf a threat as an asset in this kind of situation. If she went
through the door and some bad guy was just inside, he could
grab her before she had a chance to use it. Or grab the gun.
And she was more than twenty stories up, high enough that—
she looked out and down through the glass wall of the lift
and took a deep breath of relief. "Oh, that's okay," she muttered, as the obvious explanation occurred to her just before
the lift bell dinged for attention: Skyscrapers didn't need
doppelgängering against attack from another world where
concrete and structural steel were barely known.

Miriam stepped out into the thickly carpeted hallway and
stopped. Pulling out her mobile phone, she dialed Roland's
number. It rang three times.

"Hello?"

"Roland, what happens if you're on the twenty-fourth
floor of a tall building, say a hotel, and—" quick glance in
either direction—"you try to world-walk?"

"You don't do that." He chucked dryly. "That's why I
chose it. I wasn't expecting you so soon. Come right on up?"

"Sure," she said and rang off, abruptly dizzy with relief
and anticipation.

I hope this works out, she thought, dry-swallowing as she
walked down the corridor, hunting for room 2412. *Hell, we
hardly know each other—*

She reached the door. All her other options had run out.
She put the card in the slot and turned the handle.

Three hours later they came up for air. The bedding was a
tangled mess, half the fluffy white towels were on the bathroom floor and the carpet was a wasteland of discarded
clothing—but it had worked out.

"I have missed you *so* much," she murmured in his e: then leaned close to nibble at his lobe.

"That makes two of us." He heaved up a little, braci against the bed head, turning to look at her. "You're beautiful

"I bet you say that to every naked woman you wake up bed with," she replied, laughing.

"No," he said, in all seriousness, before he realized wh: he'd done. Then he turned bright red. "I mean—"

He was too late. Miriam pounced. "*Got* you," she giggle holding him down. Then she subsided on top of him. "Lik that?" she asked. "Or this?"

"Oh." He rolled his eyes. "Please. A few minutes?"

"Frail male reed!"

"Guilty, I'm afraid." He wrapped an arm around her "What's with the early appearance? I thought there was sup- posed to be a reception this evening?"

"There was, past tense." Miriam explained about the can- celation.

"So you came over early, just in case I was here?"

"No." She felt very sober, all of a sudden, even though they hadn't been drinking—and felt the need to remedy the condition, too.

"Why, then? I thought you were sticking with the program?"

"Not when people try to kill me twice in one day."

"*What?*" His arms tensed and he began to sit up.

"No, no—lie down. Relax. They can't come through here and I took steps to throw off the trail." She kissed him, again, tasted the sweat of their lovemaking. "Wow. What did I do to deserve someone like you?"

"You were really, really wicked in a previous life?"

"Nonsense!"

"The killers." She'd broken the magic, she realized with a sense of desolation.

"They won't follow us here, but there's a lot to tell," she said. "How about we dig a bottle out of the minibar and have a bath or something while I tell you?"

"I think we can do better than that," he said with a glint in his eye. He reached for the bedside phone. "Room service,

lease. Yes? It's room 2412. Can you send up the item I ordered earlier? Leave it outside."

"Huh?" She raised her eyebrows.

"My surprise." He looked smug.

"I thought *I* was your surprise." He'd been surprised
enough when she came through the door—but he'd kissed
her, and one thing led to another, and they hadn't even made
it as far as the bed the first time. Now she sat up on the rum-
pled sheets, brushing one hand up and down his thigh and
watching his face. "About your uncle's plans. What do you
think Olga makes of them?"

Roland looked pained. "She doesn't get a say in it. She's a
naïve little dutiful contessa who'll do as Angbard tells her
parents to tell her."

"If that's what you and Angbard think, you may be in for
a nasty surprise." Miriam watched him carefully. "You don't
know her very well, do you?"

"I've met her a time or two," he said, slightly puzzled.

"Well, I have just spent several days in her company and
that little minx may be young and naïve, but she isn't dumb. In
fact, it's lucky for me she's smart and doesn't want to marry
you any more than you want her—otherwise I wouldn't be
here now."

"What—"

"She nearly shot me."

"Holy Crone Wife! What *happened*?"

"Let go! You're hurting—"

"Sorry." He sat up and gently put an arm around her
shoulders. "I'm sorry. You caught me by surprise. Tell me all
about it. Everything. Don't leave anything out. My gods—I
am *so* glad you're here and safe now." He hugged her. "Tell
me everything. In your own time."

"Time is the one thing I don't think we've got." She leaned
against him. "Someone sent Olga an unwelcome gift—a rape-
o-gram. Luckily for me, but unluckily for the thug concerned,
Olga's childlike enthusiasms include embroidery, violins,
haute couture, and semiautomatic weapons. She found a commission in his back pocket, with my seal on it and a purse of

coin sufficient to pay the kind of maidenprice Oliver mig
ask for someone he really didn't like much. Roland, I didn
even know I *had* a seal."

" 'A seal.' " He looked away just as someone knocked c
the door. Miriam jumped. "I'll get it—"

"No! Wait!" Miriam scrabbled for her jacket, fumbled i
its pockets. "Okay, now you can open the door. When I'r
out of sight."

Roland glanced at her as he tied his bathrobe. "It's onl
room service, isn't it?"

"I'm not taking any chances." She crouched against the
wall around the corner from the door, pistol cradled in both
hands.

"Will you give that up? If it's the DEA, we have very expensive lawyers who'll have us both out on bail in about
thirty microseconds."

"It's not the DEA I'm worried about," she said through
gritted teeth. "It's my long-lost family."

"Well, if you put it that way . . ." Roland opened the door.
Miriam tensed. "Thank you," she heard him tell someone.
"That's great, if you could leave it just here." A moment
later, she heard the door close, then a squeaking of wheels.
Roland appeared, pushing a trolley upon which sat an ice
bucket with a bottle of something poking out of it.

"This is your surprise?" she asked, lowering the gun.

He nodded. "You *are* on edge," he observed. "Listen, do
you want me to chain the door and hang out a 'Do Not Dis-
turb' sign?"

"I think that would be a good start." She was shivering.
Worse, she had no idea where it had come from. "I'm not
used to people trying to shoot me, love. It's not the kind of
thing that normally happens to a journalist, unless you're a
war correspondent."

She put the gun down on the bedside table.

"Listen, Château Rothschild '98. Sound all right to you?"
He brandished the bottle.

"Sounds perfect. Open it now, dammit, I need a drink!"

He peered at her. "You do, at that," he said. "One moment . . ." He popped the cork carefully, then slowly filled two fluted glasses, taking care not to spray the champagne everywhere. He passed her a glass, then raised his own. "To your very good health."

"To us—and the future." She took a sip. "Whatever the hell that means."

"You were telling me about Olga."

"Olga and I had a little conversation at cross-purposes. She was raised to never unintentionally cause offense, so she gave me time to confess before she shot me. Luckily, I confessed to the wrong crime. Did you know that you're an, uh, 'dried-up prematurely middle-aged sack of mannered stupidity'? She doesn't want to marry you—trust me on this."

"Well, it's mutual." Roland sat in the chair opposite the end of the bed, looking disturbed. "Have you any idea how the man got into her apartments?"

"Yup. Through my own, by way of the roof. Turns out that the rooms Baron Oliver assigned me aren't doppelgängered— or rather they are, but the location on this side is unprotected. And aren't I supposed to have bodyguards or something? Anyway, that's why I came here. I figured it was safer than spending the night in an apartment that has a neon sign on the door saying ASSASSINS THIS WAY, with cousins next door who seem to have opened a betting pool on my life expectancy."

"Someone tried to rape Olga?" Roland shook his head. "That doesn't make sense to me."

"It does if I was their first target and they meant to kill me, but couldn't get at me directly: it was a contingency plan, to set up a blood feud between us." Briefly, she told him about the open staircase, and her instructions to lock and bolt all the doors on the inside. "I don't feel safe there, I really don't."

"Hmm." He took a mouthful of wine. "I don't know." He looked thoughtful rather than shocked. "I can eliminate some suspects, but not everybody." He glanced up at her, worry writ large across his face. "First, it's not official. It's family, not Clan business. If it was the Clan, they'd have sent soldiers. You've seen what we've got over here." She nodded. "Our enforcement teams—you don't bother resisting.

They're better armed, better trained, and better paid than the FBI's own specialist counterterrorism units."

"Well, I guessed that much," she said.

"Yes. Anyway, for seconds it's too damned blatant—and that's worrying. Whoever did it is out of control. Olive Hjorth might dislike you and feel threatened, but he wouldn't try to kill you in his own house. Not offering you a guard of honor is another matter, but to be implicated—no." He shook his head. "As for Olga, that's very disturbing. It sounds as if someone set her up to kill you or cause a scandal that would isolate you—one or the other. And you are probably right about being the intruder's first target. That means it's an insider—and that's the frightening part. Someone who knows that you don't know the families well, that you can be cut apart from the pack and isolated, that you are unguarded. Someone like that, who is acting like they're out of control. A rogue, in other words."

"Well, no shit, Sherlock." She drained her glass and refilled it. "Y'know something? One of these days we may eventually make an investigative journalist out of you."

"In your dreams—I'm a development economist." He frowned at the floor in front of her feet, as if it concealed an answer. "Let's start from where we are. You've told Olga about us. That means if we're *lucky* she doesn't tell Angbard. If she does, if Olga tells him about us, he could—do you have any idea what he could do?"

"What?" She shook her head. "Listen, Roland, I didn't grow up under the Clan's thumb. Thinking this way is alien to me. I don't really give a flying fuck what Angbard thinks. If I behave the way they seem to expect me to, I will be dead before the week is out. And if I survive, things won't be much better for me. The Clan is *way* out of date and overdue for a dose of compulsory modernization, both at the business level and the personal. If the masked maniac doesn't succeed in murdering me, the Clan will expect me to go live like a medieval noble lady—fuck that! I'm *not* going to do it. I'll live with the consequences later."

"You're—" he swallowed. "Miriam." He held out his arms

to her. "You're strong, but you don't know what you're talking about. I've been trying to resist the pressure for years. It doesn't work. The Clan will get you to do what they want you to do in the end. I spent years trying to get them to do something—land reform on their estates, educating the peasants, laying the groundwork for industrialization. All I got was shit. There are deeply entrenched political groupings within the Clan who don't want to see any modernization, because it threatens their own source of power—access to imported goods. And outside the Clan, there are the traditional nobility, not to mention the Crown, who are just waiting for the Clan nobility to make a misstep. Jealousy is a strong motivating force, especially among the recently rich. If Angbard hadn't stood up for me, I'd have had my estate forfeited. I might even have been declared outlaw—don't you see?" There was anguish in his eyes.

"Frankly, no. What I see is a lot of frightened people, none of whom particularly like the way things work, but all of whom think they'll lose out if anyone else disrupts it. And you know something? They're wrong and I don't want to be part of that. You've been telling me that I can't escape the Clan, and I'm afraid you're right—you've convinced me—but that only means I've *got* to change things. To carve out a niche I can live with." She stood up and walked toward him. "I don't like the way the families live like royalty in a squalid mess that doesn't even have indoor plumbing. I don't like the way their law values people by how they can breed and treats women like chattels. I don't like the way the outer family feel the need to defend the status quo in order to keep from being kicked in the teeth by the inner families. The whole country is ripe for modernization on a massive scale, and the Clan actually has the muscle to do that, if they'd just realize it. I don't like the dehumanizing poverty the ordinary people have to live with, and I don't like the way the crazy fucked-up feudal inheritance laws turn an accident of birth into an excuse for rape and murder. But most of all, I don't like what they've done to *you.*"

She leaned down and pulled him up by the shoulders,

forcing him to stand in front of her. "Look at me," she insisted. "What do you see?"

Roland looked up at her skeptically. "Do you really think you can take them all on?"

"On my own?" She snorted. "I *know* I can," she said fiercely. "All it takes is a handful of people who believe that things *can* change to start the ball rolling. And that handful has to start somewhere! Now are you with me or against me?"

He hugged her right back, and she felt another response. He was stiffening against her, through his robe. "You're the best thing that's happened to me in years. If ever. I don't want to lose you."

"Me too, love."

"But how do you think you're going to make it work?" he asked. "And stop whoever's trying to kill you."

"Oh, *that*." She leaned into his arms, letting him pull her back in the direction of the bed. "That's going to be easy. When you strip away the breeding program, the Clan is a business, right? Family-owned partnership, private share-holdings. Policy is set at annual meetings twice a year, next one at Beltaigne, that sort of thing."

"So?" He looked distracted, so she stopped fumbling at his belt for a moment.

"Well." She leaned her chin against the hollow of his neck, licked his pulse spot slowly. "It may have escaped your attention, but I am an expert in one particular field— I've spent years studying it, and I think I probably know more about it than anyone else in the family. The Clan is an old-fashioned unlimited-liability partnership, with a dose of family politics thrown in. The business structure itself is a classic variation on import/export trade, but it's cash-rich enough to support a transition to some other model. All I need is a lever and an appropriate fulcrum and then a direction to make them move in. Business restructuring, baby, that's where it's at. A whole new business model. The lever we need is one that will convince them that they have more to lose by *not* changing than by sticking with the status quo.

)nce we're in the driver's seat, *nobody* is going to tell us we
:an't shack up on this side and live the way we want to."

He lifted her off her feet and lay down beside her. "What
.everage do you need?" he asked alertly. "I spent years look-
.ng and didn't find anything that powerful . . ."

"It's going to be something convincing." She smiled hun-
grily up at him. "And they'll never know what hit them. We
need to establish a power base by Beltaigne. A pilot project
that demonstrates massive potential for making money in
some way that relies on the Clan talent without falling into
the classic mercantilist traps. It'll make me worth much
more to them alive than dead, and it'll give us the beginning
of a platform to recruit like-minded people and start building." She looked pensive. "A skunk works within an established corporation, designed to introduce new ways of
thinking and pioneer new business opportunities. I've written up enough stories about them—I just never thought I'd
be setting one up myself."

She stopped talking. There'd be time to work out the details later.

BUSINESS PLAN

Miriam dozed fitfully, unable to relax her grip on consciousness. She kept turning events over in her mind, wondering what she could have done differently. If there was anything in the past two weeks that she could have changed, what might have come of it? She might not have accepted the pink and green shoebox. She wouldn't be in this mess at all.

But she wouldn't have met Brill, or Roland, or Angbard, or Olga, or the rest of the menagerie of Clan connections who were so insistently cluttering up her hitherto-straightforward family life with politics and feuds and grudges and everything else that went with the Clan. Her life would be simpler, emptier, more predictable, *and safer*, she thought sleepily. *With nobody trying to exploit me because of who I am.*

Who I am? She opened her eyes and stared at the ceiling in the dark. *Is it me they're after or someone else?* She wondered. *If only I could ask my mother.* Not the mother who'd loved her and raised her, not Iris—the other one, the faceless woman who'd died before she'd had a chance to remember her. The woman who'd borne her and been murdered, her only legacy a mess of—

She glanced sideways. Roland was asleep next her her, his face smooth and relaxed, free of worry. *I've gone from being completely independent to* this *in just two weeks.* Never mind Brill and Kara back in the palace, the weight of Angbard's expectations, the Clan's politics . . . Miriam wasn't used to having to think about other people when planning her moves, not since the divorce from Ben.

She glanced at the alarm clock. It was coming up to seven o'clock—too late to go back to sleep. She leaned over toward Roland's ear. "Wake up, sleepyhead," she whispered.

Roland mumbled something into the pillow. His eyelids twitched.

"Time to be getting up," she repeated.

He opened his eyes, then yawned. "I *hate* morning people," he said, looking at her slyly.

"I'm not a morning person, I just do my best worrying when I should be asleep." She took a deep breath. I'm going to have to go find that lever to move the Clan," she told him. "The one we were talking about last night. While that's going on, unless we can find out who's really got it in for me, we may not be able to meet up very often."

"We can't talk about this publicly," he said. "Even if Olga keeps her mouth shut—"

"No." She kissed him. "Damn, I feel like they're all watching us from behind the bed!"

"What are you going to do today?" he asked diplomatically.

"Well." She rolled up against him. "First, we're going to order breakfast from room service. Then you're going to go and do whatever it is that Angbard expects of you this morning. If you come back here, I'll probably be gone, because I've got some research to do and some stuff to buy. There's someone I've hired—" he raised an eyebrow— "Yes, I've established a pattern of drawing out cash against that card, for as long as it'll hold out. I'm paying a friend who I trust, implicitly, to keep an eye out for me. I'm not going to tell you any more about it because the fewer people who know, the better. But when you come back to this room, even if I'm not here, you'll find a prepaid new mobile phone. From time to time, I want you to check for voice mail. Only three people will know the number—you, me, and my employee. It's for emergencies only. There'll be a single number programmed into it, and that's for me—again, I'll only check for voice mail occasionally. I figure if I can't even hide a mobile phone, there won't be anything you can do to help."

"So you're going away," he said. "But are you going back to court or are you going underground?"

"I'm going back to face the music," she replied. "At least for this evening, I need to be seen. But I'm going to hole up on this side at night, at least until I can find a safely doppelgängered room or figure out who's after me. And then—" she shrugged. "Well, I'll have to play it by ear. For now, I'm thinking about setting up a new startup venture, in the import/export field."

"That's not safe—they'll kill you if they find out! Clan business ventures are really tightly controlled. If you splinter off, they'll assume you're setting up as a rival."

"Not if I do it right," she said confidently. "It's a matter of finding a new business model that hasn't occurred to any of them. Then get it going and deal the Clan shareholders in before they know what's happening. If I can finesse it, they'll have a vested interest in seeing me succeed."

"But that's—" Roland was at a loss for words. "A *new* business? There *is* no scope for anything new! Nobody's come up with a new trade since the 1940s, when the drug thing began taking over from gold and hot goods. I was thinking you were going to try and do something like bootstrap reforms on your own estate, not—"

"That's because you're thinking about it all wrong." She reached out and touched his nose. "So are they. You did the postgraduate research thing," she said. "Economic history, right?"

"Right. What's that got to do with it?"

"Well. The family business structure is kind of primitive,

n't it? So you went looking for a way to modernize it,
dn't you? Using historical models."

"Yes. But I still don't see—"

"Historical models are the wrong kind. Look at me. They
ied to train you up to improve things, but there's not a lot
ɔu can do when the management tree is defined by birth, is
ere?"

"Correct." He looked frustrated. "I did some work on this
ide, cutting overheads and reorganizing, but there's stuff I
ouldn't touch—I just wasn't allowed anywhere near it, in
act. There's no easy way to apply the European model in
he Gruinmarkt. No investment banking infrastructure, no
imited liability, all property rights ultimately devolve to the
king—it's straight out of the late-feudal period. Lots of really competent, smart people who are never going anywhere
because they can't world-walk and lots of time-wasting
prima donnas who are basically content to serve as couriers
on a million-dollar salary." He caught her eye and flushed.

"Whether I approve or not doesn't matter, does it?" she
said tartly. "The families are dependent on drug money and
weaning them off it will be a huge job. But I'd like you to
think on this. You said that their company structure is basically fifteenth- or sixteenth-century. They're still stuck in a
mercantilist mode of thinking— 'What can I take from these
other guys and sell at a profit?', rather than ways of generat-
ing added value directly. I am absolutely *certain* that there is
a better way of running things—and one that doesn't run the
risk of bringing the FBI and DEA and CIA down on everybody's heads—some way that lets us generate value directly
by world-walking. It's just a matter of spotting it."

"The legality of the Clan's current business isn't a problem, at least not from the commercial point of view; I think
we spend a couple of hundred million a year on security because of it." He shrugged. "But what can we do? We're limited to high-value commodities because there's a limit to
how much we can ship. Look, there are roughly three hundred active inner family members who can shuttle between

the worlds, five days on and five days off. Each of us
carry an average of a hundred pounds each way. That me
we can shift three-quarters of a ton each way, each day.]
maybe half of that is taken up by luxury items or stuff
need just to keep sane. There's the formal personal
lowance. So we really only have a little over a third of a ?
per day—to fund an entire ruling class! The fixtures and ?
tings in Fort Lofstrom alone amount to a year's gross prc
uct for the family. That'd be, in U.S. dollar terms, seve.
billion. Wouldn't it?"

"So what? Isn't it a bit of a challenge to try and figure c
a better way of using this scarce resource—our ability
ship stuff back and forth?"

"But two and a half tons a week—"

"Suppose you were shipping that into orbit, instead of to
world where the roads are dirt tracks and the plumbin,
doesn't flush. It doesn't sound very impressive, but that
about the payload to orbit capacity of Arianespace, c
NPO–Energiya, or Boeing–Sealaunch." Miriam crossed he
arms. "All of whom make billions a year on top of it. Ther
are high-value, low-weight commodities other than drugs
Take saffron, for example, a spice that's worth three time
its weight in gold. Or gold, for that matter. You said the}
used to smuggle gold, back when bullion was a governmen
monopoly. If you can barter your aristocratic credentials fo
military power, you can use modern geophysics-based
prospecting techniques to locate and conquer gold-mining
areas. A single courier can carry maybe a million dollars'
worth of gold from the other side over here in a day, right?"

Roland shook his head. "First, we have transport problems. The nearest really big gold fields are in California, the
Outer Kingdom. Which is a couple of months away, as the
mule train plods, and assuming the Comanche or the Apache
don't murder you along the way. Remember, M-16s give our
guards a quality edge, but quantity has a quality all of its
own and ten guards—or even a hundred—aren't much use
against an army. Other than that, there're the deposits in
South Africa, the white man's graveyard. Do I need to say

y more about that? It'd take us years to get that kind of peline running, before we had any kind of return on investent to show the families. It's *very* expensive. Plus, it'd be eflationary over here. As soon as we start pumping cheap old onto the market, the price of bullion will fall. Or have ou spotted something all of the rest of us have been missing or fifty years? When I was younger, I thought I might be ble to change things. But it's not that simple."

She shrugged. "Sure it's hard, and in the long term it'd be eflationary, but in the long run we're all dead anyway. What 'm thinking is: We need to break the deadlock in the Clan's hinking wide open. Come up with a new business model, not one the existing Clan grandees have seen before. Doesn't matter if it isn't very lucrative at first, as long as it can fund textbooks—going the other way—and wheelbarrows. While we wean the families off their drug dependency problem, we need to develop the Gruinmarkt. Right now, the Clan could implode like *that*—" she snapped her fingers— "if Congress canceled the war on drugs, for example. The price would fall by a factor of a hundred—overnight—and you'd be competing against pharmaceutical companies instead of bandits. And it's going to happen sooner or later. Look at the Europeans: Half of them have decriminalized marijuana already and some of them are even talking about legalizing heroin. Basing your business on a mercantilist approach to transshipping a single commodity is risky as hell."

"That would be bad, I agree." He looked grave. "In fact—" his eyes unfocused, he stared into the middle distance— "Sky Father, it could trigger a revolution! If the Clan suddenly lost its supply of luxury items—or antibiotics—we'd be screwed. It's amazing how much leverage you can buy by ensuring the heir to a duchy somewhere doesn't die of pneumonia or that some countess doesn't succumb to childbed fever."

"Yeah." Miriam began collecting her scattered clothes. "But it doesn't have to go that way. I figure with their social standing the Clan could push industrialization and development policies that would drag the whole Gruinmarkt into the

nineteenth century within a couple of generations, and a
tle later it would be able to export stuff that people over h
would actually want to *buy*. Land reform and tools to bo
agricultural efficiency, set up schools, build steel mills, a
start using the local oil reserves in Pennsylvania—it co
work. The Gruinmarkt could bootstrap into the kind of ma
itime power the British Empire was, back in the Victori
period. As the only people able to travel back and for
freely, we'd be in an amazing position—a natural mono
oly! The question is: How do we get there from here?"

Roland watched her pull her pants on. "That's a lot
think about," he said doubtfully. "Not that I'm saying it can
be done, but it's . . . it's *big*."

"Are you kidding?" She flashed him a smile. "It's not ju:
big, it's enormous! It's the biggest goddamned managemer
problem anyone has ever seen. Drag an entire planet out c
the middle ages in a single generation, get the families out o
the drugs trade by giving them something productive an
profitable to do instead, give ourselves so much leverage w
can dictate terms to them from on high and make the likes o
Angbard jump when we say 'hop'—isn't that something yo
could really get your teeth into?"

"Yeah." He stood up and pulled open the wardrobe where
he'd hung his suit the evening before. "What you're talking
about will take far more leverage than I ever thought . . ."
Then he grinned boyishly. "Let's do it."

Miriam went on a shopping spree, strictly cash. She bought
three prepaid mobile phones and programmed some numbers in. One of them she kept with Roland's and Paulette's
numbers in it. Another she loaded with her number and
Roland's and mailed to Paulie. The third—she thought long
and hard on it, then loaded her own number in, but not
Paulette's. Blood might be thicker than water, but she was
responsible for Paulette's safety. A tiny worm of suspicion
still ate at her; she was pretty certain that Roland was telling

he truth, straight down the line, but if not, it wouldn't be the
first time a man had lied to her, and—

*What the hell is this? This is the guy you're thinking about
spending the rest of your life with—and you're holding out
on him because you don't trust him completely?* She confronted herself and answered: *Yeah. If Angbard told him my
life depended on him giving Paulie away, how would I feel
then?*

Next she collected essential supplies. She started by
pulling more cash from an ATM. She stuffed three thousand
dollars into an envelope, wrapped a handwritten note
around it, and FedExed it to Paulette's home address. It was
an eccentric way to pay an employee, but what the hell—it
wasn't as if she'd set up a safe bank account yet, was it? After posting the cash, Miriam hit on a couple of department
stores, one for spare socks (*There are no washing machines
in history-land*, she reminded herself) and another for some
vital information. A CD-ROM containing the details of
every patent filed before 1920 went in her pocket: She had
difficulty suppressing a wild grin as she paid ten bucks for
it. *With the right lever, I will move worlds*, she promised
herself.

She left the suitcase at the Marriott, but her new spoils
went in a small backpack. It was late afternoon before she
squeezed into a cab and gave directions back to the warehouse. *I hope I'm doing the right thing*, she thought, wistfully considering the possibility of spending another night
with Roland. But he'd gone back to Cambridge, and she
couldn't stay until he returned to New York.

Yet again there was nobody to challenge her in the warehouse office. It seemed even more deserted than usual, and a
strange musty smell hung over the dusty crates. She went
upstairs, then knelt and checked for the thread she'd left
across the top step.

It was gone. "Hmm." Miriam glanced around. *Nobody
here now*, she decided. She walked over to the spot that was
doppelgängered with her bedroom chamber, took a deep

breath, pulled out the locket, and stared at it. The knotwor intricate and strange, seemed to ripple before her eyes, di torting and shimmering, forming a pattern that she coul only half-remember when she didn't have it in front of he Odd, it was a very simple knot—

The world twisted around Miriam and spat out a four poster bed. Her head began to throb at the same time. Sh closed the locket and looked around.

"Mistress?" It was Kara, eyes wide open. She'd been ben over Miriam's bed, doing something.

"Yes, it's me." Miriam put her backpack down. "How di the assassination attempt go last night?"

" 'Assassination'?" Kara looked as if she might explode. "It was horrible! Horrible, mistress! I was so scared—"

"Tell me about it," Miriam invited. She unzipped her jacket. "Where's Brill?"

"Next door," Kara fussed. "The reception tonight! We don't have long! You'll have to listen—"

"Whoa!" Miriam raised her hands. "Stop. We have what, three hours? I thought you were going to brief me on who else will be there."

"Yes, my lady! But if we have to dress you as well—"

"Surely you can talk at the same time?" asked Miriam. "I'm going to find Brilliana. I need to discuss things with her. While I'm doing that, you can get yourself ready."

She found Brilliana in the reception room, directing a small platoon of maids and manservants around the place. She'd already changed into a court gown. "Over there!" she called. "No, I say, build it in front of the door, not beside it!" She glanced at Miriam as she came in. "Oh, hello there, my lady. It's hopeless, absolutely hopeless."

"What is?" asked Miriam.

"The instructions," said Brilliana. She sidestepped a pool of sawdust as she approached. Miriam glanced around as she added, "They're no good at following them. Even when I tell them exactly what I want."

"What have you been up to?" Miriam leaned against a tapestry-hung wall and watched the artisans at work.

"You were right about the door," said Brilliana. "So I summoned a locksmith to change the levers, and I am having this small vestibule added." She smiled, baring teeth. "A little trap."

"I—" Miriam snapped her fingers. "Damn. I should have thought of that."

"Yes." Brilliana looked happy with herself. "You approve?"

"Yes. Tell them to continue. I want a word with you in my room." She retreated into the relative peace and quiet of her bedroom, followed by the lady-in-waiting. With the door shut, the noise of sawing outside was almost inaudible. "What's the damage?"

"There were holes in your blankets—and scorch marks around them—when I checked this morning." Despite her matter-of-fact tone, Brilliana looked slightly shaken. "I had to send Kara away, the poor thing was so shocked."

"Well, I had a good night's sleep." Miriam glanced around the room bleakly. "But I was right about the lack of a doppelgängered space on the other side. It's a huge security risk. This is serious. Did anyone tell Baron Hjorth?"

"No!" Brilliana looked uncertain. "You said—"

"Good." Miriam relaxed infinitesimally. "All right. About tonight. In a while Kara's going to come back and sort me out for the reception. In the meantime, I need to know what I'm up against. I think I'm going to need to sleep in Lady Olga's apartment tonight. I want to vary my pattern a bit until we find whoever . . . whoever's behind this." She sat down on the end of the bed. "Talk to me."

"About tonight?" Brilliana caught her eye and continued. "Tonight is the formal ball to mark the opening of the winter session of his majesty's court tomorrow morning. There will be members of every noble family in the capital present. This is the session in which his majesty must assemble tribute to the emperor beyond the ocean, so it tends to be a little subdued—nobody wants to look too opulent—but at the same time, it's essential to be seen. To be present in Niejwein at the beginning of winter used to mean one was snowed in, wintering here. Noble hostages at his majesty's

pleasure. We don't do that these days, but still, it's a mark o
good faith to be seen to offer obedience and at least on
older family member. Your uncle sent word by way of hi
secretary that you be asked to bend the knee and pledge hi
obedience, by the way."

"He did, did he?" muttered Miriam.

"Well!" Brill paced across the room in front of her. "Wha
this means is that it will be an assembly of some sixty families of note and their representatives and champions." She
spotted Miriam's surprised expression. "Did you think we
and ours were the sum and the end of the nobility? This is a
small fraction of the whole, but thanes and earls from distant
towns and estates cannot appear at court, and so many of
them make supplication by proxy. We, the Clan families, are
merely a small fraction—but the cream."

"So there are going to be, what, several hundred people
present?"

Brilliana nodded, looking very serious. "At least that," she
said. "But I'll be right behind you to remind you of anyone
important."

"Whew! Lucky me." Miriam raised an eyebrow. "How
long does it go on for?"

"Hmm." Brill tilted her head over to one side. "It would
be rude to leave before midnight. Are you going to be . . . ?"

"This time, I don't have a three-day coach journey behind
me." Miriam stood up. *And this time I'm going to do business,* she added mentally. "So. What do I need to say when
greeting people, by order of rank, so as not to offend them?
And what have you and Kara decided I'm going to wear?"

This time it only took Kara and Brill an hour to dress
Miriam in a midnight-blue gown. But then they insisted on
taking another hour to paint her face, put up her hair, and
hang a few kilograms of gold, silver, and precious stones off
her. At the end of the process, Miriam walked in front of the
mirror (a full two feet in diameter, clearly imported from the

other side) and took a comic double-take. "Is that me?" she asked.

"Should it not be?" Brilliana replied. Miriam glanced at her. Brilliana's outfit looked to Miriam to be both plainer and more elegant than her own, not to mention easier to move in. "It is a work of art," Brilliana explained, "fit for a countess."

"Hah. 'A work of art!' And here I was, thinking I was a plain old journalist." Miriam nodded to herself. *All face*, she thought. *All the wealth goes on the outside to show how rich you are. That's how they think. If you don't display it, you ain't got it. Remember that.* This outfit seemed marginally less overblown than the last: Maybe she was getting used to local styles. "Is there," she asked doubtfully, "anywhere that I can put a few small items?"

"I can assign a maid to carry them, if it pleases you—" Brilliana caught her expression. "Oh *that* kind of item."

"Yes." Miriam nodded, afraid that smiling would crack her makeup.

"She could use a muff, for her hands?" suggested Kara.

"A 'muff'?" asked Miriam.

"This." Kara produced a cylindrical fur hand-warmer from somewhere. "Will it do?"

"I think so." Miriam tried stuffing her hands in it. It had room to spare—and a small pocket. She smiled in spite of herself. "Yes, this *will* do," she said. She walked over to her day sack and fished around in it. "Dammit, this is ridiculous—got it!" She stood up triumphantly clutching the bag and pulled out a number of small items that she proceeded to stuff into the muffler.

"Milady?" Kara looked puzzled.

"Never go out without a spare tampon," Miriam told her. "You know, tampons?" She blinked in surprise. "Well, maybe you don't. And a few other things." Like a strip of beta-blocker tablets, a small bottle of painkillers, a tarnished silver locket, a credit card wallet, and a mobile phone. *That should cover most eventualities*, she told herself.

"Milady—" Kara looked even more puzzled.

"Yes, yes," Miriam said briskly. "We can go now—or as soon as you're ready, right? Only," she held up a finger, "it occurs to me that it would be a good idea to keep our carriage ready to return at a moment's notice. Do you understand? Against the possibility that my mystery admirer turns up again."

"I'll see to it," said Brilliana. She looked slightly worried.

"Do so." Miriam took a deep breath. "Shall we leave now?"

Traveling by carriage seemed to involve as much preparation as a flight in a light plane and was even less comfortable. A twenty-minute slog in a freezing cold carriage, sandwiched between Kara and Brilliana, didn't do anything good to Miriam's sense of tolerance and goodwill. The subsequent hour of walking across the king's brilliantly polished parquet supporting a fixed, gracious grin and a straight back wouldn't normally have done anything to help, either—but Miriam had done trade shows before, and she found that if she treated this whole junket as a fancy-dress industry event, she actually felt at home in it. Normally she'd use a dictaphone to record her notes—a lady-in-waiting in a red gown would have been rather obtrusive at a trade show—but the principle was the same, she decided, getting into the spirit of things. "Is that *so?*" she cooed, listening attentively to Lord Ragnr and Styl hold forth on the subject of the lobster fishermen under his aegis. "And do they have many boats?" she asked. "What kind do they prefer, and how many men crew them?"

"Many!" Lord Ragnr and Styl puffed up his chest until it almost overshadowed his belly, which was proud and taut beneath a layer of sashes and diadems. "At last census, there were two hundred fishing crofts in my isles! And all of them but the most miserable with boats of their own."

"Yes, but what type are they?" Miriam persisted, forcing a smile.

"I'm sure they're perfectly adequate fishing boats; I

shouldn't worry on their behalf, my lady. You should come and visit one summer. I am sure you would find the fresh sea air much to your favor after the summer vapors of the city, and besides—" he huffed— "didn't I hear you say you were interested in the whales?"

"Indeed." Miriam dipped her head, chalking up another dead loss—yet another feudal drone who didn't know or wouldn't talk about the source of his own wealth, being more interested in breeding war horses and feuding with the king's neighbors. "May I have the pleasure of your conversation later?" she asked. "For I see an old friend passing, and it would be rude not to say hello—"

She ducked away from Ragnr and Styl, and headed toward the next nobleman and his son—she was beginning to learn how to spot such things—and wife. "Ambergris, Brill, may be available from Ragnr and Styl. Make a note of that, please, I want to follow it up later. Who's this fellow, then?"

"This is Eorl Euan of Castlerock. His wife is Susan and the son is, um, I forget his name. Rural aristocracy, they farm and, uh, they're clients of the Lords Arran. How do you spell Ambergris?"

Miriam advanced on Eorl Euan with a gracious smile. "My lord!" She said. "I am sorry, but I have not been gifted with the privilege of your acquaintance before. May I intrude upon your patience for a few minutes?"

It was, she had discovered, a surprisingly effective tactic. The manners were different, the glitz distracting, and the products and press releases took a radically dissimilar form—but the *structure* was the same. At a trade show she was used to stalking up to a stand where some bored men and women were waiting to fall upon such as she and tell her their business plans and their life stories. She'd had no idea what happened at a royal court event, but evidently a lot of provincial nobility turned up in hope of impressing all and sundry and carving out a niche as providers of this or that— and they were as much in search of an audience with a bright smile and a notepad as any marketing executive, did they but know it.

"What are you doing, mistress?" Brilliana asked during one gap in the proceedings.

"I'm learning, Brill. Observe and take notes!"

She was nodding periodically and looking seriously, as Lord Something of This told her about Earl Other of That's infringement upon his historically recognized deer forest in pursuit of coal in the Netherwold Mountains down the coast, when she became aware of a growing silence around her. As Lord Something ran down, she turned her head—and saw a posse advancing on her, led by a dowager of fearsomely haughty aspect, perhaps eighty years old but as dry as a mummy, with curiously drooping eyelids, two noble ladies to either side, and a train borne by no less than three pages astern. "Ah," said the dowager. "And *this* is the Countess Thorold Hjorth I have heard so much about?" she asked the younger of her two companions, who nodded, avoiding Miriam's eyes.

Miriam turned and smiled pleasantly. "Whom do I have the honor of addressing?" she asked. *Where's Brill?* She wondered. *Dammit, why did she have to wander off right now?* The dowager was exuding the kind of chill Miriam associated with cryogenic refrigerants. Or maybe her venom glands were acting up. Miriam smiled wider, trying to look innocent and friendly.

"This is the grand dowager Duchess Hildegarde Thorold Hjorth, first of the Thorold line, last of the Thorold Hjorth braid," announced the one who'd spoken to the dowager.

Oh. Miriam dipped as she'd been taught: "I'm honored to meet you," she said.

"So you should be." Miriam nearly let her smile slip at that, the first words the duchess had spoken to her. "Without my approval, you wouldn't be here."

"Oh, really?" Her smile was becoming painful. "Well, then I am duly grateful to you." *Brilliana! Why now? Who is this dragon?*

"Of course." The dowager's expression finally relaxed, from an expression of intense disapproval into full-on contempt. "I felt the need to inspect the pretender for myself."

'*Pretender*'? "Explain yourself," Miriam demanded, tens-

ng. There must have been something frightening about her
expression: One of the ladies-in-waiting took a step backward
and the other raised a hand to her mouth. "Pretender to *what?*"

"Why, to the title you assume with so little preparation
and polish, and manners utterly unfitted to the role. A mere
commoner from the mummer's stand, jumped up and
gussied up by Cousin Lofstrom to stake his claim." The
dowager's look of fierce indignation reminded Miriam of a
captive eagle she'd once seen in a zoo. "A pauper, dependent
on the goodwill and support of others. If you were who you
claim to be, you would be of substance." Duchess Hildegarde Thorold Hjorth made a little flicking motion, consign-
ing her to the vacuum of social obscurity. "Come, my—"

"Now you wait right here!" Miriam took a step forward,
right into the dowager's path. "I am not an imposter," she
said, her voice pitched low and even. "I am who I am, and if
I am not here happily and of my own free will, I will *not* be
spoken to with contempt."

"Then how *will* you be spoken to?" asked the duchess,
treating her to a little acid smile that showed how highly she
rated Miriam in this company.

"With the respect due my station," Miriam threw at her,
"or not at all."

The dowager raised one hooded eyebrow. "Your station is
a matter of debate, child, but not for you—and it is a debate
that will be settled at Beltaigne, when I shall take great pleasure in ensuring that it is brought before the Clan council
and given the consideration it deserves. And you might wish
to give some thought to the matter of your competence, even
if your identity is upheld." The little smile was back, dripping venom: "If you joust with the elite, do not be surprised
when you are unhorsed." She turned and walked away, leaving Miriam gaping and angry.

She was just beginning to realize she'd been outmaneuvered when Brilliana appeared at her elbow. "Why didn't
you warn me?" she hissed. "Who *is* that poisonous bitch?"

Brilliana looked astonished. "But I thought you knew!
That was your grandmother."

"Oh. *Oh.*" Miriam clapped a hand to her mouth. "I have
grandmother?"

"Yes and a—" Brilliana stopped. "You didn't know," sh
said slowly.

"No," Miriam said, looking at her sharply.

"Everyone says you've got the family temper," Brill le
slip, then looked shocked.

"You mean, like—*that?*" Miriam looked at her, aghast.

"Hmm." Brill clammed up, her face as straight as a gam
bler with an inside flush. "Oh look," she said, glancing be
hind Miriam. "Isn't that—"

Miriam glanced around, then turned, startled. "I wasn'
expecting to see you here," she said, trying to pull herself together in the aftermath of the duchess's attack.

The duke's keeper of secrets nodded. "Neither was I, until
yesterday," he said stone-faced. He looked her up and down.
"You appear to be settling in here."

"I am." Miriam paused, unsure how to continue. Matthias
looked just as intimidating in Niejwein court finery as he
had in a business suit. It was like having a tank take a
pointed interest in her. "Yourself? Are you doing all right?"

"Well enough." Matthias noticed Brilliana. "You. Please
leave us, we have important matters to discuss."

"Humph."

Brill turned and was about to leave. "Do we?" Miriam
asked, pointedly. "I rather think we can talk in front of my
lady-in-waiting."

"No we can't." Matthias smiled thinly. "Go away, I said."
He gestured toward the wall, where secluded window bays,
curtain-lined against the cold, provided less risk of being
overhead. "Please come with me."

Miriam followed him reluctantly. *If they ever make a
movie about the Clan, they'll have to hire Schwarzenegger to
play this guy,* she decided. *But Arnie has a sense of humor.*
"What is there to talk about?" she asked quietly.

"Your uncle charged me to deliver this to you." Matthias
held out a small wooden tube, like a miniature poster holder.

"For the king, a sworn affidavit testifying to your identity." His expression was unreadable. "I am to introduce you to his majesty on behalf of my master."

"I, uh, see." Miriam took the tube. "Any other messages?"

"Security." Matthias shook his head. "It's not so good here. I gather that Baron Hjorth assigned you no guards? That's bad. I'll deal with it myself in the morning." He leaned over her like a statue.

"Um." Miriam looked up at him. "Is that all?"

"No." His cheek twitched. "I have some questions for you."

"Well. Ask away." Miriam glanced around, increasingly uncomfortable with the way Matthias had corraled her away from the crowd. "What about?"

"Your upbringing. This is important because it may help me identify who is trying to kill you. You were adopted, I believe?"

"Yes." Miriam shrugged. "My parents—I was in care, the woman I was found with was dead, stabbed, a Jane Doe. So when Morris and Iris went looking for a child to adopt, I was around."

"I see." Matthias's tone was neutral. "Was your home ever burgled when you were a child? Did anyone ever attack your parents?"

"My—no, no burglaries." Miriam shook her head. "No attacks. My father's death, that was a hit-and-run driver. But they caught him; he was just a drunk. Random chance."

" 'Random chance.' " Matthias sniffed. "Do not underestimate random chance."

"I don't," she said tersely. "Listen, why the third degree?"

"Because." He stared at her unblinkingly: "I take a personal interest in all threats to Clan security."

"Bullshit. You're secretary to the duke. And a member of the outer families, I believe?" She looked up at him. "That puts a glass ceiling right over your head, doesn't it? You sit in Fort Lofstrom like a spider, pulling strings, and you run things in Boston when the duke is elsewhere, but only by proxy. Don't you? So what's in it for you?"

"You are mistaken." Matthias's eyes glinted by candle light. "To get here, I left the duke's side this morning."

"Oh, I get it. Someone gave you a lift across and you caught the train."

"Yes." Matthias nodded. "And here is something else you should understand, your ladyship. I am *not* of high birth. Or rather, but for an accident of heredity . . . but like many of my relatives I have reached an accommodation with the Clan." He took her arm. "I know a little about your history. Not everyone who lives here is entirely happy with the status quo, the way the Clan council is run. You have a history of digging—"

"Let go of my wrist," Miriam said quietly.

"Certainly." Matthias dropped his grip. "Please accept my apologies. I did not intend to give offense."

Miriam paused for a moment. "Accepted."

"Very well." Matthias glanced away. "Would you care to hear some advice, my lady?"

"It depends," she said, trying to sound noncommittal, trying to stay in control. *First a hostile grandmother, now what . . . ?* She felt slightly dizzy, punch-drunk from too much information, much of it unwelcome. "In what spirit is the advice offered?"

Matthias's face was as stiff and controlled as a mask. "In a spirit of friendly solicitude and perfect altruism," he murmured.

She shrugged uncomfortably. "Well, then, I suppose I should take it in the manner in which it is intended."

Matthias lowered his voice. "The Clan has many secrets, as you have probably realized, and there are things here that you should avoid showing a conspicuous interest in. In particular, the alignment of inner members, those who vote within the council, is vulnerable to disturbance if certain proxies were realigned. You should be careful of embarrassments; the private is public, and you never know what seeming accidents may be taken by your enemies as proof of your incompetence. I say this as a friend: You would do well to find a protector—or a faction to embrace—before you become a target for the fears of every conspirator."

"Do you know who's threatening me? Are *you* threatening me?" she asked.

"No and no. I am simply attempting to educate you. There are more factions here than anyone will admit to." He shook his head. "I will visit you tomorrow and see to your guards—if that meets with your approval. I can provide you with a degree of protection if you choose to accept it. Do you?"

"Hah. We'll see." Miriam backed away from him, trying to cover her confusion. She retreated back into the flood of light shed by the enormous chandeliers overhead, back toward the torrent of faces babbling in their endless arrogant status games and power plays, just as Brilliana came hurrying up to her. "You have a summons!" Brill said hastily. "His royal highness would like you to present before him."

"Present what, exactly? My hitherto-undiscovered family tree, a miracle of fratricidal squabbles and—"

"No, your credentials." Brilliana frowned. "He gave them to you?"

Miriam held up the small scroll and examined the seal. It was similar to the one Olga had shown her, but different in detail.

"Yes," she said, finally.

"Was that all he wanted?" Brilliana asked.

"No." Miriam shook her head. "Time for that later. You'd better take me to his majesty."

The royal party held their space in another window bay backed by curtains and shutters. All the cloth didn't completely block the chill that exuded from the stonework. Miriam approached the king as she'd been shown, Brilliana—and a Kara she'd found somewhere—in tow, and made the deepest curtsy she could manage.

"Rise," said his high majesty, Alexis Nicholau III. "I believe we have met? The night before last?"

He smelled of stale wine and old sweat. "Yes, your majesty." She offered her scroll to him. "This is for you."

He cracked the seal with a shaky hand, unrolled it, the nodded to himself and handed it to a page. "Well, if you'r good enough for Angbard, you're good enough for me."

"Um. Your majesty?"

He waved vaguely at the curtains. "Angbard says you'l do, and what he says has a habit of sticking." One of the two princes sidled up behind him, trailing a couple of attendants "So I've got m'self a new countess."

"It would appear so, your majesty."

"You're his *heir*," said the king, relishing the last word.

Miriam's jaw dropped. "M-majesty?"

"Well, *he* says so," said King Alexis. "Says so right there." He stabbed a finger at the page who held the parchment. "'N, who d'you think really runs this place?"

"Pardon me, please. He hadn't told me."

"Well, I'm telling you," said the king. The prince—was it Creon or Egon? She couldn't tell them apart yet—leaned over his majesty's shoulder and stared at her frankly. "Doesn't matter much." The king sniffed. "You won't fill that man's shoes, girl. The man you marry might, though. If you both live long enough."

"I see," she said. The prince was clearly in his twenties, had long dark hair, an embroidered gold blouse, and a knife at his belt that looked to be a solid mass of gemstones. He regarded her with an expression of slack-jawed vacancy. *What* is *this?* Miriam wondered with growing fear. *Shit, I knew it! They're trying to set me up!*

"There's one way of seeing to that," the king added. "I believe you've not been introduced to my son Creon?"

"Delighted, absolutely delighted!" Miriam tried to smile at him. Creon nodded back at her happily.

"Creon is long past an age to marry," the king said thoughtfully. "Of course, whoever he took to wife would be a royal princess, you realize?" He looked down his nose at her. "Of course anyone who would be pledged to a royal household would need a very *special* dowry—" his glance was dark and full of veiled significance—"but I believe Angbard's relatives might find the price affordable. And the

ince would benefit from the intelligent self-interest of an
nderstanding wife."

"Uh-huh." She looked past the king, at Prince Creon. The
rince beamed at her, a delighted, friendly expression that
as nevertheless undermined by the way he simultaneously
rooled on his collar. "I'd be delighted to meet with the
rince later, under more appropriate circumstances," she
ushed. "Delighted! Of course!" She beamed, desperately
acking her brain for platitudes recovered from a thousand
nd one annual shareholders' meetings gone bad. "I'd love
o hear from you, really I would, but I am still being intro-
uced to so many fascinating people and I owe you my full
attention, it would be awful to devote less than my full ener-
gies and attention to your son! I quite appreciate your—"

"Yes, yes, that's enough." The king beamed at her.
"There's no need for sycophancy. *I* have heard so much I am
far beyond its reach, and he—" he nodded—"will never be
within it."

Gulp. "I see, your majesty."

"Yes, he's an idiot," King Alexis said genially. "And
you're too old." Some instinct for self-preservation made
Miriam swallow an automatic protest. "But he's *my* idiot,
and were he to marry his child would be third in line to the
throne, at least until Egon's wife bears issue. I urge you to
think on this, young lady: Should you meet anyone suitable,
I would be most interested to hear of them. Now begone
with you, to these vastly important strangers who fascinate
you so conspicuously. I won't hold it against you."

"Uh—thank you! Thank you most kindly!" Miriam fled in
disarray, outmaneuvered for the third time this evening. *Just
what is it with these people?* She wondered. The king's over-
ture was undoubtedly well-meant; just alarming and demor-
alizing, for it highlighted the depths of her own inadequacy
in trying to play power politics with these sharks. *The* king
*wants to marry his son into the Clan, and he thinks I'm a
useful person to talk to?* It was desperately confusing. And
why had Angbard named her his heir? That was the real
question. Without an answer, nothing else seemed to make

sense. What was he trying to achieve? Didn't it make
some kind of target?

Target.

She stopped, halfway from pillared bay to dancing flo
as if struck in the head by a two-by-four.

"Milady Miriam? What is it?" Brilliana was tugging
her sleeve.

"Shush. I'm thinking."

Target. Thirty-two years ago someone had pursued a
murdered her mother, while she was en route to this very cou
to pay attendance to the king—probably Alexis's father. Du
ing the civil war between the families, before the Clan peac
was installed. Her mother's marriage had been the peace se
tlement that cemented one corner of the arrangement.

Since she'd come here, someone had tried to kill her
least twice.

Miriam thought furiously. *These people hold long grudge*
Are the incidents connected? If so, it could be more tha
Baron Hjorth's financial machinations. Or Matthias's myste
rious factions. Or even the dowager grandmother, Duches
Hildegarde Thorold Hjorth.

Someone ignorant of her past. Of course! If they'd known
about her before, or on the other side, she'd have been pushed
under a subway train or run over by a car or shot in a random
drive-by incident long before she'd discovered the way back.
How common is it to conceal an heir? She wondered.

"Mistress, you've got to come."

"What is it?" Something about Brilliana's insistent nudg-
ing attracted Miriam's attention. *It's not me, it's something*
to do with who I am, she realized vaguely, groping for the
light. *I'm so important to these people that they can't con-*
ceive of me not joining in their game. It would be like the
vice president refusing to talk to the Senate. Even if I don't
do *anything, tell them I want to be left alone, that would be*
seen as some kind of deep political game. "What's happening?" She asked distractedly.

"It's Kara," Brill insisted. "We've got a problem."

"I'm here," she said, shaking her head, dazed by her in-ght. *I've got to be a politician, whether I like it or not . . . What is it now?"*

As it happened, Kara was somewhat the worse for wear, not ⸱ say steaming drunk. A young Sir Nobody-in-Particular had ⸱een plying her with wine, evidently fortified by freezing—⸱er speech was slurred and incoherent and her hair mussed—⸱uite possibly with intent to climb into her clothing with her. ⸱le hadn't got far, perhaps because Kara was more enthusias-⸱c than discreet, but it wasn't for want of trying. Though Kara ⸱rotested her innocence, Miriam detected more than a minor ⸱ote of concern on Brill's part. "Look, I think there's a good ⸱eason for going home," Miriam told the two of them. "Can ⸱ou get into the carriage?" she questioned Kara.

"Course I can," Kara slurred. "N'body does 't better!"

"Right." Miriam glanced at Brilliana. "Let's get her ⸱ome."

"Do you want to stay, mistress?" Brilliana looked at her doubtfully.

"I want—" Miriam stopped. "What I want doesn't seem likely to make any difference here," she said bleakly, feeling the weight of the world descend on her shoulders. *Angbard named me his heir because he wanted me to attract whatever faction tried to kill my mother,* she thought. *Hildegarde takes against me because I can't bring back, or be, her daughter, and now I've got these two ingenues to look out for.* Not to mention Roland. Roland, who might be—

"Got a message," announced Kara as they were halfway to the door.

"A message? How nice," Miriam said drily.

"For th' mistress," Kara added. Then she focused on Miriam. "Oh!"

From between her breasts, she produced a thin scrap of paper. Miriam stuffed it in her hand-warmer and took Kara by the arm. "Come on home, you," she insisted.

The carriage was literally freezing. Icicles dangled from the steps as they climbed in, and the leather seats crackled as they sat down. "Home," Brilliana told the driver. Wit[h] shake of the reins, he set the horses to walking, their bre[ath] steaming in the frigid air. "That was exciting!" she sa[id] "Shame you spoiled it," she chided Kara. "What were y[ou] arguing about with those gentles?" she asked Miri[am] timidly. "I've never seen anything like it!"

"I was being put in my place by my grandmother, I thin[k]," Miriam muttered. Hands in her warmer, she fumbled for [a] blister-pack of beta-blocker tablets. She briefly brought [a] hand out and dry-swallowed one, along with an ibuprofe[n]. She had a feeling she'd be needing them soon. "What do y[ou] know about the history of my family, Brill?" she asked.

"What, about your parents? Or your father? Families [or] braids?"

Miriam shut her eyes. "The civil war," she murmure[d]. "Who started it?"

"Why—" Brilliana frowned. "The civil war? 'Tis clea[r] enough: Wu and Hjorth formed a compact of trade, east coas[t] to west, at the expense of the Clan; Thorold, Lofstrom, Arne[r]-sen, and Hjalmar returned the compliment, sending Andru Ar[-] nesen west to represent them in Chang-Shi, and he wa[s] murdered on his arrival there by a man who vanished into thi[n] air. Clearly it was an attempt to prevent the Clan of four from competing, so they took equivalent measures against the gang of two. What made it worse was that some hidden members of each braid seemed to want to keep the feud burning. Every time it looked as if the elders were going to settle things up, a new outrage would take place—Duchess Lofstrom abused and murdered, Count Thorold-Arnesen's steading raided and set alight."

"That's—" Miriam's eyes narrowed. "You're a Hjalmar, right?"

"Yes?" Brilliana nodded. "Why? What does it mean?"

"Just thinking," Miriam said. *Left-over grudges, a faction that didn't want the war to stop, to stop eating the Clan's guts out.* She hit a brick wall. *It's as if someone from outside had stepped in, intervened to set cousins against each other* . . . She sat up.

"Weren't there originally seven sons of Angmar the Sly?"

"Um, yes?" Brill looked puzzled.

"But one was lost, in the early days?"

Brill nodded. "That was Markus, or something. The first head west to make his fortune."

"Aha." Miriam nodded.

"Why?"

"Just thinking." *Hypothesis: There is another family, outside the Clan. The Clan don't know about them. They're not numerous, and they're in the same import/export trade. Won't they see the Clan as a threat? But why? Why couldn't they simply marry back into the braids?* She shook her head. *I should have tried those experiments with the photograph of the locket.*

The carriage drew up at the door of the Thorold Palace, and Miriam and Brilliana managed to get Kara out without any untoward incidents. Then Kara responded to the cold air by stumbling to the side of the ornate portico, bending over as far as she could, and vomiting in an ornamental planter.

"Ugh," said Brilliana. She glanced sidelong at Miriam. "This should not have happened."

"At least the plants were dead first," Miriam reassured her. "Come on. Let's get her inside."

"No, that's not what I meant." Brill took a deep breath. "Euen of Arnesen plied her with fortified wine while she was outwith my sight. I should have seen it, but was myself beseiged when not following your lead." She frowned. "This was deliberate."

"You expect me to be surprised?" Miriam shook her head. "Come on. Let's get her up to our rooms and see she doesn't—" a flashback to Matthias's warning—"*embarrass us further.*"

Brill helped steer Kara upstairs, and Miriam ensured that she was sat upright on a chaise longue, awake and complaining with a cup of tea, before she retreated to her bedroom. She started to remove her cloak then remembered the handwarmer, and the message Kara had passed her. She unrolled it and read.

I have urgent news concerning the assassin who has
been stalking you. Meet me in the orangery at midnight

Your obedient servant,
Earl Roland Lofstrom

"*Shit,*" she mumbled under her breath. "Brill!"

"Yes, Miriam?"

"Help me undress, will you?"

"What, right now? Are you going to bed?"

"Not immediately," Miriam said grimly. "Our assassin
seems to have gotten tired of trying to sneak up on me and
trying to reel me in like a fish. Only he's made a big mistake." She turned to present her back. "Unlace me. I've got
places to go, and it'd be a shame to get blood on this gown

Black jeans, combat boots, turtleneck, and leather jacket:
gun in her pocket and a locket in her left hand. Miriam
breathed deeply, feeling naked despite everything. She felt
as if the only thing she was wearing was a target between her
shoulder blades.

Across the room Brilliana looked worried. "Are you sure
this is the right thing to do?" she asked again. "Do you want
me to come? I am trained using a pistol—"

"I'll be fine. But I may have to world-walk in a hurry." *I
won't be fine*, Miriam corrected herself silently: *But if I
don't deal with this trouble sooner or later, they'll kill me.
Won't they?* And the one thing an assassin wouldn't be expecting would be for her—not one of the Clan-raised hot-
heads born with her hands on a pistol, but a reasonable,
civilized journalist from a world where that sort of thing just
didn't happen—to turn on them. She hoped.

Miriam hitched her day sack into place and checked her
right pocket again, the one with the gun and a handful of
spare cartridges. She didn't feel fine: There were butterflies
in her stomach. "If there's a problem, I'll stay the night on
the other side, safely out of the way. But I need to *know*. I

nt you to wait half an hour, then take Kara around to Olga
d sit things out with her there. With your gun, and Olga,
d her own guards, in a properly doppelgängered area, you
ould be safe. But I don't want her tripping and falling
wnstairs before we learn who gave her that note. D'you
derstand? Matthias promised to sort me out some guards
morrow, but I don't trust him. If he's in on this—or just be-
g watched—there'll be an attempt on my life tonight. Ex-
pt this time I think they got sloppy, expecting me to turn
p for it like it's an appointment. So I'm going to avoid it
ntirely."

"I understand." Brill stood up. "Good luck," she said.

"Luck has nothing to do with it." Miriam took two steps
oward the door, then pulled out her locket.

Dizziness, mild nausea, a headache that clamped around
er head like a vice. She looked around. Nothing seemed to
have changed in the warehouse attic, other than the dim light
getting dimmer and the bad smell from somewhere nearby. It
was getting worse, and it reminded her of something. "Hmm."

Miriam ducked behind a wall of wooden crates, her head
pounding. She pulled the pistol out, slightly nervous at first.
It was a self-cocking revolver, reliable and infinitely reassur-
ing in the gloom. *Stay away from guns*, the training course
had emphasized. But that was then, back where she was a
journalist and the world made sense to rational people. But *if
they're trying to kill you, you have to kill them first*, was another, older lesson from the firearms instructor her father
had sent her to. And here and now, it seemed to make more
sense.

Carefully, very slowly, she inched forward over the edge
of the mezzanine floor and looked down. The ground floor
of the warehouse was a maze of wooden cases and boxes.
The mobile home that constituted the site office was blocked
up in the middle of it. There was no sign of anybody about,
none of the comforting noises of habitation.

Miriam rose to a crouch and scurried down the stairs as
quietly as she could. She ducked below the stairs, then from
shadow to shadow toward the door.

There was a final open stretch between the site office
the exit. Instead of crossing it, Miriam tiptoed around
wall of the parked trailer, wrinkling her nose at a faint,
smell.

The site office door was open and the light inside was
Holding her gun behind her, she stood up rapidly a
climbed the three steps to the door of the trailer. Then
looked inside.

"Fuck!"

The stench was far worse in here, and the watchman seem
to be smiling at her. Smiling? She turned away blindly, stic
ing her head out of the door, and took deep breaths, despe
ately trying to get her stomach back under control. *Cultiva
your professional detachment*, she told herself, echoing a ha
forgotten professor's admonition from med school. Reflex
left over from anatomy classes kicked in. She turned back
the thing that had surprised her and began to make observ
tions, rattled to her core but still able to function. She'd see
worse in emergency rooms, after all.

It was the old guy she'd met with the clipboard, and h
was past any resuscitation attempt. Someone had used an ex
tremely sharp knife to sever his carotid artery and trachea
and continued to slice halfway through his spine from be
hind. There was dried blood everywhere, huge black puddle:
of it splashed over walls and floor and the paper-strewr
desk, curdling in great thick viscous lumps—the source of
only some of the smell, for he'd voided his bowels at the
same time. He was still lying on top of his tumbled chair, his
skin waxy and—she reached out to touch—cold. *At least
twelve hours*, she thought, gingerly trying to lift an arm still
locked in rigor mortis, *but probably no longer*. Would the intense cold retard the processes of decay? Yes, a little bit.
*That would put it before my last trip over here, but after I
saw Paulette.*

"Goodfellas," she whispered under her breath: It came out
as an angry curse. During her night with Roland, someone
had entered the warehouse, casually murdered the old man,
climbed the stairs—breaking the hair—and then, what?

ought the attacker who'd gone up on the roof and tried to
ack Olga? Then he came back later, crossed over to the
ier side, and emptied a pistol into the dummy made of pil-
ws lying in her bed? Gone away? *Correlation does not im-
y causality*, she reminded herself and giggled, shocked at
rself and increasingly angry.

"What to do?" Well, the obvious thing was to use her most
ingerous weapon. So she pulled out her phone and speed-
aled Roland.

"Yeah?" He picked up at the fourth ring.

"Roland, there's a problem." She realized that she was
anting, breathing way too fast. "Let me catch my breath."
he slowed down. "I'm in the warehouse on the doppel-
änger side of my rooms. The night watchman's had his
hroat cut. He's been dead for between twelve and thirty-six
ours. And someone—did you send me a note by way of the
eception on the other side, saying to meet you in the or-
ingery at Palace Thorold?"

"No!" He sounded shocked. "Where are you?" She gave
him the address. "Right, I'll tell someone to get a team of
cleaners around immediately. Listen, we're wrestling alliga-
tors over here tonight. It looks like the Department of
Homeland Security has been running some traffic analysis
on frequent fliers looking for terrorists and uncovered one of
our—"

"I get the message," she interrupted. "Look, *my* headache
is that I planted a hair across the top step when I came
through last night, and it was broken when I went back over
this morning. I'm fairly sure someone from the Clan came
here, killed the watchman, headed up to the mezannine
that's on the other side of my suite—breaking the hair—and
crossed over. There was another attempt to kill me in my
suite last night, Roland. They want me dead, and there's
something going down in the palace."

"Wait there. I'll be around in person as soon as I can get
unstuck from this mess."

Miriam stared at the phone that had gone dead in her
hand, paranoid fantasies playing through her head.

"Angbard set me up," she muttered to herself. "Wha[...]
Roland's in on it?" It was bizarre. The only way to be [...]
would be to go to the rendezvous, surprise the assassin. [...]
had come over from this side. Yes, but if they could get [...]
her apartment, why bother with the silly lure?

"What if there are *two* groups sending assassins?" [...]
asked the night watchman. He grinned at her twice ov[...]
"The obvious one who is clearly a Clan member, and, a[...]
the subtle one—"

She racked her brains for the precise number of pa[...]
from the stairs up to her room to the back door opening i[...]
the grounds of the palace. Then she remembered the cra[...]
laid out below. *The entrance will be next door*, she realize[...]
She jumped out of the trailer with its reek of icy death a[...]
dashed across to the far wall of the warehouse—the one co[...]
responding to the main entrance vestibule of the palace.
was solid brick, with no doors. "Damn!" She slipped arour[...]
to the front door and out into the alley, then paced out th[...]
fifty feet it would take. Then she carefully examined the ne[...]
frontage.

It was a bonded warehouse. Iron bars fronted all the dus[...]
smeared windows, and metal shutters hid everything withi[...]
from view. The front door was padlocked heavily and looke[...]
as if nobody had opened it in years. "This has got to be it,'[...]
she muttered, looking up at the forbidding façade. What bet[...]
ter way to block off the entrance to a palace on the othe[...]
side? Probably most of the rooms behind the windows wer[...]
bricked off or even filled with concrete, corresponding to the
positions of the secure spaces on the other side. But there
had to be some kind of access to the public reception area,
didn't there?

Miriam moved her locket to her left hand and pulled out
her pistol. "How the hell do they do this in the movies?" she
asked herself as she probed around the chain. "Oh well." She
carefully aimed the gun away from her, at the hasp of the
padlock. Then she pulled the trigger.

The crack of the gun was deafeningly loud in the night-
time quiet, but the lock parted satisfyingly easily. Miriam

nked it away, opened the bolt, and pushed the door in.

An alarm began to jangle somewhere inside the building. e jumped, but there wasn't anything to be done about it. e was standing at one end of a dusty linoleum-floored cordor. A flick of a switch and the dim lights came on, lighting path into the gloom past metal gates like jail cell doors that locked access to rooms piled ceiling-high with large barls. Miriam closed the door behind her and strode down the orridor as fast as she dared, hoping desperately that she was ght about where it led. There was a reception room at the nd: cheap desks and chairs covered in dust sheets and a ocked and bolted back door. It was about the right distance, he decided. Taking a deep breath, she raised her locket and ocused on the symbol engraved inside it—

—And she was *cold,* and the lights were out, and her skull elt as if she'd run headfirst into a brick wall. Snowflakes fell on her as she doubled over, trying to prevent the intense nausea from turning into vomiting. *I did that too fast,* she thought vaguely between waves of pain. *Even with the beta-blockers.* The process of world-walking seemed to do horrible things to her blood pressure. *Good thing I'm not on antidepressants,* she thought grimly. She forced herself to stand up and saw that she was just in the garden behind the palace—outdoors. Anyone trying to invade the palace by way of the doppelgänger warehouse on the other side would find themselves under the guns of the tower above—if the defenses were manned. But it was snowing tonight, and someone obviously wanted as few witnesses around as possible . . .

An iron gate in the wall behind her was the mirror image of the door to the warehouse office. "Orangery," she muttered through gritted teeth. She slid along the wall like a shadow, letting her eyes grow accustomed to the night. The orangery was a familiar hump in the snow, but something was wrong. The door was ajar, letting the precious heat (and how many servants did it take to keep that boiler fed?) escape into the winter air.

"Well, isn't that just *too* cute," she whispered, tightening her grip on her pistol. *'Welcome to my parlor' said the spider to the fly,* she thought. *The style is all wrong. Assassin #1 breaks i[nto] my room and shoots up the bedding. Twice. Assassin #2 trie[s to] bounce Olga into shooting me for him, then sends an RSVP [on] an engraved card. Assassin #3 shows me an open door. Wh[ich] of these things is not like the other?* She shivered—and n[ot] from the cold: the hot rage she'd been holding back ever sin[ce] she'd first been abducted was taking hold.

The wall at this end of the orangery was of brick, and t[he] glassy arch of the ceiling was low, beginning only about t[en] feet up. Miriam gritted her teeth and fumbled for finger an[d] toe holds. Then she realized there was a cast-iron drain pip[e] half-buried under the snow where the wall of the orangery m[et] the corner of the inner garden wall. *Aha.* She put the pistol [in] her pocket and began to climb, this time with more confidence.

On top of the wall she could look out across a corrugate[d] sheet of whiteness—the snow was settling on the oranger[y] faster than the heat from below could melt it. Leaning for[-]ward, she used her sleeve to rub a clear swathe in the glas[s.] Paraffin lamps shed a thin glow through the orangery, help[-]ing with the warmth and providing enough light to see by. To Miriam's night-adapted vision it was like a glimpse into a dim subterranean hell. She hunted around and saw, just be[-]hind the door, a hunched shadow. And after a minute of watching—during which time her hands began to grow numb—she saw the shadow move, shifting in position just like a man shuffling his feet in the cold draft from outside.

"Right," she whispered tensely, feeling an intense, burn-ing sense of hatred for the figure on the other side, just as the door opened further and someone else came in.

What happened then happened almost too fast to see— Miriam froze atop the window, unable to breathe in the cold air, her head throbbing until she wondered if she was com-ing down with a full-blown migraine. The shadow flowed forward behind the person who'd entered the orangery. There was a flurry of activity, then a body collapsed on the floor in a spreading pool of . . . of— *Holy shit,* thought Miriam, *he's killed him!*

Shocked out of her angry reverie, she slid back down the rainpipe, scraping hands and cheek on the rough stone-work, and landed in a snowdrift hard enough that it nearly knocked the breath out of her. *Quick!* Fumbling for her pistol, she skidded toward the door and yanked it open. She brought the gun up in time to see a man turning toward her. He was dressed all in black, his face covered by a ski mask or something similar: The long knife in his hand was red with blood as he straightened up from the body at his feet. "Stop—" Miriam called. He didn't stop, and time telescoped in on her. Two shots in the torso, two more—then the dry *click* of a hammer on a spent cartridge. The killer collapsed toward her and Miriam shook her head and took a step back, wishing she hadn't heard the sound of bullets striking flesh.

Time caught up with her again. "Shit!" She called out, heart lurching between her ribs like a frightened animal. A sense of gathering wrongness overcame her, as if what had just happened was impossible. Another old reflex caught up, and she stepped forward. "Gurney—" she bit her tongue. There were no gurneys here, no hemostats, no competent nurses to get the bleeding staunched and no defibrillators—and especially no packets of plasma and operating theaters in which to struggle for the victim's life.

She found herself an indefinite time later—probably only seconds had passed, although it felt like hours—staring down at a spreading pool of blood around her feet. Blood, and the body of a man, dressed from head to foot in black. A long curve-bladed knife lay beside him. Behind him—"Margit!" It was Lady Margit, Olga's chaperone. The fat lady had sung her last: There was nothing to be done. She still twitched, and maybe a modern ER room could have done something for her—but not here, not with a massive exsanguinating chest wound that had already stopped pumping. *Probably the dorsal aorta or a ventricle*, she realized. *Oh hell. What was she doing here?* For a moment, Miriam wished she believed in something—someone—who'd look after Margit. But there wasn't time for that now.

She turned back to the assassin. He was alive—but that was just residual twitching, too. She'd actually nai him through the heart with her first two shots, the seco double-tap turning his chest into a bloody mess. There v already a stench of excrement in the air as his bowels laxed. She pulled back his hood. The assassin was shave headed and flat-faced: *He looks Chinese*, she realized with mixture of astonishment and regret. She'd just *killed* a ma but—there was a chain around his neck.

"What the fuck?" she asked through the haze of h headache and anxiety, then she pulled out a round seale locket, utterly unadorned and plain. "Clan." She put it in h pocket and glanced at Margit's cooling body. "What o *earth* possessed you to come down here at midnight?" sh asked aloud. "Was it a message for—" she trailed off.

They're after Olga, too, she realized, and with that real ization came both a sick fear. *I have to warn Olga!*

Miriam left the orangery and headed toward the palace half-empty for the evening with its noble residents enjoying the king's hospitality. She wouldn't be able to world-walk from her own rooms any more, but if Brilliana was in, they'd have a little chat. *She knows more than she's saying*, Miriam realized. Slowing. *What a mess!* The implication was just beginning to sink in. "Wheels within wheels," she muttered. Her hands were shaking violently and the small of her back was icy cold with sweat from the adrenaline surge when she'd shot the assassin. She paused, leaning against the cold outside wall of the orangery while she tried to gather her composure. "He was here to kill me." The chill from the wall was beginning to penetrate her jacket. She dug around in her pocket for spare cartridges, fumbling as she reloaded the re-volver. *Got to find Olga. And Brill.*

And then she'd have to go undercover.

One way of looking at it was that there was a story to dig up, a story about her long-dead mother, blood feuds, and civil war, a tale of assassins who came in the night and drug-dealing aristocrats who would brook no rival. Just like any other undercover investigativeexpose—not that Miriam was

sed to undercover jobs, but she'd be damned if she'd sur-
ender to the editorial whims of family politics before she
roke that story all over them—at the Clan gathering on
Beltaigne night.

"Get moving, girl," she told herself as she pushed off the
wall and headed back toward the palace. "There's no time to
ose . . ."

PART 5

RUNAWAY

ENCOUNTER

The snow was falling thickly when Miriam reached the wall of the orangery, and she was shivering despite her leather jacket. It was dark, too, in a way that no modern city ever was—*No streetlights to reflect off the clouds*, she realized, fumbling with her pocket torch. The gate was shut, and she had to tug hard to open it. Beyond the gate, the vast width of the palace loomed out of the snow, row upon row of shuttered windows at ground level.

"Shit," Miriam muttered in the wind. *No guards*, she realized. Wasn't this the east wing, under the Thorold tower, where Olga was living? She glanced up at the towering mass of stonework. The entrances were all round the front, but she'd attract unwelcome attention going in. Instead she trudged over to the nearest window casement. "Hey—"

It wasn't a shuttered window: It was a doorway, designed to blend in with the building's rear aspect. There was a handle and a discreet bell-pull beside it. Cursing the architectural pretensions of whoever had designed this pile, Miriam tugged the rope. Something clanged distantly, behind door. She stepped sideways and steeled herself, raising pistol with a sick sense of anticipation in her stomach.

Rattling and creaking. A slot in the door, near eye lev squeaked as it moved aside. "Wehr ish—" quavered a hoar voice.

"Unlock the door and step back now," Miriam said, ai ing through the slot.

"Sisch!"

"*Now*." A click. Two terrified eyes stared at her for a m ment, then dropped from view. Miriam kicked the door har feeling the impact jar through her foot. For a miracle, the e derly caretaker had dropped the latch rather than shootin the bolt before he ran: Instead of falling flat on her ass wit a sore ankle, Miriam found herself standing in a dark hal way facing a door opposite. *Did he understand me?* Sh wondered. No time for that now. She darted forward, pullin the door closed behind her as she headed for the other end o the short hall. Then she paused. There was a narrow staircas beside her, heading up into the recesses of the servants' sid of the wing, but the old guy who'd let her in—*gardener or caretaker?*—had vanished through the door into the reception room off to one side. *Right*. Miriam took the stairs two at a time, rushed past the shut doors on the first landing as lightly as she could and only paused on the second landing.

"Where *is* everybody?" she whispered aloud. There should be guards, bells ringing, whatever—she'd just barged in and instead of security all she'd encountered was a frightened groundskeeper. The butterflies in her stomach hadn't gone away, if anything they were stronger. Either her imagination was working overtime or something was very wrong.

There were doors up here, doors onto cramped rooms used by the servants, but also a side door onto the main staircase that crawled around the walls of the tower's core, linking the suites of the noble residents. It was chilly, and the oil lamp mounted in a wall bracket hardly lightened the shadows, but it was enough to show Miriam which way to go. She pushed the side door open and stepped out onto the

aircase to get her bearings. It was no brighter in the main
all: The great chandelier was unlit and the oil lamps on
ach landing had been turned right down. Still, she was just
ne flight of stairs below the door to Olga's chambers. She
was halfway to the landing before she noticed something
wrong with the shadows outside the entrance. The door was
open. Which meant, if Brill had gotten through in time—

Miriam crept forward. The door was ajar, and something
bulky lay motionless in the shadows behind it. The reception
room it opened onto was completely dark, but something
told her it wasn't empty. She paused beside the entrance, her
heart hammering as she waited for her eyes to adjust. *If it's
another hit, that would explain the lack of guards*, she
thought. Memories of a stupid corporate junket—a "team
building" paintball tournament in a deserted office building
that someone in HR thought sounded like fun—welled up,
threatening her with a sense of déjà vu. Very slowly, she
looked round the edge of the door frame.

Something or someone clad in light-absorbing clothes
was kneeling in front of the door at the far end of the room.
Another figure stood to one side, the unmistakable outline of
some kind of submachine gun raised to cover the door. They
had their backs to her. *Sloppy, very sloppy*, she thought
tensely. Unless they *knew* there was nobody else in this wing
because they'd all been sent away.

The inner door creaked and the kneeling figure stood up
and flowed to one side. Now there was another gun. *This is
so not good*, Miriam realized sickly. She was going to have
to do something. Visions of the assassin in the orangery raising his knife and moving toward her—the two before her
were completely focused on the door, preparing to make
their move.

Then one of them looked around.

Afterward, Miriam wasn't completely sure what had happened. Certainly she remembered squeezing the trigger re-
peatedly. The evil sewing-machine chatter of automatic fire
wasn't hers, as it stitched a neat line of holes across the ceiling. She'd flinched, dazzled and deafened by the sudden

noise, and there'd been more hammering and she'd fal.
over, rolling aside as fast as she could, *then* what souno
like a different gun. And silence, once she discounted ❘
ringing in her ears.

"Miriam?" called Olga, "is that you?"

I'm still alive, she realized, wondering. Taking stock:
she was still alive, that meant the intruders weren't. "Yes
she called faintly. "I'm out here. Where are you?"

"Get in here. Quickly."

She took no second warning. Brill crouched beside th
splintered wreckage of the door, a brilliant electric lam
held in one hand, while Olga stood to the other side. He
face cast sharp shadows that flickered across the walls as sh
scanned the room, gun raised. "I am going to have harsʜ
words with the Baron," she said calmly as Miriam scuttle
toward them. "The guards he assigned me appear to have
taken their leave for the evening. Perhaps if I a flog a few un
til the ivory shows, it will convince him of my displeasure."

"They're not to blame," Miriam said hoarsely, feeling her
stomach rise. The smell of burned cordite and blood hung in
the air. "Brill?"

"I bought Kara hither, my lady. I did as you told me."

"She did." Olga nodded. "To be truthful, we did not need
your help with such as these." She jerked a thumb at the
darkened corner of the room. "There's an alarm that Oliver
does not know of, the duke insisted I bring it." The red eye
of an infrared motion sensor winked at Miriam. "But I am
grateful for the warning," she added graciously.

"I—" Miriam shuddered. "In the orangery. An assassin."

"What?" Olga looked at her sharply. "Who—"

"They killed Margit. Sent a note to lure me there, but I
was expecting trouble."

"That's terrible!" Brill looked appalled: The light swayed.
"What are we going to—"

"Inside," Olga commanded. Brill retreated, and after a
moment Miriam followed her. "Close the door, damn you!"
Olga called, and after a moment a timid serving maid scurried forward and began to yank on it. "When it's shut, bar it.

hen get that chest braced across it," Olga added, pointing to
wardrobe that looked to Miriam's eyes to be built from
most of an oak tree. She stopped and turned to Miriam.
This was aimed at you, not me," she said calmly, lowering
her machine pistol to point at the floor. "They're getting
overconfident. Margit—" she shook her head—"Brilliana
old me of the note, you are lucky to have escaped."

"What am I going to do?" Miriam asked. She felt dizzy
and sick, the room spinning around her head. There was a
stool near the fireplace: She stumbled toward it tiredly and
sat down. "Who sent them?"

"I don't know," Olga said thoughtfully.

A door in the opposite wall opened and Kara rushed in.
"My lady! You're hurt?"

"Not yet," Miriam said, waving her away tiredly. "The
killer in the orangery was of the Clan, he had a locket," she
said.

"That could tell us which braid he came from," Olga said.
"Have you got it?"

"I think—yes." Miriam pulled it out and opened it. "Shit."

"What is it?" asked Olga, leaning close. "Oh my."

Miriam stared at the locket. Inside it was a design like the
knotwork pattern she was learning to loathe—but this one
was subtly *wrong*. Different. A couplet with a different
rhyme. One that she knew, instinctively, at a gut level, would
take her somewhere *else* if she stared at it too long and hard.
Not to mention making her blood pressure spike so high it
would give her an aneurism—if she tried it in the next few
hours.

She snapped it shut again and looked up at Olga. "Do you
know what this means?" she asked.

Olga nodded very seriously. "It means you and Brilliana
will have to disappear," she said. "These two—" a sniff and
a nod at the barricaded doorway—"are of no account, but
this—" a glance at the locket—"might be the gravest threat
to the Clan in living memory." She frowned uncertainly. "I
had not imagined that such a thing might exist. But if it
does—"

"—They must stop at nothing to kill anyone who kno— they exist," said Brill, completing the thought for her. S— looked at Miriam with bright eyes. "Will you take me w— you wherever you go, mistress? You'll need someone guard your back . . ."

Two hours later.

Painkillers and beta-blockers are wonderful thing Miriam reflected as she glanced over her shoulder at Bri— She'd managed to relax slightly as Olga organized cleanup, marshaling a barricade inside the doorway an— chivying Kara and the servants into making themselves use— ful. Then Olga had pointed out in words of one syllable wha— this meant: that two factions, at least one of them hithert— unknown, were after her and it would be a good idea to mak— herself scarce. Finally, still feeling fragile but now accommodating herself to the idea, Miriam had crossed over. With— her passenger. Who wore a smart business suit and an expression of mild bemusement. "Where are we?" asked Brill.

"The doppelgänger warehouse." Miriam frowned as she transferred her locket to her left hip pocket. "Other side from my own chambers. Someone should have cleaned up by now."

Fidgeting in her pocket, she pulled out some cartridges. She shuffled quietly closer to the edge of the mezzanine and looked over the side as she reloaded her pistol.

"This wasn't what I expected," the younger woman said in hushed tones, staring up at the dim warehouse lights.

"Stay quiet until I've checked it out." She let a sharp note creep into her voice. "We may not be alone here."

"Oh."

Miriam crept to the edge of the platform and looked down. There was no sign of movement below, and the front door of the warehouse—past the dismounted trailer that served as a site office—was shut. "Wait here. I'll call you down when it's safe," she said.

"Yes, Miriam."

She took a deep breath, then darted down the stairs
ghtly, her gun raised. Nobody shot at her from conceal-
1ent. She reached the bottom step and paused for a couple
f seconds before stepping off the metal staircase onto dusty
vooden floorboards, then duck-walked over to the side of
he site office, out of sight from its windows and the door.
Creeping again, she sidled around the wall of the trailer and
crouched next to the short flight of steps leading in to it. She
spent about a minute staring at the threshold, then stood up
slowly, lowered her gun, and carefully returned it to her
jacket pocket. She rubbed her forehead, then turned. "You
can come down now, as long as you come right over here.
Don't touch anything with your hands!"

Brilliana stood up and dusted herself off, lips wrinkling in
distaste as she tried to shake the warehouse cobwebs from
the sleeve of her Chanel suit. Then she walked down the
stairs slowly, not touching the guard rail. Her back was
straight, as if she was making a grand entrance rather than a
low-life departure.

Miriam pointed at the steps to the trailer. "Don't, whatever you do, even *think* about going in there," she warned.
Her expression was drawn. Brill sniffed, conspicuously, then
pulled a face in disgust.

"What *happened* there?"

"Someone was killed," Miriam said quietly. Then she bent
down and pointed to something in the threshold. "Look. See
that wire? It's hair-thin. *Don't* touch it!"

"What wire—oh."

A fine wire was stretched across the threshold, twelve
inches above the floor.

"That wasn't here when I came this way three hours ago,"
Miriam said tonelessly. "And nobody's been to clear up
what's inside. Going from what Roland was telling me, that
means that first, this is a trap, and second, it's not the kind
where someone's going to jump out and start shooting at us,
and third, if you touch that wire, we probably both die. Wait
here and don't move or touch *anything*. I'm going to see if
they're belt-and-suspenders people."

Miriam shuffled gingerly over toward the big wood doors of the warehouse—there was a smaller access door in the side of one of them—with her eyes focused on t ground in front of her, every step of the way. Brill stay where she was obediently, but when Miriam glanced at h she was staring up at the lights, an odd expression on h face. "I'm over here," she said. "I'm *really* on the oth side!"

Miriam reached the inner door, bent low, looked up, an made a hissing noise through her teeth. "Shit!"

"What is it?" called Brill, shaking herself.

"Another one," Miriam replied. Her face was ghost-white "You can come over here and look. This is the way out."

"Oh." Brill walked over to the door, stopping short a Miriam's warning hand gesture. She followed Miriam'. pointing finger, up at something in the shadows above the door. "What's that?" she asked.

"At a guess, it's a bomb," said Miriam. "Probably a . . . what do you call it? A Claymore mine." The green package was securely fastened to two nails driven into the huge main warehouse door directly above the access door cut in it. Miriam's compact flashlight cut through the twilight, tracing a fine wire as it looped around three or four nails. It came back to anchor to the access door at foot level, in such a way that any attempt to open the door would tug on it. Miriam whistled tunelessly. "Careless, very careless."

Brill stared at the booby trap in horror. "Are you just going to leave it?" she asked.

Miriam glanced at her. "What do you expect me to do?" she asked. "I'm not a bomb disposal expert, I'm a journalist! I just learned a bit about this stuff doing a feature on Northern Ireland a couple of years ago." For a moment, an expression of helpless anger flashed across her face. "We've got to get out of here," she said. "I know somewhere safe, but 'safe' is relative. We need to hole up where nobody is going to ask questions you can't answer, assassins can't find us, and I can do some thinking." She glanced at the Claymore

ine. "Once I figure out a way to open this door without
lling us both."

"That was another, in the office?" asked Brill.

"Yes." Miriam shrugged. "I figure the idea was to kill any-
ne who comes sniffing. But the only people who *know*
vhat's in there are me and whoever . . . whoever murdered
he night watchman."

"What about Roland?"

"Oh, yes. I told Roland. And he could have told—" for a
moment Miriam looked wistful. "Damn, this means I can't
trust *anyone* who works for Angbard, can I?" She glanced
obliquely at Brill.

"I don't work for Angbard," Brill said slowly. "I work for
you."

"Well, that's nice to know." Miriam gave her a lopsided
grin. "I hope it doesn't get you into trouble. Worse trouble,"
she corrected.

"What are we going to do?" asked Brill, frowning as only
a twenty-something confronted by fate can frown.

"Hmm. Well, I'm going to open this door." Miriam gestured. "Somehow or other. Then . . . there's a lot you don't
know, isn't there? The door opens on an alley in a place
called New York. It's a big city and it's after dark. I'm going
to call a car service, and you're going to do what I do—get
in after me, ride with me to where we're going, wait while I
pay the driver, and go inside. I'll do all the talking. You
should concentrate on taking in whatever you can without
looking like a yokel. Once we're in private, you can talk all
you want. All right? Think you can do that?"

Brill nodded seriously. "It'll be for me like when you first
arrived? On the other side?" she asked.

"Good analogy." Miriam nodded. "No, it'll be worse,
much worse." She grinned again. "I had an introduction; the
whole world didn't all get thrown at me all at once. Just try
not to get yourself killed crossing the road, okay?" Then she
glanced around. "Look, over there below the mezzanine, see
those crates? I want you to go and sit down on the other side

of them. Shield your head with your arms, yes, like they
about to fall on you. And keep your mouth open. I'm go
to try and get this door open without blowing us to pieces
figure it should be possible because they were expecti
people to come in from outside, not to materialize right i
side the warehouse."

"We're already supposed to be dead, aren't we?"

Miriam nodded. "Go," she said.

Brill headed off toward the stack of tea chests. Miria
bent down and followed the near-invisible wire off to or
side. *I really don't like the look of this*, she thought, her hea
hammering at her ribs. She glanced up at the green casing
ominous as a hornet's nest suspended overhead. "Let's see,
she mumbled. "The door opens inward, pulls on the wire . .
or the warehouse door opens inward, also pulls on the wire
But if it's spring-loaded, releasing it could *also* set the fuck
ing thing off. Hmm."

She examined the wire as it ran around a rusting nail
pounded into the wall beside the door. "Right." She stood up
and walked back across to the trailer with its own booby trap
and its cargo of death. Climbing the steps, she paused for a
moment, took a deep breath, and stepped over the wire.

Nothing happened. *I'm still here*, she told herself. She
took another deep breath, this time to avoid having to
breathe in too close to the thing sprawled across the fallen
office chair at the far side of the office. She'd called Roland,
told him to send cleaners—instead, these booby traps had
materialized. *When the Clan wants you dead, you die*, she
realized bleakly. *If indeed it is the Clan . . .*

There, on a rusting tool chest propped against the other
wall, was exactly what she was looking for. She picked up
the heavy-duty staple gun and checked that it was loaded.
"Yup." She hefted it one-handed, then mustered up a smile
and picked up a pair of rusty pliers and stepped back out of
the trailer.

Two minutes later, she had the door open. The wire, firmly
stapled to the door frame, was severed: The mine was still
armed, but the trigger wire led nowhere. "Come on," she

alled to Brilliana. "It's safe now! We can leave!" Brill hurried
ver. As she did so, Miriam glanced up and shuddered once
nore. *What if they'd heard of infrared motion detectors?*

Well, that was the Clan all over.

It was snowing lightly, and Miriam phoned for a taxi when
they reached the main road. Brill kept quiet, but her eyes
grew wide when she saw Miriam talking into a small gray
box—and wider still as she took in the cars that rumbled
past in the gloom. She glanced from side to side like a caged
cat in a strange, threatening environment. "I didn't know it
would be like this!" she whispered to Miriam. Then she
shivered. "It's really cold."

"It's winter, kid. Get used to it." Miriam grinned, slightly
manic from her success with the bomb.

"It's colder on the other side, isn't it?"

A cab pulled alongside, its light turned off. Miriam
walked over. "Cab for Beckstein?" she asked. The driver
nodded. She held open the rear door. "Get in and slide
across," she told Brill. Then she gave directions and got inside, shutting the door.

The cab moved off. Brill looked around in fascination,
then reached down toward her ankles. "It's *heated*!" she said
quietly.

"Of course it's heated," said the driver in a Pakistani accent. "You think I let my passengers freeze to death before
they pay me?"

"Excuse my friend," Miriam told him, casting a warning
glance at Brill. "She's from Russia. Just arrived."

"Oh," said the driver, as if that explained everything.
"Yes, very good, that."

Brill kept her eyes wide but her mouth closed the rest of
the way to the Marriott Marquis, but watched carefully as
Miriam paid off the cabbie using pieces of green paper she
pulled from a billfold. "Come on, follow me," said Miriam.

Miriam felt Brill tense as the glass doors opened automatically ahead of them, but she kept up with her as she headed

for the express elevator. "One moment," Miriam muttered
her, pushing the button. "This is an elevator. It's a room, su
pended on wires, in a vertical shaft. We use it instead of th
stairs."

"Why?" Brill looked puzzled.

"Have you ever tried to climb forty flights of stairs?
Miriam shut up as another elevator arrived, disgorging
couple of septuagenarians. Then the express doors opened
and she waved Brill inside. "This is easier," she said, hitting
the second from top button. The younger woman lurched
against the wall as the elevator began to rise. "We'll be there
in no time."

The glass-walled elevator car began to track up the outer
wall of the tower. "That's—oh my!" Brill leaned back
against the far wall from the window. "I'd rather walk, I
think," she said shakily.

A thought struck Miriam at the top. "We'd better be careful going in," she commented before the doors opened. "I
want you to wait behind me."

"Why?" Brill followed her out of the lift into an empty
landing. She looked slightly green, and Miriam realized she
hadn't said anything on the way up.

"Because," Miriam frowned, "we're safe from the other
side, here. But Roland knows which room I'm using." *He
won't have told anybody*, she reasoned. *Even if he has, they
can't have booby-trapped it from the inside, like the warehouse. Not on the twenty-second floor. I hope.*

"All right." Brill swallowed. "Which way?" she asked,
looking bewildered.

"Follow me." Miriam pushed through the fire doors,
strolled along a hotel corridor, trying to imagine what it
might look like to someone who'd never seen a hotel—or an
elevator—before. "Wait here."

She swiped her card-key through the lock, then stood aside,
right hand thrust in her jacket pocket as she pushed the door
open to reveal an empty suite, freshly prepared beds, an open
bathroom door. "Quick." She waved Brill inside then followed
her, shut and locked the door, and sagged against it in relief.

"Oh shit, oh shit . . ." Her hands felt cold and shook until ...e clasped them together. *Delayed shock*, the analytical ob-...rver in her brain commented. *Tonight you killed an assas-...n in self-defense, defused a bomb, discovered a murder ...nd a conspiracy, and rescued Brill and Olga. Isn't it about ...me you collapsed in a gibbering heap?*

"Where is—" Brilliana was looking around, eyes nar-...owed. "It's so *small*! But it's hot. The fireplace—"

"You don't have fireplaces in tall buildings," Miriam said ...utomatically. "We're twenty-two floors up. We've got air-...:onditioning—that box, under the curtains, it warms the air, ...eeps it at a comfortable temperature all year around." She ...ubbed her forehead: The pounding headache was threaten-...ing to make a comeback. "Have a seat."

Brill picked a chair in front of the television set. "What now?" she asked, yawning.

Miriam glanced at the bedside clock: It was about one o'-clock in the morning. "It's late," said Miriam. "Tonight we sleep. In the morning I'm going to take you on a journey to another city, to meet someone I trust. A friend. Then—" she instinctively fingered the pocket with the two lockets in it, her own and the one she'd taken from the assassin— "we'll work out what to do next."

They spent a nervous night in the anonymous hotel room, high above any threat from world-walking pursuers. In the morning Miriam pointed Brill at the shower—she had to ex-plain the controls—while she called room service, then went to check the wardrobe.

A big anonymous-looking suitcase nearly filled the lug-gage niche, right where she'd left it. While breakfast was on its way up, Miriam opened it and pulled out some fresh clothing. *Have to take time to buy some more*, she thought, looking at what was left. Most of the suitcase was occupied by items that wouldn't exactly render her inconspicuous on this side. *Later*, she resolved. Her wallet itched, reproaching her. Inside it was the platinum card Duke Angbard had sent

her. Two million dollars of other people's blood money.
ther it was her "Get Out of Jail Free" card, or a death tr
depending on whether whoever had sent the first bunch
assassins—her enemy within the Clan, rather than wi
out—was able to follow its transactions. Probably th
wouldn't be able to, at least not fast enough to catch up w
her if she kept moving. If they were, Miriam wasn't the on
family member who was at risk. *It's probably safe as long*
it keeps working and I keep moving, she reasoned. *If som*
body puts a stop on it, I'm in trouble. And better not go bu
ing any air tickets. Not that she was planning on doir
that—the idea of introducing airline passenger etiquette
Brill left her shaking her head.

There was a discreet knock at the door. Miriam picked u
her pistol and, hiding it in her pocket, approached. Th
peephole showed her a bored bellhop pushing a trolley. Sh
opened the door. "Thanks," she said, passing him a tip
"We'll keep the trolley."

Back inside the suite, Brill emerged from the bathroom
looking pink and freshly scrubbed—and somewhat confused. "Where does all the water *come from?*" she asked, almost complaining. "It never stopped!"

"Welcome to New York, baby," Miriam drawled, lifting
the cover off a plate laden with a full-cooked breakfast.
"Land of plenty, home of—sorry," she finished lamely and
waved Brill toward a chair. "Come on, there's enough food
for both of us." *Damn,* she thought. *I don't want to go rub-
bing her nose in it. Not like that.*

"Thank you," Brill said, primly picking up a knife and
fork and going to work. "Hmm. It tastes slightly . . . odd."

"Yeah." Miriam chewed thoughtfully, then poured a couple of cups of coffee from the thermal jug. "The eggs aren't
as good. Are they?"

"It's *all* a little different." Brill frowned, inspecting her
plate minutely. "They're all the same, aren't they? Like
identical twins?"

"It's how we make things here." Miriam shrugged. "You'll

e lots of things that are identical. But not people." She be-
n working on her toast before she noticed Brill surrepti-
ously following her example with the small wrapped parcels
butter. "First, I'm going to call my friend. If she's all right,
e're going to go on a journey to another city and I'm going
 leave you with her for a few days. The way we tell it is:
ou're a relative from out of state who's coming to stay. Your
arents are weird backwoods types, which is why there's a lot
f stuff you haven't seen. My friend will know the truth. Also,
he's got a contact number for Roland. If I—" she cleared her
hroat— "she'll get you back in touch, so you can go home.
To the other side, I mean, when you need to."

"'When I need to'," Brill echoed doubtfully. She glanced
around the room. "What's *that?*"

"That?" Miriam blinked. "It's a television set."

"Oh. Like Ser Villem's after-dinner entertainments. I remember that! The cat and the mouse, and the talking rabbit,
Bugs." Brill smiled. "They are *everywhere*, here?"

"That's one way of putting it." *Kid, I prescribe a week as a
dedicated couch potato before we let you go outdoors on
your own*, she resolved. "I've got a call to make," she said,
reaching for her mobile.

The first thing Miriam did was switch her phone off, open
the back, and replace the SIM chip with one she took from
her billfold. Then she reassembled it. The phone beeped as it
came up with a new identity, but there was no voice mail
waiting for her. Steeling herself, she dialed a number—one
belonging to another mobile phone she'd sent via FedEx a
couple of days before.

"Hello?" The voice at the end of the line sounded posi-
tively chirpy.

"Paulie! Are you okay?"

"Miriam! How's it going, babe?"

"It's going messy," she admitted. "Look, remember the
other day? Are you still home?"

"Yes. What's come up?"

"I'm going to come pay you a visit," said Miriam. "First,

I've got a lot of things to discuss, stuff to get in order—
a down payment. Second, I've got a lodger. How's your sp
room?"

"Oh, you know it's been empty since I kicked that b
Walter out? What's up, you wanting him to stay with me?

Miriam glanced at Brill. "It's a she, and I think you
probably like her," she said guardedly. "It's part of that d
we made. I need you to put her up for a few weeks, on
company—I mean, I'm paying. Trouble is, she's from, u
out of state, if you follow me. She doesn't know her w
around *at all*."

"Does she, like, speak English?" Paulette sounded inte
ested rather than perturbed, for which Miriam was im
mensely grateful. Brilliana was toying with her coffee an
pretending not to realize Miriam was discussing her, on a
intimate basis, with a talking box.

"Yeah, that's not a problem. But this morning was the firs
time she'd ever met an electric shower, and *that* is a problem
for me, because I've got a lot of traveling to do in the nex
few weeks and I need to put her where someone can keep ar
eye on her as she gets used to the way things are done over
here. Can you do that?"

"Probably," Paulette said briskly. "Depends if she hates
my guts on first sight—or vice versa. I can't promise more
than that, can I?"

"Well—" Miriam took a deep breath. "Okay, we're coming
up today on the train. You going to be home in the afternoon?"

"For you, any day! You've got a lot to tell me about?"

"Everything," Miriam said fervently. "It's been crazy."

"Bye, then."

Miriam put the phone down and rubbed her eyes. Brill
was watching her oddly. "Who was that?" she asked.

"Who—oh, on the phone?" Miriam glanced at it. So Brill
had figured out that much? Bright girl. "A friend of mine. My,
uh, business agent. On this side." She grinned. "For the past
few days, anyway. We're going to see her this afternoon."

" 'Her'?" Brill raised an eyebrow. "All the hot water you
want, no need to feed the fire, and women running busi-

esses? No wonder my mother didn't want me coming
ere—she was afraid I'd never come back!"

"That seems to go with the territory," Miriam agreed
dryly.

After breakfast she chivvied Brill into getting dressed
again. Her tailored suit and blouse would blend into the
background just fine: another business traveler in the heart
of New York. Miriam thought for a moment, then picked another jacket—this time a dressy one rather than one built for
bad weather. She'd have to keep her pistol in her handbag,
but she'd look more in keeping with Brill, and hopefully it
would distract any killers hunting for a lone woman in her
early thirties with thus-and-such features.

Miriam took the large suitcase when they left the room
and headed downstairs. Brill's eyes kept swiveling at everything from telephones to cigarette ads, but she kept her questions to herself as Miriam shepherded her into a nearby bank
for ten minutes, then flagged down a taxi. "What was that
about?" Brill murmured after Miriam told the driver where
to go.

"Needed to take care of some money business," Miriam
replied. "Angbard gave me a line on some credit, but—" she
stopped, shrugged. *I'm talking Martian again*, she realized.

"You'll have to tell me how this credit thing works some
time," Brill commented. "I don't think I've actually seen a
coin since I came here. Do people use them?"

"Not much. Which makes some things easier—it's harder
to steal larger amounts—and other things more difficult—
like transferring large quantities of money to someone else
without it being noticed."

"Huh." Brill stared out of the window at the passing traffic, the pedestrians in their dark winter colors, and the bright
advertisements. "It's so *noisy!* How do you get any thinking
done?"

"Sometimes it's hard," Miriam admitted.

She bought two tickets to Boston and shepherded Brill
onto the express train without incident. They found a table a
long way from anyone else without difficulty, which turned

out to be a good thing, because Brill was unable to cont[...]
her surprise when the train began to move. "It's so diffe[...]
ent!" she squeaked, taken aback.

"It's called a train." Miriam pointed out of the windo[...]
"Like that one, only faster and newer and built for carryin[...]
passengers. Where we're going is within a day's walk [...]
Angbard's palace, but it'll only take us three hours to g[...]
there."

Brilliana stared at the passing freight train. "I've see[...]
movies," she said quietly. "You don't need to assume I'[...]
stupid, ignorant. But it's not the same as being here."

"I'm sorry." Miriam shook her head, embarrassed. Sh[...]
looked at Brill thoughtfully. She was doing a good job o[...]
bluffing, even though the surprises the world kept throwing
at her must sometimes have been overwhelming. A brigh[...]
kid, well-educated for her place in time, but out of her depth
here—*How would I cope if someone gave me a ticket to the
thirtieth century?* Miriam wondered. At a guess, there'd be
an outburst of anger soon, triggered by something trivial—
the realization that this wasn't fairyland but a real place, and
she'd grown up among people who lived here and withheld
everything in it from her. *I wonder which way she'll jump?*

Opposite her, Brilliana's face froze. "What is it?" Miriam
asked quietly.

"The . . . the second row of thrones behind you—that's interesting. I've seen that man before. Black hair, dark suit."

"Where?" Miriam whispered, tensing. Feeling for her
shoulder bag, the small pistol buried at the bottom of it. *No,
not on a train . . .*

"At court. He is a corporal of honor in service to Angbard.
Called Edsger something. I've seen him a couple of times in
escort to one or another of the duke's generals. I don't think
he's recognized me. He is reading one of those intelligence
papers the tinkers were selling at the palace of trains."

"Hmm." Miriam frowned. "Did you see any luggage
when he got onboard? Anything he carried? Describe him."

"There is a trunk with a handle, like yours, only it looks

ike metal. He has it beside him and places one hand on it
every short while."

"Ah." Miriam relaxed infinitesimally. "Okay, I think I've
got a handle on it. Is the case about the same size as mine?"

Brill nodded slowly, her eyes focused past Miriam's left
shoulder.

"That means he's probably a courier," Miriam said quietly. "At a guess, Angbard has him carry documents daily
between his palace and Manhattan. That explains why he
spends so little time at court himself—he can keep his finger
on the pulse far faster than the non-Clan courtiers realize. If
I'm right, he'll be carrying a report about last night, among
other things." She raised a finger to her lips. "Trouble is, if
I'm right, he's armed and certainly dangerous to approach.
And if I'm wrong, he's not a courier. He's going to wait for
the train to stop, then try to kill us." Miriam closed her hand
around the barrel of her pistol, then stopped. *No, that's the
wrong way to solve this*, she thought. Instead she pulled out
her wallet and a piece of paper and began writing.

Brilliana leaned forward. "He's doing it again," she murmured. "I think there's something in his jacket. Under his
arm. He looks uncomfortable."

"Right." Miriam nodded, then shoved the piece of paper
across the table at Brill. There was a pair of fifty-dollar bills
and a train ticket concealed under it. "Here is what we're going to do. In a minute, you're going to stand up while he isn't
looking and walk to the other end of this carriage—behind
you, over there, where the doors are. If—" she swallowed—
"if things go wrong, don't try anything heroic. Just get off
the train as soon as it stops, hide in the crowd, make damn
sure he doesn't see you. There'll be another train through in
an hour. Your ticket is valid for travel on it, and you want to
get off in Cambridge. Go out of the station, tell a cab driver
you want to go to *this* address, and pay with one of these
notes, the way you saw me do it. He'll give you change. It's
a small house; the number is on the front of the door. Go up
to it and tell the woman who lives there that I sent you and

I'm in trouble. Then give her this." Miriam pushed anoth[e]
piece of paper across the table at her. "After a day, te[ll]
Paulette to use the special number I gave her. That's a[ll.]
Think you can do that?"

Brill nodded mutely. "What are you going to do now?"
she asked quietly.

Miriam took a deep breath. "I'm going to do what we i[n]
the trade refer to as a hostile interview," she said. "What wa[s]
his name, again?"

"Hello, Edsger. Don't move. This would not be a good place
to get help for a sucking chest wound."

He tensed and she smiled, bright and feral, like a mon-
goose confronting a sleepy cobra.

"What—"

"Don't move, I said. That includes your mouth. Not very
good, is it, letting your mark turn on you?"

"I don't know what you're talking about!"

"I think you do. And I think it's slack of you, nodding off
just because you're on the iron road and no world-walkers
can sneak up from behind." She smiled wider, seeing his unnerved expression. "First, some ground rules. We are going
to have a little conversation, then we will go our separate
ways, and nobody will get hurt. But first, to make that possible, you will start by *slowly* bending forward and sliding that
pistol of yours out into this shopping bag."

The courier leaned forward. Miriam leaned with him,
keeping her pistol jammed up against his ribs through her
jacket. "Slowly," she hissed.

"I'm slow." He opened his jacket and slid a big Browning
automatic out of the holster under his left armpit—two-
fingered. Miriam tensed, but he followed through by dropping it into the open bag.

"And your mobile phone," she said. "Now, kick it under
the table. Gently." He gave it a half-hearted shove with one
foot.

"Put your hands between your knees and lean back slowly," she ordered.

"Who *are* you?" he asked, complying.

"First, you're going to tell me who you're delivering that case to at the other end," she said. "Ordinary postal service—or Angbard himself?"

"I can't—"

She shoved the gun up against him, hard. "You fucking *can*," she snarled quietly. "Because if you don't tell me, you are going to read about the contents of that case on the front page of *The New York Times*, are you hearing me?"

"It goes to Matthias."

"Angbard's secretary, right." She felt him tense again. "That was the correct answer," she said quietly. "Now, I want you to do something else for me. I've got a message for Angbard, for his ears *only*, do you understand? It's not for Matthias, it's not for Roland, it's not for any of the other lord-lieutenants he's got hanging around. Remember, I've got your number. If anyone other than Angbard gets this message, I will find out and I will tell him and he will kill you. Got that? Good. What's going to happen next is: The train's stopping in a couple of minutes. You will stand up, take your case—*not* the bag with your phone—and get off the train, because I will be following you. You will then stand beside the train door where I can see you until it's ready to move off, and you will stay there while it moves off because if you *don't* stand that way I will shoot you. If you want to know why I'm so trigger-happy, you can ask Angbard yourself—after you've delivered his dispatches."

"You must be—" his eyes widened.

"Don't say my name."

He nodded.

"You're going to be an hour late into Boston—an hour later than you would have been, anyway. Don't bother trying to organize a search for me because I won't be there. Instead, go to the Fort Lofstrom doppelgänger house, make your delivery to Matthias as usual, say you missed the train or something, then ask to see the old man and tell him about meeting me here."

"What?" He looked puzzled. "I thought you had a message."

"*You* are the message." She grinned humorlessly. "And you've got to be alive to deliver it. We're slowing up: Do as I tell you and it'll all be over soon."

He shook his head very slowly. "They were right about you," he said. But when she asked him who he meant, he just stared at her.

epilogue

There was an old building on Central Avenue, with windows soundproofed against the roar of turbofans. Whenever the wind was from the southwest and inbound flights were diverted across the city, the airliners would rattle the panes. But perhaps there were other reasons for the soundproofing.

Two men sat in a second-floor office, Matthias leaning back behind a desk and Roland perched uncomfortably close to the edge of a sofa in front of it.

"Consignment F-12 is on schedule," said Matthias. "It says so right here on the manifest. Isn't that right?"

He fixed Roland with a cold stare.

"I inspected it myself," said Roland. Despite his stiff posture and the superficial appearance of unease, he sounded self-confident. "Contractor Wolfe has the right attitude: businesslike attention to detail. They vet their workers thoroughly."

"Well." Matthias leaned across his desk. "It's a pity the

cargo is laid over in Svarlberg while a storm blows itself ou~~t~~ isn't it?"

"Damn." Roland looked annoyed. "That's recent, I take it?"

"Two days ago. I did a spot inspection myself. Impresse~~d~~ Vincenze to carry me across for the past week. I think you'~~d~~ better warn Wolfe that F-12 is going to be at least four day~~s~~ late, possibly as much as seven."

"Damn." A nod. "Okay, I'll do that. Usual disclaimers?"

"It's in the warranty small-print." Neither of them cracke~~d~~ a smile. The Clan provided its own underwriting service— one that more than made up for the usurious transport charges it levied. The customer code-named Wolfe would damn well swallow the four- to seven-day delay and smile, because the cargo *would* arrive, one way or another, which was more than could be said for most of the Clan's competitors. If it didn't, the Clan would pay up in full, at face value, no question. "We have a reputation to guard."

"I'll get onto it." Roland pulled out a small notebook and scribbled a cryptic entry in it. He caught Matthias staring. "No names, no pack drill." He tucked the notebook away carefully.

"It's good to know you can keep a secret."

"Huh?"

"There's something else I wanted to talk to you about." He didn't smile. "Look at this." Reaching into a desk drawer, Matthias pulled out a slim file binder and slid it across the desk. Roland rose and collected it, sat down, opened it, and tensed, frowning.

"Page one. Our prodigal dresses for dinner. Nice ass, by the way."

A glare from the sofa. If looks could kill, Matthias would be ashes blowing on the wind.

"Turn over. That's her, leaving her room, shot from behind. Someone ought to tell her she oughtn't to leave security camera footage lying around like that, someone might steal it. Turn over." Reluctantly, he turned over. "That's her, in the passageway to a room in—" Matthias coughed discreetly into his fist. "And over, and oh dear, there seems to

e a camera behind the bathroom mirror, doesn't there? I
onder how that got there. And now if you turn over, you'll
ee that—"

Roland slammed the folder shut with an inarticulate growl,
hen slapped it down on the desk. "What's your point?" he
demanded, shaking with anger. "What the fuck do you *want*?
Spying on me—"

"Sit down," snapped Matthias.

Roland sat, shoulders hunched.

"You've put me on the spot, did you know that? I could
show this to Angbard, you realize. In fact, I *should* show it to
him. I've got a *duty* to show it to him. But I haven't—yet. I
could show it to Lady Olga, too, but I think neither you nor
she would care about that unless I embarrassed her publicly.
Which would raise too many questions. What in Lightning
Child's name were you *thinking* of, Roland?"

"Don't." Roland hunched forward, eyes narrowed in pain.

"If Angbard sees this, he will rip you a new asshole. To be
fair, he might rip *her* a new asshole too, but she's better positioned to survive the experience. You—" he shook his
head. "I see a long future for you as Clan ambassador to the
Iroquois. Or maybe the Apache nation. For as long as any
Clan ambassador lasts in one of those posts."

"You haven't told him, though." Roland stared at the floor
in front of the desk, trying to hide his suspicions. Surely
Matthias wouldn't be telling him this if he was just going to
go straight to the duke?

"Well, no." His interrogator fell silent for a while. "I'm
not a *robot,* you know. Loyal servant, yes—but I have my
own ambitions."

" 'Ambitions'?" Roland looked up, his expression strained.

"The Clan doesn't offer an ideal career track for such as
I." He shrugged. "I expect you to understand that better than
most of them."

Roland licked his lips. "What do you want?" he asked quietly. "What are you after?"

"I'm after the status quo ante." He picked up the file and
slid it into a desk drawer. "Your little . . . servant . . . made

waves where she shouldn't have. I want her out of the p:
ture: I hasten to add, this doesn't mean dead, it just mea
invisible."

"You want her to disappear." For an instant, an expressic
of hope flickered across Roland's face.

"Possibly." He nodded. "I think you'd like that—if yc
went with her. Wouldn't you?"

"Damn you, three years was all I had . . . !"

"If you do as I say, then the folder and its contents—an
all the other copies—will vanish. And the Clan won't b
able to touch you ever again. Either of you. What do yo
say?"

Roland licked his lips. "I thought this was blackmail."

"What makes you think it isn't?"